The Last of the
Angels

A Modern Iraqi Novel

Fadhil al-Azzawi

Translated by
William M. Hutchins

FREE PRESS
New York   London   Toronto   Sydney

FREE PRESS

A Division of Simon & Schuster, Inc.
1230 Avenue of the Americas
New York, NY 10020

First Free Press trade paperback edition July 2008

FREE PRESS and colophon are trademarks of Simon & Schuster, Inc.

For information about special discounts for bulk purchases,
please contact Simon & Schuster Special Sales:
1-800-456-6798 or business@simonandschuster.com

The first chapter has appeared under the title "Hameed Nylon" in a slightly different form
in the online journal wordswithoutborders.org and in the anthology *Literature from the
"Axis of Evil,"* edited by Words Without Borders (The New Press, 2006). The second chapter
has appeared under the title "Burhan Abdallah's Secret Chest" in a slightly different form
in *Banipal: Magazine of Modern Arab Literature,* Number 26, Summer 2006.

Manufactured in the United States of America
1 3 5 7 9 10 8 6 4 2

The Library of Congress has catalogued the Free Press edition as follows:
'Azzawi, Fadil.
[*Akhir al-mala' ikah*. English]
The last of the angels: a modern Iraqi novel / Fadhil al-Azzawi;
translated by William M. Hutchins.
p. cm.
I. Hutchins, William M. II. Title.
PJ7814.Z92A6413 2008
892.7'36——dc22   2007047102
ISBN-13: 978-1-4165-6745-5
ISBN-10: 1-4165-6745-3

What turned into wine yesterday is today vinegar, and never will vinegar turn back to wine. Never.

Herman Hesse, "Der schwere Weg," *Märchen*

The Last of the
Angels

One

Hameed, who had yet to learn the nickname by which he would be known for the rest of his life, entered the house, which emitted a fresh country scent. With his foot, as usual, he shoved open the heavy door, which was made of walnut and decorated with large, broad-headed nails. Only at night was it closed by a bolt with protruding teeth. Verdigris had spread across this till its edges looked bright green. He climbed a few steps, making his way to the two small rooms over the entryway that led to the courtyard.

It was the first time Hameed had returned from his job at the oil company so early. It was barely eleven, and this fact surprised his wife Fatima, who was not expecting him till afternoon. He interrupted her innocent laughter as she stood on the steps discussing her nightly pleasures over a low masonry wall with a neighbor next door. Her happiness actually was tinged with bitter anxiety, since she had been married for more than a year without conceiving. She had sought out most of the better-known and even less well-known imams in the city for charms against barrenness to neutralize the magic that the many women envying her had clearly concocted to her detriment. Although she had never said so openly, her suspicions, from the beginning, had focused on Nazira—her husband's sister—and on Nazira's mother, Hidaya, a plump old woman who made no secret of her collaboration with the devil, for her house was always cluttered with herbs and dried flowers, ground bones, and assorted chemical substances purchased from Jewish druggists in al-Qaysariya, at the entrance to the old souk.

Among the imams Fatima consulted was a blind man who charged her a dirham to write a charm. He told her, "This amulet will set on fire any devil that dares approach you." As an additional precaution, however, she consulted another Turkmen imam, who lived in a nameless alley branching off from the Chay neighborhood. A month or two later, since her belly had not swollen up yet, her neighbor advised her to tour the tombs of the dead imams, since the living ones were not useful anymore and only wrote charms for money. Thus Fatima, enveloped in her black wrap, headed to Imam Ahmad, whose tomb lay in the center of the main thoroughfare linking al-Musalla district with the old souk. She wept and pleaded, deliberately prolonging the time she spent there so the imam would not ignore her request. A passing car almost ran into her, since in her spiritual rapture—tears streaming from her eyes—she had forgotten she was sitting in the middle of the street. After that she visited the tomb in al-Musalla cemetery of a Kurdish imam said to have been able to converse with birds, which understood and obeyed him. A month later, when no change had occurred in her, even though she made her husband sleep with her more than once a night, her visiting mother said, "This time you're going to head for the tomb of a Jewish saint, for no one is on better terms with the devil than Jews; evil is only negated by evil." The next morning, however, when she related that to her neighbor, the woman advised her to go to the citadel and ask a Christian household there for a hog's tooth. She said they put those, normally, in water jugs. She should slip it under her husband's pillow, since Satan fears nothing more than hogs' teeth. Perhaps because of all of this advice she was receiving from here and there, and also, possibly because she was disillusioned with saints whose blessed powers had failed, she decided to call off, at least temporarily, these unsuccessful attempts while increasing the number of times she slept with her husband, since she knew, perhaps with good reason, that—more than any other location—bed was where the issue would be settled, if only because this was the resting place for the saints closest to God.

Even so, Fatima would not have paid much attention to this matter had it not been for her mother's persistent entreaties and the insinuating comments of the old woman Hidaya and her daughter Nazira, who deliberately spoke in riddles, saying, for example, "The cow that doesn't give birth is slaughtered." On the whole she was content with her nightly trysts with her husband, who had never given a thought, not even once, to having children, since love for women eclipsed all other loves in his life. He especially wished to preserve for as long as possible his sense of being a young man little burdened with responsibilities, so that he could leave in the morning for his job at the oil company and not return home till he felt like it. He occasionally returned in the afternoon but frequently stayed out until ten or eleven p.m. without upsetting Fatima, who had no way of discovering anything about his work except from the stories he told her. She knew he drove a private car belonging to an English engineer and his wife, conveying them from one place to another and waiting for them. She grasped that this type of work might force him to work late more often than not. He was occasionally obliged to travel to other cities and areas, accompanying his boss. Then he would return home bringing—especially during Christian holidays—chocolates from London or locally produced pieces of sugared coconut, which she had not tasted before. The moment she saw her husband enter, she raced to him since this was the first time he had returned so early, a fact that made her feel uncomfortable and anxious. She fought to control her emotions and to keep herself from asking why he was early. He, however, spoke first, saying with a smile, "I want to lie down a little." Only then did she find the courage to ask anxiously, "I hope you don't feel ill?" As he climbed toward their two rooms over the house's entryway, he replied, "No, not at all. I'm just tired." This answer satisfied her enough that she said, "Fine. I'll start cooking right away so we can have lunch together." She went off to prepare the food, feeling on the whole contented and delighted that her husband was home with her. Even if something were the matter, he would certainly tell her, she was sure of that.

Her husband kept uncharacteristically silent this time, however. In fact, he did not leave his bed to go to the coffeehouse or to visit with his friends, not even that afternoon. Neither did he go out to chat with the neighborhood youth, who met each evening in front of a shop located near the community's mosque. Even worse than that, he did not leave home for work the next day. Only then did Fatima realize that something was wrong, something he was hiding from her and did not care to divulge. It had to be something serious. Her fears led her to beg him to tell her the truth, but he merely told her he had taken a few days' holiday. She felt somewhat relieved but not entirely reassured, for he might be trying to deceive her, thinking that he should not alarm or upset her.

She knew that when he was in a good humor he would tell her one story after another about Mr. McNeely; his flirtatious wife, Helen; and the other Englishmen who worked in the Baba Gurgur region for the Iraq Petroleum Company in Kirkuk. She knew that every Englishman was called "Boss" and that the company belonged to them. Fatima and Hameed would laugh a lot when he told her how Englishwomen were not at all embarrassed about showing their naked bodies to employees and how they wore undershirts and shorts in the presence of their cuckolded husbands, who bragged about their wives to one another. In fact, he had discovered that his boss's wife had more than one English lover. He was equally well versed in his boss's affair with the daughter of Khamu, an Assyrian Christian, who enjoyed the rank of a "first-class" employee with the firm. That was not all; her father encouraged the girl to continue this relationship with the man. As for the boss and his wife, they did not attempt to conceal their affairs from him, leaving the impression that these were extremely natural. In fact, his boss's beautiful, bronzed wife would leave the home of one of her lovers and climb into the waiting automobile as if returning from prayers. Once, when they were on the lakeshore in al-Habaniya, Helen removed every stitch of clothing. When she noticed that Hameed was staring wildly and lustfully at her, she was surprised and winked at him, smiling as she sank into the water. Fatima had frequently teased him, laughing, "What more do you want? Many men would pay good money to have such enjoyable work."

Hameed, however, did not actually find in his work the kind of satisfaction his wife imagined, for he felt humiliated most of the time as he sat behind the steering wheel, waiting for Helen to leave an assignation. They occasionally invited him inside and served him lemonade in the servants' quarters while he listened to his mistress's moans from a bed in another room where she lay with the lover she was visiting. That would drive him crazy, agitating him, although he did not dare protest or refuse the invitation. He assumed it not unlikely that she would fancy him someday and invite him to sleep with her, but that day never came. After the incident in which Mrs. Helen McNeely appeared naked at al-Habaniya and after her conspiratorial wink, he spent more than a month feeling uncertain about his standing with her, wanting her but lacking the audacity to cross the line separating them. The image of her standing naked before him never left his head, since he often thought of her while he slept with his wife. That did not, in his opinion, constitute any diminution of his love for his wife, everything considered, for Mrs. Helen McNeely was no better than a whore. He, as a man, had a right to seize this opportunity. He was sure he would show her in bed that he was superior to all her other lovers. He would thus avenge himself and erase the humiliation he felt whenever she climbed into the car to head for one of them.

Hameed never returned to work and there must have been some secret reason, which would eventually surface, even though he attempted to postpone this moment, day by day. People in the Chuqor neighborhood learned from other men who worked for the company that Hameed had been fired. Instead of trying to console him, however, they burst into laughter, and his story traveled by word of mouth until the whole city knew it. Thus he acquired a nickname that remained linked to his given name forever, as if it actually were a real part of his name. Even innocent children always called him by this name—Hameed Nylon—which he himself finally accepted, adding it to his given name.

The story these workers told, based on reports from the oil company, was that Hameed, who was the personal driver for Mr. McNeely and his wife, wishing to try his luck with the wife and to win her affection, had returned one day from a trip to H3 and Rutba, carrying a simple present for her—a pair of nylon stockings—but that Mrs. McNeely, who considered him a servant, had tossed the stockings back at him and thrown him out. Some said that she had initially accepted his present but had asked him the reason for it. Then, taking his cues from films he had seen, he had leaned over her and tried to kiss her. At that point she had slapped his face, screamed, and accused him of trying to rape her. Others asserted that she had slept with him but had tired of him and had then used the nylon stockings as a pretext to sack him. Neighborhood women asserted that he had befriended the Englishwoman and actually had given her nylon stockings but that her husband, who was suspicious about this affair, had used the stockings as an excuse to separate him from his wife and thus had fired him. Hameed Nylon remained silent for many days, refusing to say anything about the incident. Once he regained his composure he made one comment, simply this: "The only true thing in any of these stories is the nylon stockings."

Although the people of the Chuqor neighborhood considered his termination by the firm a natural event that no one could influence, some men who worked there, and most of the neighborhood youth who trained each day in the gym they had created in an abandoned building adjacent to the house where Hameed Nylon lived, tried to incite the people of the neighborhood against the oil company. The imam of the Chuqor community even mentioned in his study sessions, which began spontaneously every night after evening prayer at the mosque: "The English have deprived one of our community's young men of his livelihood because of a pair of stockings. This matter cannot be acceptable to God or His Prophet." Some women's zeal was so aroused that they swore at the poor kerosene vendors and snubbed them. They would open the taps of the drums

8

that were pulled by donkeys, letting the kerosene spill onto the street. They told the sellers, who had absolutely no comprehension of the affair, "You should pour kerosene down that Englishwoman's crotch." Once again the community's sages objected: "How are these poor fellows to blame?" Oil workers' families certainly did not want to lose the privilege of buying gas at reduced rates through coupons sold to workers. Moreover, the secret labor union that was organizing oil workers distributed a handbill that attacked the firing of Hameed Nylon and called for his reinstatement, although no one in the Chuqor neighborhood knew about the pamphlet, and that was just as well, for if the people had felt the case was political, they definitely would have been afraid. Although the Chuqor neighborhood had never at any time in its history, which stretched back at least a hundred years, participated in a protest demonstration, many residents had heard of them. Indeed, some had seen the demonstration in the great souk a few months before. There were also some butchers who had assisted the police by attacking the demonstrators and clubbing them, after they were told that these demonstrators advocated female licentiousness, once a week, every Friday.

Thus a month after Hameed Nylon had lost his job, it was decided that one Friday the neighborhood would set out on a demonstration to seek the reinstatement of their son who had been fired from his position with the firm. Everyone became excited by the idea after it was lengthily discussed in the coffee shops, which turned into free-for-all houses of debate each afternoon. The matter evolved into a quasi-religious duty once Mullah Zayn al-Abidin al-Qadiri declared that since all Muslims constitute a single body, when one member suffers, the rest of the body rallies on its behalf with a vigilant defense. Consequently, an aged artist, known for carving words on marble tombstones, undertook the creation of protest signs, devising the texts himself.

One day, after the Friday prayer, a procession that included women and children set forth. Athletes from the Chuqor neighborhood, along with those from other communities, carried signs written in a variety of scripts—Ruq'a, Farsi, and Kufic—"There is no god but God; Muhammad is the Messenger of God," "In the

9

name of God the Merciful, the Compassionate," "Traitor, Your Time's Up," "Hameed Nylon's Innocent," "Hameed Nylon Has a Family to Support," and "Long Live Hameed Nylon!" Raised alongside these were green flags brought from the mosques. Thus the tops of their standards read, "God," "Muhammad," and "Ali." When the children saw these, they rushed home and returned with any scraps of cloth they could find. They tied these to sticks, which they began to wave as they hopped about inside the crush of people or at the front. The neighborhood's dervishes brought their swords and lances, which they brandished, striking in time to the ululations of the women or whenever anyone cried, "God is Most Great!" There were also three or four—among them the thief Mahmud al-Arabi, who broke into houses by night (outside of the Chuqor neighborhood, naturally)—who brought their revolvers, since they felt responsible for their community's inhabitants. They fired into the air until the mosque's imam forbade them from doing that. They stopped firing but kept their revolvers in their hands. Many children had stained their faces black with soot so that they resembled Africans or afreets. Others, who wore goat heads attached to skins that reached down to their feet, butted the air with their horns. At the same time some shaykhs sprinkled rose water from small bronze vessels with long necks over the assembled people. Others carried pictures of al-Hasan and al-Husayn, the dragon-slaying saint, the child king Faisal II, King Ghazi, and Kemal Atatürk. Indeed, there was even a framed portrait of the renowned artiste Samanchi Qizzi—taken from the coffeehouse in the great souk.

Finally the demonstration set off, but where was it heading? No one knew. It traversed the Chuqor neighborhood, back and forth, entering alleyways and bursting out of them. When they saw the soot-stained faces and the goat heads, women watching from rooftops thought the procession was a prayer for rain and started pouring water over the heads of the demonstrators for good luck. After they had crisscrossed the neighborhood, someone shouted, "Let's go to the company and present our complaints!" Another person cried, "No, let's go to the barracks and present the matter to the government!" Mullah Zayn al-Abidin al-Qadiri, the mosque's imam, who was marching in the lead with the neighborhood's shaykhs beside him, stopped to deliver a speech that everyone remembered for a long time. He said, "It is unreasonable to think we can march from here to the company in Baba Gurgur to present our petition to the Englishman and his wanton wife, who is a Christian. We would die of fatigue before we reached there. Moreover, God and His Messenger have forbidden Muslims from bowing their heads before infidels. If we go there, we will be forced to act in a submissive and subservient way when we appeal for merciful treatment from a harlot and her procurer husband. This approach would ill befit the honor of the Chuqor neighborhood. I have heard others demand that we head for the barracks or the palace, but how is the government involved in Hameed Nylon's firing? It's the English who fired him, and they're not our fellow countrymen. Only red Communists pick fights with the police and the government, and praise God we're not Communists or Muscovites."

When the Imam Zayn al-Abidin al-Qadiri reached this point in his speech, voices from enthusiastic members of the crowd asked, "What should we do then?" A profound silence reigned while the imam responded. His answer was decisive and dumbfounding this time: "We will turn toward God." The multitude did not quite comprehend the meaning of this lofty phrase. Therefore, he added, "It's true that Hameed Nylon was sacked, but the affliction is even greater than that, for we are all threatened by the drought, since not a single drop of rain has fallen. If God does not show compassion by sending His clouds over the city of Kirkuk, we shall starve to death. So let's all go to the open area in al-Musalla to pray to God and His Messenger for the advent of rain and the diffusion of goodness and blessings to everyone."

Thus, to the beating of drums and the rattle of tambourines, people carrying their green flags and their placards demanding justice for Hameed Nylon headed to al-Musalla Square, which they crossed to the open cemetery, which concealed among its gravestones hoopoes and larks that took flight and soared into the air, until the human throng reached the open space that Turkmen called Yeddi Qizlar, where remains of abandoned stone grist mills could be found. Everyone stood facing God with dignified submission, raising their hands to the sky in common prayer and tearful, heartfelt entreaty for rain to fall and for Hameed Nylon to be reinstated to his job. They remained there more than an hour, asking God to cleanse their soot-stained faces with copious amounts of rain. Suddenly the sky darkened as black clouds approached from the east. Then affirmative cries glorifying God's compassion and might resounded in thanks to Him for hearing the appeal of the inhabitants of the Chuqor neighborhood. In fact, there was thunder and lightning; the prayerful demonstrators were caught in the rain and only reached home by the skin of their teeth, soaked and nearly drowned in the torrents that swept through all the neighborhoods. The miracle that had occurred made them forget the story of Hameed Nylon, who could now joke with the others about his escapades with Mrs. Helen McNeely.

This miracle left an indelible impression on people's memories. They debated and quarreled for a long time about who deserved credit for it. Had God answered the plea of anyone in particular, or simply their joint appeal?

They reached a degree of consensus on the notion that God would not have answered the prayer of one of the few Arabs participating in the procession, for they never washed off their butts and would be regarded as traitors for ever and a day because they had assisted the infidel English in the war against the Muslim Ottomans, fighting against their Turkish brethren without any consideration whatsoever for the religion uniting them. Since the Turkmen disparaged the Arabs in any quarrel that erupted between them with references to "traitorous Arabs" or "those shit-assed Arabs," many Arab children began to wish that God had created them Turkmen. Some Arab children even joined with Turkmen children in their enthusiasm and support for Turkish political parties, of which many Turkmen youth considered themselves members. The portrait of Kemal Atatürk, recognizable by his lengthy face, military uniform, and medals, was displayed on the walls of most homes, whereas only Arabs dared hang a picture of the king, the prince regent, or even of Queen Aliya, who was loved by many, especially

women, perhaps because she was a widow or possibly because it was
the English who according to widespread rumors had killed her husband, King Ghazi, in revenge for his campaign to slay the Assyrians
who had wanted to establish an independent state for themselves in
Iraq under the leadership of Mar Sham'un, who escaped with his
life, fleeing to America. Women told their children with pride how
the people of Kirkuk had once gone out to welcome the return of
the victorious soldiers and armed men of some northern tribes,
each of whom carried the head of an infidel Assyrian in his hands.
The women said that the eyes in these heads were impudent and
kept staring at them, casting impertinent glances their way, so that
many women had been forced to pull their headscarves around their
faces as they cursed Satan and the Assyrians.

Similarly, if the Arabs were ruled out as deserving any credit for
this miracle, there was naturally no cause for the Kurds to claim
such a favor. The truth was that the Kurds themselves, the two or
three families that had settled in the Chuqor neighborhood, denied
playing any role in this case, which was God's doing alone.

It would not have been possible, in any event, for them to claim
the opposite, since they were not very bright and could not even distinguish black raisins from dung beetles. (Everyone in the Chuqor
neighborhood knew that a group of Kurds who were served a plat-
ter of raisins mixed with dung beetles had begun capturing fugitive
beetles to devour, telling each other, "Eat the runaway raisins first;
the others will stay where they are.") Would it have been conceivable
for God to answer the prayer of such ignoramuses? The matter
deserved no debate or reflection.

It was clear that God had answered the Turkmen's prayer and not
anyone else's, but had He answered their communal prayer, or that of
one or two of them only? It was admittedly difficult to be sure about
a complicated matter like this, for opinions were totally irreconcilable.

Some claimed that this miracle should be credited to the madman Dalli Ihsan, who had raised his head to the sky, as he always
did, and ordered the clouds to give rain, so that it rained. These people had an irrefutable argument, namely that Dalli Ihsan was not a
human being but a jinni, one of the Muslim faction of the jinn. This

was no secret, since everyone said so every day. He would walk through the Chuqor neighborhood, stroll through the great souk, and stop repeatedly to scream in the faces of jinn who apparently were trying to pick a fight with him or to upset him. Then he would continue on his way only to turn round once more and curse the void. He was allowed to stop at any stall and take whatever he wanted without anyone asking him to pay, although to tell the truth he never took more than he needed for himself: an orange from here and an apple from there. At times he would sit in a deserted corner of a coffeehouse and drink a tumbler of tea—without paying for it, naturally—and listen attentively to the coffeehouse's rhapsodist as he recited the story of Antara ibn Shaddad or Sayf ibn Dhi Yazzan or the choice exploits of Mullah Nasr al-Din. He would smile, shake his head, and leave. Then some patrons of the coffeehouse would mutter, "What a lucky fellow! The queen of the jinn has summoned him."

The story of his relationship with the jinn had come to light many years before, and even the children of the Chuqor neighborhood knew it. What actually happened was that al-Hajj Ahmad al-Sabunji, a wholesale cereals merchant and the community's richest man, was awakened one night by a voice, which did not sound human, outside his bedroom. He pretended to be asleep while sharpening all of his senses. Someone whispered in the dark, "Harun, Harun, are you ready?" The query came from a cat he had never seen before. Then he saw Harun, the household cat, join the other cat, which he greeted. He said, "I've borrowed some of my master's clothes for us." The second cat replied, "I was afraid you'd forgotten or succumbed to fatigue and fallen asleep." Harun replied, "No other night's like this one. How could I forget our annual party?" They leapt quietly onto the wall and from there descended to the street.

Curiosity got the better of al-Hajj Ahmad al-Sabunji, who also went out to the street and followed the pair from a distance. The two cats, each carrying a bag by the neck, set off in the direction of the souk. Then they turned right, slunk down a side alley, and ended up on the public street parallel to the citadel. Slowly and calmly they continued on their way to the women's baths. He saw his cat Harun and the other one change into men in front of the side door to the baths, open their sacks, and then put on the jilbabs they had brought. Next they shoved open the door and disappeared inside. For a time, al-Hajj Ahmad heard heady, inebriating music coming from within, from the courtyard of the baths. His heart pounded fiercely, for he had recognized one of the two men as none other than Dalli Ihsan.

Al-Hajj Ahmad hesitated for a few moments, not knowing what to do. Should he enter too or not? He was terrified but recited, "In the name of God the Compassionate, the Merciful" and then the Throne Verse from the Qur'an. After that, he thrust open the door and entered, surrendering his fate to destiny. There he beheld a sight no human eye had ever seen before—nor would al-Hajj Ahmad al-Sabunji ever see anything comparable for the rest of his life.

The courtyard of the baths, which his wife visited once a week with the children, taking along her bundle of clothes, had been transformed into an astonishing chamber of colored glass. Hanging from the ceiling were huge chandeliers of pearls. Around the sides were solid gold benches on which were engraved magical inscriptions he could not decipher, not a word. Green, blue, red, yellow, and white birds soared through the higher reaches of the chamber, making music like jinn singing. Al-Hajj Ahmad inhaled the fragrance of intoxicating incense that made him forget he was in the Kirkuk baths. In fact, he forgot he was in this world at all. He was especially incredulous when he discovered something he could in no way explain: the chamber opened onto the shore of a vast ocean traversed by ships arriving from afar in the command of cats of every variety. These leaped to shore the moment the ships and vessels reached it and then changed into young men and women of ravishing appearance. He knew, since he had spent his entire life in the city, that there is no ocean in Kirkuk and that the Khasa Su, which runs through town, is an unusual type of river, since it dries up completely in the summer but turns into a torrential, raging river in the winter, flooding its banks at times and threatening to drown the Chay neighborhood. The many people present wore the most splendid clothes. At the center of the hall sat the king and queen on a throne studded with pearls and rubies. Surrounded by their ministers and courtiers, they were served by comely youths and maidens, who were clad in silk and who carried around platters of pure gold containing finger foods and fruit. Al-Hajj Ahmad realized that these were Muslim jinn and that the names of their king and queen, respectively, were Hardhob and Murjana.

Dazzled by the lights and the elegance of the place, al-Hajj Ahmad al-Sabunji mingled with the guests without anyone noticing him. When he saw people singing and doing line dances, he joined them so that no one would realize that a human being had crashed their party. They were all singing in unison to a beat like a magical incantation:

I saw my Love with my heart's eye.
Then he asked: Who are you? I said: You,
You who surpass every limit
To erase "where"; so where are You,
Now that there is no "where," where You are
And there is no "where" wherever You are
And there is no image for imagination to use to imagine You
So that imagination can know where You are?

Al-Hajj Ahmad al-Sabunji personally memorized these verses, passed down from al-Husayn ibn Mansur al-Hallaj, and started repeating them along with the others. He learned from the partygoers that this poet, who was crucified on a palm trunk in Baghdad, was actually not a human being. He was, rather, one of the God-fearing jinn. They cherish him very highly, and his standing with them is just below that of King Solomon the Wise, who possesses limitless sovereignty over all factions of the jinn.

During the exuberant enjoyment shared by everyone, al-Hajj Ahmad al-Sabunji decided to make a mark that would provide irrefutable proof later on. Thus he approached Harun, who was wearing his navy-blue jilbab, and burned the sleeve of the garment from the rear with a cigarette butt that left a small hole, without Harun noticing. Finally he found an opportunity to slip back to the street again, more than a little concerned for his safety. On the way home through a darkness attenuated at intervals by feeble street lamps, he met thieves carrying their bags on their back, sentries who blew their whistles from time to time, solitary drunks singing Turkmen folk songs as loudly as possible while drunks in other streets responded with their songs in response to the songs they had just heard as they awaited an answering song. But al-Hajj Ahmad al-Sabunji, plunged into another world, was oblivious to everything—the stealthy thieves, the night watchmen, and even the Turkmen folk songs, which he normally enjoyed. Shaking with stress and fright, he might almost have been a prophet upon whom divine inspiration had been bestowed.

As soon as he reached home, he slipped into bed to ponder the events of his amazing night. He tried to sleep but could not and stayed awake until dawn, when he heard Harun jump onto the wall once more, slink into the house, and then—through the keyhole in the door—tell Dalli Ihsan, who had apparently stayed outside, "It was a great night, wasn't it?" He heard Dalli Ihsan whisper, "Naturally, of course," and then add, "Good-bye." Harun replied affectionately, "May the Prophet Solomon be with you." Al-Hajj Ahmad did not close an eyelid all night long and did not leave bed save to perform the dawn prayer, when he saw Harun stretching by the threshold, as if nothing had happened. Al-Hajj Ahmad deliberately donned his navy blue jilbab, in which he found the hole he had created with his cigarette butt. Then he turned to Harun and—to his wife's astonishment—asked the cat, "Do you see, Harun? You've burned my jilbab. You ought to have asked my permission before you wore it." Harun understood that al-Hajj Ahmad had found him out. Lowering his head, he left the house, never to be seen there again.

From that day forward, ever since al-Hajj Ahmad al-Sabunji had told his story in the coffeehouse, Dalli Ihsan wore a halo of sanctity. It is true that most people, especially the unsophisticated and the children, feared him, but the neighborhood's sages considered him a gift from God and a blessing for them from Him. As a Muslim jinni in human form, he could only bring them good fortune. This madman, unlike all the other ones in the city, was quite fastidious, always wore clean clothes, and acted with admirable composure, except for his public conversations with the jinn. He naturally did not have a staff he rode like a hobbyhorse the way other madmen did. Moreover, not a single child dared follow him or chase after him, even though the neighborhood was crawling with children. Not one man could think, even think, of teasing or taunting him, since a matter like that could have cost him his life.

There was thus no doubt in anyone's mind concerning Dalli Ihsan's true nature. Indeed, they were even able to trace his jinni lineage. There was first of all the account of al-Hajj Ahmad al-Sabunji, whose piety, righteousness, and honorable actions no one could question. But this was merely one of the proofs, since Dalli Ihsan's mother had been forced, when an elderly woman of more than a hundred years, to admit under pressure from her neighbors that a king of the jinn named Qamar al-Zaman had been her lover, visiting her secretly at night, and that she had married him according to the precedent established by God and his prophet Muhammad. Ihsan was his son, although she had attempted to conceal his identity from everyone. Her spouse, who had later been taken prisoner in one of the wars he waged against Jewish jinn, had died of grief and sorrow at being separated from his wife and son.

Clearly the madman, who would not have spoken to anyone, was responsible for the miraculous rain that suddenly inundated Kirkuk, for who else would be able to order the sky to fill with clouds and have it obey, or to order the clouds to rain and have them do so? As always, however, there were people ready to wrangle and to express extreme opinions recklessly. They claimed that the rains had fallen in torrents for Hameed Nylon's sake, since had he not been sacked by the company and had there not been a demonstration on his behalf in which the Chuqor neighborhood had participated fully, the miracle would never have occurred. This theory seemed rather logical but did not clarify the miracle. Others responded to this theory, saying, "If we were to adopt this logic, then it would be necessary for us to proceed even a step beyond Hameed Nylon." By this they referred to the flirtatious Englishwoman, since without her affairs with men and her fickleness, Hameed Nylon would not have been sacked. They concluded, "Such an opinion would inevitably lead us to a denial of the faith."

Mullah Zayn al-Abidin al-Qadiri was disturbed by all these views, which he considered heretical and noxious. He announced that neither the jinn nor Hameed Nylon was responsible for the miracle. God had quite simply accepted the plea of the Muslims and had caused the rain to fall abundantly on them. Truth to tell, this view appeared totally logical and was welcomed by the hearts of the inhabitants of the Chuqor neighborhood, especially since Hameed Nylon himself had joked about the idea that he had caused the miracle, saying, "If I were able to cause miracles, I would have made the English whore sleep with me." And he meant what he said.

The rain fell for three consecutive days without cease until low-lying houses were filled with water, the roofs of many homes collapsed, and the Khasa Su River flooded its banks, submerging the neighborhoods closest to it. People reached the point of praying again, but this time for the rain to stop. On the third day of what he termed Noah's flood, Hameed Nylon lifted his head to inspect the sky and told his wife, who had seized the opportunity to spend most of the time in bed with him, "It seems the sky is peeing a lot, after having to hold it in for months." His wife Fatima replied, nervously, "Don't blaspheme, Hameed; it's a miracle." Then Hameed, laughing, answered, "True, it's a miracle, but the sky should not get carried away." During this nonstop torrential rain, Hameed Nylon remained trapped in the two upper rooms they rented in the home of his sister Nazira and her husband—the itinerant butcher Khidir Musa—who lived in a large room downstairs at the end of the courtyard with their three daughters, the eldest of whom was five and the youngest less than a year old.

During these rainy days, Hameed Nylon only descended to the large room once. Then he sat on the carpet near a charcoal brazier with ash covering its embers, a plate of Ashrasi dates and walnuts before him. He affectionately told his sister to pour him a tumbler of tea, and then his niece Layla came to sit on his knee. Khidir Musa expressed his concern: "How will I be able to sell my lambs if this rain lasts much longer?"

Hameed Nylon teased him, "Think of the rain as a holiday, man. Your money will last a thousand years."

Khidir Musa laughed, "That's the rumor my sister Qadriya spreads about me, God curse her; she says I place dinar bills under my mattress and sleep on them, ironing them that way."

Hameed Nylon answered, "What's wrong with that? They're your dinars. Do whatever you want with them." Then he fell silent, gazing by the lamp's faint light at the cabinets. Their gold and silver doors were painted with red and blue peacocks, which had symmetrical tail feathers, and with larks sitting on boughs. There were flowers around the edges.

Khidir Musa said, "There's not much work left in Kirkuk. There are as many butchers here as grains of sand. I'm going to move to al-Hawija, where there's not even one butcher."

Hameed Nylon knew that Khidir Musa craved money and that his avarice was so extreme he only rarely patronized the coffeehouse. Indeed, Hameed Nylon thought Qadriya's assertion justified. He did not realize that the person who really ironed dinar bills was his own sister Nazira, who earned at times more than Khidir Musa—trading in fabrics and women's wear. She would travel and buy her goods from other cities that no one else visited. It was even reported that she had been to Aleppo, a city that women said was in Syria or Lebanon. She would bring back colored fabrics, beautiful blouses, and the famous Raggi Abu al-Hil brand soap, which she sold to the women in the neighborhood (and nearby ones) on credit, but for high prices. Moreover, her mother, Hidaya, a crone who lived in the adjacent Jewish quarter, ran a depilatory service for women's faces (using ceruse), practiced magic, and read fortunes. In fact, it was said that she could turn stones to gold by reciting arcane incantations she had learned from her Jewish neighbors. The two women—Hidaya and her daughter—took care to adorn their sturdy ankles with anklets, their wrists with bracelets, and their necks with coins fashioned into gold chains.

Hameed Nylon had barely finished drinking his first tumbler of tea when his wife Fatima came for him, pretending to be annoyed at being left home alone. As a matter of fact, she was concerned instead that Nazira might be plotting to turn her husband, Hameed, against her. She knew also that Khidir Musa, who was incapable of opposing his wife, would join the plot against his sister-in-law. Hameed Nylon, who was tired of sitting in a darkness dissipated only by the flame of an oil lamp with a dirty globe, rose, saying, "The best thing a man can do during rain and gloom like this is to sleep." His wife followed him. On the steps to their pair of rooms he heard one of Khidir Musa's lambs bleat. He answered sarcastically, "And upon you peace." His wife, climbing behind him, cautioned him about the broken steps. He responded in the dark, "I know each of them by heart." Fatima was happy they were returning once more to their suite, where he was safe from his sister's snares. Perhaps he would feel like sleeping with her, too.

Hameed Nylon stretched out on his back in bed, but did not hear her until she asked if he wanted some tea, since he had been dreaming, and his dream had outstripped the Chuqor neighborhood and the city of Kirkuk to reach a vast, open space, a strange, limitless area he had never seen before in his whole life.

Two

The Chuqor neighborhood actually had only two concerns: poverty and afreets. Poverty had driven many, especially migrant Arabs, to adopt theft as a profession, so that they broke into shops and houses by night. And the afreets, with which the neighborhood teemed since it was near the cemetery, similarly had led many residents, primarily the Turkmen, to become dervishes and sorcerers, devoting much of their time, which was always freely given, to encounters with the ghosts that had chosen the Chuqor neighborhood for their home. People thought it odd when Burhan Abdallah, who was a boy of seven at the time, told them one day that afreets follow poverty and thieves follow afreets. When they asked him what this meant, he did not reply, for he himself did not understand the sentence. When his father, Abdallah Ali, who worked for the Iraq Petroleum Company, wanted to learn the source of that statement and whether the mullah with whom the boy studied Qur'anic recitation had taught it to him, the boy insisted stubbornly, "No, I dreamt it in my sleep." Then he recounted the story of his dream.

He had been sitting on a hill that overlooked the Chuqor community, fearfully watching the afreets and the thieves who thronged the region. He was screaming, but three old men, who had long beards dyed with henna and who were wearing white robes, came to him and, placing their hands on his head, said, "Don't be afraid, my son, for afreets follow poverty, and thieves follow afreets." Then they planted a green banner where the boy sat and departed.

The boy's father nodded thoughtfully and told his wife Qadriya, "I believe our son will be a prophet." His wife, however, objected to this idea, explaining instead that the flag represented leadership and that he would become a police officer. The boy's father asked him to keep this dream quiet and to refrain from telling it to anyone.

Qadriya Musa, in point of fact, when disclosing her hopes that her son would become a deputy lieutenant, was merely disclosing her envy for the good fortune enjoyed by the household of the gravedigger's daughter Husniya, who had worked herself to the bone until her son became a deputy lieutenant. Then jugs of oil, sacks of rice and wheat, coops of chickens, and baskets of eggs began to arrive at her home every day as bribes offered to her son. These were always delivered by uniformed policemen. In fact, over and beyond that, Deputy Lieutenant Najib, who was no more than twenty, would always arrive in a Jeep that brought him to the door of his home, while every policeman he encountered, even those he did not know, saluted him smartly. All this had generated widespread envy, and the hearts of neighborhood girls pounded whenever he passed. They would deliberately peek out at the street or raise the curtain normally blocking the doorway of their home, hopeful that his eye would light on one of them and that he would send his mother to ask for her hand in marriage.

No matter how it might be, the statement that the boy Burhan Abdallah had not understood at the time was destined to influence his later life. It was true that the three men with long beards and white robes had said that in his dream, but he had heard it previously in a fog-shrouded, magical valley where he had found himself on opening a secret box bequeathed by his ancestors, for he had stumbled upon a wooden chest in a forgotten corner of his home. The boy was really an artful fellow and even thought of himself as an original thinker. He was fascinated by his father's prediction that he

23

would be a prophet, since he considered himself worthy of such a mission because he had memorized the whole Qur'an in only a few months. During that time, from observing the letters and discovering their relationship to the spoken words, he had learned to read and write, although he had not confided this secret to anyone, especially since neither of his parents was well placed to discover this fact because neither of them had ever learned to read or write. Mullah Zayn al-Abidin al-Qadiri, for his part, spent most of his time placing the feet of student troublemakers in a foot press so he could beat their soles with his stick.

Burhan Abdallah came upon that amazing chest by accident. There was a large chamber in the house with two marble benches, as was typical, and a dirt entryway served as a kitchen. This earth-floored foyer stretched back to a dark, decaying room that had no natural light. Alongside the large chamber was a kind of abandoned storeroom, which hardly anyone entered, since it was overrun by scorpions. Above this abandoned pantry was an upper room, which was stuccoed with gypsum and which had two small, square windows opening on the street. Reached by broken stone steps, the upper room was also abandoned, even though light entered it during the day. Spread across one side were bits and pieces of strange and discarded items left there for years or perhaps even a century. No one in the household had ever thought of investigating these forgotten artifacts. The room was simply there, offering neither threat nor benefit. Perhaps no one felt like cleaning away the dust of the past, but another, more important consideration was the fact that this part of the house was swarming with jinn and therefore forgotten, as if it did not exist.

The boy—who had never seen a jinni—stealthily slipped away once, however, and climbed to the upper room, thinking that he might find the house's good jinni, about whom his mother had told him tales, for every home has a good jinni guarding it. Although this escapade was not devoid of danger, a powerful drive encouraged the boy to persevere. He had decided that he should not be afraid when the jinni put in an appearance. Indeed, he was determined to talk with it, just as he would talk to any other individual, even if the jinni did not treat him to a trip. He would not mind such an excursion into the jinn's strange worlds, featured in stories his father told him. All the same, Burhan Abdallah was actually carrying a list of requests that he hoped to present to the house's good jinni, for the jinn can accomplish anything. He thought he would ask the jinni to change all the doors of the Chuqor neighborhood to gold, to turn the old woman Hidaya into a cow, and to provide him with a cap of invisibility, which he needed so he could smite some of the older boys.

The boy continued to sit in a corner of the upper room, day after day, waiting for the jinni, which never showed itself to him, until he started to doubt its existence. Finally he grew convinced that the jinn show themselves when no one is expecting them. For that reason, he deliberately stopped waiting to see them and began to dig around in the discarded residue of past centuries. To his astonishment, he stumbled across a small, coffee-colored chest, a closed box on which there were carved cryptic designs and inscriptions that resembled charms and talismans. It was coated with dust and wrapped in spider webs. So he wiped it off with the end of his dishdasha's sleeve and sat leaning back against the wall, gazing at it breathlessly. Since the inscriptions on the cover, in gold, were lovely, delicate, and quite similar to the Qur'anic inscriptions with which he was familiar, he supposed at first glance that he had stumbled on a copy of the Qur'an inside a box. For that reason, he kissed the chest and held it to his forehead. No sooner had he opened the box, though, than the earth shook mightily and a brilliant light flashed through the upper room, leaving him curled up in a ball. Then everything vanished and he found himself cast into the void. He shut his eyes, perhaps on account of the surprise. There he heard the four winds blowing from their directions, blending together into a sweet music. Then everything quieted down. All that remained was the music, which could still be heard in the distance. When the boy opened his eyes once more, he found himself seated in a grassy valley. In the distance, by a boulder, a blind man stood playing a flute. Farther down the valley he observed three old men wearing white, as if they were angels that had just descended from the heavens. They came toward him, smiling and leaning on the staffs in their hands. On their shoulders were sacks that shook with each step.

At this point exactly, while he was in the valley, he heard his mother call him, but tarried to await the arrival of the three angels. Finally one of them accosted him: "Hello, Burhan. You've finally made it."

Staring at the valley, Burhan replied in confusion, "Made it? Where?"

The man, who kept smiling, answered, "Go now; your mother is calling you."

Burhan Abdallah asked, "How can I go, when I'm here in the valley with you?"

"Close the chest the way you opened it. We will always be with you from now on."

It happened that the moment the boy closed the box, he found himself seated in the upper room, leaning against the wall. So he sped down the steps, his heart pulsing with light and thunder.

His father was drinking tea, and his mother suggested to him, "Today is Wednesday, your father's weekly payday. He doesn't begin work till after noon, but we need the cash. Would you like to go with him to bring the money home?" The boy Burhan Abdallah was happy to be entrusted with tasks like this and to be treated like a reliable adult. In the past his father had taken him along when going to work and had placed the envelope of money in Burhan's pocket, advising him to take care that it not get lost or stolen. In fact, his father, who boasted of his son's cleverness and of his ability to recite the Qur'an and to chant it, had taken him to Baba Gurgur more than once. Burhan had been overwhelmed by the sight of the huge, white pipes, the giant storage tanks, the circular dials with needles resembling the hands of a clock, the flames that shot into the red sky, and the sand. He could not get that unforgettable stink—a mixture of oil and soil odors—out of his nostrils.

Burhan Abdallah went with his father this time as well to the remote location where money was distributed in sealed envelopes, each with the recipient's name on it. He walked beside his father, who always carried an aluminum lunch pail with two trays. In the top one was the rice and in the lower one the stew. A spoon was inserted into a handle on the side of the pail after it was closed. His father sent him on his way with a smile, and Burhan Abdallah headed home. He was supposed to walk all the way, but covered some of the distance clinging to the rear gate of a cart pulled by two horses. He did not let go of the cart until the driver noticed him and flicked his whip carelessly toward the back, striking him painfully on the shoulder. He walked across the stone bridge that stretched over the Khasa Su River and saw, opposite the citadel, on the dry side of the river, many men, women, and children squatting on the pebbles with their possessions beside them. A number of policemen had them surrounded. They were clearly all Kurds. Many other people had gathered to stare at them from a distance and to laugh. From time to time the prisoners raised their voices to shout in Kurdish the equivalent of, "The Truth! The Truth!" The crowd then would respond to a beat that fit the words—in Kurdish too—"Put your hand on the hammer."

The boy was led to believe, from what he overheard from the people standing around him, that these were the followers of a Kurdish prophet who had recently appeared with a revelation that a man could marry his sister and mother and plunder the goods of the upper classes. Apparently this prophet thought everything to be the ultimate truth: life, death, woman, sex, and even the stars in the sky and the rocks on the ground.

The boy Burhan Abdallah—instead of joining in the laughing throng's cry of "Put your hand on the hammer"—felt compassion and affection for these strangers, who perhaps were actually right, for who could prove they were not? At the same time, however, the boy was bitter because he himself wanted to be a prophet, and here was someone who had beaten him to it. He told himself, "Never mind, I've still got a lot of time till I grow up." He felt hungry and descended toward the right on the bank of the Khasa Su River, heading toward the great souk, for he saw food vendors placing their kettles on the quay. He put his hand in his pocket to extract ten fils his father had given him and ordered a plate of cabbage from a Turkmen vendor, who said he had spent ten years as a prisoner of war in Russia, where he had worked as a baker. He squatted down to eat beside three porters, who were sitting on the cushions they placed

27

on their backs when they worked. He could have made his way to the great souk, which led to al-Qaysariya and then on to the Chuqor community but instead headed to the nearby livestock market, which was located opposite the river at the entrance to the Chay community. He liked looking at the donkeys, horses, sheep, goats, and cattle bought and sold there. He saw a small donkey standing at the corner of the square, in the midst of all the commotion and the yelling that came from all sides. He approached it and put his hand on its head, combing its mane. Then he told it affectionately, "Here I am, donkey. How are you?" The boy Burhan Abdallah was flabbergasted to see the donkey lift its head and reply in an equally affectionate whisper, "I became a donkey because I didn't go to school. Do you want to become a donkey too?"

The boy dashed off as fast as his feet could carry him and did not stop running until he entered his home, breathless. He told the story to his mother, who laughed to calm him. She told him, "You say you're a man, and then you're frightened by something like this!" Then she added, "It definitely wasn't a donkey. It must have been a playful jinni wanting to tease you." She told him that some jinnis enjoy teasing, jesting, and playing practical jokes. Then she told him a story he had already heard her repeat more than once.

Her father, who was a herdsman, had gone out early one day—at dawn—with his flocks to the pasture. He noticed a strange ram in the herd, so he approached it and began groping under its belly toward the rear, the way shepherds do, when the ram suddenly turned its head back toward him to ask, "Ha! Do you like your uncle's balls?" Her father was frightened, but remained steadfast and recited the Throne Verse from the Qur'an. The playful jinni, who had certainly only meant to have a laugh and joke around—perhaps because it was bored or lonely—vanished.

The next day Burhan Abdallah's father took his hand and led him to al-Musalla Elementary School for Boys, which faced the cemetery, after buying him gray shorts, a shirt, and shoes from a shop that belonged to a relative in al-Qurya Souk. He told his son, "If that donkey wanted this, we won't deny its request." His mother sensed that her hopes of her son becoming a police officer were beginning

28

to be realized. Although the boy, who was wearing shorts for the first time in his life—and this was the only pair of shorts he had to wear, even in the winter when he shivered from the stinging cold—was greeted with insults and sarcasm by most of the neighborhood children, who chased after him when he returned from school, he felt proud of himself. He carried in his hand the book that had been given to him, notebooks, and orange pencils, the fragrance of which enchanted him, and paid no attention to these children, not returning their abuse or quarreling with them. From then on, he had an obscure sense of power that never left him.

He spent the whole afternoon in his house—renouncing the temptation to play in the neighborhood with the other children—after devouring a flat loaf of bread so hot that it burned his fingers, since his mother had just plucked it from the oven, which was flaming in a corner of the courtyard near a small plot where he had planted sunflowers with large blossoms. In his mind's eye, he reviewed what had happened to him that morning in school. The principal had told his father, who had addressed the man as "effendi," "You should have started your son in school before now."

His father had replied, "Effendi, the boy was with the mullah. I wanted him to finish memorizing the Qur'an. You know how important that is."

Then the boy had surprised the principal with a challenge: "Effendi, you can examine me. I know how to read."

The principal's eyes had twinkled as he reached to pluck a book from the table. He had opened it to a certain page, saying, "Fine. Take this and read!"

The boy had read several sentences with ease and fluency. Then the principal had called the school messenger and had instructed him, "Take this boy to First B and tell the teacher he's a new pupil." He had left without even a word to his father, who was thanking the principal.

After the boy Burhan Abdallah came home from school, he read the book the teacher had given him through to the final page as he paced back and forth in the court between the door to the large room and the well, which was located on the other side by an open booth leading to a recently constructed room, which was rented to a man and his wife—Faruq and Gulbahar—who had only been married for two months. Gulbahar spent most of her days in her family's house in the nearby community of Piryadi, and so would not return till evening. Faruq, for his part, left early each morning and did not return till nightfall—almost as if he did not reside in the house. Finally Burhan Abdallah stopped by the opening to the well, which was enclosed by a wall approximately a meter high. He cranked the rather tall winch, which was fastened to one side, arm over arm, as the water bucket's rope twisted slowly but surely at the center of the winch, raising the bucket filled with water ever so gently toward the top. It was light at first but grew heavier as it rose higher. The hardest part was clinging with his left hand to one of the winch's arms while pulling the bucket out—once it reached the lip of the well—with the other hand. His mother had warned him that the bucket was heavy and might drag him back down with it toward the bottom, but he had always been able to pull the bucket out, deliberately not filling it too full of water to make it easier to lift. He poured the cold water into another pail and carried it over to sprinkle on his small garden. His mother had told him, "Don't overdo the water. The plants don't need a lot of water during the winter." Since he saw that his mother was preoccupied with her work at the oven, he slipped unobserved to the upper room to open his box and the valley of the angels.

He remained cloistered there until late afternoon and did not descend until he heard through the two windows, which were open to the street, the commotion that kids were making as they played in the neighborhood. Then he joined three other children in a game they called "The Duped Jew." One child would fetch a banknote from his house, unbeknownst to his mother or family, of course. They would pierce one side of it, pass a fine thread through the hole, and then cover the thread, which they stretched all the way to their hiding place, with dirt. They would wait until they saw a Jew approaching in the distance. Then they would leave the banknote in the middle of the street while they hid in some corner. They were sure that Jews always search the ground for something as they walk, since they do not raise their eyes toward the heavens except to pray for God to send destruction and every conceivable and inconceivable

30

calamity down on the Muslims. The Jew's eyes would normally spot the banknote from afar and glow with delight and greed. He would speed his steps toward the abandoned money, glance right and left, and then lean over to grab it. Before his fingers could touch the money, however, the laughing children would yank it away. Then the Jew would see the practical joke and raise his hands to the heavens to incite God to slay them or else mumble some incomprehensible words. If the children could not lay their hands on a banknote, they would amuse themselves by digging in the center of the street a small ditch that they would fill with water and cover, topping it off with dirt, in hopes that a Jew would pass by on his way home from his shop in the souk and plunge into it. Adults usually drove them away when they did that or chased them, cursing, back to their homes.

This time the children placed the money in the middle of the street and waited for a long time without any Jew passing. Finally the children gave up, took the money, and headed to the abandoned building used as a gym, where they watched weightlifting exercises practiced by young wrestlers in a zurkhaneh pit. After that they stood behind some young men who were gambling, playing Twenty-One with cards, but one who had lost some of his money sent them packing: "Scram! I can't bear to have people look over my shoulder." So Burhan Abdallah went home, where he found his father, his maternal uncle Khidir Musa, and Hameed Nylon standing in front of the house, conversing. The moment his father saw him, he asked his son, "So, how was school?"

The boy replied tersely, "Super."

Abdallah Ali proudly told the other two men, "Burhan has started school."

Khidir Musa complained, "Then I've lost him. I wanted him to work with me." The boy snapped resentfully, "I'm not going to be one of your lambs."

His maternal uncle teased him by cursing him, but Hameed Nylon laughed and said, "I like this boy; he's self-confident."

The boy, however, had gone inside and climbed to the upper room again in the pale evening light, which was still entering the two windows.

Many days passed without anything unusual happening in the Chuqor community. Everything went according to the norm. The men left for their jobs in the morning, and numerous disputes flared between the women concerning the children. These were normal quarrels, and the men tried to stay out of them, despite the many words of abuse the women flung at each other while standing in front of the doors of their homes or poking their heads out through the curtains of their doors. Each day, Arab salt vendors, leading their donkeys, would pass through the neighborhood as did Turkmen vendors with thick mustaches that covered their mouths. The latter came from the nearby village of Tis'in and sold bottled rose water. The children, who were excited by these men's mustaches, would follow them, shouting, "Uncle, where's your mouth?" Then a vendor would seize his mustache with a hand, hold it back, and expose his mouth, saying, "What's this? Your mother's cunt?"

There were blacksmiths and cutlers whose machines with turning, knife-sharpening stones would emit sparks whenever a knife touched them. There were men who bought scrap metal and vendors with small blocks of ice in the summer. From time to time, Bedouins came. These were poets who sat in front of the door of each home as they played their fiddles and recited odes in praise of the house-holder, whose name they had known since childhood. They would not leave their station until the master of the house had displayed his generosity toward them. There were Turkmen and Kurds who came with monkeys and bears to present dramatic performances in the neighborhood. The monkeys would pinch the women and provoke them. The bears would make people laugh by imitating old ladies walking. Even the Gypsies, whose women fastened red kerchiefs around their heads, would circulate through the community, offering sieves for sale. Mothers would warn their children to stay away from them, since they would not hesitate to kidnap children, especially girls, whom they would teach to sing and dance in their tents, which they erected on fields at the city's outskirts. Of all these, the appearance of Hanna the Christian, who was charged with killing stray dogs, caused the greatest commotion in the neighborhood when he chased this dog or that with the rifle he always carried on his shoulder.

One evening, almost everyone in the Chuqor community went out to al-Musalla Square, where a large vehicle had stopped. Written in Arabic on the side was, "British Information Agency." A sheet of white fabric was stretched over the wall of the school, and in front of it on the ground in the open air sat hundreds of men, women, and children, who had come from the neighboring communities to watch a film about the war. The film was an old newsreel from the British War Office about the Allies' victorious battles against Germany and the Axis nations. The sight of tanks and aircraft firing excited many people, especially the women, some of whom trembled with fear. Even though the war had been over for some time, people went home with sarcastic and derisive smiles on their lips at this "British propaganda," since they believed that Hitler's armies were still inflicting losses on the British, punishing them. Some said that Yunus Bahri had broadcast that very day on "Here Is Berlin" that the English had lost the war.

Once, the Chuqor headman, Salman, who lived in the Arab section, came to Hameed Nylon's house in a Jeep with three policemen and a police officer. They searched the two rooms over the entryway without discovering anything incriminating, but carted Hameed Nylon off to the police station anyway. His wife Fatima kept on weeping and wailing, since she did not know what to do. Her neighbor Qadriya came and took her home with her in an attempt to calm her. Many neighborhood women gathered there, for they were scared.

A rumor spread through the community that Hameed Nylon had been trafficking in arms, but many discounted this, claiming the affair must inevitably relate to the flirtatious Englishwoman. Others rejected this theory, since many months had passed since that incident. Three or four whispered, "Perhaps he's a Communist. Who knows?" But they quickly dismissed this idea from their minds: "No, no; he's too bright to be a Bolshevik." They were right, for Hameed Nylon returned that very evening, cursing all the English, everywhere. Someone had fired a few shots at the woods in the English enclave of the oil company—from outside the fence—and that had caused the company's police to make inquiries and to investigate anyone they could think of, based solely on conjecture.

Two or three weeks after this misadventure, Khidir Musa took his wife and their three daughters to al-Hawija so that he could work as a butcher there. His sister Qadriya began to make critical remarks about him to her husband, Abdallah Ali, saying that her brother had fled there because he was scared when he saw the police take Hameed Nylon to the police station, but that his fear was certainly unjustified. Now, Khidir Musa, who saw no point in life besides making money, had mapped out this project months earlier, believing that it would make him rich and prosperous. No one, certainly, missed Khidir Musa or his wife Nazira, but the transfer of the old lady Hidaya to the home the couple had left vacant seemed ill-omened to many, who sought God's protection against the evil caused by cunning witches. Fatima, who was forced to live in the same building with the old woman, was one of these.

Actually, this crone had scarcely moved from the Jewish neighborhood to the Chuqor community when the curse moved with her. Men began to beat their wives in an unprecedented fashion. Indeed, many quarrels broke out among the men themselves for no real reason, and many children contracted typhoid, malaria, and trachoma. Other people lost their jobs. And prices rose, while folks became increasingly impoverished. They substituted barley bread for wheat bread and brown sugar—and finally dates—for the white sugar slabs they broke into lumps small enough for a person to hold between his thumb and index finger while he drank tea. The worst, however, was what happened next.

For the first time in the city's history, the government inaugurated a cabaret on al-Awqaf Street and filled it with female dancers and singers, whom the neighborhood women referred to as whores in every discussion they had of this new plague, which lured many of the neighborhood youth, who would pounce on the last penny in a house or sell anything they could lay their hands on—with no regard for the needs that women felt after being beaten—so they could head for the Bliss Cabaret in hopes that this dancer or that would smile at them. They had to content themselves, naturally, with drinking a bottle or two of beer, since they did not have the wherewithal to keep pace with the tribal chiefs, who would offer whiskey to the dancers and light their cigarettes with five-dinar notes—according to rumors in the Chuqor neighborhood, which was writhing with hunger.

One summer night, the whole community was awakened. Some people were content to stand at the ledges of their roofs watching the spectacle from there, calling down in a loud voice to this person or that in the street, as others abandoned their beds. Even the women left the white-curtained sleeping areas on the roofs and went out to say to one another, "This is what we've been expecting." Everyone had been sound asleep on rooftops open to a sky strewn with stars and traversed from time to time by shooting stars, trailing behind them long tails of light, when they heard in the night a shrill shriek that came from the cul-de-sac adjoining the mosque. The wailing was followed by a hullabaloo, loud screams, and gunfire. Some at first believed it was a clash between thieves, but the sight of a police car parked at the entrance to that alley apparently eliminated this possibility, since the police were not particularly interested in what the thieves did and could not be expected to come to the Chuqor community to chase robbers. Moreover, everyone knew that the police always received their cut from each heist. Thus the matter concerned something else, unrelated to the thieves, and this was in fact the case, for the police had arrested Abbas Bahlawan, who owned an automobile repair shop in the Rafidayn Garage and who would not eat rice unless arak was poured all over it—so the women said—although this claim was highly exaggerated, since all it amounted to was that he added a little arak to the broth normally eaten with rice, not for a buzz, as he himself said, but to add aroma. Thus Abbas Bahlawan was led away, handcuffed, after policemen had been forced to chase him from one roof to another and to fire on him to frighten him. He finally surrendered, inebriated enough to curse the government in front of the throngs of the Chuqor neighborhood: "This is a shitty government that protects prostitutes." No one, however, paid any attention to what he said.

There was no protest against the police's rude intervention this time, for the matter was too big for anyone to fuss about. In only a few moments, everyone had learned the story. They shook their heads, saying, "We expected this." Whether or not they had, someone had been killed by Abbas Bahlawan, who was a regular at the Bliss Cabaret, where he admired the dancer Kawakib, whom he adored and upon whom he showered everything he had gained by working during the day. It seems that, on this night, two of his friends had accompanied him and that he had boasted to them that she loved only him. Unfortunately, that very night, she had chanced upon a better catch. At first he invited her to their table very politely, but she refused, since she was busy with some Kurdish dignitaries. He returned and sat down but avoided the eyes of his two companions, who started to joke and laugh about his claims. He drank and drank and grew increasingly sorrowful and tipsy. His two friends laughed mockingly while they stared at his sweetheart Kawakib, who roamed from the embrace of one dignitary to the next.

It was impossible for Abbas Bahlawan to endure the pain of his suffering any longer. He rose, headed for the dignitaries' table, and stood there staring at Kawakib. One of the three gents asked in Kurdish, "What's this man want?"

A friend replied, "Leave him alone; he seems to be infatuated with the whore."

The dancer Kawakib noticed him as he stood staring angrily at her. "Don't be an ass!" she snapped at him. "Get out of my face!" He forced his mouth open: "You're nothing but a whore!"

Instead of trying to calm or cajole him, however, she spat in his face: "Your mother's the whore!"

That was more than he could bear, for he was cocky to the point of conceit. All at once he noticed that his hand had reached for his small revolver—which he had purchased four years earlier from a Polish soldier whose English unit had been garrisoned for a period of time in tents near the Kirkuk Railroad Station—and had raised it toward Kawakib, who was aghast by this act and gazed at him in consternation. He pressed the trigger, and the gun fired once, twice, three times. Then he came to his senses, perhaps because of the blood that gushed forth. When he felt it sprinkling on his hand, he threw the revolver to the ground and dashed out, forgetting even his two comrades.

The death of the dancer Kawakib meant the cabaret's death as well because Ahmad Sulayman, the governor, who had only quite recently obtained his post, issued orders to keep the doors of the cabaret closed, at least temporarily. A week later, when the owners of the cabaret—after paying bribes to the police chief and after the cabaret's artistes had exerted themselves with city officials—reached an understanding to open the cabaret's doors once more, Abbas Bahlawan's aging mother, who thought it unjust that her son should be imprisoned for killing some whore, marshaled the women of the Chuqor neighborhood who rallied many other women—even from distant communities like the Citadel, al-Qurya, Shatirlu, Imam Qasim, and Sari Kahiya—and all these women poured into the streets, wailing and shouting, "The prostitutes' cabaret has destroyed our homes!"

Some boys, who were skipping back and forth in front of them like demons, showed them where the cabaret was located on al-Awqaf Street. On the way there, many dervishes joined the band of women. They carried placards that read, "Jerusalem Belongs to the Muslims," "Down with Communism," and "There's No Place for Jews in Our Country." This outraged the Communists, who were caught off guard by the demonstration, which they considered a provocation organized by the government. This belief seemed confirmed when the policemen stood idly by, watching women throw stones at the cabaret and break its windows. Some of the artistes who lived in the cabaret itself, because there was no hotel that would accept them, were terrified and forced to flee via the roofs of neighboring buildings, even though they were half-naked.

Apparently the governor took advantage not only of these disturbances, which he had been expecting, but also of the danger to public safety, which he exaggerated in the report that he sent up to the minister of the interior, to cast all the blame on the shoulders of the previous governor, who had not given a moment's thought to the disasters that opening a cabaret in this city would shower on its innocent inhabitants.

Thus the cabaret was closed once and for all and its doors were sealed with red wax, and the female dancers and singers were forced to move to Baghdad again to look for whatever work was available at short notice under difficult circumstances. The Egyptians among them returned to Cairo. One, however, succeeded in staying in Kirkuk, and—with the patronage of the police chief—set up a clandestine brothel frequented by prominent figures, near the Government Guest House. She brought in some second-rate whores from al-Maydan in Baghdad and others from a whorehouse in Mosul.

At the same time, the police chief earned a sterling reputation for himself in the city by ordering, a few days after the attack on the cabaret, the release of Abbas Bahlawan. In fact, no charges were brought against him after everyone, on the advice of the governor, refused to testify against him. Thus the incident was recorded as unsolved, and his widowed mother as well as the Chuqor community welcomed Abbas Bahlawan back with drums and tambourines as if he were a pilgrim returning from Mecca. She was so carried away by patriotic fervor that she began yelling, "Long Live King Ghazi!" as though he had tired of lying dead in his tomb, which was situated in al-A'zamiya in Baghdad.

If this affair had ended in a way that pleased the Chuqor community—after an anxious period that fortunately did not last long—there were, however, other incidents that occurred during this season as well to upset and distress the neighborhood and even disconcert it, for despite the fact that the thief Mahmud al-Arabi was responsible in a general way for protecting the neighborhood against break-ins by night, there had been a number of evening robberies that he was unable to explain, even though everyone knew that Mahmud al-Arabi was closely linked to the other thieves of Kirkuk. Because of his status as a professional thief, it was inconceivable that he would violate the maxim, which was almost a religious conviction, that a thief's home turf was off-limits for theft. So a theft in his community threatened the thief's honor and prestige. Indeed, some thieves took it upon themselves to make restitution for any loss, even if they were required to pay from their own pockets, if they could not track down the culprits and force them to return what had been stolen. Something like this would happen—and then only rarely—if the solidarity among the thieves was threatened and disagreement and conflict arose between them or when new, inexperienced robbers who lacked savoir-faire or who did not acknowledge the geographical division of the city between different thieves began to steal. Far-sightedness and wisdom would occasionally force this thief or that to buy back stolen items from these thieves to return, with a word of apology and the assurance that this would never happen again, to their owners in his home district.

Many houses in the Chuqor community were broken into that summer while people lay sleeping securely on their rooftops. One of these was the home of al-Hajj Ahmad al-Sabunji, who was famous for his wealth. These houses were completely rifled, as if a magic broom had swept them clean. That embarrassed the thief Mahmud al-Arabi, who swore to the outraged citizens of the community, placing his hand on the holy Qur'an, that he would track down the perpetrators who had treated his presence in the community so disrespectfully and then settle accounts with them one by one, no matter how much protection the police provided them. He actually left the neighborhood, after he had thrust his revolver into his belt, and no one doubted that he would be as good as his word.

He was gone for three days, during which time he apparently did not sleep a wink. When he returned, he was stressed to the breaking point. He announced hopelessly, "There is no connection between these robberies and the thieves of the city." The Chuqor community learned that the thieves of Kirkuk, most of whom were Arabs and Kurds, had declared, with the holy Qur'an before them, that they could never commit an outrage of this kind and moreover that they had announced a general alarm to confront this vicious challenge. The thief Mahmud al-Arabi proclaimed to a private assembly, which was held in the courtyard of the home of al-Hajj Ahmad al-Sabunji and which was attended by headman Salman Hanash, Mullah Zayn al-Abidin al-Qadiri, and other elders and notables of the community, that he was not rich enough to compensate the victims and that for this reason he would consent to any decision the community would take with reference to him, even if that meant moving to a different area. He affirmed that given the time and opportunity he would catch the robbers, even if they came from some other city, and that no further thefts would occur in the Chuqor community.

Everyone was convinced by what he said and therefore they declared that they needed him now more than ever before. At that, the thief Mahmud al-Arabi stood up and said, "This will be my responsibility. You all should go home and sleep with confidence about your possessions and your lives."

Afterwards, a strange rumor spread through the neighborhood. At first senior citizens confided it to one another but then it spread to other people like fire through chaff. Neighborhood residents were telling each other that the thieves were not human beings, but the jinn.

Some people became so alarmed that they headed for the home of the madman Dalli Ihsan to entreat him to intervene to put an end to the nightly raids on their community by the jinn and the afreets. Dalli Ihsan did nothing more than look into their eyes and then stand up to begin roaming aimlessly through the city, leaving them with his mother, who said, "He's gone to muster the angelic armies against the Satanic ones." The matter grew even worse when some boys, who lacked a proper upbringing, began to jump out of corners suddenly at night—while cloaked in their mothers' wraps and standing on wooden stilts like legendary giants—to surprise women out alone. Many women collapsed from fear and terror, falling to the ground where they lay kicking and choking on foam that filled their mouths and mixed with the dirt of the alley. Some pregnant women among them suffered miscarriages. Then strict fathers felt compelled to tie these boys up with ropes at home. Finally, the community discovered a foolproof way to control the jinn, afreets, and demons and to drive them from the Chuqor neighborhood. People began to attach copies of the Throne Verse from the Qur'an to the doors of their homes at the suggestion of Mullah Zayn al-Abidin al-Qadiri and also in response to a plea from the thief Mahmud al-Arabi, who said candidly, "Spare me the evil of the jinn, and I'll spare you human evil." Some people got carried away and attached horseshoes and circles of blue beads over the entrances to their homes. Some expectant mothers also placed knives of all types under their pillows and those of small children to ward off evil spirits, especially a certain spirit that was fond of pregnant women. Called Ayyi, she assumed the shape of a kindly old lady but kidnapped women to serve as food for bears or to drown in the river. Men, occasionally, noticed the abduction of a spouse and followed the evil spirit, rescuing the victim from certain death, sometimes at the very last moment.

Thus, when the Chuqor community took steps to clamp down on the jinn and evil spirits and to drive them away, the thief Mahmud al-Arabi fulfilled his pledge. Every night more than twenty masked men came, sporting revolvers in their belts, to stand at the points of entry and the alleyways leading into the Chuqor community, while others patrolled the neighborhood all night long, till morning.

The Chuqor residents went all out to honor these thieves and to show them respect. Many left the doors of their homes open to them, allowing them to come in if they needed a drink of water or to respond to a call of nature. Some households took turns offering them food and tea. Even more important than all this was the community's desire to show its total confidence in them, and they certainly did not err in this. The arrival of these masked men brought universal security and peace to the community to an unprecedented degree. Indeed, one of the thieves befriended the young men of the neighborhood and joined in their zurkhaneh exercises. Another fell in love with a girl, who—apparently—for her part, encouraged him. A new spirit entered the Chuqor community, a powerful, engaging spirit that the other neighborhoods began to envy. Jealousy in these other neighborhoods blinded some weak souls, who secretly contacted the thief Mahmud al-Arabi to propose that he move in exchange for free lodging and a monthly stipend to be paid by that community. Mahmud al-Arabi, however, rejected them decisively, saying that he possessed first and foremost a profession that rained gold on him and that he would never stoop so low as to take a bribe from his fellow countrymen, fleece them, or beg from them in return for doing his duty. Over and beyond that, a man should not betray his fatherland merely for a scrap of bread, and by "fatherland" he meant the Chuqor community.

Three

The summer that thieves violated the Chuqor community, a deep friendship developed between Hameed Nylon, Abdallah Ali, and Gulbahar's husband, Faruq Shamil, who worked in the municipality of Kirkuk's print shop located on Queen Aliya Street. In the course of time, a young Turkmen with a delicate, calm face—Najat Salim—joined their group. He was studying in the vocational training program sponsored by the Iraq Petroleum Company in New Kirkuk. Usually they met in the neighborhood or went to a nearby coffee shop to play backgammon or dominoes. Although their meetings seemed innocent to most people in the Chuqor community, where people thought of themselves as each others' friends even without any declaration of friendship, the matter was much more than that this time. A destiny stronger than friendship united these men, for they had begun to savor new ideas that were not common knowledge among most residents of the Chuqor neighborhood. They would curse the English, mock them, and dub them imperialists who exploited their workers. The son of Mullah Zayn al-Abidin al-Qadiri—Fathallah—who owned a bottling plant for Namlet, laughed when talking with Hameed Nylon: "I can barely understand you, Hameed. Why curse the English? Don't you know they benefit this city? How can you say they exploit their workers when the oil company pays a worker many times more than he could earn working for the state?"

As a matter of fact, the position adopted in discussions by Hameed Nylon and the others was weak, and they had trouble convincing people, for even bakers, butchers, and chauffeurs acknowledged the benefits the English bestowed on the city and envied the well-off employees of the oil company. Moreover, the company compensated employees it forced to retire on account of age with hundreds of dinars and a gold medal for those who had served a long time. This English compassion had made an impression on people's hearts. Even Mullah Zayn al-Abidin al-Qadiri himself once proclaimed in a Friday sermon that the English were more compassionate than many Muslims. In response to this, Hameed Nylon and his friends spread a rumor that Mullah Zayn al-Abidin al-Qadiri received each month a fat envelope filled with cash from the English, and women began to speak contemptuously of the mullah, asserting that he drank arak, too, normally concealing the glass under his turban. The workers earned their money by the sweat of their brows, the mullah by propaganda for the English. The image of Mullah Zayn al-Abidin al-Qadiri became so tarnished in the community that many people boycotted his mosque and frequented a nearby one, which had a zealous young imam, who called for war against the Jews in Palestine and the defense of Jerusalem. Thus Mullah Zayn al-Abidin al-Qadiri felt compelled to deliver a fiery sermon in which he cursed the English, for no reason at all, and announced a jihad against them throughout the Islamic world. The following morning, slogans scrawled in red paint appeared on the walls: "Down with English Imperialism," "Down with Zionism," "Long Live the Oil Workers' Union," and "Long Live the Iraqi Communist Party."

These slogans excited a great commotion among the people, who did not understand the meaning of the words "Union" or "Communist Party," although they grasped, after a fashion, the danger of these terms when around noon they saw a Jeep enter the community. Policemen wearing khaki Bermuda shorts leapt from it. They carried a bucket filled with white paint and some brushes and proceeded to cover the red slogans with their paint. Because they could not read, they also smeared paint over insults that kids had recorded on the walls against each other. The children, who were delighted by the serious interest the police displayed in their handiwork, began to show the police all the slogans written on the walls. Once they realized that the policemen's goal was to obliterate only the Communist slogans, they filled the neighborhood's walls—out of sight of the police—with the slogans "Long Live the Communist Party" and "The Oil Workers' Union Lives." Then they would return to show these to the policemen. The children's mischief-making exhausted the police, who never caught on to this deceit and worked until evening, when they were forced to withdraw even though they had not obliterated all the slogans because they had run out of paint. They promised to return the next day but did not keep their promise, although the children covered the community's walls with more slogans than had been effaced and actually created some new slogans that were even more damaging and critical attacks on the state's honor.

The policemen who came the next day were in plain clothes. The women who normally sat in front of their houses noticed three strangers entering the mosque, as if to pray there, only to leave in a few minutes with Mullah Zayn al-Abidin al-Qadiri, who appeared terrified. He raised his hands toward the heavens, protesting almost in a scream. The women learned from the children, who had also left the mosque, following the group, that the three men were secret government agents who were taking Mullah Zayn al-Abidin al-Qadiri away with them to lock him up on charges of nationalist agitation. The women then rose, leaving behind their small children, who began to crawl across the ground between people's feet. The women started cursing the security agents, who refrained from responding to them for fear of scandal but who urged the mullah, since he was dragging his feet, to step lively. Some of the women known for their boldness and insolence, however, allowing their wraps to flutter open in the breeze, caught up with the group and cursed the government and the English all the way to the little souk, where it became impossible to stay abreast of the men. At that point, one of the security agents turned to his two comrades to say, "Praise God who has delivered us from those women." Then, directing his words to Mullah Zayn al-Abidin al-Qadiri, he asked provocatively, "If you're such a scaredy-cat that you crap in your pants, why ask for trouble by cursing the government?" The mullah swore that he had always supported the government and Nuri al-Sa'id in particular and had attacked Rashid Ali al-Gaylani in his Friday sermon after that leader's movement collapsed, holding him responsible for Muslim blood that was shed in the battle of Sin al-Dhubban in al-Habaniya against the British. The security agent laughingly told him, "These are old stories that no longer concern anyone."

In the barracks, which were on the other side of the city, overlooking the river, they sat the mullah down on a wooden chair before an old desk, behind which sat a man he recognized as Deputy Lieutenant Husayn al-Nasiri, who told Mullah Zayn al-Abidin al-Qadiri, "Fine, mullah; given that you are one of the religious men we respect, you should not have become a Communist."

The mullah's face blanched and he was unable to keep from shaking: "God's forgiveness, my son; God's forgiveness!"

Noting how frightened he was, the deputy lieutenant procured a glass of water for him along with a tumbler of tea with sugar, to calm him. Then he asked him critically, "If you're not a Communist, why do you attack the government?"

Since the mullah thought it pointless to explain his real reasons, to excuse himself he said, "I won't deny that I attacked the English, but that was because they fired Hameed Nylon, and this matter has nothing to do with our government, may God preserve it. I am known throughout Kirkuk for my support for His Excellency Nuri al-Sa'id."

Then the public security deputy lieutenant laughed to lighten the atmosphere: "This doesn't matter; you can even support the Socialist Salih Jabr, since I myself am an enthusiastic Socialist. My concern is stamping out Communism and clandestine unions that advocate disbelief and atheism."

Mullah Zayn al-Abidin agreed: "God's curse on Stalin and all the Reds in the world!"

At that point, the deputy lieutenant, who did not hide his affection for the mullah, proposed that he should act as a security representative in his neighborhood in return for seven dinars a month. He would only need to keep an eye on the Communists and enemies of the government and to inform on them. He reminded the cleric that the walls of the Chuqor community had been covered with Communist slogans, a fact that indicated that Communists lived there. Mullah Zayn al-Abidin al-Qadiri thanked him for the government's expression of confidence, but denied that there were any Communists in his community. He suggested that those who had written the slogans had perhaps come from other neighborhoods. Then he added that God had bestowed His goodness on him, so that his family owned a bottling plant for the soft drink Namlet and another for making ice, in addition to an up-to-date flour mill. He concluded his apology by saying, "My station does not permit me to serve as a spy, but I'll talk with the student who lives with me in the mosque. He's poor and needy and one of God's people. He might be willing to act as a secret agent for you."

Smiling, the deputy lieutenant said, "Never mind about your student; it's not that big a deal." Then he apologized for upsetting the mullah and, escorting him to the door, said, "I hope you won't meddle in politics from now on. If you feel you need to say something, curse Communism; that's the only party a person is allowed to curse in this country."

Mullah Zayn al-Abidin al-Qadiri, however, after being humiliated in this fashion, definitely did not meddle in politics again, not even to curse Communism, for if the commissioner himself was a Socialist, who could guarantee that the police chief was not a secret supporter of Communism? As a matter of fact, Mullah Zayn al-Abidin al-Qadiri was wrong about certain points, especially about his student Aziz Shirwan, whom he had proposed to the deputy lieutenant as a secret agent. The mullah knew that this young Kurd, who had come from Sulaymaniya to study Islamic jurisprudence with the mullah, lived in the mosque and knocked on doors each afternoon in hopes of receiving a loaf of flat bread or a section of one—since people deemed it a religious duty to feed him. He did not know that he was not merely a Communist but had transformed the mosque itself into a secret drop point for Party mail. He had thought about fleeing when the security men led the mullah away but had returned and decided against it when he learned the truth. He reassured the distraught mullah by telling him that security men often try to exert pressure on religious figures to frighten them.

From that day forward, Mullah Zayn al-Abidin al-Qadiri enjoyed unprecedented respect, for people began to speak of him as a stalwart nationalist who held firm to the principles of his faith. Indeed, some people spread a rumor that he had slapped the police chief himself and had proceeded to open the prison gate and set the prisoners free without anyone daring to stop him. Mullah Zayn al-Abidin actually felt proud when he heard these rumors, which he greeted with a crafty smile. He declined to comment on them, although he became more cautious and adhered to the deputy lieutenant's advice to avoid wading into politics. Instead, he turned his attention to the gender of angels: were they male or female? His opinion—which differed from that of many Muslim religious scholars—was that angels are female and that there are no male angels. He supported this opinion by reference to the fact that a male inevitably possesses a penis, which would not be something an angel would need, since they naturally do not copulate. If they are not males, then logically they must be females. At any rate, a sound intellect would reach this conclusion. Hameed Nylon—once during a discussion overheard by men in the coffeehouse—replied, "If we follow your logic, we should conclude that the angels are eunuchs, for what need would a female angel have for genitals if there are no male angels?" His view was convincing, although all the men present rejected it, since they scorned eunuchs. Then Hameed Nylon smiled and told the mullah, "I agree with you, mullah, for God's taste is too refined to create male angels resembling us ugly men when He could make them like the heavenly maidens who delight the heart." The men guffawed, but the mullah said, "Damn you, Hameed. You turn everything into a joke." All the same, Hameed Nylon's argument made an impact on Mullah Zayn al-Abidin al-Qadiri, who began to search for irrefutable arguments for his position.

Mullah Zayn al-Abidin al-Qadiri's assertion to Deputy Lieutenant Husayn al-Nasiri that there were no Communists in the Chuqor community was credible, for there were no Kakaiyeen with the thick mustaches that were considered a sure sign of Communism. People were right to believe this, for Communists in the city during World War II had deliberately adopted Stalin's mustache as a symbol of their nationalist struggle. That made the job easier for security agents, who recognized and pursued them. Of course, law student Aziz Shirwan, Hameed Nylon, and all the other men in the community had mustaches, since a man would not be considered manly without one. Thus the worst insult exchanged in a quarrel was for one man to threaten another, "I'll shave off your mustache!" Their mustaches, however, were thin, not thick, and more like two strokes under the nose from a draughtsman's brush than anything else. Indeed, the mustache of the oil worker Abdallah Ali, who was thin, brown, and lanky, was trimmed on both sides to look almost like Hitler's. Thus it was impossible for anyone to imagine that these men were connected to politics in any way.

Except for the law student Aziz Shirwan, who was already a Communist when he moved to the neighborhood, and for Faruq Shamil, who met Communists in the print shop where he worked—and in any case he had moved into the Chuqor community from elsewhere—there were no dyed-in-the-wool Communists in the neighborhood. The others—including Hameed Nylon, who had begun to transport passengers between Kirkuk and al-Hawija in an old, wood-sided vehicle that belonged to a Jew named Shamu'il, who had a shop selling watches in al-Awqaf Street and who was the sole agent for Swiss Felca and Nivada watches—were preoccupied with a single thought: a union that would defend the rights of its members. The police considered unions to be simply another face of Communism and pursued them mercilessly. Hameed Nylon, however, believed firmly that had there been a public union for oil workers, Mr. McNeely and his prostitute-wife, Helen, would not have been able to toss him out on the street like a rat. Indeed, he was so touched when he learned that the clandestine union had issued a flyer defending him that his eyes were bathed in tears. When Najat

Salim showed him the flyer, he read it again and again. Then he hid it carefully in a bag at home. That same day, he asked Najat Salim to introduce him to these folks. Najat Salim asked him, "Why should I introduce you? They are closer than you think." Hameed Nylon was perplexed. So Najat Salim said, "Let's go have tea at the union." He led Hameed to the room where Faruq Shamil lived with his wife Gulbahar, right next to his own house. Hameed Nylon burst out laughing and ruffled the evening calm of the Chuqor neighborhood, exclaiming, "What an ass I am!"

Thus Hameed Nylon found his way to the trade union, for although Faruq Shamil did not work for the oil company, he was a member of the cell that directed the work of the city's unions. At this session, Faruq Shamil told him to attempt—circumspectly—to interest working men in the Chuqor neighborhood in joining the unions and to put them in contact with the leadership of the workers' movement in the city. Hameed Nylon disappeared then for a full week. When he returned, he brought with him a list of the names of twenty-one individuals in the Chuqor community—including four oil workers—who wished to join a union. Hameed Nylon apologized that he had not had enough time to contact more people. The men admittedly belonged to diverse professions and included an officer at the rank of second lieutenant, a policeman, three soldiers, and a dervish known in the neighborhood for sticking skewers through his cheeks and swallowing glass. He was a member of the Qadiriya Brotherhood and affiliated with a Sufi lodge located in the Kurdish regions of the city. Faruq Shamil was puzzled to find the name of the thief Mahmud al-Arabi on Hameed Nylon's roster as well. He asked Hameed gravely, "What did you say to get a person like the thief Mahmud al-Arabi to side with the union?" Hameed Nylon replied, laughing, "Oh, it was easy with Mahmud. I suggested that he should head a union that would embrace all the thieves of Kirkuk, and that was exactly what he wanted."

Hameed Nylon had scarcely joined the union and contacted the oil workers when a marked difference was observed in their relationship with the firm, which they held responsible for the injustices they felt, especially after it sacked several employees whom it considered saboteurs.

These men eventually fell into the hands of the police, who tortured them with special German-made, nail-pulling pincers that the minister of the interior had purchased himself during his annual holiday in Turkey. This gross attack led the workers to call a strike, since they felt their personal honor had been impugned.

During the week preceding the oil workers' strike, neighborhood men, who as a matter of course met each afternoon in front of their homes, noticed a stranger in a dishdasha riding into the community on a bicycle. He traversed the community several times, going back and forth, before stopping in front of the mosque to watch the young men gathering. They had spotted him: "Look! He's an undercover agent come to spy on us." Hameed Nylon wanted to challenge and beat the stranger, but Faruq Shamil stopped him: "That's not how it's done, Hameed. Wait just a moment." Faruq Shamil went home. He was gone a few minutes and then returned, laughing. He did not even look at the man, who had taken a seat on the mosque's bench, withdrawing from his pocket a dark loaf of military-issue bread, which he proceeded to gnaw on greedily.

A few moments later, the men standing there heard Gulbahar's voice screaming at the man with the bike, "Dog, scamp, for days now you've been annoying women in our community. Don't you have an ounce of shame or honor?" Before the man could swallow the morsel he was chewing, she pulled off her sandals to beat him. Suddenly the women who had been sitting in front of their homes burst out screaming. Other women left their chores indoors to attack the man, who cried as he fled, "No, by God, I've done nothing." Blows landed on his head from every direction, and the children took part in the screaming and drubbing too. One even caught the man off guard from behind and attempted to sodomize him with a metal rod as punishment for his insolence toward the women of the community. It was Abbas Bahlawan who rescued him by grabbing hold of him as if he were a scared rat. Then he slapped him a few times, until he fell into the narrow, open sewer that passed through the neighborhood, lifted him again, and gave him a kick that sent him sprawling on his face and made his nose bleed profusely. He tried to flee, but the children seized him and he fell once more. Abbas

Bahlawan raised the bicycle into the air and threw it so far that it broke. He grasped the man and lifted him up, threatening, "If you enter this community again, you can kiss your ass good-bye." The man swore, "I'll never set foot in this community again so long as I live." Then Abbas Bahlawan turned toward the women and children to say, "Let him go. You'll never see his filthy face again." The man—whose dishdasha was ripped and soiled with muck and blood—left, dragging his bicycle, which was too damaged to ride. He actually was never seen there again.

The day of the strike, Hameed Nylon stood with more than twenty workers on the train tracks that connected the city and the company to prevent frightened and hesitant workers from going to work, calling them cowards and stooges of the English. Many brawls broke out between strikers and non-strikers during which the food in the men's lunch buckets spilled onto the ground and some men used their cutlery to defend themselves. That first day the police stood at a distance, watching the workers fight one another, ready to intervene at an opportune moment. Hameed Nylon, along with three other workers, retreated to the rear, back to the mouths of the alleyways leading to the main thoroughfare. Whenever he saw an oil worker in his blue uniform, he greeted him, saying casually, "Go home. They've sent us home today. Enjoy your holiday, brother." The worker would ask in astonishment, "Holiday? What holiday?" Then Hameed Nylon would respond quickly, "Don't you know? The king is visiting Kirkuk today." This was the way he approached the unsophisticated. For those who seemed more on the ball, he would pretend to be fleeing, after having escaped with his life, claiming that battles had erupted between the police and the workers and that the police were arresting people—indeed, that they were firing indiscriminately on any worker they encountered. He advised them to go back home. Many believed him without even asking any more questions. In fact, his reasoning was only rarely rejected, even by workers who knew what was happening. He would tell these men that the strike's goal was to increase their salaries and to realize gains for them and that it was in their self-interest to join the strike in defense of their own welfare—if nothing else—instead of weakening the operation and harming others. In any event, they would not be held accountable, even if the strike failed, because they could always claim to their bosses that the striking workers had prevented them from getting to work. His spiel was quite seductive: "Share our victory, or, in the event of a failure, blame it all on us."

Seventeen days of the strike passed without bringing a settlement. True, work at the firm was crippled once the number of strikers increased, but no one thought of yielding to the workers. That would have been, quite simply, a violation of principle and was therefore intolerable to the police chief, the governor, and the minister of the interior. Mr. Tissow, the head of the firm, actually would have liked to bargain with the strikers because he himself had once been a member of the Labour Party when he was a student at Cambridge University, but the governor told him politely, "I understand your humane sentiments, Mr. Tissow, for you Englishmen are fond of democracy, but how can you practice democracy with donkeys?"

The translator whom the governor had brought along was apparently less than fluent in English and became confused, substituting "monkeys" for "donkeys," so that Mr. Tissow then smiled and replied, "Your Excellency, you should address this question to Darwin."

As a matter of fact, the issue was bigger even than the governor himself, although he attempted to project an image of being a decisive man of action, for the minister of the interior contacted him by telephone and ordered him to suppress the strike at any cost. The minister of the interior had himself received a comparable order from the prime minister, who had decided to resort to force on the advice of the British High Commissioner, who unfortunately was a member of the Conservative Party and hated workers because his party had lost the most recent election to them.

The workers met every day, from early in the morning, in Gawirbaghi, which was a parched garden not far from the offices of the oil company. There they recited poems by Muhammad Mahdi al-Jawahiri, Ma'ruf al-Rasafi, and other less well-known poets. Naturally, half the inhabitants of Kirkuk found their way to Gawirbaghi—especially the women and children—not to show their support, which was assumed, but because the strike was a thrilling song fest, which lasted from morning till evening and which differed from any Kirkuk had ever witnessed. The strikers' children and wives brought them food, even from the furthest communities in the city. The women's trills, which rang out continually, re-energized those men who were quaking with fear inside. Thus they came to see the affair as a question of personal honor, as if it were a clash with a hostile tribe.

The first hours of the seventeenth day of the strike passed like the others. The workers delivered harangues and chanted slogans in the garden. Men, women, and children gathered round to watch. Security men, who were circulating on their bicycles, observed them. Children sat on the branches of olive trees that grew here and there. Even the armored police vehicle was still parked where it had been: at the head of the street leading to the garden. Everything seemed normal until noon, when someone arrived to say that large numbers of mounted policemen were massing at the beginning of the street. Fear drove the workers to greater zeal and they shouted even louder, although everyone expected some face-saving resolution. Finally a Jeep with a rifle-mount appeared. In the back stood three policemen and a lieutenant. The crowd surrounding the area fearfully moved back at first, although they soon returned cautiously when the lieutenant, from his place in the open Jeep, began to address the workers: "We warn you to evacuate the area, end the strike, and return to your jobs. You are the victims of a Communist plot. The Communists are exploiting you and deceiving you. The Communists are friends of the Jews and wish to get you into trouble. Unless you disperse now, the police will intervene."

Even before the lieutenant had concluded his threatening oration, cries and curses resounded in the garden: "Scum, return to your masters and kiss their asses!" Many people broke branches from the trees and trimmed them into staffs in preparation for a battle. A worker somewhere started a chant that others repeated: "Strike till death!" At that, the Jeep retreated amid the worker's guffaws and catcalls, "The cowards are fleeing." It was, however, only a few minutes before the armored vehicle returned, followed by a large number of mounted policemen armed with truncheons. Only then did most of the onlookers grasp the danger of the situation. They raced off in every direction, while continuing to watch the spectacle with interest. Others stayed where they were because they felt allied with the workers, or perhaps because they had misunderstood the situation.

Silence reigned over the strikers who had held their ground. They grasped green tree limbs as if these would suffice to ward off the danger confronting them. Suddenly an intermittent round of gunfire resounded. The striking workers lowered their heads amid the universal turmoil and screaming. The first round was followed by a second and a third. The workers looked about and sought shelter behind the trunks of the garden's few trees. Terror-stricken onlookers mixed together with the strikers till they formed a single bloc. Just then, the ground shook from the hooves of the horses that had reached the garden. Their riders, truncheons in hand, were oblivious to any of the crowd of humans who fell beneath their horses' hooves. Occasional shots were fired by policemen and security agents. A number of workers clashed with policemen who had fallen off their horses. In this battle, Hameed Nylon, who—like all the strikers—had concealed his identity by winding a cloth around his head, although short, demonstrated bravery that surprised even himself. From inside his shirt he drew out a dagger, which he carried in defiance of the union's instructions, and began to stab the bellies of the horses from the rear till they were writhing with pain and threw their riders or fell down with them. A Kurdish dervish, who had come from Erbil to present a display of his supernatural powers in a nearby Sufi lodge, seized a policeman who had fallen to the ground, dragged him behind some trees, and then butchered him, after reciting the opening prayer of the Qur'an for his soul.

The battle ended with the flight of the striking workers, who left behind them thirteen slain, including a child—struck by a bullet—who remained lodged where he had been sitting in the branches of a tree, two women, and a vendor of cooked broad beans, who had fallen in a heap over his cart. More than twenty of the wounded were placed under arrest. Others managed to escape from the hands of the police and security agents. Of the attackers, three policemen were killed, including the one slaughtered by the dervish. All the attackers listed themselves as wounded in order to receive the ten-dinar bonus that the minister of the interior had earmarked for casualties.

Many from the Chuqor community and from those recruited by Hameed Nylon witnessed the carnage only to emerge unscathed, with nothing more than bruises, which this person or that received, but Hadi Ahmad received a blow to the head. He was a ten-year-old boy whose father owned a portable camera of the old-fashioned type that ends with a black cloth into which the photographer sticks his head while the customer sits against a plain sheet placed in front of a wall—on the quay at the head of the stone bridge opposite the barracks—while he too is shrouded in black as he faces the moving lens. The blow that the boy received from the truncheon of a mounted cop left him unconscious. Had Abbas Bahlawan not plucked him up and carried him home, he would certainly have died beneath the horses' hooves. When he regained consciousness, the sight in one of his eyes was gone. Worse than that, he had suffered some neural trauma and permanently lost his sense of equilibrium, a condition that stumped all attempts by imams and physicians to find a cure. His left eye, however, quickly regained its sight, thanks to the genius of a young ophthalmologist who had studied in Turkey after despairing of gaining entrance to the Medical College in Baghdad, first because his marks did not average more than fifty and second because he was an Arts Faculty graduate. All this, however, did not prevent the doctor from venturing on an experimental treatment that American ophthalmologists would only adopt forty years later. This Turkmen physician realized that the boy Hadi Ahmad had suffered a detached retina, which needed to be lifted and reattached in its previous location. The challenge did not lie in lifting the retina, for even a nurse could do that, but in reattaching it where it belonged. Since there seemed to be nothing to lose because that eye was sightless, no matter what, he had a simple idea that not even the devil could have dreamed up. This was to fix the retina back in place with a normal adhesive. That resulted in another miracle for the Chuqor neighborhood, although this time it was a medical one, for after half a minute the boy rose and could see better than ever, since the doctor had placed the retina precisely where it belonged, bypassing some of nature's shortcomings.

The bloodbath was followed by a wave of arrests, including those of all the leaders of the strike. The police turned the facts upside down, asserting that the strikers had launched the attack and had fired on the lieutenant when he came to ask them to evacuate the area. The Chuqor neighborhood escaped these arrests, however, since the police focused on suspects already known to them, and these were not from the Chuqor community. All the same, Hameed Nylon disappeared, without his absence exciting any suspicion, for his wife Fatima claimed that he had traveled to Lebanon on business and that he would be gone for several months. Some people in the neighborhood spread a rumor that he had gone to Turkey, where he had enlisted in the Turkish division sent to Korea in order to plunge into the war on the Americans' side against the Communist revolutionaries. Others said he was actually fighting for the Communists against the Americans.

The massacre in Gawirbaghi Garden scared the striking workers, who returned to their jobs at the oil company the next day as if nothing had happened, although they avoided each other's eyes for fear their hearts' shame would show. They had lost their battle and had no alternative to returning to work, without any preconditions and most of all without a union.

At the same time as the workers acknowledged their defeat, Mr. Tissow undertook to comply with all the demands the workers had advanced during the strike, except for recognition of the union. That, he said, was an issue for the regional authorities, not for the Iraq Petroleum Company. He declared that he did not want the workers and the company to be separated by an iron curtain like the one the Communists had erected in Europe. He appropriated this phrasing from Winston Churchill, who had originated it a few months earlier. The magazine *Qarandal*, published in Baghdad, reported it for the first time, attributed to the firm's director general.

In point of fact, Mr. Tissow adopted his conciliatory posture after holding a private meeting with British Intelligence at the Iraq Petroleum Company. The meeting was also attended by Mr. John

Brown, who was known as "the Arab" and who served as a political attaché at the British Embassy, which was located in Baghdad on the Tigris River on the Karkh side. Mr. Brown had assigned exceptional importance to the oil workers' strike—even more than the Iraqi government itself—affirming that the strike was considered a link in the chain of an international Communist conspiracy, led by Stalin himself, to end British influence in the world and to establish people's dictatorships like those Communism was then founding in Eastern Europe, in Greece, which borders the Middle East, in Iran's Kurdistan, which touches Iraq, in China, where Mao Tse-tung controlled most of the territory, and likewise in Korea and Vietnam. Mr. Brown explained that the Iraqi government was totally isolated, "But thank God for this nation's tribal structure, for citizens here normally follow their chiefs, and the chiefs are in the pocket of our friend Mr. Nuri al-Sa'id. This is the only guarantee of our presence in this country now; there's nothing else." Then Mr. Brown revealed that the central headquarters of British Intelligence in London possessed information that indicated the probability that some of the firm's British employees had themselves played a role in inciting the Iraqi workers to strike. He offered a list of names of English employees who were associated with the British Communist Party or who had been active in left-wing politics in Britain. At the end of his remarks, Mr. Brown said, "If it was possible to tolerate a situation like this for tactical reasons in wartime, it's not possible now."

At this meeting, which lasted more than two hours, they finally decided it was necessary both to impose covert surveillance on leftist English employees until they could be transferred back to England and to contact the Iraqi authorities to explain that the best posture to take toward the strikers was a conciliatory one, rather than a severe one, for fear of arousing nationalist feelings—especially since many Iraqis held Britain responsible for the massacres that Jews were committing against Arabs in Palestine.

Afterwards Mr. Tissow escorted his guest Mr. Brown and the members of the British Intelligence team attached to the firm to a banquet held at the British Club. A dance followed, but Mr. Brown did not attend, because he felt tired after his strenuous trip from

Baghdad to Kirkuk. He was unaccustomed to the intense heat, which affected his chronic low blood pressure. Thus he retired for the night apologetically, expressing his wish that Mr. Tissow enjoy himself.

The following day, Governor Ahmad Sulayman was puzzled when Mr. Tissow, emphasizing the danger of doing anything to increase tensions at that time, requested that he treat the imprisoned workers leniently and even release them after a trial that would merely be a formality. The governor, who was trying to suppress his own rebellious emotions, looked at him: "If the workers learn of your humane stance, none of them will dare open his mouth to call for a strike."

Mr. Tissow smiled proudly, "Yes, Your Excellency, we place flowers every day on the tomb of Karl Marx in London."

The governor contacted the police chief, relaying to him Mr. Tissow's desire that he go easy on the incarcerated prisoners. The police chief said, "I don't know if that will be possible, for two have already died of torture and others are as good as dead."

The governor quickly responded, "That makes no difference. You can add those to the other fatalities and claim they died in hospital as a result of their wounds, but keep your men from beating the others. Indeed, provide medical care for them before you present them in open court. Then release them, which will affirm that we are actually democratic."

Thus the court, which was convened six weeks later, found no grounds for conviction of the strike's leaders and pronounced them innocent of all the charges directed against them. In fact, the court displayed such exceptional impartiality that it issued an order for the arrest of the lieutenant and the three policemen who were with him in the armored vehicle, charging them with planning the massacre. The police chief, however, later tore up this order himself, telling the head of the court, "It's true that we asked you to be impartial in issuing your verdict, but not to the point of sending my men to prison." The security men were upset when they saw the strike leaders hug each other in delight at being liberated. They approached them to whisper, "Don't think that you've escaped from our hands. We'll find a way to crush your skulls if you so much as breathe again." The workers, however, displayed no reaction to this provocation; they

58

were puzzled by the spirit of impartiality that had suddenly descended on the government. There was something suspicious about the matter, but they attributed it to the government's retreat in the face of public pressure. They were content to save their skins, which still bore scars from the whips.

As a matter of fact, the only one from the Chuqor community who attended this trial, which was held in the first courtroom on the second floor of the Palace of Justice and which lasted for seventeen days, was Mullah Zayn al-Abidin al-Qadiri, who wanted a closer look at the Communists. The trial helped him form a somewhat more positive impression of these people, whom he termed atheists. He returned, saying that the only difference between them and other people was their blindness and adherence to a heresy called Communism. He declared that any type of heresy is an error, espe-cially a godless heresy. All the same, he explained to the men attending his study session in the mosque that as a point of fact Communism was not a creation of Stalin's thought, as Communists claimed, but an invention of Ahmad ibn Qarmat, who had estab-lished the first communist society while attempting to destroy the Islamic state.

Between the failure of the oil workers' strike and the general Jewish migration to Palestine two or three years later, no events excited the interest of the Chuqor community except for their sup-port of the execution in Baghdad of the Jewish spy Adas, which the people supported, and the parade the Chuqor community mounted, with drums and tambourines, to mark the return of three of its sons: soldiers who had gone with the Iraqi army to combat the Jews in Palestine. They were the very same soldiers whom Hameed Nylon had recruited for the union drive.

The three told many tales, which were transformed with time into legends. They said that the Jewish army would not have been able to stand up for even a few days to the Iraqi forces, which were advanc-ing on Haifa, Jaffa, and Tel Aviv, had it not been for the treachery of Nuri al-Sa'id, who ordered the military commanders, each time, to withdraw from any site they occupied. In fact, they swore they had witnessed Jews holding up pictures of Nuri al-Sa'id and chanting his name. The crowd laughed each time they mentioned the terror that overcame the Jews whenever they heard any reference to the Iraqi army, since they believed that the Iraqis were cannibals. Iraqi forces had once taken prisoner a number of Jewish Hagana and placed them in detention. Then the Iraqi commander had come and examined them, one after the other, finally choosing five of them saying, "Take these five and slaughter them. Then prepare them for cooking today: three for lunch and two for supper." These terrified Jews were led away to two isolated tents: ingredients for lunch in one tent and those for supper in the other. The Iraqis allowed supper to escape so they would carry the frightening news to the Jews, namely that the Iraqis ate their prisoners, which was precisely the message the Iraqi commander wanted conveyed to the Jewish soldiers.

An earlier event that had roused the entire city, not just the Chuqor community, was the crash of a small, two-passenger airplane, for this was the first time a plane had crashed in Kirkuk. It fell on some trees in the garden of the Officers' Club and demolished a side of the outer wall, leaving its right wing visible from the street. Children used it as a see-saw, clinging to it despite the presence of a police guard, who occasionally was obliged to visit a nearby coffeehouse to pee or drink tea. Hadi Ahmad—the boy whose retina the ophthalmologist had reattached with glue—managed to slip inside the plane through its wrecked door. There he found a compass, which he carried around his neck for years to come as a good luck charm, not even removing it when he entered the public bath.

After the return of the three soldiers to the Chuqor community from the Palestine War, the Iraqi government expelled Jews from the country, placing them and their suitcases in open trucks that conveyed them through the desert to Transjordan and from there to Israel. Many wept, asking to stay, saying, "Iraq is our homeland," but the police arrested such refuseniks, charging them with spying and Communism, and then transported them in police vehicles that dropped them off beyond the nation's borders. The only persons to escape from this expulsion were some young Jewish women who were in love with young Muslim men: they eloped after professing Islam.

The whole Chuqor community welcomed the Jewish woman Hayat Sasson, who had changed her name to Hayat Yusuf, after she married Najat Salim, who had completed the training program at the oil company and acquired a first-rate post there. He had gained an excellent command of English from his passionate reading of English-language editions of Maxim Gorky's works, which the Eugene Bookstore, located near Cinema al-Alamein, imported without ever arousing the suspicions of the police, who, naturally, did not know any English. The women of the Chuqor community, accompanied by their children, had gone to view the Jewish/Muslim woman and to welcome her. On the morning of the wedding day, Najat Salim's mother and some other women danced. Seized by a musical euphoria, they partnered the male dancer, a Turkmen known professionally as "Sprout," who shook his midriff to the rhythmic music of his troupe, which consisted of a drummer and a folk oboist. The women were not embarrassed to be around male dancers like these, who attended women-only parties dressed in women's outfits and sporting rouge and powder on their faces. From time to time a woman would stick a coin in his hand and tell him a name. Then he would stop dancing, yell very loudly, "A tip!" and announce the name of the donor's family. His companion would begin drumming again, and he would swivel his hips swiftly to the music.

During this party, someone came in to say that Hayat's parents were standing outside the house and wanted to spirit away their daughter. Then Najat's mother went out and threw stones at them, scolding them. She said, "Hayat's become a Muslim; there's no hope for you now." Thus they were forced to withdraw, weeping. When the children wanted to pursue them, Najat's mother stopped them. She said, "Come back to the wedding. They're Hayat's parents, in spite of everything."

Trucks came every morning to the Jewish community, who opened the doors of their houses to Muslims, selling everything they could, from household furniture to cooking pots and tea tumblers. Burhan's mother bought an iron bed for half a dinar, and the boy usurped it the moment it arrived in their house. Although he fell off it repeatedly while he slept, he finally got the knack of sleeping on it. In fact, it became his favorite place to write and read, and he prevented the others from getting on it.

Hameed Nylon appeared again after an absence of more than three months, as if he had suddenly emerged from the belly of the earth. He affirmed that he had been in Lebanon, although there was no indication that he had made his fortune there, for he returned to work on the Kirkuk-to-al-Hawija route, driving a Jeep that transported Arabs along with their sheep, goats, and chickens. As a matter of fact, he kept the secret of his disappearance even from his wife Fatima. When the strike that the government had met with a hail of bullets had failed, he had ridden off heading toward Chamchamal, which lies between Kirkuk and Sulaymaniya. From there, he had made his way on foot, without a guide, to the nearby mountains. He was searching for Khula Pees, a Kurdish brigand who had killed three policemen and had then sought refuge as an outlaw on a mountain, where men with problematic relationships with the government had followed him. When the police had tried to pursue him later, he had killed tens of them, forcing them to retreat, humiliated and defeated. Hameed Nylon went from one mountain to another in search of him and finally discovered him one day in front of a cave at the head of a valley. Starting with this first meeting, he attempted to persuade the brigand to transform his gang into a people's liberation army modeled after that of Mao Tse-tung, but this robber, who was illiterate and near-sighted, after staring at Hameed Nylon for some time, asked, "What would I gain from that?" Hameed Nylon replied with the astuteness of a person who can read other men's minds, "You'll become the people's hero." The thief smiled and retorted, "But I already am the people's hero." After that, none of Hameed Nylon's efforts during the three months he spent with the thief panned out. In the man's head, there was only one idea, which was to kill the greatest number of policemen he could.

This was the first time that Hameed Nylon had ever failed to sell a person one of his ideas. He considered proclaiming a liberating, armed rebellion in the style of Mao Tse-tung, whom he greatly revered, but realized that he did not possess even a single rifle with which to fire the revolution's opening shot. Thus, Hameed Nylon retraced his steps home, but without losing hope, since a trip of a thousand miles begins with a single step, as Mao Tse-tung had said. This was a phrase that Faruq Shamil had frequently repeated to him.

Four

After a stay of several years, livestock dealer Khidir Musa returned from al-Hawija, but without the fortune he had dreamt of. In fact, he would have ended up in prison had he not paid many bribes: to the county manager, the police lieutenant, and the deputy lieutenant, not to mention the policemen who hovered around him like flies.

Actually, at first he had enjoyed a streak of good luck and in only a few months had become an influential figure who gambled on a regular basis with the county manager, the police lieutenant, and several tribal chiefs. First, he had worked as a butcher. Then he quickly switched professions to open, in a location near his home, a shop that sold sugar, tea, and cereals. Eventually he became—in return for the sum of one hundred dinars, which he used to bribe the government (in other words, the county manager and some police officers)—the sole government contractor approved to provision the county. In time, he learned that he should lose, although not too frequently, when he gambled with government officials. He was also obliged to demonstrate his support for the government on a regular basis with sacks of sugar and cereals and with Ceylon tea boxes, which usually contained small black elephants with ivory tusks. Policemen would, as a matter of course, volunteer to convey these souvenirs to their superiors at the behest of the contractor Khidir Musa. They were themselves gratefully satisfied with a scoop of sugar or a tea packet that the contractor would generously present to them.

All the same, truth be told, this trade did not compare with his previous career as a livestock dealer and butcher. At the beginning he had established strong ties with the tribal Arabs who came from the villages around al-Hawija by purchasing their sheep and goats, which he would dispatch to Kirkuk. In time, however, he had discovered that dealing in livestock drew him away from his store and demanded a lot of time and effort, which were not repaid by commensurate profits. So he had therefore retired from this trade, at least partially, after stumbling across another, more beneficial one. He had noticed that no commerce was as profitable as that in smuggled weapons, especially in Czech BRNO rifles, which every farmer who lived on the outskirts of al-Hawija coveted, for in these villages, which lay on the plains, the rifle symbolized social power and honor insofar as it was an instrument of death and a frightening weapon used to plunder and pillage or to confront hostile tribes, between which there were endless wars. Indeed, it was difficult for a tribal Arab to find a bride unless he was prepared to offer her father an excellent rifle as dower that he could reclaim if she left him or was barren. Because there was not a single tribal Arab man who did not think of procuring a wife or two, with the passing of time, ever since tribesmen had first acquired rifles from irregular Ottoman army units at the beginning of the nineteenth century—or perhaps even before that—the rifle had gained an exceptional value that not even gold itself could equal. Thus Khidir Musa had entered a new world that could easily have left him dead or in prison. It is true that he had readily purchased the government's blind eye and made lots of money, but matters had turned against him in the end in an unexpected way. He attributed this, quite simply, to luck or fate, the course of which was beyond his powers to influence.

One night, farm workers—and this was something that had only happened once before in ten generations—attacked the palace of the head of their tribe, Shaykh Mahmud al-Hindi himself, in a region beyond government control, in retaliation for the seizure of their lands and eviction from them. Shaykh Mahmud al-Hindi, however, had prepared for this eventuality by transforming his palace into an impregnable fortress. He and his men, who were armed to the teeth, counterattacked the attacking farmers and launched flares to unmask their foes' positions. These flashes of light were visible as far away as al-Hawija itself. Indeed, people say that his son sped to his aid in a helicopter that bombed the farmers. This battle, which lasted one whole night, resulted in the death of twenty-seven farm workers, whose bodies were transported by the police to al-Hawija the next day because there was not enough room for them all in the police station and perhaps because of the stench, which had begun to disrupt people's breathing—given the intense heat—after the police had lined up the corpses beside each other, uncovered, on the ground in front of the coffeehouse, which was opposite the police station, and beside a small waterwheel so that the feet of some corpses dangled in the water.

Although Khidir Musa was certainly not responsible for the deaths of these men, he had sold the rebels enough rifles to proclaim their rebellion against their chief. The county manager, the police commissioner, and the investigative officers who arrived in al-Hawija took advantage of this opportunity to strip Khidir Musa of all his profits, especially after Shaykh al-Hindi swore to kill him as punishment for his misdeeds. They nearly threw him in prison, but he offered bribes to everyone down to the lowest-ranking policeman in the county. Then, to save his skin, he fled with his family and never showed his face there again.

Khidir Musa returned to the Chuqor community, not knowing where to begin. He felt bitter, disillusioned, and world-weary—having turned fifty. He surrendered all the money he had to his wife Nazira, who was in business with her mother, the crone Hidaya, buying and selling fabric. For his part, he did nothing but sit for long hours, staring at people. During cold weather he would balance on the lip of the clay oven and dangle his feet in it, once the oven had cooled slightly after his wife had finished baking bread. He was the butt of his wife's complaints, to which he only rarely responded.

Then, suddenly, although he had never entered a mosque before, he began to pray. Hameed Nylon presented him with a set of amber prayer beads, which he never allowed to slip from his fingers, not even while he slept. Each Friday evening, he attended a Sufi dhikr service during which the brotherhood's master teacher would pierce his followers with swords and lances, which remained lodged in their bodies without a drop of blood falling or the scar of a wound showing. Tambourines rattled to the beat of Sufi chants that glorified the prophet and celebrated his memory. The dhikr's euphoria would overwhelm one or another of them as the word "Allah" was endlessly repeated rhythmically. Then people present would seize that man forcefully or shove him to the ground until after a while he calmed down once more, as they repeated the word "Allah" time and again. Khidir Musa would occasionally take with him his sister's son Burhan Abdallah, who was very excited to watch the dervishes tread on live coals and swallow glass, or see the brotherhood's shaykh slay one of his disciples. Once he had done that, they would throw a piece of cloth over the corpse to cover it. After murmuring his secret prayer, the shaykh himself would lift the cover, shouting in a voice that all could hear, "Rise now!" Then the man would rise as though he had never been slain. On a few occasions the man did not rise. When that happened, the dervishes would call out to the audience, "Someone here did not perform ablutions after having sex. He should please leave." The slain man would not rise from the dead until one of those present had slipped out and left. Joyous chanting of the Islamic creed would echo through the Sufi circle when the spirit returned to the slain man and he rose again.

Khidir Musa would occasionally tell his nephew on their way home that the Sufi master, or shaykh, was a member of the Naqshbandi brotherhood and that not even bullets could harm him. He had once leaned against a wall and demanded that one of his followers empty the bullets of his revolver at him. So he did, and the bullets did not even scratch the shaykh. The boy thought the government should offer this Naqshbandi shaykh an appointment in the army to transform all the soldiers into dervishes. Then the government could send them to fight Israel. "Who do you suppose could defeat them then?"

Eventually Khidir Musa performed a retreat at a Sufi lodge located between the Chuqor and al-Musalla communities. He withdrew from human contact for a period of forty days, during which he spoke to no one and his food was shoved through an opening in a closed door. This was the ordeal chosen by persons who sought the truth and the saints. At first, people were surprised by the spiritual transformation that had befallen the livestock dealer, whose whole world had revolved around treasuring wealth. Indeed, even his sister Qadriya mocked him, saying, "You can bet he's found a path that allows him to cheat God and make more money." Hameed Nylon suggested, "God disclosed to him the truth in the faces of the farmers killed by his rifles."

Just as soon as livestock dealer Khidir Musa left his spiritual retreat, he announced in the mosque of the Chuqor community—to the astonished admiration of the other worshipers—that during his retreat he had received from the spirit world a message to set forth to search for his two brothers, who had been missing since World War I. These two older brothers had gone with the Ottoman forces to fight the Russians, but nothing had been heard from them since. Years later a rumor had spread to the effect that they had been killed in the war and buried in the Caucasus Mountains. Eventually people had forgotten the story of these two young men, whose effects Burhan Abdallah had discovered in the upper room. Here, however, was a message from the other side, revealed to their brother Khidir Musa more than thirty years later. It informed him that they were still prisoners in Russia and were waiting for someone to come and take them back to their home in the Chuqor community. Khidir Musa said, "I'll go; I won't return without them." Although no one dared to question a message from the spirit world, even one that was scarcely credible, many hastened to convince him to set aside this impossible mission, declaring that Russia was now ruled by the Bolsheviks, who would not hesitate to behead him once they saw him pray. Hameed Nylon used logic on him, affirming first, that he did not possess his brothers' address and that Russia was an extremely large country; second, that he did not speak Russian and could not ask about the two prisoners; and third, that if they had not been killed in World War I, they probably had been killed in World War II. His wife Nazira accused him of being senile and insane. She threatened to tie him up with a rope and lead him to an Arab sayyid who lived in a hut at the edge of the city so this healer could cast out the demons from his spirit. People scolded her angrily, however, telling her that he was one of those whose heart God had enlightened, opening before their eyes the secrets of the Unknown.

Thus commenced Khidir Musa's one thousand attempts to escape from his home. They all ended in failure, for his wife Nazira overtook him every time and brought him back. The first time, she grabbed hold of his collar as he was crossing the stone bridge heading toward al-Qurya. The second time, she brought him back from climbing the hill of the water treatment and distribution facility at the garden of Umm al-Rabi'ayn as he headed for the village of Shawan. The third time, she did not catch him until he was in the city of Alton Kopri. The fourth was in Daquq. The fifth was in Rawanduz, the sixth in Qurna, the seventh in Wadi al-Dhahab in the western desert. She bewailed her luck: "Wolves will devour him or bears dismember him before he reaches his brothers, and all that's left of them is their bones." He found it perplexing to be forced to set out in no matter what direction, as if he would reach Russia whichever way he headed.

Finally, after many failed attempts, Khidir Musa disappeared, and his wife searched for him for three months, going from city to city and town to town without finding any trace of him. In despair, she returned, cursing the Ottomans, who had taken his two brothers away and left them to be slain by the spears of Russian soldiers somewhere in the Caucasus Mountains. Qadriya Musa, Khidir's sister, wept and said, "It's certain he'll die in the rugged mountains or in the desolate deserts." Her son Burhan Abdallah was on the verge of tears too, under his mother's influence, but resolved instead to climb to the upper room and then descend into the valley of the angels to ask the three old men, who had been journeying since eternity—as they headed to the Chuqor community to bring it spring—for news of his enlightened uncle, who had gone in search of the two men killed in World War I. He hoped they might disclose his uncle's fate to him.

The three shaykhs, who resembled angels, were traveling through a desert that stretched without obstruction to the horizon and making footprints in the sand, which the wind was skimming. The sun was shining over their heads, and the earth, which was spotted with camel's thorn and Indian fig plants, blazed beneath their feet. In the distance Burhan Abdallah saw a camel caravan that was heading toward the golden domes of a legendary city on the horizon. He assumed that this must be a mirage and asked himself, "Why do you suppose these old men are traversing this desolate desert?" Then he told himself, "The route to the Chuqor community must pass this way." The three men who resembled angels saw him and shouted, "So, you've come again, Burhan!" One of them teased him, "Come walk before us and share our exhaustion."

Burhan Abdallah hesitated a little, however. He gazed at them and then said, "I've come to ask you about my uncle Khidir Musa's fate."

One of them demanded, "What about him?"

Burhan Abdallah replied sadly, "He's gone to search for his two brothers. They've been lost for a long time in Russia."

Smiling, one of the men asked, "Wouldn't you search for your brother if he were lost?"

Burhan Abdallah responded, "But they've been lost for a long time."

Then one of the men put his hand on Burhan's shoulder and said, "Time does not bury the truth. Memorize that maxim, Burhan, and don't forget it."

So Burhan Abdallah left the upper room, not knowing whether his uncle was on a true or false path.

That evening, Burhan Abdallah attended a special meeting in a house located in the Piryadi community. He had been invited by an Arabic-language teacher who belonged to "The Afterlife," an association that had established a center at the head of Atlas Street, opposite the barracks' jail. No sooner had the youth entered the long chamber furnished with carpets and rugs and seated himself on the ground at the rear by the door, than the lights were extinguished. By the faint light slipping into the room he saw a ghost suddenly emerge from the ceiling, slowly descend, and then assume a cross-legged position at the center of the gathering. The audience, who numbered more than forty, reacted noisily, declaring the unity and ultimacy of God. The specter was a man with a wide, luminous face and eyes that shone in the dark like a cat's. Burhan Abdallah asked the person sitting on the floor beside him, "Who is this man?" His neighbor whispered back, "Don't you know? It's the supreme master himself." Burhan Abdallah felt that this event would stay engraved in his memory for a long time.

The man's dramatic descent from the room's ceiling—as if he were a saint alighting from the heavens—was doubtless a master stroke. Since he commenced his sermon in the dark, his voice seemed to come from no one and nowhere. The voice in the darkness was more like a timeless summons that entered the heart and terrified it, since it could not be attributed to any source. The supreme master began to speak as if singing, and the walls resounded with the vibrato of his voice. He opened his sermon with some verses from the Holy Qur'an. Then he came to the heart of his message: "I have come to teach you a trade that surpasses all others. Consider the souk's vendors who hawk their wares using words that endear them to shoppers. Consider the Communists, who ornament their principles, seducing youth to socialism. Consider the West, which lauds freedom and democracy. Our duty is to sell Islam and to hawk it with terms even more attractive."

After speaking for an hour or more about the tragedy of Kashmir, the tyranny of Abd al-Nasir in Egypt and of Mossadegh in Iran, he asked his audience to work to combat the atheism that was so widespread in the world. This was a matter that depended most of all on the way a person proved God's existence: "Spare no effort in arriving at this goal, for it is more beneficial than any of the sciences that reach us."

Then he stood up and presented a final display; perhaps this was his way of proving the existence of God. He raised his hands, held them out in front of him, and then began to flutter them as if he were a sparrow. Next he ascended through the darkness toward the ceiling, as though drawn by a magnetic force, while he said, "Farewell." Then he vanished like a star suddenly eclipsed by clouds or like smoke dispersing into thin air. At that same moment, the lights came back on. Then the audience made a ruckus, praising and glorifying God, for they had been touched by the magic of the miracle that had occurred before their eyes. This was a miracle that no one could reject on that sacred day, even though the room had been as dark as night.

On his way home the youth reflected that this did not prove the existence of God, for the feat lay within the powers of any sorcerer, who could present an even better display. He had once seen, at the Sporting Club during a religious festival, a magician eat his own head; indeed one magician had vanished even without dimming the lights. From that moment Burhan Abdallah resolved to perform a miracle even more stirring than simply disappearing in the dark. Ill-defined doubts, moreover, gripped him about the whole affair; perhaps it had been a scripted act that the man had rehearsed for a long time till he had perfected it. Thus Burhan Abdallah began, the very next day, an exhaustive search to master the secrets of sorcery, purchasing every book that discussed magic and hypnotism. Most of these were cheap, yellowing books sold on the sidewalk. He also contacted the astrologers who were dispersed up various alleys in the city. In fact he tried to tempt even that crone Hidaya to reveal her secret ways of contacting the demons, but she threw him out, cursing his mother for not knowing how to raise her children. He thought of joining the dervishes, but hesitated fearfully because they only knew how to slay people and thrust spears and skewers into them. He did not wish to take a chance on that. In the end, after collecting a large number of books about magic, hypnotism, astrology, and flying saucers from other worlds, he sat and read them attentively, taking to heart all their instructions and suggestions.

One magic book said that a man could vanish from sight if he recited the Qur'anic sura called "al-Nas" a hundred and fifty times without stopping, so he did that and went into the courtyard to test the result. He was deeply saddened when he heard his mother ask, "Why are you staring at me that way, like an idiot?" He felt sure that he was still visible. He went back inside and recited the sura once more, but to no avail. He gave up finally, believing that there was some catch he did not know how to resolve.

71

From another book he learned a method by which a person could master other people. It combined magic and hypnotism: "Walk behind anyone on the street and focus your mind and eyes on the nape of his neck until you sense that you control him. Then order him to turn right or left or even toward the rear. In fact, you can order him to stop, turn around, and head off in another direction." Burhan Abdallah actually realized better results here than with his previous experiment, for occasionally one of his subjects would turn—after he had exerted a tremendous effort—even if in a direction other than the one the youth had chosen. When this attempt proved less than fruitful, he switched to hypnotism. After assembling a number of his classmates, who used to meet every afternoon in one room or another, he chose one of them for his subject and hypnotized him by having him focus on the tip of his index finger, which he moved back and forth before his subject's eyes as he repeated close to his ear, "You feel sleepy. Relax. Sleep. You will do everything I suggest." This would continue at times for up to an hour. Then the subject would fall asleep or pretend to sleep in the quiet of the darkened room. Next, Burhan Abdallah would instruct him to identify what was passing by on the street at that instant. His subject would open his mouth to say, perhaps, "I see a soldier walking past." One or two of them would then rush to the street to see whether he had been telling the truth.

Finally, for fifty cents, he purchased a telescope from a shop in the souk and started to observe regions of the pure blue sky from a position on the roof in hopes of seeing one of the flying saucers that visit our terrestrial world from other solar systems.

One of the books he purchased from a vendor who spread his books out on the ground by the wall of the mounted police headquarters furnished accounts from pilots, priests, policemen, teachers, and housewives who had witnessed with their own eyes foreign bodies coming from non-terrestrial cultures. In fact, the American Air Force had itself pursued these flying saucers more than once, but in vain, for these alien visitors always escaped. The book also contained stories about people who were able to contact these visitors, but, to tell the truth, Burhan Abdallah realized it was often a matter of luck whether someone saw a flying saucer or not, even with a telescope.

When these experiments with sorcery, hypnotism, and contacting alien solar systems failed, Burhan Abdallah climbed to the upper room to ask the assistance of the three angels, who were journeying through time on their way to the Chuqor community. He said, "I've come to request the secrets of power."

One of the three old men smiled: "Power? What do you mean by that?"

The boy replied calmly, "For a rope to stand up straight when I tell it to, for the sun to rise at night, for the cock to bray and the ass to bark, should I so desire."

The three shaykhs laughed and sat down to rest beneath a leafy tree. Then one said, "Now you're asking for the impossible, Burhan. You're asking to be God."

Burhan Abdallah was perplexed. He answered skeptically, "I would like to have miracles like the others. The Messiah walked on water. Moses cast down his staff, which turned into a slithering serpent. The supreme master flapped his hands like a sparrow and flew."

The three old men gazed silently at the boy. Then one of them said pensively, his head bowed, "We're just three tired old men who travel through time with nothing in our bags but spring, which we are carrying to Chuqor." Then the three men rose, hoisted their sacks to their shoulders, and departed like ghosts that had emerged from the past. The boy Burhan Abdallah returned even more bewildered than before.

Notwithstanding the despair pervading Burhan Abdallah's heart, in a month or less, his life underwent a radical transformation that made him forget his previous, unsuccessful experiments, for his father, Abdallah Ali, decided to run electricity into the house. Indeed he also purchased a large, wooden-cased radio, which he turned on every day at full blast to humor the neighbors, who wished to listen to the songs and the sermons. The residents of the Chuqor community were also delighted when the municipality paved the street. Their cheerful thanks, however, soon turned to curses against the municipality when it asked them to pay the cost of the paving, calculated according to a house's front-footage on the street. Eventually people submitted to their destiny after the municipality agreed to allow payment by installments. People were habitually so tardy in these payments that the municipality finally despaired of receiving them and decided to write them off.

Burhan Abdallah realized in an obscure way that times were changing, for the gramophones with the seated dog on the speaker disappeared from coffeehouses to be replaced by radios set on a high shelf at the front. These almost always broadcast the songs of Lami'a Tawfiq and Khudayr Abu Aziz. By night, the voice of Abd al-Basit filled the whole city's space, illuminating the spirits of the poor with Qur'anic verses, which he would chant over and over again until it seemed that his voice flowed from a spring in eternity. One summer night, many people in the Chuqor community looked down from their rooftops and some of them even went down to the street to hurry to the home of Izzat, a young man who was his elderly parents' only child and who ran a neighborhood shop with them. His aged parents were quarreling, insulting each other in loud voices, and revealing each other's defects in a way that other people should not be hearing. Concerned citizens hurried to hush them up and to make peace between them but were flabbergasted to find the couple seated in front of their house, begging their son to let them into their locked home. People asked in astonishment, "Who are quarreling so loudly on the roof?" Izzat's mother replied, "I don't know. It's a devil. I quarreled with the old man this noon, and here the devil is repeating our quarrel, word for word, tonight." Thus people became acquainted with the tape recorder, which entered the Chuqor community through a public quarrel between two senior citizens.

The tragic disappearance of Khidir Musa caused his sister Qadriya, who had forgotten all her previous slanders against him, to weep for him each day. Nazira, his wife, awaited his return for three months, but then donned mourning clothes. The shaykhs of the Chuqor community said a special prayer reserved for missing persons for his spirit. This constituted an announcement that the man, who had set off to search for his two lost brothers, could be forgotten.

This period of forgetfulness did not last long, however, for less than a year after the disappearance of Khidir Musa, people saw a zeppelin hovering over the city one morning. This was definitely the first blimp that Kirkuk had ever witnessed. Its appearance over the city stirred people's curiosity and also the fears of the governor, the police chief, and the commander of the Second Division, who initiated the necessary defensive maneuvers for fear that the zeppelin was the vanguard of a hostile attack. Somehow news reached the correspondent of one of the foreign news agencies, and thus the news spread, bringing a state of alert to the armed forces, which anticipated further developments. People kept running from one street to another, following the track of the blimp, which soared high over the city. Finally the zeppelin landed in al-Musalla garden, where thousands of people congregated, surrounding the spot but at the same time fearful to come too close. Their fears faded, however, when they saw three men leave the zeppelin and wave to the crowds. As they swarmed closer, those who hailed from the Chuqor community shouted, "Here's Khidir! He's back! But, by God, what a difference!"

They saw that the livestock dealer Khidir Musa, who had never in his whole life worn anything but a jilbab, was attired in a stylish, navy-blue suit, sported a hat, and wore prescription glasses. Khidir Musa stood before the throngs and delivered a brief statement in which he explained that he gone to search for his two brothers—Ahmad and Muhammad—who had been lost for many years. He had discovered them in their exile and brought them home. Khidir Musa's two brothers gazed smilingly at the people's faces. Once the governor and the police chief arrived in person, Khidir Musa asked them calmly, "Could we discuss this affair somewhere else?" The three men from the zeppelin climbed into the cars of the governor and police chief, who disappeared from sight as policemen surrounded the blimp, preventing people from reaching it.

After three or four hours, the three brothers returned in the governor's own automobile, which was escorted by a police cruiser, to the Chuqor community, which welcomed them with a party the likes of which the neighborhood had never seen. Attached to the electric poles were banners and placards that read, "The Chuqor community welcomes the return of its absent sons." The truth is that half the inhabitants of Kirkuk came to this forgotten neighborhood to see the three men from the blimp. Thus many women and children were trampled underfoot, and even the police were unable to hold back this human wave that swept everything before it.

The police chief asked Khidir Musa to say a few words and to ask the mob to disperse, since the continued presence of this throng in the Chuqor community could lead to disturbances that would be hard to control. Given the difficulty of finding a location in the neighborhood that could accommodate this horrific crush of human beings, Mullah Zayn al-Abidin al-Qadiri suggested that Khidir Musa should give his speech from the mosque's minaret, which was equipped with four loudspeakers. Thus Khidir Musa climbed the minaret and delivered a short, stirring oration in which he thanked the governor, the police chief, and the other officials for their fine welcome for him and his brothers. He also thanked the citizens of the Chuqor community and of the city of Kirkuk for their elevated sentiments and declared that he had returned with his two brothers to the homeland after a long absence to work for its uplift and betterment. Then he requested that the crowd disperse so that he and his two brothers could get some sleep after the long, exhausting trip that they had made by zeppelin. Grudgingly, people began to depart, although some dragged their feet sluggishly—especially those who had come from distant neighborhoods to listen to the story of the shepherd who had returned with his two brothers from Russia in a blimp that had carried them thousands of kilometers.

All the same, the true story of this adventure was on every tongue by the next day, since people had relayed it without feeling a need to embellish it with imaginary touches, which were deemed unnecessary. Why would they add anything when the truth was even more thrilling than fiction? In any event, Khidir Musa himself was forced to narrate his story time and again, without ever growing bored, and the newspaper Kirkuk published it first. Then it appeared in a condensed and distorted fashion in *al-Zaman,* a newspaper published in Baghdad. Finally, journalists arrived from America, England, Germany, and France, seeking to buy his story. Thus Khidir Musa's old taste for money returned. He sold his story, all at the same time, to several different newspapers and to an American magazine that

offered him ten thousand dollars in exchange for rights to his memoirs, provided he would soar over the city of Kirkuk once more in
the zeppelin and allow them to take photographs. He agreed after the
governor—in whose office the negotiations took place—told him
that this sum was more than thirty thousand dinars. Khidir Musa,
who earned more than fifty thousand dinars in one fell swoop, after
presenting suitable financial tributes to the governor, the police chief,
and the head of the municipality, decided to be magnanimous this
time and divided twenty thousand dinars among his two brothers
and his two sisters Qadriya and Salma, his wife Nazira and her
mother the old witch Hidaya, Hameed Nylon and his wife Fatima,
and even young Burhan Abdallah, who collected a hundred dinars
from his uncle. Khidir Musa also distributed five thousand dinars
among the households of the Chuqor community, without omitting
any, in appreciation for the festive welcome they had afforded him
and his brothers. He only kept back for himself half of the sum that
had landed on him from the sky, as he put it. Financial gain was not
all that accrued to him, for he suddenly became a person of note in
Kirkuk. The governor even offered to move him into one of the
city's more prestigious neighborhoods. But he declined, explaining
that he could not desert the community in which he had been born.

Khidir Musa actually recounted the story, which brought him
renown and wealth before anyone else had heard it—while he and his
brothers were seated on the ground in the Chuqor community, and
supplied details then he did not mention even to the newspapers and
the foreign magazines that paid him so liberally. As residents of the
Chuqor community laughed, the livestock dealer explained how he had
tricked his wife Nazira and managed to escape from her as she pursued him from one place to another. He had headed first toward the
Kurdish mountains, proceeding on foot until he reached the Hajj
Umran valley, where he contacted the Barzan tribe's chief, who presented him with a mule and provided him a companion for his difficult
journey to Russia. Thus Khidir Musa, with his guide, followed the very
same secret mountain trail that Mullah Mustafa Barzani had traversed
years before during his retreat with his army of Kurdish peasants as
they made their way to Russia amid savage battles with the Iraqi and

Iranian armies that pursued him. Finally, after an arduous trip, Khidir Musa and his guide reached the Russian border, where they saw the red flag with its hammer and sickle fluttering above a Soviet border control post. The guide headed for it and knocked on the closed door. The man in charge welcomed both of them, thanks to the guide, who had brought him presents of the type Barzanis customarily presented each time they crossed the border. The man running the control post demonstrated his generosity by bringing out three bottles of vodka, which he placed before them and invited them to share. They gently declined, even though he persisted and insisted. Finally the man said, "Never mind; I'll drink your share." So he swallowed the contents of the three vodka bottles before saying good-bye to Khidir Musa and his guide al-Barzani, without ever showing any sign of intoxication. He even performed a Caucasian dance for them with feet as steady as a bear's.

The two men traveled for three more days until they reached a village where Kurdish refugees lived under a form of self-government, according to the Soviet system. Since the livestock dealer from Iraq was in a hurry, he took the train the next day, heading for Tashkent. He carried with him only a letter of introduction from the commissar of the Kurdish Kulkhuz to the mufti of Tashkent and a few rubles that men of the village had slipped into his pocket. Khidir Musa arrived in Tashkent in the morning and found that the people there spoke the same language as in the Chuqor community. Before proceeding to the mufti's residence, he entered a coffeehouse to drink a tumbler of tea. The proprietor of the coffeehouse refused to allow him to pay once he discovered that Khidir Musa was from Iraq. He asked him to bring him a copy of the Holy Qur'an whenever he visited Tashkent again. Indeed, the man was so gracious that he left his work at the coffeehouse, which belonged to the state, and accompanied him to the mufti's residence, which would have been difficult for a foreigner like Khidir Musa to find on his own. The mufti was extremely happy, once he had read the letter from his friend the Kulkhuz commissar, and joked, "He should at least have given you a lamb to bring me." Then he offered Khidir Musa a position as muezzin in the great mosque of Tashkent, since God had granted the Arabs the gift of correct pronunciation of Arabic words. Khidir Musa accepted the offer, which was a perfect fit for his aptitudes. He explained to the mufti that he had been motivated to come to Tashkent by a desire to find his brothers, who had been prisoners of the Russians. The mufti then promised to contact his friend the police chief, who would search for them in all possible locations.

Khidir Musa spent many rough months in exile while waiting each day for news the police chief might send him. Had it not been for the hope that filled his heart, he would have returned to Iraq again. He could not, however, return empty-handed, for that would have made him the laughingstock of the whole Chuqor community. For this reason, he held firm in the mosque's lodge where he lived. His only consolation was climbing up to the minaret's balcony five times a day to deliver the call to prayer, inviting believers to pray.

Out of the blue, one day at noon, the mufti entered the mosque accompanied by the police chief and trailed by two old codgers. Khidir Musa rose to greet the men. In a flash of recognition he identified the two men, who gazed at him in astonishment. He embraced them even before asking anything, for they were his spitting image. The Turkmen mufti said, "We've brought you your two brothers. What more than that can you ask for?" His brothers, who took him to their home, where they lived together, told him how they had been imprisoned and brought to Tashkent, where they had witnessed the horrors of the civil war, which had lasted for several years. After that—like other fellow-countrymen—they had been forbidden to leave the country, although they had never lost hope of returning one day to the Chuqor community. For this reason they had refused to marry, since they were unwilling to trade their homeland for a spouse.

They now had to plot their return. The police recognized their status as foreigners and lifted all travel restrictions on them. Khidir Musa wanted to take them back by the secret route he had followed through the mountains of Kurdistan, but the police chief vetoed that idea, declaring that should they fall into the hands of the Iranian or Iraqi border patrols—and this was always a possibility—they would be shot as spies, even before anyone bothered to listen to their story. Worse still, they did not have Iraqi passports. The police chief was forced to consult the bureau of secret intelligence, and the mufti presented their case to the central committee, of which he was himself a member, in hopes of finding a solution to the brothers' problem. The issue was extraordinarily complicated, and the central committee was forced to meet three times, without finding a solution. Thus it was required to seek assistance from the intelligence bureau, which was able to consider anything, even minutiae.

Koliyanovsky, who was the director of the intelligence bureau, smilingly told the mufti, "Don't worry. Everything will be fine." At first, Khidir Musa was frightened when told that they were flying to Kirkuk in a zeppelin, since he had only a vague notion of what that was, but his two brothers, who had worked in many war-related factories, told him that flying in a zeppelin would be a rare delight. In point of fact, the intelligence bureau, which had decided to send them to Iraq in a blimp, had thought through all the eventualities. First and foremost, diplomatic relations between the Soviet Union and Iraq had been severed. This meant that the men would be exposed to extreme danger if intelligence agents were simply to deposit them beyond the country's borders, even if they were provided with forged documents. Traveling by blimp, however, meant that they would reach Iraq quickly. The three ageing men would thus be spared a rough trip that might prove too arduous for them. Even more important, when the men asserted that they had fled from Communism in a zeppelin, their perfectly confected story would mislead the Iraqi authorities, who would pardon them for everything. They repeated the story time and again, so that they would not forget any details, and this was the very tale that they repeated to everyone—from the governor to the American magazine, which published Khidir Musa's memoirs with the thrilling headline: "They Fled by Blimp from Communist Hell."

As a matter of fact, the Soviet intelligence bureau, which conceived this operation, had conjectured that the Americans' propagandistic spirit would prevent them from seeing anything else. It is true that Soviet intelligence saw nothing wrong with returning the three men to their homeland, but they were more interested in pinning down the sites of military bases that the Baghdad Pact had begun to establish and in determining whether these stocked any nuclear weapons. Thus they filled the zeppelin with a special, highly classified gas, which emitted special rays that located the site of every military base and even its types of weapons. Naturally the three age-ing men, and even the mufti, the police chief, and the members of the central committee knew nothing of all this, and in any case it was not a matter that concerned them. The zeppelin voyage, which lasted seventeen days, was truly enjoyable, although they were exposed to some dangers on the way. For example, an eagle, apparently upset by this strange, heavenly apparition, attacked the blimp, frightening Khidir's brothers who were piloting the craft. They thought the eagle would cause them to crash. It flew off, however, once they started screaming as loudly as they could and pelting it with anything they could find to throw. Moreover, en route, some Kurdish mountaineers fired on them, believing the craft to be a ship piloted by the devil. This forced the three men to climb higher into the sky. Otherwise, everything proceeded according to plan. They guided themselves at times by compass and at others by Khidir Musa's visual memory, for he had learned by heart all the important landmarks on the way.

Khidir Musa's return by blimp with his two brothers to the Chuqor community left an indelible impression on the heart of the boy Burhan Abdallah, whose belief in science and modern technology increased. He abandoned his fascination with soaring and disappear-ing the way the supreme master had done and dedicated a lot of effort, instead, to creating a scientific theory, or possibly a mathematical one, that would disclose the secret of existence, for this was a question to which he had found no answer—not even in religion.

As a matter of fact, the impact was not limited to the boy Burhan Abdallah, for the lives of all of the Chuqor community were turned upside down as well. Many residents repaired their homes and filled their storage bins with cereals and rice. Some pur-chased small shops in the souk. Hameed Nylon abandoned—at least temporarily—the notion of founding a people's liberation army once he had purchased his own vehicle and discovered a prostitute, whom he visited on the sly twice a week to escape the crying and screaming of the twins his wife had delivered in response, she believed, to the fervent prayers she had submitted through the imams.

The Chuqor community received a high honor when King Faisal II came to the city of Kirkuk in a Rolls-Royce preceded by two policemen on motorcycles and trailed by a police Jeep in which stood three secret service guards. Released from class, school children lined up on al-Awqaf Street to await their young king, who greeted his people, smiling from behind the glass of his vehicle. Khidir Musa personally slaughtered a yearling sheep in front of the limousine and Burhan Abdallah, who had been chosen to represent his school, shouted, "Long live His Majesty our beloved King Faisal II!" The royal limousine, however, had already sped past him, and so the king did not hear his greeting. That evening the youthful king received Khidir Musa and his brothers who had returned from Russia and conferred on them the Medal of the Two Rivers, second class, to recognize their rare courage and their love for their homeland, for these qualities had caused the whole world to talk about them. This human touch, coming from the youthful monarch, deeply moved those present. Even the governor's eyes were wet with tears. Others struggled hard to avoid displaying the emotions that the king's personal appearance had awakened.

Five

No sooner had people heard about the municipality's plan to cut a road through the nearby cemetery in al-Musalla than they contacted Khidir Musa, asking him to intercede to halt this gross sacrilege and to present their concerns to the governor—or even the king. For the municipality deliberately to challenge the feelings of the Muslims was really more than the citizens of Kirkuk could stand. A man could tolerate almost anything, but when the government set about digging up the graves of his fathers and grandfathers—many of whom were pious saints—that was sheer paganism.

The delegation, which as usual formed spontaneously, was composed of distinguished citizens from the community and some of its elders, including Mullah Zayn al-Abidin al-Qadiri, even though he had decided definitively to wash his hands of politics after being dragged to the police station and interrogated about the fiery insults he had directed against the English. This time, however, he considered the matter to be a religious duty that could not be overlooked. True, he had told the young deputy lieutenant when saying good-bye to him at the door, "I'll avoid mentioning Abu Naji since that upsets our stalwart government." He had not, however, pledged to avoid God. Indeed, the deputy lieutenant himself had told him to cleave to God's Book and to the Prophet's sacred precedent. Politics was for politicians and religion for men of the cloth; it was inappropriate for either side to meddle in the other's affairs. This position was absolutely correct according to Mullah Zayn al-Abidin al-Qadiri, and the cemetery was the bailiwick of men of religion and no concern whatsoever of Abu Naji's—or even of the government's.

Khidir Musa declared, after a lengthy silence that exhausted the other men, who were beginning to think he had forgotten how to speak, "We will contact the mayor first off and present our grievance to him. We shouldn't undertake any rash action before we clarify the situation. There is a lot we can do." Salman Hanash, the headman of the Chuqor community, replied, "I'm sure the mayor is a Muslim like us and will oppose the desecration of his ancestors' tombs." Mullah Zayn al-Abidin al-Qadiri broke in, addressing Khidir Musa, "I'd have liked you to contact King Faisal himself so everyone realizes the Chuqor community is not a tasty morsel for any passing opportunist." Smiling, Khidir Musa replied, "We shouldn't trouble the king with every issue great and small. He is there for us to contact at any time if the other doors are shut in our faces. Remember that the cemetery serves not only the Chuqor community but all of Kirkuk. We're not the only ones responsible for it."

Thus the delegation, which was led by Khidir Musa and which included Mullah Zayn al-Abidin al-Qadiri, the headman Salman Hanash, and the merchant al-Hajj Ahmad al-Sabunji, set off the next day for the mayor's office, which was located opposite al-Alamein Park. The attendant who stood at the door led them to the office of the mayor, who, for his part, emerged to greet them, welcoming them warmly. The mayor—a man of about forty—wore a red rose in the left lapel of his blue suit jacket and sported black "Jam Jam" shoes with toes that curved up. These derived their odd name from the Indian song "Jam Jam" that was popular in that era—oddly enough—in Kirkuk and other Iraqi cities.

Although his appearance was a bit droll—for now that early-onset male-pattern baldness had cleared the top of his head, he was attempting to thatch this area with thicker hair from his temples and to hold the strands in place with hairspray, which was sold in most of the shops on al-Awqaf Street, and ministered carefully to his short mustache—he was the kind of person who easily gained the affection of other folk, without letting familiarity diminish the dignity of his position. The fragrance of green-colored sticks of incense—inside a glass container on a wooden shelf, above which a portrait of King Faisal II and one of Crown Prince Abdul'ilah hung on the wall—lent a convivial air to the long, elegant room, which ended with a gray metal table. On two sides stood some chairs, covered in a yellow fabric that had faded with age but remained pristine. The attendant entered with tumblers of tea, which he placed on small tables beside the chairs, and the mayor rose to offer them John Player cigarettes from a black plastic case, which was inscribed with gold words in Latin characters.

Mullah Zayn al-Abidin al-Qadiri said, "May God repay you with blessings, my son."

Al-Hajj Ahmad al-Sabunji exclaimed, "I think I know you. Tell me: aren't you the son of Izzat Effendi?"

The mayor smiled: "Of course, Uncle. My father always has good things to say about you."

Al-Hajj Ahmad al-Sabunji asked fondly, "How is he? I haven't seen him for a long time."

The mayor replied, "He's enjoying his time now in Turkey. You know how my father loves Istanbul."

Al-Hajj Ahmad al-Sabunji said, "I remember now. You must be Ihsan."

The mayor laughed, "You've finally recognized me." Then, looking at Khidir Musa and Mullah Zayn al-Abidin al-Qadiri, he added, "I know all of you, and it is a great honor for me to receive a visit from men like Khidir Musa and Mullah Zayn al-Abidin al-Qadiri and from a personal friend of my father's like al-Hajj Ahmad al-Sabunji."

At this moment, Khidir Musa decided the time had come to introduce their concern: "You know no one has the right to disturb the dead in the next life, especially when the deceased are our fathers and grandfathers, who expect us to defend them and to shelter them from harm.

Now the municipality intends to dig up the graves of our dead to build a new road. We have come to petition you to stop this project, which will engender intense unrest among all the citizens of Kirkuk."

Khidir Musa had actually said everything he wanted to say, or at least most of it, in a concise form, while pointing out the dangerous consequences of this type of action. Mayor Ihsan Izzat Effendi bowed his head, as if to collect his thoughts, while Mullah Zayn al-Abidin al-Qadiri repeated under his breath, "I seek the forgiveness of God, the Exalted, the Mighty. I seek the forgiveness of God, the Exalted, the Mighty."

Finally, the mayor said with a diffidence inspired by his embarrassment: "My distress is equal to yours. The cemetery of al-Musalla contains all of our history in this city. If it held nothing more than the remains of Sayyid Qizzi, that alone would suffice. But the matter is out of my hands. The order has come from above."

Concerned to avoid any appearance of opposition to the English after having taken a vow before the deputy lieutenant, Mullah Zayn al-Abidin al-Qadiri interjected, "There's no way the English can be implicated in this matter, which only concerns Muslims."

The mullah, however, was wrong this time. The mayor shook his head and said, "The oil company wants to build this road through al-Musalla to its new oil fields."

This bombshell shook the delegation from the Chuqor community so severely that the most Khidir Musa could find to say was, "We'll give this matter a second look."

The mayor pledged to place himself and his administrative staff and employees at the disposal of the Chuqor community to further their just cause, so the delegation returned even more anxious than they had set forth. All the same, these prominent community leaders did not abandon hope of stopping this tyrannical project. After all, there was Khidir Musa, who would contact the king and tell him about this abominable injustice should the English persist in building their road through the graves of the Muslims.

Mullah Zayn al-Abidin al-Qadiri felt himself honor-bound to contact Deputy Lieutenant Husayn al-Nasiri to renounce—in his presence—the vow he had made to avoid attacking or opposing the

English, for this time the matter was not susceptible to any qualifications. It was, as Mullah Zayn al-Abidin al-Qadiri commented to the youthful official, "A jihad in defense of what Muslims hold sacred." Overwhelmed by his feelings of Islamic solidarity, the mullah even dared to ask Husayn al-Nasiri, as well as his police officers, including the secret service, to join forces with the Muslims of the Chuqor community and oppose this flawed project, which did not respect the repose of the dead. The deputy lieutenant, however, smiled and said, "There must be some mistake. It's inconceivable that the English would do something that stupid. Even so, we entreat you to calm people's minds to allow us time to investigate. Rest assured that everything will be just fine." Mullah Zayn al-Abidin al-Qadiri left the barracks feeling pleased with himself, for he had finally freed himself from a vow that he had made in a moment of weakness. This time the deputy lieutenant had not asked him to avoid insulting the English. Instead, he had requested him to work to calm people's minds. He felt empowered as he repeated to himself: "It's true that God forbade a man to throw himself to destruction, but jihad is a duty for each Muslim, male and female."

Two gatherings were held in the Chuqor community. The one on the roof of the mosque, after evening prayers was, as usual, attended by community elders. The other was in the abandoned building used for the zurkhaneh and was attended by the community's young men, most of whom were athletes, and by women who clustered around the ramshackle structure in their black wraps, their young children clutched to their breasts. In these two meetings, which were held without any invitations being issued, the Chuqor community announced its rebellion against the municipality and its will to frustrate the plan to build a road through the cemetery—no matter the cost. Support for this decision was overwhelming in both meetings, although there was a difference of opinion about the methods to employ. The athletic youth decided to resist by force the municipality's attempt to build the road, while the community's elders, who had assembled on the roof of the mosque, decided to contact the governor and ask him to intervene to halt this despotic aggression.

The next day, the labor union's local representative council released an announcement, which was written by hand with carbon paper, calling for the municipality's workers to strike to show their solidarity with the Muslim dead whose graves the imperialist English oil company wished to exhume.

The situation really was tense, despite a deceptive surface calm that would not have prevailed had not the elders of the community insisted that people avoid clashes with the police and with government employees until they saw what their contacts with responsible officials could achieve. Many actually put their trust in the good offices of Khidir Musa, whom some, on their own, had begun to refer to as "Pasha," although Khidir Musa disliked this title, for he told the citizens of his community that people are as alike one to another as the teeth of a comb and that there is no superiority even of an Arab over a non-Arab, for merit only accrues to a person more God-fearing than another. Khidir Musa also realized that a trial lay in wait for him and that failure was not an option. Since God had bestowed His grace on him and granted him this high position among the citizens of Kirkuk, it was up to him to show that he merited it. The question of contacting the king, however, made him nervous, for should the king reject his plea, he would have placed himself in an awkward position.

His two brothers who had returned from Russia and who possessed considerable experience in negotiating with bureaucratic structures advised him to begin his work from the bottom, before he sought out the bigger fish, especially the king, because occasionally a low-ranking official can solve a problem that a prime minister cannot. They counseled him to offer presents, for an appropriate gift can soften even the most recalcitrant heart. Thus Khidir Musa filled a wagon, which was drawn by two horses, with presents, and he and a delegation of prominent citizens and elders from the Chuqor community set forth in two other wagons, heading to the governor's home, which was located in the Shatirlu region on the other side of the city of Kirkuk.

Their departure was marked by the trills of the community's women and their prayers and supplications to Imam Ahmad and

Shaykh Abd al-Qadir al-Gilani, who could do anything. The women chose to appeal to these two spiritual leaders because Imam Ahmad, whose story no one knew precisely, was considered the guardian imam for the entire region of al-Musalla, in which the Chuqor community is located, and because Shaykh Abd al-Qadir al-Gilani, who was unquestionably on a higher spiritual plane than Imam Ahmad, became enraged whenever he confronted a tyrant. Once when he was performing his ablutions in Baghdad, he saw Sultan Humayun pass an unjust verdict against a poor Indian Muslim in Agra, which was later known as Akbarabad after Humayun's son Akbar, who ruled for more than fifty years. Then Shaykh al-Gilani called out to him, "Change your verdict, Sultan Humayun, since you are the representative of God's will on earth. Set the man free, for he has a family waiting for him at home." The sultan, however, apparently did not care to listen to the voice of truth. So Shaykh Abd al-Qadir al-Gilani burst into a fury, seized his wooden clog—which he had placed beside him on the rim of the basin in which he was bathing at a Gilani lodge located near al-Rasafa in Baghdad and flung it at the tyrannical Sultan Humayun in India, striking him on the chin and knocking him from the throne on which he was sitting to the ground. The women of the Chuqor community were sure that no army could withstand, even for a moment, Shaykh al-Gilani's clog should he decide to lend a helping hand to Kirkuk's Muslims in defense of the graves of their dead.

One morning, the three wagons, one behind the other, traversed the small souk and then the large one, where butchers sat on chairs placed directly in front of their meat hooks from which hung slaughtered carcasses. Their knives were stashed in leather belts that they fastened around their waists over their dark, blood-stained dishdashas. Their jamdaniyat head cloths distinguished them as being Turkmen, not Arabs or Kurds. Also present were proprietors of small stores that sold elixirs and aromatic herbs, vendors of fruit and vegetables, which were displayed in straw baskets placed on the pavement, and people selling kebabs, for which the city of Kirkuk is renowned, since they are prepared in an almost secret way. The meat is mixed with dry bread that has been pulverized and ground while special spices are added. The Jewish merchants of aromatic herbs procured these from a village called Turcham, located in Afghanistan on the Khyber Pass, which Alexander the Macedonian traversed with his armies long ago on his way to India. All these men rose to show their respect and greeted the elders of the Chuqor community as they headed to the governor's home in the open, black, horse-drawn wagons. Even the patrons of the great souk's male public bath, which was to the left of the market up an alley that linked the great souk with a street leading to the Chay community, came out to the street—clasping red cloths around their waists, while some held tumblers of cinnamon tea, which they drank after eating an orange in the baths—to present their respects to the elders, whose renown had reached every locale in the city.

The three wagons crossed the narrow, stone bridge, descending toward the other side of the city. After almost half an hour the wagons came to a halt in front of the governor's residence, which was guarded by a policeman who was sitting in the garden on a wooden chair. He wore khaki Bermuda shorts and had set his rifle on the grass. The policeman sprang to his feet in surprise when he saw the men descend from the wagon. Meanwhile the drivers started unloading the delegation's presents, which consisted of cans of shortening, molasses, and sesame oil, sacks of sugar, and boxes of tea. Khidir Musa called to the policeman, "Come lend a hand." Another man, who was obviously a servant, emerged from the house, and a gardener working in the front yard hurried over too. Assisted by the coachmen, they carried the presents inside. Then the servant returned to the four gentlemen waiting in the garden and invited them to enter, escorting them to the reception room, where he served them orange juice.

The seated men expected the governor to appear from one minute to the next. Khidir Musa collected his thoughts and even the sentences he would use with the governor, but the wait lasted so long that the men began to feel anxious. Finally the servant returned to announce, regretfully, that the governor had been forced to travel to Baghdad that very morning and that Madam thanked them for the presents. If they cared to tell him what was on their minds, he would convey their concerns to the governor when he returned. The men, who grasped instinctively that "madam" referred to the governor's wife, assumed that the servant had misspoken because the city of Kirkuk normally applied the term 'madama' to a woman who showed her hair and wore high-heeled shoes. The absence of the governor troubled the men somewhat, but Khidir Musa managed to cloak their discomfort by saying, "It's nothing urgent. Merely convey to him the best wishes of the Chuqor community when he returns."

The men departed, but anxiety overwhelmed them once more and they felt desperate. Khidir Musa surprised them, however, and restored hope to their hearts when he remarked, "It seems we shall be forced to contact the king." Mullah Zayn al-Abidin al-Qadiri agreed, saying as if he were uttering a maxim, "It's always better for a man to address the head rather than plead with the tails." Thus the men climbed into the wagon, which was still waiting for them, and headed this time for the post office, which was located on the banks of the Khasa Su River, opposite al-Alamein Garden, in order to place a call to the king. For no apparent reason, the other two wagons trailed along behind them.

The postal clerk, who was a young man of about twenty-five and who had transferred from the district of Tuzkhurmatu to Kirkuk some six months before, was alarmed when Khidir Musa approached and asked in a friendly way, "Could you place a call to al-Zuhur Palace in Baghdad? I would like to speak to the king." The young man continued to stare openmouthed at Khidir Musa—as if awaiting further instructions. So Khidir Musa said, "I can speak Turkmen if you don't know Arabic: I said I would like to speak to the king." The young man nodded and replied, "One moment please." He rose and entered a side room. He disappeared for a few minutes and then returned, accompanied by a portly man who wore thick prescription glasses. Khidir Musa introduced himself: "I'm Khidir Musa, recipient of the Medal of the Two Rivers, second class." The man shook hands with the elders of the Chuqor community, one after the other, and then invited them to have a seat in his office. Since there were not enough chairs, he asked Khidir Musa to sit in his chair, behind the desk, while he was content to perch on a small tea table after covering it with a copy of the newspaper *al-Nahda*, which was lying in front of him on the desk. The man said welcomingly, "It is a great honor for us to receive a visit from men of your caliber."

Al-Hajj Ahmad al-Sabunji burst in, "May God repay you with blessings."

The man said, "Unfortunately we don't have the king's secret telephone number, although the number for al-Zuhur Palace is available, to be sure, in a directory we keep for our own use."

Mullah Zayn al-Abidin al-Qadiri beamed as he observed, "What's the difference? The king lives in al-Zuhur Palace; everyone knows that."

The man stammered, "That's true." So he rose, lifted the receiver of the telephone that stood in front of him on the desk, and asked the operator to connect him with al-Zuhur Palace in Baghdad.

Soon the telephone rang. The postal employee lifted the receiver, listened to something, and then handed it to Khidir Musa, saying, "Here's al-Zuhur Palace. Go ahead and speak."

Khidir Musa felt extremely uncomfortable. His heart was pounding rapidly, and his face was flushed. He no longer knew what to say. He took the receiver but did not place it near his ear, for this was the first time he had used a telephone. Silent and awestruck, the elders from the Chuqor community waited to hear what Khidir Musa would say in this historic conversation. The postal employee rose and, gently pressing on Khidir Musa's hand, suggested, "Move the receiver closer to your ear." Then the terrified men seated there heard Khidir Musa open his mouth and say, "Greetings! With whom I am speaking? Is this His Majesty King Faisal II?" There were several moments of silence after which Khidir Musa, whose face was now streaming with perspiration, announced "I am Khidir Musa, recipient of the Medal of the Two Rivers, second class. I am speaking from Kirkuk." Khidir Musa suddenly beamed and then laughed affably. "So you know who I am then. Yes, I'm the man who flew to Iraq from Russia in a zeppelin." There were some more moments of silence as Khidir Musa listened to the speaker on the other end. Then he said, "A delegation of prominent citizens of Kirkuk would like to have the honor of being received by His Majesty King Faisal II, may

God preserve him and bestow on him a peaceful reign." He listened again attentively and then said, "That is most convenient: next Thursday at ten a.m. We will be there, God willing. Convey my greetings to His Majesty the King as well as those of Mullah Zayn al-Abidin al-Qadiri, al-Hajj Ahmad al-Sabunji, and Headman Salman Hanash. May God reward you with blessings. Good-bye." Thus ended a conversation of which the residents of Kirkuk continued to speak with pride and satisfaction until the king's death in the revolution conducted by Brigadier Abd al-Karim Qasim many years later.

The man with whom Khidir Musa had been speaking at al-Zuhur Palace in Baghdad was not actually the king, but was definitely a member of the royal family, as Mullah Zayn al-Abidin al-Qadiri observed, since the man had immediately recognized Khidir Musa and teased him, asking, "Weren't you afraid you'd fall out of the blimp? His Majesty and the Crown Prince were highly diverted by your escapade." Mullah Zayn al-Abidin al-Qadiri was not too far from the mark because only an insider close to the king would have known that King Faisal and Crown Prince Abdul'ilah were impressed by Khidir Musa's courage. Headman Salman Hanash, who felt proud when he heard Khidir Musa mention his name when passing on his greetings to the king, said, "Perhaps the speaker was the Pasha." Khidir Musa rejected that suggestion, however, affirming that if the speaker had in fact been Nuri al-Sa'id, he would definitely have spoken to him in Turkish, since he was fluent in that language. Khidir Musa openly blamed himself for neglecting to ask the man his name, but al-Hajj Ahmad al-Sabunji, who had difficulty keeping famous people straight, said, "You did the right thing. It would not have been appropriate for you to ask his name, for he represents the king, and when you speak with him it is as if you are speaking with the king himself."

Khidir Musa asked the postal employee, "How much for the telephone call, son?"

The employee protested: "Don't even think about it. The call's on me."

Mullah Zayn al-Abidin al-Qadiri told him firmly, "That's not right; you have to make a living."

The embarrassed employee answered, "It's a trivial amount; three dirhem. What does that amount to?"

Al-Hajj Ahmad al-Sabunji intervened again, preventing Khidir Musa from reaching into his pocket while placing a banknote, which obviously was a quarter dinar, in the employee's hand.

The four men exited to find their three drivers waiting for them by the wagons. Mullah Zayn al-Abidin al-Qadiri proposed that they should go to the teashop of al-Hajj Ahmad Agha to drink a tumbler of heavy black tea after their successful day's effort and to meet with al-Qurya's prominent citizens, who could normally be found there, smoking a water pipe. So they all climbed into the first wagon again, and the driver began to spur his horses on with his long, wood-handled goad. The other two wagons trailed along too as everyone headed for al-Hajj Ahmad Agha's teashop. It soon became clear that there was not much to do in the teashop, since the notables ordinarily frequented it in the afternoon. The men spent about an hour there while each of them drank two tumblers of tea, and Khidir Musa played backgammon with al-Hajj Ahmad al-Sabunji, who beat him. Then Mullah Zayn al-Abidin al-Qadiri suggested that they return to the Chuqor community: "We must carry the good news of the telephone conversation with the king to our people in Chuqor."

The procession of three wagons went along al-Awqaf Street in the direction of the stone bridge. The wagons had scarcely descended alongside the Citadel on the way to the great souk when the four men were caught off guard by something they had not been expecting. Lined up there were the men who worked in the souk, women shoppers wearing black wraps and veils over their faces, and children who had come out on the street in dirty dishdashas. They lined up on both sides of the street and began to applaud the four men, who responded to their greetings by raising their hands. The three other men insisted that Khidir Musa should at least stand, so that the people, who loved him, could see him. Mullah Zayn al-Abidin al-Qadiri suggested, "Perhaps it would be best if you sat beside the coachman." So Khidir Musa climbed over the partition, trailing behind him the tail of his striped underwear, to sit beside the driver, raising his hands on high, and saluting the loyal citizens of his city. He was greatly touched by this scene and oblivious even to the tears that filled his eyes.

The Chuqor community experienced a true festival; animals were slaughtered, and the rich distributed alms to the poor. Khidir Musa and the three men with him did not understand how the entire city had learned about his telephone call to al-Zuhur Palace only an hour or two after that historic conversation had taken place. The fact was that the three coachmen had spread the word to passersby when Khidir Musa and the other men entered the post office. Then the news reached an advertising genius, a young man who handled publicity for the films shown at al-Alamein Cinema in an attractive manner, standing in front of a giant poster of a still from the film while acting out scenes from it in a voice loud enough to be heard by pedestrians even on other streets: "Most powerful champion in the world! . . . Hand-to-hand combat! . . . Bow and arrows! . . . Warring pirates! . . . Tarzan King of the Jungle fights the lion and splits it in two! . . . Return of Superman!" Deciding to exploit this opportunity to attract the public's attention, he added Khidir Musa's call to al-Zuhur Palace to his film promotions: "Attention! Attention! Latest news! Dutiful son of Kirkuk, Khidir Musa, contacts King Faisal II! After an exchange of greetings the king tells him, 'It will be a big honor for me to receive a man like you!' Long live Khidir Musa! Fatin Hamama in her finest film yet! Samia Gamal, Queen of Eastern dance, captivates hearts with her extraordinary scenes! Invitation from His Majesty King Faisal II for Khidir Musa to attend the Coronation!" In this way the news was spreading even before Khidir Musa had concluded his conversation with al-Zuhur Palace.

This conversation made a big impression not only in the Chuqor community but throughout Kirkuk. Everyone was delighted, especially the mullahs, many of whom dedicated their Friday sermons to praising the royal concern with defending the sanctity of the graves of the Muslims. They mentioned Khidir Musa's name directly after those of the king and the governor. There were as well, however, some pessimists, who expected good from no one—not even from the king. In their opinion the king was still a callow youth dominated by his uncle, who collaborated with the English. He was led by Nuri al-Sa'id, whom they considered, whether correctly or not, England's number one agent in Iraq.

In point of fact, Khidir Musa faced many problems that he was obliged to handle with the wisdom and patience for which he was known and most of all with his instinctive understanding of human nature and of ways to deal with people. He realized that a single false move by anyone could torpedo everything.

The Communists, for example, stirred up a contrived row, claiming that one community could not represent the entire city. They also spread a rumor that the delegation would include only Arabs and Turkmen, without even a single Kurd, as a deliberate slight aimed at the Kurds, who in turn asserted their right to direct things, since they considered Kirkuk to be part of Iraq's Kurdistan. This claim was denied by the Turkmen, who thought that Kirkuk was their homeland. Indeed, Shakir Effendi, who published a local newspaper in both Arabic and Turkmen, intentionally wrote an editorial in which he affirmed that Kirkuk had been distinguished by Turkmen characteristics for more than a thousand years. In response to that, some Turkish families with deep roots in the city also decided to raise with Khidir Musa the subject of including in the delegation that would see the king the genuine elite of the city, not hoi polloi like Mullah Zayn al-Abidin al-Qadiri or Headman Salman Hanash, who was actually a secret agent. This was only the beginning, however, for the same animosity made itself felt in the Chuqor community. Khidir Musa learned that the young athletes, perhaps at the suggestion of Hameed Nylon and Faruq Shamil, had met in the zurkhaneh and decided to form a gang, which they called "The Giants." Its mission was to prevent the municipality, by force, from building the road through the cemetery of al-Musalla. Placing their hands on the Holy Qur'an, they had sworn to sincere and wholehearted defense of the dignity of their fathers and grandfathers.

While everyone was preoccupied with hatching intrigues and conspiracies, using the construction of the road through the cemetery and the Baghdad trip to meet with the king as a pretext for rallying any type of support, even if merely verbal, Khidir Musa stepped from his house after slinging over his shoulders a piece of camel hide embroidered in green and red that the Jiburi tribe's chief, to whom he was related, had presented to him, even though winter was almost over and the weather was mild. Since he had returned from Russia, he had grown accustomed to wearing this whenever he wanted to be alone. Ideas were surging and clashing in his head as he walked along Piryadi Street, heading for the Valley of Adam's Horse. It was said that Adam had landed there, mounted on his horse, when he descended from paradise. As he proceeded, Khidir Musa passed by the tannery, which opened onto the street, and its stench stopped up his nostrils. In the past, that smell had seemed normal, back when he carried skins from his sheep on his back. He had received a quarter dinar for a lamb's skin and more than that for a ewe's. He was not in a mood to visit his former friends and greet them, but one of them recognized him and called to him from a distance, "You don't bring us skins anymore, Khidir. Have your lambs run away from you?" So Khidir Musa replied, without moving closer, "No, I'm the stray runaway. I can't trust my hand with the knife anymore." He went along a path that cut through a field of cucumbers. Leaning down, he plucked one and wiped it on his sleeve before biting into it. When he reached the lettuce bed, he returned to the dirt road to avoid the shit that the city's night-soil men carted to the lettuce patches, whose owners paid them ten fils a barrel.

Khidir Musa found himself outside the city in an area frequented by quarry workers, who cut chunks of stone from the rocky earth and carried them on their donkeys to the city, where these blocks were used to build houses. The quarrymen left behind them many pits, which filled with rain water and became dangerous ponds where children from nearby communities swam when it was scorching hot. No summer passed without a child or two drowning. The quarrymen, who were known for their sexual perversions, would stand on protruding boulders to try to attract the most radiant youth. This time there were only a few masons breaking rock with their pickaxes in the distance. Khidir Musa climbed the rocky road, looking at the scarecrows in the fields that lay on the slope of the Valley of Adam's Horse and at the crows that were scattered over the rocks. He was wondering how to escape from the crisis into which he felt himself slipping. He could simply choose the people he wanted to accompany him to see the king. He realized, though, that this approach might expose him to the wrath of the city's elite, toward whom he felt a special respect and whose wrath he would definitely like to avoid. At the same time, he was afraid that the zealous young men of the city would resort to violence when confronting the municipal workers or would even clash with the police, thereby calling into question his relationship with the state, which had demonstrated its trust in him. What made him most anxious of all was the possibility that the king might reject his effort, or merely ignore it. He understood from long experience and from his grasp of life's realities that this was not out of the question. His walk eventually brought him to a fig tree in front of a cave on the flank of the mountain. He removed his camel hide, spread it on the ground, and sat down cross-legged upon it, after taking off his shoes and setting them to one side. Then he began to gaze at the wild flowers that grew from gaps between the rocks to announce the imminent arrival of spring.

Khidir Musa raised his head to contemplate the blue sky, which was dotted with white clouds that scurried by in the wind. Some birds rose slowly, flapping their wings and then gliding high overhead for a time before swooping back to the grass-covered plains that extended to the horizon. Khidir Musa reflected on his life's trajectory: its decline and rise, poverty and riches, humiliation and glory. "That's the way the world is, Khidir ibn Musa; that's the world. Don't be beguiled by its perfidious smile." He bowed his head, held his forehead with his right palm, shut his eyes, and contemplated nothingness. In the gloom that encompassed him, in that nameless darkness, he succumbed to an intense bout of weeping. He wept for himself and perhaps for the world. "Weep, Khidir ibn Musa, weep for yourself." He began to sob under the stormy influence of emotions and memories from throughout his past. Then as he remembered words his grandfather had spoken while holding him as a small boy in his arms he felt suffused with a new peace. His grandfather had said, "Weep, Khidir, for tears cleanse the soul."

He was weeping silently, and his soul felt inebriated by the scent of spring, which was descending upon the mountain, when he sensed a hand pat him on the shoulder. A gruff voice said, "Stand up, son. You'll be my guest in this cave of mine." The livestock dealer, who had not been expecting anyone, was startled and glanced up at the person who had interrupted his weeping. "I didn't know anyone lived here," he said. The old man who had emerged from the cave had a thick beard. His clothing was black and his skullcap red, and he had clogs on his feet. He replied, "This is God's cave, which is open to all His creatures." The old man entered the cave followed by Khidir Musa, who had been taken by surprise by the man's invitation and thus prevented from thinking of an excuse to decline it. The entryway was a gap between two boulders. Then a brief hall led to an extensive, marble chamber with a fountain spouting water at its center. The cave's resident said in an almost compassionate voice, "I was performing my ablutions when I heard you crying. You've done the right thing, Khidir, for tears cleanse the soul."

Khidir Musa was startled: "You know my name, too."

The old man responded rather gravely, "Yes, Khidir, and I've heard that you are going to visit the king and are concerned about the whole affair. Don't worry, Khidir. We'll find a solution for your problem."

Overwhelmed by anxiety, Khidir Musa said, "If I weren't a Muslim, I would believe you're God."

The aged dervish looked down at the ground for such a long time that Khidir imagined he did not care to reveal his identity. Finally he looked up and, gazing at the aged livestock dealer with eyes that were suddenly all ablaze, said, "No, Khidir, I'm Death."

Khidir Musa began to tremble. His whole body was shaking, but he gained control of himself and said, as if to himself, "So, this is Death. I did not expect him to be so gracious."

The old man known as Death guffawed till he showed his dentures, which were clearly visible to Khidir Musa. He felt suspicious about Death's need for dentures. The man grasped Khidir Musa's uncertainty and asked him jestingly, "Did you think time would leave no mark on me? Even I age, Khidir."

Khidir Musa shook his head again: "So this is death: a cave a man enters accidentally."

Death said, "Death is something totally different, Khidir. Don't be alarmed, for you are still at the cave's entrance and will return to your family." Then he rose and gently grasped the shoulder of Khidir Musa, who no longer understood anything. He said, "Come look at death if you wish."

There was an opening covered with thin glass, in the wall of the cave. Through it poured light that created a shadow in the room. The old man cast a fleeting look through the pane and then drew back, saying, "Go ahead and look. You may learn something from what you see."

Khidir Musa's heartbeat felt irregular, but he stepped forward and peeked into the other kingdom, the kingdom into which he too would pass one day. He was astonished by what he saw. Countless groups of men, women, and children, all with sad, pale faces, were shoving past one another on an endless bridge, screaming sound-lessly. He stepped back and asked the cave's master, "Where do you suppose all these massive crowds are heading?"

Death smiled and said, "Not even I know the answer to that question."

Khidir Musa peeked through the aperture again. Then he said, "My God, they're miserable. They don't seem the least bit happy."

Khidir Musa leaned against the curving wall of the cave as he floated on an invisible wave that beat against the pit of his soul. In the pale light filtering into the cave he looked like an alien from another world. The old man, whose clogs clicked against the marble floor as he walked, granted him time to catch his breath after he had glimpsed something no living person had ever seen before. Death wondered whether the sight was more than a man's nerves could bear. Khidir Musa knew that he too would one day walk along that bridge that had no end. Since he had not opened his eyes, Death addressed him in a voice that was determined but tender. Khidir Musa opened his jet-black eyes and looked attentively at the man's face, which was devoid of any expression. Then his pale lips opened, and he asked, "If my hour has not come, what do you want from me?"

Death was silent for a moment before he replied, "Nothing at all." Then he looked at Khidir Musa as though he wished to remind him of something he had forgotten: "I thought you needed me."

Khidir Musa did not venture a response because he could not understand how he could need death. Death, with his thick, black beard speckled with white and his lanky physique, seemed rather embarrassed when he asked politely to be included in the delegation heading for Baghdad to visit the king. Khidir Musa, who was surprised by this unusual request, which almost made him laugh, felt compelled to ask, even before the smile left his eyes, "But why? What distinction do you lack that you would seek to meet the king?"

Death, who seemed to understand Khidir Musa's reticence, said, "I have learned to distrust distinctions that are destined to disappear, that are a 'concern and a striving after the wind.'"

This man who called himself Death had excited Khidir Musa's admiration with his calm, humility, wisdom, and eccentricities. All the same, Khidir Musa waged an inner struggle to resist giving in to him, for if this resident of the cave represented annihilation, he himself represented continued existence. There ought to be a counterweight, at least as long as he remained alive. Death said, "I have more right to join your delegation than anyone else. Don't forget that the matter concerns the dead first and foremost, not the living. The dead too have a right to voice their opinion. Isn't that so?"

A fleeting radiance glowed inside Khidir Musa's mind, for the idea dazzled him and he felt Death was right. So he shook Death's hand and said sincerely, "Sir, I'm honored for you to join my humble delegation." He headed toward the cave's entrance, preparing to leave, but twirled around suddenly as if he had remembered something and asked, "Do I need to hunt you down here when I want you?"

Death replied, "You will never discover this cave a second time. You will find me wherever you need me. Don't tell anyone what you have seen because people lend greater credence to phantoms of the imagination and superstitions than to self-evident truths."

Khidir Musa answered, as if setting down a basic axiom: "There are some secrets that a man keeps to himself forever; you know that for certain."

When Khidir Musa walked outside the cave, he was dazzled by life, which he felt he was seeing for the first time: in the rocks on which green moss grew, in the blend of voices he heard from afar, and in the awe that filled his heart. He descended once more to the wide valley that led down toward the city, startling some wild doves, which soared off into the distance when he approached. He heard a roar in the air and automatically looked up to gaze at the birds fleeing from a helicopter that was flying toward the city. He would have liked, as he returned to the Chuqor community, to forget what he had seen, but the sight of the dead people crowding against each other on the bridge that extended perhaps to infinity was still stuck in his mind. It haunted him. In that massive crowd he thought he had seen—despite the distance—faces of people he had met in his lifetime, but he was not certain: If living people resemble one another, then so do the dead. He felt he could still hear the faint, monotonous wail that rattled his skull and that originated in the kingdom of the dead. It might have been the screech of a siren or a distant, subdued music playing outside of time.

He turned to cast one last look at the cave where he had seen Death, perhaps to satisfy himself that what he had seen had not been a dream. The cave was on fire. Then he heard an explosion that shook the ground beneath his feet. He saw boulders rise into the air and then disappear into the white clouds. The quarrymen working at the far side of the valley raised their heads to study the explosion, which had taken them by surprise. Then they went back to work again, assuming that some other quarrymen were responsible for the blast—a common occurrence for them.

At that moment, when Khidir Musa saw the cave collapse and suddenly disappear, only a thin thread held him fast to life. In his heart there was something that seemed greater to him than life itself: life's secret, which he had seen in the face of the cave's master—that buffoon who called himself Death. What he felt was not fear of death, or even alarm at being in its presence, but an indescribable sense of power resulting from his rapprochement with Death, who would be a member of his delegation, which was going to visit the king. The cave's master had inspired in him a high degree of wisdom. Thus although Khidir Musa returned to the Chuqor community without a definitive list of those who would accompany him to the royal palace, his indecision did not last long, for that afternoon, while

he sat in the coffeehouse near Nakishli Manarsi, he observed a portrait on the wall of an awe-inspiring man who had thick hair and a
thick beard and who made a person think of the saints. When he
asked Mullah Zayn al-Abidin al-Qadiri, who was sitting beside him
on the bench, about the man, the mullah replied with a smile, "He's
the greatest poet Kirkuk has ever produced. This is the great Dada
Hijri." Then Mullah Zayn al-Abidin al-Qadiri started reciting stanzas
of his poetry, composed in Turkmen, as Khidir Musa felt his spirit
soaring into a different sky inhabited only by angels. Khidir Musa
remarked, "I think we ought to include him in our delegation."

The mullah, after a short hesitation, replied, "That's an excellent
idea, but I'm not sure whether he's still alive."

Others seated near them said, "Yes, he's alive and well. Every day
he walks in gardens near here to compose poems about the birds
and the trees."

One of them volunteered, "Would you like us to bring him to the
coffeehouse? He lives in the Citadel."

Thus the great Dada Hijri became a member of the delegation, to
which was later added the madman Dalli Ihsan, who was included in
response to his aged mother's entreaties and assurances to the delegation's members that even angels had a right to kiss the king's hand.
She was naturally referring to her son Dalli Ihsan. Meanwhile, the
Communists, of whom Khidir Musa had said that they excelled only
in the art of stirring up needless strife, had agreed that Hameed
Nylon should represent them—although they did not announce
this—since he was to be the chauffeur who drove the delegation to
Baghdad. Fathallah Isma'il, Kirkuk's director of public security,
imposed himself on the delegation at the last moment, alleging that
the government wished to assure the delegation's security. Previously
Khidir Musa had accepted the participation of other delegations,
which were chosen respectively by the Turkmen, Kurds, Arabs, and
Assyrian Christians, in addition to a delegation from the Chuqor
community and the special delegation that he had selected himself.
The understanding was that all these delegations, representing the
entire city of Kirkuk, would meet half an hour prior to the appointment in front of al-Zuhur Palace.

In advance of the appointed day, the vehicles left for the capital, the seat of government of the king of Iraq. In front was Hameed Nylon's vehicle, which flew the flag of Iraq. Khidir Musa, who was awarded pride of place, sat in front with Hameed Nylon. Trying to emphasize his importance, Fathallah Isma'il, the director of public security, squeezed himself in between Khidir Musa and Hameed Nylon. He took out his revolver once or twice to brandish it, but Khidir Musa forbade him from doing that, saying, "Put away your revolver. No one will try to interfere with a delegation like ours." Among those in the back seat was Death, who had introduced himself—to mask his identity—as Dervish Bahlul, a name that Hameed Nylon joked about sarcastically throughout the trip, without, however, upsetting Death, who smiled slyly from time to time and said, "Nothing's better in life than laughter." As usual, Dalli Ihsan remained silent as he contemplated a terrifying emptiness that stretched as far as his eye could see. Between them sat the poet Dada Hijri, who looked like a saint who had descended from a mountaintop.

Behind this automobile came the other vehicles, which carried prominent citizens of the Chuqor community and the city of Kirkuk. These men took a special pride in having been selected to represent their factions in a visit to the king, whom they loved fervently. They were indebted for this chance to Khidir Musa, whose great authority no one could any longer question. They considered his prestige a distinction for their city, for which they wished a deservedly illustrious position. People had actually emerged early that morning to line Railroad Station Street, which was the anticipated route of the delegation as it headed toward Baghdad. Schools had been given the day off, and teachers came with their pupils, carrying Iraqi flags and lining up on both sides of the street. The military band also turned out, and the musicians in their dress uniforms played drums and cymbals. An enormous, dark-complexioned sergeant marched at the head of the troupe. He carried a staff with two metal heads and twirled it with awe-inspiring skill to the beat of the music. Overwhelmed by the jovial mood, Hameed Nylon—to the crowd's applause and laughter—began to drive his car in reverse. He did not cease driving this way, even though his vehicle was at the head of the procession, until they left the city and reached an area where the undulating plains that encircled the city spread out.

The procession had scarcely left Kirkuk when the poet Dada Hijri sank into a soul-chilling despair. He was seized by such anxiety that not even Dervish Bahlul could banish it from the poet's breast. The smile did not return to his bronzed face until a sonnet was born— near the Hamreen Mountains, which are a rocky chain that stretch from Iraq to Iran. He refused to share a single couplet from it, however, despite their persistent pleas, alleging that he wanted to revise it in different circumstances when he would be better able to judge it, since the circumstances might even get the better of the poetry itself and leave it an awkward mishmash. He was seconded here by Dalli Ihsan, who seemed more affected than the others by Dada Hijri's words, which Kirkuk's director of public security declared incomprehensible. Khidir Musa pointed out that a person cannot understand everything and that some matters are perceived directly by the senses, independent of any logical reflection.

At noon the motorcade reached Khan Bani Sa'd, where the vehicles stopped in front of a ramshackle, whitewashed mud-brick structure where food and tea were served. In front and inside, the establishment had old platforms, on top of which had been placed straw mats, and long wooden tables, which were covered with oil-cloth sheets that could easily be wiped clean. In this filthy setting, which was unprotected from the dust and swarming with flies, Khidir Musa delivered a brief oration to the Turkmen, Kurdish, Arab, and Assyrian members of the Kirkuk delegation. He said that the delegation's members had a right to enjoy their visit to Baghdad however they wished. Perhaps some had relatives or friends they also wished to visit. For this reason he granted each of them an appropriate freedom of movement. All he asked of them was to appear at least half an hour prior to the appointment in front of al-Zuhur Palace, so that they could enter as a group to see the king. Then he invited them to enjoy—at his expense—stew, which was the only dish this restaurant offered to travelers to or from Baghdad. Everyone relished this repast, but when the tea, which was an indispensable sequel to the stew, arrived in sawn-off bottles cut down to half their original size, Khidir Musa, who was enraged by this, scolded the restaurant's proprietor, demanding that he serve their tea in proper tumblers. The man apologized, protesting that tea tumblers cost a lot and that he saw little difference between a tumbler and a bottle bottom. The tea a person drank was the important thing, not its container. Even so, Khidir Musa paid this man, who was clearly greed incarnate. Khidir Musa had himself once resorted to cups made from bottle bottoms, during the war era when the price of tumblers had increased in such an obscene way that the poor could not afford them. He remembered how he had filled a bottle half full with kerosene and then placed an iron rod, which had been heated red-hot on a fire, inside the bottle. The moment the rod touched the kerosene, the bottle would split apart at the level of the kerosene. All that was in the past now, though, even if the restaurant's owner claimed otherwise.

The vehicles shot off again and later that afternoon reached Baghdad, where most of the cars disappeared in the maze of streets. No one was concerned about this, for they had all agreed where they would meet the next day. Of the motorcade there remained only Hameed Nylon's car and a second one transporting prominent citizens from the Chuqor community. That was driven by Salim Arab, who normally worked as a driver on the Kirkuk-Sulaymaniya road.

These two vehicles headed toward al-Rashid Street and then stopped in the region of al-Maydan, the red-light district of Baghdad at the time. There Hameed Nylon escorted the men to the River Bank Hotel, the entrance of which adjoined that of the Shams Restaurant, which was filled with soldiers, country folk from every corner of Iraq, petty bureaucrats, pimps who supervised prostitution in the nearby alleys branching off from al-Rashid Street, and detectives who were close to their employment in al-Saray Station, which was located on the other side of the street, behind some houses that once had been mansions inhabited by top Ottoman officials. The men from Kirkuk climbed the stairs to find themselves face-to-face with a man of about sixty wearing an Arab head cloth held in place by a band. He rose to greet and direct the men, of whom only six remained. The public security director had withdrawn, explaining that he was obliged to stay in al-Fadl in the home of a cousin who would never forgive him if he chose to stay in a hotel. Al-Hajj Ahmad al-Sabunji had gone to the home of a friend who was a merchant in al-Shurjah Market. Mullah Zayn al-Abidin al-Qadiri had sought out an old friend whom the government had named as the imam of the Haidarkhana Mosque, which was located a few steps from the hotel. The remaining men could have had beds in a number of different rooms, but Khidir Musa preferred to reserve a single room for their party so they could talk matters over that evening. Thus Khidir Musa, Dervish Bahlul, Dalli Ihsan, and Dada Hijri had their beds in a room that was reserved for them alone. Hameed Nylon and Salim Arab were assigned a different room, which they were to share with other men currently absent. They preferred to separate from their companions, for they wanted to enjoy their stay in Baghdad, free of any oversight.

In fact, barely half an hour had passed when these two were back on the street again, slipping down the alleys where love was for sale. The doors of the houses were open and whores stood in the doorways chatting idly with young pimps, who leaned against walls or light poles while watching the action from a distance. A young prostitute called to Hameed Nylon and Salim Arab, "Come in here. You won't find any finer girls than us." There was an open courtyard where a few men were seated on benches. Two women were chatting with them. They were obviously waiting for the appearance of their favorite girls, who were with other patrons. At the front of the courtyard sat a corpulent old woman, whom the girls referred to as al-Hajja. She took the money before a man entered and met a girl. The girl who had been standing in front of the door entered and asked Hameed Nylon, "Don't you like me?" The madam, who clasped a string of prayer beads, called to Hameed Nylon in a tone that was almost a command, "Go with Awatif, man. She's hot for you, as you can see." Awatif tugged on his hand, saying, "You won't regret this." Salim Arab went with another girl who had just returned from Mosul and who was bragging about her boyfriend, who was an officer, and her visit to him. Al-Hajja told her the moment she arrived, "Your fun with your friend the officer is over. Now it's time

107

to work." This romantic escapade, which cost each of the men a hundred and fifty fils, restored the equilibrium after their tiring road trip. Hameed Nylon confided to his friend his true feelings about women: "Nothing is sweeter than what's forbidden." This made Salim Arab laugh. He agreed that this was a matter that scarcely two men in the entire world would dispute. He told Hameed Nylon about a carpenter who owned a shop in al-Nujum Street in Kirkuk. The man would proclaim his wife divorced whenever he threw himself upon her only to regret later what he had done. Hameed Nylon smiled and said, "Without sin, there's no pleasure. What is licit is a duty. It is what's forbidden that's special."

On their return to the hotel they met Dervish Bahlul, who was coming back from a visit to the hotel's only toilet, which was located in the hall. He told them in a low voice that Khidir Musa had asked where they were, indicating that he might wish to speak with them. Khidir Musa, who was stretched out on one of the beds listening to Dada Hijri recite some of his poetry in a quavering voice as he leaned his elbow against the pillow, told them that the men did not want to spend all their time in this putrid hotel, for when a person comes to Baghdad, he needs to see some of it. They agreed to leave the hotel shortly. Dada Hijri said, "We thought we could sleep, if only for half an hour, but that proved difficult, as you can see. When a man senses that he is in Baghdad, he feels alert. It's a sensation I experience each time I visit this city." As the men prepared to leave the room, Dada Hijri said, "Previously I would head for the Parliament Café, where I would find Jameel Sidqi al-Zahawi and Ma'ruf al-Rasafi waiting for me, but death's tyrannical hand has not spared them." Dada Hijri was merely making a casual observation, and Dervish Bahlul fought to retain his self-control. Only Khidir Musa remarked the angry flash in his eyes when he responded, "This is man's destiny on earth. No one is exempt. Death is the ultimate price of life."

Dada Hijri was astonished by this profound maxim that Dervish Bahlul had volunteered. He answered this deep insight by repeating a quatrain of Turkmen verse in the style of the people of Kirkuk:

Beyond the mountains
I awoke to the call of my beloved.
My beloved is a gazelle. I am a hunter
Who pursues her.

Dervish Bahlul smiled then and responded with a quatrain that left Dada Hijri in tears as emotions exploded in his heart:

Don't weep.
Today will also end. Don't weep.
He who has closed this door
Will open it again one day. Don't weep.

Hameed Nylon placed a brotherly hand on Dervish Bahlul's shoulder, telling him, "I like you a lot, dervish. People who see you for the first time don't grasp your true worth. Only now have I understood why Khidir Musa chose you as a member of this delegation. A fellow rarely meets someone as wise as you." Dervish Bahlul smiled almost apologetically: "Hold your compliments, Hameed Nylon. Perhaps meeting me will one day be something you will hate more than anything else in life." Naturally, no one understood the real meaning of this statement except for Khidir Musa, who said in an attempt to end this awkward conversation, "I think the time has come for us to hit the streets. The city's calling us." So the six men descended to al-Rashid Street to give themselves a chance to blow off steam, for the smell of dust from the desert had made them giddy.

Six

Having had more experience of life than most men, Khidir Musa understood the dangers of frequenting kings, for the honor a king bestows on those he embraces can vanish in a moment. Indeed, it may change into a disaster, often for no apparent reason. He knew from stories he had learned from his father that the ancient Arab kings would—from time to time—chop off their favorites' heads, either for the sake of change or as the result of an intrigue hatched by persons with influence over the monarch's mind or heart. His father had become acquainted with some Ottoman pashas who resorted to stratagems that were almost ludicrous. The Ottomans would place prominent men with whom they were annoyed on donkeys, backwards. Then a herald would lead them through the city's markets, loudly enumerating their vices and treacheries, while citizens, who were delighted by the misfortunes of others, attacked these victims, who were seated on an ass, by pelting their heads with filthy shoes or beating them with sticks. Even more atrocious than this punishment was death by impalement, when a stake was inserted in the anus of a person who was forced to sit on it in such a manner that the spearhead gradually penetrated his intestines. The Turks were known for this type of execution and reckoned the spectacle of victims suffering an agonizingly slow death a rare delight in otherwise dreary lives. For these reasons, although times had changed, Khidir Musa was the most anxious of the delegation's members, who were looking forward to meeting the king.

What made Khidir Musa nervous was not the possible loss of a benefaction, but rather possible humiliation; not the king's anger itself, but the chance of falling from grace. Khidir Musa's fears, however, were simply those of a troubled heart finding itself in the presence of Dervish Bahlul, who reminded a person of the evanescence of every glory. The following day, the delegation from the city of Kirkuk, on gathering by the gate of al-Zuhur Palace, met an officer who led them through a garden filled with trees, flowers, and fountains into a vast chamber without even one chair. Exiting by a side door, he left them there without saying a word.

At first the men remained silent, anticipating the king's appearance, but when their wait dragged on they began to whisper to each other. After half an hour of anxious waiting, some of them felt the need to walk around the room to restore circulation to their tired legs while others sat down cross-legged on the ground in the corners as their voices rose in a din that filled the whole space. Finally they summoned up the courage to smoke, and the cloud of smoke that rose from their Ghazi, Turki, and Luxe cigarettes blanketed the entire room. After two hours some members of the delegation asked Khidir Musa to do something: "We can't wait any longer." Khidir Musa shot back, "What can I do? It's customary for kings to make their subjects wait." One of them suggested, "Maybe the best thing would be for you to knock on the door and summon the king." A nearby Kurd objected, "That's not appropriate. The king might be with his family." After some minutes of this, the men—through the chamber's window—saw King Faisal II, who was dressed in white gym shorts and a blue athletic singlet, performing Swedish calisthenics in a section of the garden. Pushed to the breaking point,

Dada Hijri said, "This is too much. I'm going out to invite him to come here." Khidir Musa replied, "He doesn't know you. I'll come with you." Dervish Bahlul joined them, even without being invited. So the three went out into the garden, heading toward the king.

Their appearance was a bit alarming and incongruous. Khidir Musa was wearing a dark blue suit, a gray hat, and dark glasses, Dada Hijri wore a loose-fitting blazer over trousers with torn hems, and Dervish Bahlul was clad in a gown of white linen with ancient scuffs on his feet. When the king's companions and guards saw the three men approaching the king, they pointed their revolvers and rifles at them. The commotion attracted the attention of the king, who stood his ground but soon recognized Khidir Musa and laughed. In a loud voice he said, "I can scarcely believe my eyes. This definitely is Khidir Musa." He called to them, "Come here. What are you waiting for?"

The three men approached the king, who shook their hands. Khidir Musa introduced his two companions: "Dada Hijri, the greatest poet Kirkuk has ever produced and Dervish Bahlul, a fount of human wisdom."

The young king said jocularly, "What more than this could a king ask for? A brave man like Khidir Musa, a poet like Dada Hijri, and a sage like Dervish Bahlul!" Inviting them to sit on the grass, the king observed, "My grandfather's court was a salon for poets. He appointed Muhammad Mahdi al-Jawahiri as poet laureate, but as you know al-Jawahiri had a capricious temperament. He turned against us after a time and began to write panegyrics for our enemies. Poets are always like that. What can we do? My uncle and the Pasha know by heart the poems in which he ridicules them."

Dada Hijri commented, "But his ode praising you is considered one of the gems of Arabic poetry."

The king asked, "Do you mean his poem 'Swagger, Spring'? That truly is a beautiful poem, but a king needs something more than praise. He needs people he can trust." Then he turned to Khidir Musa: "Are you planning another adventure or have you retired?"

Khidir Musa cleared his throat and laughed, "You know, Your Majesty, that life makes demands on a person. I no longer have the heart to embark on hazardous adventures."

The king laughed, "So you're growing old then, Khidir."

The king invited his three guests to eat breakfast with him, although it was already noon, but Khidir Musa reminded him of his appointment with the Kirkuk delegation, who were still waiting in the reception chamber. This statement astonished the king, who protested that no one had told him about it. Then he relented: "If they've come all the way from Kirkuk, I ought to greet them. But what do they want?"

Dervish Bahlul replied, "They have come to defend the honor of their dead."

The king was astonished: "The honor of their dead? What do you mean, dervish? Are living men honorable enough to defend the honor of the dead?"

Khidir Musa gently intervened, "We'll tell you the whole story, Your Majesty."

The king responded jokingly, "Not before breakfast. I thought I only ruled over the living, but if the dead want me to be their king too, I have no objection."

Khidir Musa and Dada Hijri laughed at the royal jest, but Dervish Bahlul averted his face to avoid being obliged to laugh or smile to humor the king, who was still a callow youth.

Followed by Khidir Musa, Dervish Bahlul, and Dada Hijri, the king strode toward the room into which were squeezed the elite of Kirkuk. As wishes for his long life resounded, the king was received with thunderous applause. He then delivered a brief statement, mentioning that he nourished a special affection for Kirkuk's citizens, who had always proclaimed their loyalty to the Hashemite throne, that he would do everything in his power to develop the city and to resolve its problems, and that he would discuss the whole affair with his friend Khidir Musa over breakfast. He also thanked them for enduring the discomforts of the trip in order to declare their allegiance and fealty to him. The king departed, holding Khidir Musa's hand, and they were followed by Dervish Bahlul and the poet Dada Hijri. Mullah Zayn al-Abidin al-Qadiri called to Khidir Musa, "We'll wait for you at the hotel, Khidir." Hameed Nylon shushed him, saying, "Hush, man. He certainly won't get lost."

The king escorted the three to a dining room, where they enjoyed coffee and pastries. The king drank a glass of milk, took three slices of bread with butter and jam, and sipped two cups of coffee while Khidir Musa—deliberately avoiding any reference to the role of the English oil company in the case—related to him the story of al-Musalla Cemetery, which the municipality of Kirkuk was planning to plow under. At the same time he alluded to the possibility that this might lead provocateurs to incite strife and unrest. The king listened attentively to what Khidir Musa had to say. He bowed his head for a time before replying, "Although I don't like to interfere much in affairs of state, I will pass your request on to the prime minister. No matter what the circumstances, the dead should be treated respectfully in this nation." The king rose to bid farewell to his three guests in a jocular fashion. He told Khidir Musa, "Next time I expect you to visit Baghdad by zeppelin." He smiled when he shook hands with Dada Hijri: "If you ever write a panegyric poem about me, send it to me." Before shaking hands with Dervish Bahlul, he paused in silence for a moment. Then he said, almost with embarrassment, "I feel I will meet you again some day." Dervish Bahlul squeezed his hand as he said, "I know, Your Majesty." Then he stepped back, leaving the king to ponder the meaning of this sentence, which sounded odd to him, for how would this dervish know that they would meet a second time? He explained it away as one of those riddles that dervishes deliberately use to pry open the sealed doors of the Unknown.

The three men returned to the hotel like ghosts emerging from a legendary party, exchanging no more than a few terse words. They seemed to wish to review in their minds the scenes they had witnessed. Khidir Musa reflected that this young, pampered king in reality possessed no power in the state that he ruled and was merely a decorative garden gnome. The thought that the king himself did not have the power to stop the desecration of the tombs of Khidir Musa's father and grandfathers saddened him. He grasped, perhaps in a murky way, that much blood would be shed and that he was responsible. Dada Hijri was composing a poem about a poet who quaffs coffee with the king. The verses were evolving in his head:

114

The king and I drank coffee
  One morn,
  Sandwiched,
Between Life and Death.

The king appeared so innocent that Dervish Bahlul was grief-stricken, for he knew that this innocence would survive only a few years more before it was punctured by a bullet one morning, even before the king fully grasped what was happening. Dervish Bahlul knew from experience that some deaths are easy and others hard. A man can accept his death if his heart is braced to meet it. Death may also surprise a person and cause him grief. There would always be unfinished business: writing a letter, reading the final chapter of a novel, apologizing for an offense, proclaiming some love or affection, or taking a trip somewhere. Then there was always a gap between extinguished hopes and hopes delayed. No one perceived this discrepancy more clearly than Dervish Bahlul on his return from meeting with the king.

Hameed Nylon stood in front of the hotel waiting for the three men. From there, he led them to the Haidarkhana Mosque, which the members of the delegation had chosen as their meeting place. They were waiting impatiently for the news Khidir Musa would bring them about his breakfast with the king. His continued silence was so alarming that many people felt forced to ask him what was the matter. Then Khidir Musa gestured for Dada Hijri to rise, saying, "We'd best hear the poet tell the story from the beginning." The poet stood up in front of the mihrab. All eyes were fixed on him. Other men who had happened into the mosque by chance joined the group seated there, without knowing what the occasion was. Then Dada Hijri, his eyes closed, began to sing a Turkmen quatrain, rocking back and forth, as if he had risen from a long slumber:

The rose's bed:
Come let us seek the rose's bed.
I sought the rose's bed
But found thorns bedded there instead.

115

This poem the poet intoned shocked those present because it contained an overt reference to the king, although only the members of the Kirkuk delegation, who were waiting for good news from the interview with the king, caught it. The members of the delegation felt even more uneasy. They wanted to know what the king had told the three men and had no time for cryptic poetry. Their eyes turned on Khidir Musa, encouraging him to speak. His head was bowed, however, as though he was brooding about the poet's words. Dada Hijri, too, was lost inside himself, mulling over his unfinished poem about breakfasting with the king. For this reason he shook his shoulders in a theatrical fashion and mumbled some incoherent words. When he quit the mihrab, his eyes looked sad, but no one noticed besides Dervish Bahlul, who rose and headed toward the mihrab, where he delivered a short statement that left many squirming, as if simultaneously repulsed and attracted by the conflicting magnetic poles of what they knew and what they did not. Dervish Bahlul's voice sounded like thunder on a rainy day. Khidir Musa looked up at him and smiled as if to encourage him to continue speaking. "Night and day follow each other in turn, but some people who know the night deny there is a day. Drink from the gushing spring and climb to the peak of the mountain. Then descend to meet me—I who have been awaiting you since you were born. Farewell! Until we meet again!" Dervish Bahlul looked away and departed, quitting the mosque without anyone understanding a word he had said. Moreover, the people there disapproved of his obscure language and his unexplained departure. It was true that Khidir Musa had recruited the dervish, insisting that he should be a member of the delegation, even though no one had ever heard of him before, but since chance had furnished him the opportunity to sit with the king, it was wrong for him to leave the gathering in this theatrical manner after mouthing a few obscure sentences that meant nothing.

Thus Khidir Musa was forced to rise. Everyone was expecting him to say something straightforward now—unlike his two companions who had set fires blazing in the audience's hearts, even without saying anything comprehensible. Khidir Musa, who was an experienced, persuasive speaker, was obliged to apologize for any appearance of obscurity in the words of Dada Hijri and Dervish Bahlul. He hinted that perhaps their meeting with His Majesty King Faisal II, may God preserve him, had affected them strongly. In an attempt to convey a new impression to his listeners he said that the king had been deeply moved by the danger threatening the tombs of the Muslims in Kirkuk and had said he would speak to his prime minister about the matter. Although this was less than his listeners had been expecting to hear, he attempted to close off any debate by pointing out that the matter was now in the king's hands and that this was a major breakthrough, all by itself. So the gathering broke up, leaving the issue unresolved.

Since there was nothing more for the men to do in Baghdad, most of them decided to return to Kirkuk the next day because home-sickness had overwhelmed them. The group split up again. Khidir Musa, followed by the elders of the Chuqor community, headed for Souk al-Haraj, where they purchased clothing and shoes that were almost like new. Imported from Europe, these were offered at extremely low prices. The merchants among them took advantage of the opportunity to conclude some deals with merchants of al-Shurjah Market. Hameed Nylon and Salim Arab slipped away once more to the alleys where love is sold, before picking up—from a shop located in al-Iwadiya—a small Roneo printing machine con-cealed inside a wooden box. It had been smuggled across the desert from Damascus on the back of a camel and Faruq Shamil had asked Hameed Nylon to transport it to Kirkuk. Later, the delegation spread out to the nearby coffeehouses. The Turkmen went to the Parliament Coffeehouse, and the Kurds went to the Municipal Coffeehouse, where they were staying in rooms on the second floor. Others headed to the coffeehouse of Hasan Ajami. Meanwhile, Khidir Musa, Dada Hijri, and Dalli Ihsan sat in front of their hotel on chairs they placed on the sidewalk so they could watch the people with whom al-Rashid Street swarmed. All evening long Dada Hijri remained anxious about the disappearance of Dervish Bahlul—who had vanished without a trace—even though Khidir Musa reassured him more than once, suggesting that their friend had perhaps gone to the mosque of al-Hallaj in al-Karkh or to recite the opening prayer of the Holy Qur'an in al-A'zamiya at the grave of the great Imam Abu Hanifa, and noting that Dervish Bahlul frequently disappeared, moving from country to country and town to town, as if charged with a mission to which only he was privy.

When the vehicles set off the next morning for Kirkuk, which they reached by noon, the delegation's mission was over; all that was left for them to do was to wait for orders from on high, and these were expected at any moment. The surprise the men found waiting for them on their return to Kirkuk, however, was greater than anyone could have imagined, for first the Chuqor community had rebelled and then the other neighborhoods had followed suit, attacking the municipality's backhoes and bulldozers with rocks. In response, the police had sent their forces into al-Musalla and had occupied the garden in the center of the district, firing many shots over the roof of the elementary school that overlooked the cemetery. The rebels attacked municipal vehicles with stones and liberated them, turning them into barricades against any possible counteroffensive the enemy might initiate. Had a police regiment not arrived, the municipal workers would not have escaped alive, for rocks flew from the roofs of nearby buildings as if it were raining stones. Even so, the police were only able to rescue the workers after they fired repeated rounds into the air. A police armored vehicle with loud speakers disseminated nonstop appeals for the insurgents to withdraw from the area and threats of punishment for anyone who defied the law or disrupted civil order. The insurgents responded to these appeals—delivered by a cereals-market broker who was known throughout the city for the purity of his language and the loudness of his voice and who had been forced against his will to accompany the police—with their own contradictory calls, which they broadcast from loudspeakers located on the minarets of mosques in the area. After the police had occupied the roof of their school, the pupils of al-Musalla Elementary School, accompanied by their principal and teachers, formed two orderly lines and sang the patriotic anthem "My Country!" The people applauded these young pupils, who had scarcely reached the end of the garden separating the two sides before they merged with

the resistance forces, whose morale soared as they joined the pupils
in their stirring anthem:

> *My homeland . . . my country!*
> *Glory, beauty, splendor, and majesty thrive in your hills*
> *Life, success, bliss, and hope thrive in your fair weather.*
> *Will I see you*
> *Safe, blessed, successful, and honored?*
> *Will I see you,*
> *In your eminence, reach the sky?*
> *My homeland . . . my country!*

The Chuqor community proclaimed its rebellion the very same
day that Khidir Musa met with King Faisal II. This happened as a
result of an error committed by the municipality's public works
director. The police chief had ordered a halt to the grading that the
municipality had started once he learned that a delegation was heading to Baghdad to see the king. This was a judicious decision on his
part, for he wanted to stay ahead of events and thus to avoid any
untoward incidents. The municipality's public works director, who
was supervising the road construction, however, did not withdraw
the backhoes and bulldozers from the work site near the cemetery
but ordered these moved to an area on the far side of the cemetery
till the situation was sorted out. Thus, instead of asking his workers
to retreat, he ordered them to advance.

At that, the "Giants" gang, who were lurking in an alley that lay
between the Arab neighborhood and the Jewish one, rushed out in a
surprise attack against the municipal workers and the policemen
guarding them. They were followed by children, women, and old
men who carried sticks, knives, and stones. The Giants, lacking only
Hameed Nylon, who had gone to Baghdad, had armed themselves
with brass knuckles. The attack, which was led by Abbas Bahlawan,
began with cries of "God is most great," women's trilling ululation,
and stones that rained down on the workers and the policemen, who
took to their heels. Abbas Bahlawan caught up with the driver of one
of the backhoes and—clinging to the door—threw him a punch,

which the man dodged so that it hit his shoulder, causing him to throw himself to the ground on the far side. Then he fled, cursing and screaming in pain. The attackers rushed forward. At the forefront was the boy Burhan Abdallah, who carried the Iraqi flag. This surprise attack frightened the municipal workers, who fled toward the garden, where they shielded themselves behind its trees from the stones pelting them. Three policemen attempted a counterattack by firing their rifles into the air, but the members of the gang surrounded them and stripped them of their weapons after pummeling them liberally. Then they led the policemen to one of the abandoned trucks, where they bound their hands with ropes. The municipal public works director was added to this number when some women pursued him and captured him as he attempted to slip away down a side alley.

The quick and crushing victory achieved by the Chuqor community came at an unexpected price. When the Chuqor community launched its lightning raid against the municipal workers, an undercover policeman who had been sitting among the tombs drew his revolver and raced toward the attackers. Once he realized, however, that he was about to fall into a trap, he too fled, brandishing his revolver. A group of children, men, and women chased after him, calling out, "Thief! Seize him!" He raced away breathlessly with the screaming mob on his heels. Some other people terrified him when they threatened to block his escape route, so he lifted his revolver and fired three shots toward his pursuers, who were gaining on him. One of these shots hit a black barber who was seated on a chair outside his shop, which was located near the tomb of Imam Ahmad, slaying him. Even as blood gushed from the hole in his chest and his head tilted forward, his body remained seated, and thus it was some time before his two young children, who were watching the chase scene too, noticed the blood staining their father's chest. Then they began to scream loudly enough that the pursuers stopped to look at the dead man. The undercover agent thus had a chance to escape by ducking into an alley that led to the leather market.

The victim was descended from an immigrant to the city: a slave Captain Chesney, an English surveyor who had worked first for the East Asia Company and then for the Lench family, had brought with him from Africa. In April 1836, after they had endured a month of terrible discomforts aboard a steamboat called the *Tigris,* which had set out from Birejik, Chesney and his group were attacked by the lawless Khaza'il tribe, which sank the ship in the swamps of Lamlum after plundering its contents. The slave and the woman with him escaped from the bloodbath on a craft made of inflated skins. This carried them as far as al-Qurnah, where a well-armed Turkish boat plucked them from the water. Then they joined the service of the governor Rashid Pasha al-Gozlikli, who a month later after they had both embraced Islam presented them to his son-in-law Ata Effendi in the sanjak of Kirkuk. That man—Qara Qul Mahmud—was the grandfather of the barber Qara Qul Mansur, who was killed by the undercover agent. The few residents of African heritage, whose number barely exceeded ten, were absorbed into the life of the city to such an extent that they capriciously began to call themselves black Turkmen. People would pretty much have forgotten their descent had their children not frequently accosted other children on their way to or from school, and had their visages, which they allegedly anointed with a special cream, not been so dark.

Although Qara Qul Mansur died while seated on a chair in front of his barber shop, people considered him a martyr who fell in battle defending Islam and the Muslims. Many stories were repeated about his heroic death, and unrelated miracles were attributed to him. Some of these stories were certainly fabricated to stir people's emotions, which are inflamed by this type of tale. Their authors were members of the city's secret political organizations, which were interested in opposing the government by creating strife, agitation, and chaos. There were other stories that people told in the coffeehouses, though, without anyone being able to pin down the source or motivation behind them. These were imaginative tales that were scarcely credible. One mentioned that Qara Qul Mansur traced his genealogy to the Prophet's companion Bilal the Ethiopian, who was the first muezzin in Islam to call people to prayer, thus defying the pagans and polytheists. Some of these stories went so far as to allege that Qara Qul Mansur actually was Bilal the Ethiopian incarnate and that the Prophet Muhammad had loaned him Buraq, his heavenly steed, which had carried him down from the seventh heaven to the earth so he could raise high the banner of Islam once more. Hand-written pronouncements appeared, declaring that Judgment Day would begin at 10:15 a.m. on the twenty-eighth of March—in other words, exactly seven days after Qara Qul Mansur's slaying. The police chief attributed these flyers to those Jews who had remained in the city of Kirkuk, refusing to move to Israel. A number of Jews, whom the police arrested, actually confessed to drafting these declarations in order to stir up chaos and strife in the Muslim state, but the police released them two days later to avoid offending world public opinion.

Qara Qul Mansur's funeral evolved into an event unprecedented in the history of Kirkuk. People emerged from alleys and neighborhoods, sorrowfully striking their faces and wailing. They turned out in human waves, hoisting black flags, preceded by funereal drums, the beat of which could be heard throughout the whole city. Hung from the entries of roads, alleys, and streets were banners that read: "Glory and Eternal Life to the Martyr of the Insurrection Qara Qul Mansur" and "The Blood of the Martyr Qara Qul Mansur Will Not Have Been Shed in Vain." Farmers from villages near Kirkuk came with their donkeys and horses. The nomadic Arabs who pitched their tents in the desert near al-Hawija arrived with their camels, which they allowed to graze on the grass that grew between the tombs on the plain of Yeddi Qizlar. Not even the Gypsies, who staged bawdy dance performances in their tents, which were erected in the city's green plains, hesitated to descend to the streets, pulling behind them a she-bear they forced to dance in time to the funereal beat of the drums and a she-ape they had dressed in mourning clothes.

The governor, who was flabbergasted by the whole affair, was afraid that matters would get out of control and declared a state of emergency in the city after a brief meeting that he held with the police chief and the commander of the second brigade. From Baghdad, the prime minister contacted the governor to reprimand him for the disorder in his city and to demand that he get in touch with Khidir Musa and the city's other leading citizens to quell the disturbances. Khidir Musa, however, was in Baghdad with the other civic leaders. For that reason there was nothing to do but wait.

Despite the proclamation of a state of emergency, the police chief withdrew his forces from the city, leaving behind only the policemen who were camped in al-Musalla Elementary School, overlooking the cemetery. The second brigade's commander, who was an Arab from Mosul, positioned some of his troops at the city's entry points but refused to send soldiers into the streets, which the insurgents controlled. The police chief and the commander of the second brigade went up in a helicopter, which continued to hover over the cemetery for reconnaissance of the thousands of people who had come to pay their final respects to their martyr, Qara Qul Mansur, who was buried near the tomb of a plump imam, whom people had eaten back in the days of the great famine that the city had suffered during the previous century. Once his bones began to speak, the deed had been revealed, and a judge had ordered the perpetrators slain, so people had eaten them to revenge the roasted imam.

The matter did not end with Qara Qul Mansur's burial, however, for the rebels, most of them from the Chuqor community, stayed on at the barricades they had constructed at the edge of the cemetery using backhoes and bulldozers behind which they had sought shelter. They torched tires and blocked the road to the cemetery as they confronted the policemen who continued to occupy al-Musalla's elementary school. Children from nearby communities spent the evening with the insurgents, listening with attentive interest to stories that their elders related about the days of World War I, when Turkish armies had retreated from the invading English forces, impounding everything they met on their way. Their native troops would force their way into houses and spear mattresses in their search for wheat and flour. They seized jars of lentils, pulling them from the flaming fires inside bake-ovens. Then they would extract the lentils, squat down on the ground, and devour them, preventing even the household's hungry children and womenfolk from approaching the kettle. Now some women brought pots of stuffed grape leaves to the insurgents while other women were busy making tea to distribute to the rebels. The opposing police force adhered to the stern orders that had been issued and only opened fire two or three times. When, under cover of darkness and sheltering behind tree trunks, some

individuals slipped into the garden separating the two sides and
tossed at the police several Molotov cocktails that students from the
technical secondary school had concocted, the insurgents responded
to the enemy's gunfire by shooting toward the school three rifles they
had seized from the police at the beginning of the battle and some
revolvers men had placed in their belts. Three men fetched the
Ramadan cannon, which had been left in a space between the tombs,
hoping to use it in some fashion even though they had no sulfur, perhaps to intimidate the enemy and raise the spirits of the insurgents,
if nothing else.

As a matter of fact, during the night that the Chuqor community—along with nearby communities—spent beside the cemetery
by the light of lanterns placed on the marble tombs, things happened that caused the policemen, who had continued to watch
developments from the school's roof, to drop their weapons and
flee under cover of darkness, terrified by what they witnessed.
When the three men fetched the Ramadan cannon, everyone
laughed, even Abbas Bahlawan, who was commanding the battle.
He asked, "What will we do with a cannon that looks like a donkey?" The children clambered on top of it, and Burhan Abdallah
even stuck his hand inside the cannon's barrel and began to feel
around as if searching for something. Gulbahar told him not to, for
fear the cannon, about which she had no clear understanding, would
explode. Then Burhan Abdallah said to Abbas Bahlawan, "It would-
n't be hard to make some sulfur. We could use the chemicals from
matches." Abbas Bahlawan responded, "Do you know what you're
talking about, boy? I suspect the matter's not as easy as you think."
A sergeant who had fought in Palestine, however, said, "We might
need a little sulfur, but the most important thing is to get hold of a
sufficient quantity of gunpowder." Getting hold of the gunpowder
was not a problem, for the quarrymen had plenty and they were not
about to begrudge it to the insurgents. Once a bag of gunpowder
reached the cemetery on the back of a donkey, which was accustomed to transporting gypsum by day, a group of former soldiers
took charge of the cannon, shooing away the onlookers who had
gathered around them, cautioning them about the danger of being

too close. These soldiers succeeded in loading the cannon and then declared it ready to fire.

At that point Abbas Bahlawan walked over to the wall of the garden and shouted loudly at the police in the elementary school, demanding that they surrender or prepare to receive cannon fire. From the roof a defiant voice responded, "Who are you to threaten the government, you son of a bitch?" So Abbas Bahlawan replied, "I'm Abbas Bahlawan, you son of a whore. If you're a man, come down here, so I can toss you into your government's lair." Then Abbas Bahlawan gave the order to fire. People stepped back at the very same time that the soldier who had served in Palestine stepped forward and aimed the cannon toward the school. Then he lit the fuse attached to the cannon and hastily retreated, directing people to lie on the ground between the tombs. When nothing happened for a time, many bored and curious people began to poke their heads up. At last, the expected, dreadful explosion occurred and shook the ground beneath the feet of the insurgents, who saw the cannon turn into a terrifying mass of flame that rose into the sky, shot past the garden's lofty trees, and fell to the street before it could reach the school. Initially the policemen hiding behind the roof parapet of the school were frightened. Once they observed the cannon lying prostrate before them like a corpse in the street, however, they began to laugh sarcastically and loudly and to chant the first jingle that came to mind: "Your brick doesn't upset us, O Abbas ibn Farnaas."

The policemen kept chanting their jingle until Mahmud al-Arabi fired three shots toward the elementary school, hitting in the shoulder a policeman who was leaning on the parapet, smoking. The police returned fire with a hail of shots, and the donkey that had hauled the gunpowder to the insurgents was struck. It had slipped into the garden and had begun grazing there. No one noticed until the following morning, when they observed a line of coagulated blood running from a hole in the head of the donkey, which lay on its right side under a eucalyptus tree.

This failure, which tried the insurgents' resolve, certainly upset them because they had wished to teach the policemen sheltering inside the school a stern lesson, but it was not a big deal. Some of the elders of the Chuqor community actually praised God that the Ramadan cannon had flown up into the air instead of launching a projectile at the school, since that could have caused a calamity with unpredictable consequences. One of the women said, "Don't forget the police are Muslim, just like us." The strongest objection to this aborted mission, however, came from the school's teachers, who had joined the insurgents. These men disapproved of the idea of blowing up their school and at the same time questioned the supposed benefit of the whole operation: "What do you have against the policemen? Leave them where they are." Abbas Bahlawan replied nervously, "Do you believe they occupied the school to search for wisdom? They have come to terrorize us and to protect the municipal workers who want to dig up the graves. We must chase them out." Abbas Bahlawan's arguments were irrefutable, and the teachers were forced to step aside and to retreat into silence.

Some members of the Giants gang considered embarking on a virtually suicidal mission: attacking the school with Molotov cocktails, which they would launch from inside the garden while they hid behind tree trunks. Faruq Shamil, however, scoffed at this idea and pointed out its danger, affirming that it could lead to unnecessary casualties: "What's important is to win the battle with as few losses as possible." He had read this sentence in a book by a Russian about World War II. Meanwhile Burhan Abdallah and some of the other boys had obtained some pyrotechnic rockets, which they began to set off, aiming them toward the school. These would rise with a hiss, illuminating the whole area before falling back to the roof or slamming into the side of the building. Their light disclosed the policemen who were watching the area, but the men forbade them from doing that, since it also revealed the insurgents, making them an easy target for enemy fire.

The night had grown pitch-black, and those who felt sleepy retired to their nearby homes, where one would continue to discuss with another, from neighboring roofs separated only by low walls, the events of the day they had experienced. They praised the heroism of Abbas Bahlawan but poked fun at the weird outfits worn by the Giants: "Young men are always like that: a courageous heart and a tiny intellect."

As a matter of fact, not everyone shared this opinion. After Abdallah Ali seized the hand of his son Burhan Abdallah to take him home, he—for example—described the gang members to his neighbor, who ran a small kebab shop in the great souk this way: "Those young men are nothing but clowns. The battle's only a game to them. Did you see how they bragged to the people?" Later, his wife Qadriya, lauding the importance of her brother Khidir, said, "Khidir shouldn't have gone to Baghdad. If he had stayed here, this tragedy would have been averted."

At precisely this moment, when the wall clock in Abdallah Ali's home had just struck twelve times, which the boy Burhan Abdallah counted while stretched out in bed, the insurgents lying in ambush at the edge of the cemetery, the policemen on the roof of the elementary school, and people in nearby communities that overlooked the cemetery witnessed the cloudless sky flash with light two or three times. Then there was thunder so loud that the earth shook beneath their feet. All at once the moon and the stars disappeared and the street lights went out, leaving the city sunk in total darkness. The stray dogs roaming the city began to howl monotonously in unison. Cats mewed, and cocks crowed to announce a dawn that had not yet arrived. People thought this odd and puzzling. They continued to watch the sky, which had evolved into an alarming, gloomy void. Their anxiety did not last long, however, because a pillar of light suddenly shot up from somewhere in the cemetery and rose until it reached the limits of heaven, transforming night to day. Many people searched for the spot from which the light was emanating while others headed toward it with distraught and awe-struck hearts, but the light was so powerful they could not see. So they retreated or stayed where they stood. When people ascertained that the light was radiating from the grave of Qara Qul Mansur, they started glorifying God. Religious fervor seized hold of a small group of members of the Afterlife Society, who were joined by some dervishes, and they began to chant to the beat of tambourines:

The full moon has risen above us
From the folds of farewell.
O emissary to us,
Who brought the imperative command.

Women ululated and their echoing trills announced the advent of a religious festival. The insurgents shot volleys into the air, thanking God for this incontrovertible miracle. The excitement affected even the policemen, who began to beg for God's forgiveness, as fear of His anger seized hold of them. This miracle, however, was only part of a greater one, news of which spread to the entire world. Scholars of spirituality debated it in their circles, scattered throughout Iran, India, Turkey, and Azerbaijan. Brilliant light continued to flood forth for an hour or so before people saw a luminous, white horse leap from inside the grave and ascend into the air. On its back was Qara Qul Mansur, still cloaked in his shroud. The horse and its rider continued to ascend within the column of light until they came to resemble a cloud suspended over the city. The deceased Qara Qul Mansur clutched a goad, which he brandished as if waving to the thousands of astonished folks who stood staring at him. The stallion whinnied and then shot off, galloping into the heavens, which opened before him. He was illuminated by the beacon of light, which was focused on him. A comprehensive silence held sway over the city except for whispers people exchanged: "Look! There's Buraq, the Prophet's mount when he ascended to the seven heavens." One way or another people were confident that this was Buraq, sent by God to the martyr Qara Qul Mansur, because Buraq, who was pastured in Paradise, was the only horse that could fly.

Qara Qul Mansur, riding on Buraq, made a complete circuit over the city before pausing once again over the cemetery, where he raised a hand, which emerged from his shroud, as if to issue a command to a secret army hiding behind a hill. In point of fact, no sooner had his hand sunk down again than people saw waves of totally unfamiliar birds—golden birds halfway between storks and hawks—carrying in their beaks fiery rocks, which they dropped on the policemen who saved their skins by fleeing, leaving behind them even their rifles.

When the rocks hit the earth they scorched it and in some places created deep craters. Even without anyone telling them, people knew that God had sent Ababil birds to pelt the police with sijjil rocks. Finally Qara Qul Mansur raised his hand up high, ordering the birds to stop their attack, and so they retreated, wave after wave, and disappeared into the darkness. Then Qara Qul Mansur touched his steed with the goad, pointing its neck toward the sky. He shot off like a bolt of lightning and disappeared into the highest heavens.

At that very moment, the light ceased flooding out of the tomb. Then the moon and stars appeared again, the street lights came back on, and the old wall clock in the home of Abdallah Ali struck twelve times, which the boy Burhan Abdallah counted. He was perplexed because this was the second time the clock had marked midnight, making it seem as though what had just happened had been outside of time. Unable to find a satisfactory explanation for this event, the boy Burhan Abdallah laid his head on the pillow and fell asleep.

When the motorcade of the notables of Kirkuk reached the city's outskirts, where the army had positioned tanks at the intersections of major arteries, soldiers stopped the vehicles arriving from Baghdad and demanded that the notables show their papers to establish their identities. Since none of the men had any documents with him, because they had not needed them or been asked for them before, Hameed Nylon opened the door of his automobile and said to the soldier who had been addressing him, "What's all this about? I don't want to quarrel with you. Go and summon your commanding officer before there's a disaster. Tell him that Khidir Musa orders him to come." The soldier was nonplussed by the commanding tone that Hameed Nylon had adopted with him. So he bowed his head and headed to one of the many tents that had been erected beside the road. Nearby were two tanks and a military transport vehicle. In a few moments, three officers emerged from the tent the soldier had entered. They headed for Hameed Nylon and Khidir Musa, who had also alighted from the car. They lined up and offered a salute, which Khidir Musa returned somewhat haughtily, remarking, "I am Khidir Musa. I am returning directly from meeting with His Majesty Faisal II. What has happened to make you ask people for their identity papers?" One of the officers apologized for his troops' conduct in a manly tone, explaining that there had been a rebellion in the city and that martial law had been declared. He said that they had been await-ing his arrival so they could take him to the headquarters of the second brigade, where the brigade's commander, the governor, and the police chief were expecting him.

Khidir Musa, who was flabbergasted by this turn of events, replied, "Rebellion? I don't believe it. Fine; I'll proceed there at once." One of the officers informed him politely, however, that orders had been issued to transport him inside a tank, for fear something unto-ward might happen. Khidir Musa smiled and said, "Fine; if you think that's necessary." Then he asked Hameed Nylon to follow him and drive the delegation to the second brigade's headquarters. He climbed into the tank. Since it was cramped and stifling inside, he preferred to stand. The tank headed toward the city by way of Railroad Station Road, trailed by the convoy of vehicles returning from Baghdad.

Khidir Musa was received inside the second brigade's building, which resembled a walled fortress in the heart of the city, by a lieu-tenant colonel, an Arab who told him his name was Salim and who led him to an office on the right-hand side. It was near the military prison, which had windows overlooking two streets separated by a square. Summer cafés operated along the two streets and ran for a long way down them. The lieutenant colonel picked up the telephone receiver, dialed four numbers, and then spoke with someone at the other end, exchanging a few terse phrases. Afterwards he rose and said, "The group is waiting for you at the club." He referred to the officers' club, which was located on the other side of the street. The two men set off by foot, and soldiers halted street traffic so they could cross.

Khidir Musa and the lieutenant colonel passed through the tree-shaded entrance to the club and proceeded to an elegant room where five men sat. They rose to shake hands with Khidir Musa, who looked tired. Governor Ahmad Sulayman noticed this and said, "We're sorry we didn't allow you time to rest. But we need your help." Then after a brief pause he added, "I don't know if you've previously met His Excellency Sa'id Khoshnaw the interior minister, and Mr. John Tissow the director general of the oil company."

Khidir Musa replied suavely, "The honor has been culminated now."

The two other men were the commander of the second brigade Adnan al-Dabbagh and the police chief Naji al-Rawi, whom Khidir Musa had previously met, if only in passing. The interior minister, who was a Kurd from Sulaymaniya, asked him in an Arabic that was not impeccable, "How was your meeting with His Majesty?"

Khidir Musa replied sociably in Kurdish, "It was an unforgettable encounter!" Then he added in Arabic, "If all Iraqis thought the way our king does, there would not have been any problem."

Mr. Tissow, for whom the police chief was acting as interpreter, said, "But we have many problems, as you see, Mr. Musa." He attached a flattering smile to his comment.

The minister of the interior interjected, "It's regrettable that public security should collapse in a city like Kirkuk the way it has. The danger should have been averted before it could occur. It is regrettable that entire neighborhoods in the city remain in rebellion despite the declaration of martial law. But we don't want a bloodbath that will carry away innocent victims."

The chief of police said, "The problem is more the superstitious beliefs filling the city than the people. The whole city is speaking today about the dead man who rose from his grave and ascended to heaven on horseback and about the Ababil birds that supposedly attacked police headquarters."

Khidir Musa asked with concern, "When did this happen?" The police chief replied, "Overnight, or so they say. I, for one, was asleep."

The waiter entered with tumblers of tea and glasses of pomegranate juice. Addressing Khidir Musa, the minister of the interior said, "His Excellency Nuri Pasha has been informed of the discussion you have conducted. It will not be hard to find a solution to the problem of the road the firm needs. Mr. Tissow is in total agreement with us. The road can be routed around the cemetery. This is not a problem that will be much of a challenge for the engineers. Far more serious than that is the rebellion in the Chuqor community and other neighborhoods, where shots were fired at the police throughout the night. The instigators must be punished before we lose control of things. We can't allow this insurrection to continue."

Khidir Musa responded, "It will be hard to set straight what has happened during the two days we spent in Baghdad. I warned of the danger before it occurred. That's why I went to see the king. But I do not believe that taking revenge on people will solve the problem." Then he asked, "Were there any fatalities?"

The police chief replied, "An African black who worked as a barber was accidentally slain when rebels were pursuing one of our men."

Khidir Musa frowned and observed, "I knew him; may God be merciful to him."

Mr. Tissow, who had remained silent for most of the time, volunteered, "I'm inclined to agree with Mr. Musa. Appeasement works best with the masses. Otherwise, a bad situation will only grow worse. We actually have no wish to intrude into your internal affairs. We will, however, make every effort to improve our relations with the residents of the city. With this in mind, I announce in your presence, Mr. Musa, the cancellation of the road through the cemetery. Our engineers will devise an alternative route that will avoid any cemeteries. We will make compensatory payments to anyone whose house we are forced to demolish because it lies on the route. Moreover, the firm will undertake construction of a wall around the cemetery and restoration of the tombs of all of the Muslim saints buried there. We will also provide a monthly salary for two men to guard the cemetery."

Khidir Musa thanked him for this fine gesture, which he said would restore people's confidence in the oil company, which was considered a vital part of the city's life. He suggested to Mr. Tissow that he should present an appropriate sum of money as compensation to the family of the man who had been killed. Mr. Tissow approved of this idea and said he had simply not thought of it.

At that point, the police chief said confrontationally, "Fine! We've yielded enough to the rebels. If they don't release my men and return the weapons they've seized, I'll make them see bloody hell."

That was a clear threat, rife with hostility, but Khidir Musa chose to ignore it. He asserted, "Have no fear. Everything will be sorted out." Then he added as though pressuring the police chief, "But at the same time, the killer policeman must be punished. I certainly hope he will not be rewarded for his deed." Then he rose, excusing himself to rejoin the delegation's members who had been detained in the headquarters of the second brigade.

As he left the club, the commander of the second brigade joined him, trailed by his guards. He led him once more to the stone fortress where he indicated his intentions to Khidir Musa in a veiled manner, "You can count on me. The army will never disappoint the people."

Khidir Musa had remarked that Adnan al-Dabbagh had remained silent throughout the meeting, and grasped that the man was made of a different metal. The commander shook hands with the notables of Kirkuk, one after the other, and apologized for inconveniencing them. When he bade farewell to Khidir Musa at the outer gate, pressing his hand firmly, he said, "Don't forget to visit me. I would like that." Khidir Musa replied respectfully, "I certainly will."

After eating some kebab in the restaurant of Uthman Kebabchi, which was not very far from the second brigade's headquarters, the notables headed in an awe-inspiring motorcade to al-Musalla's cemetery, which the insurgents still occupied, cutting through both the police's and the insurgents' barricades. Many of them shook their heads in sorrow over the chaos to which the city had reverted. They felt as if a portentous wave from some unknown time had slammed into it, filling its heart with tears.

"Not everything has been lost, so long as hope lingers here." So thought Khidir Musa as he gazed through his prescription lenses at the collapsing houses on which dust and time lay heavy. Dada Hijri, who grasped nothing but his own dreams, was overcome by longing so bitter that it seemed to be the colocynth he sipped each time poetry transported him to the cavern of madness. This longing—as dark as a blot of China-ink and dotted with glowing, luminous spots of white and red—was for Dervish Bahlul, who had vanished in Baghdad. The man's face had reminded him of the ancient Torah prophets, whose portraits were sold on the other side of the city on dirt pathways for ten cents apiece along with pictures of the Imam Ali seated on his horse spearing the viper-like wild beast attacking him and of Shim'r holding al-Husayn's head, which is dripping blood as his eyes stare at death. Hameed Nylon had preceded them and joined the insurgents, who had been waiting for him perhaps more than for anyone else, for Hameed Nylon's presence among them made them feel they could thumb their noses at the entire world. Hameed Nylon sensed that he had missed something big. He wished he had been with his brothers from the community in their battle against the enemy but comforted himself with the thought, "Perhaps there will be more to come. Our struggle is greater than a fight to protect the dead." He was so distracted by these hopes that he neglected to deliver the Roneo press entrusted to him in Baghdad, oblivious even to the danger of having the police discover it in his vehicle—an offense that could lead to his spending long years in prison. A man like Hameed Nylon, however, could not brood about such things, for it was danger itself that liberated him from fear. Surging deep within him, a dreamy intoxication, comparable to what he felt when he was with women, possessed him.

When Kirkuk's notables reached the cemetery, vast numbers of women swathed in black suddenly emerged from among the tombs, wailing and slapping their faces in grief, as if they were part of a theatrical performance. Khidir Musa shouted at them, "What are you doing?" Since none of them answered, he brushed past them and headed for the area where the men were congregated. He called out to Abbas Bahlawan and to the Chuqor community's young men, who were standing there with the others, "For the love of God, make those women be quiet. What's all this wailing about?" Then Khidir Musa climbed on the remnants of a ruined wall and delivered a speech he had been composing on the way. In it he said, "Noble sons of Kirkuk, God has annihilated the iniquity. The travesty has been destroyed." He announced that the cemetery would not be touched, that a wall would be built around it, that the tombs of the saints would be restored, that two guards for the cemetery would be appointed, and that the family of the martyr Qara Qul Mansur would be compensated. He also communicated to them King Faisal II's personal greetings. Once Khidir Musa had reported all this heartwarming news to them, applause immediately resounded everywhere throughout the cemetery along with the women's trilling ululation. A voice from the crowd protested, however, "We want the killer policeman executed publicly here and his body displayed for people to see." Another man declared that the police chief should himself be punished. A Communist student, whose face was covered to conceal his identity, demanded that the English imperialists be thrown out of Kirkuk and the oil company nationalized so that its profits could be distributed to the workers and the poor.

Khidir Musa listened to all this with calm self-confidence. "None of these requests seems out of reach, since the king himself stands beside us." Then he added, "Now I think it is our duty to recite the opening prayer of the Holy Qur'an by the grave of our martyr Qara Qul." Thus he left no room for further protest. The grave was still there, even though many of those who had witnessed the miraculous ascent to paradise of Qara Qul on Buraq's back believed they would find the grave empty. Some of these dismayed observers muttered, "We saw him with our own eyes ascend to heaven." Mullah Zayn al-Abidin al-Qadiri, who stepped forward to lead the throng in a recitation of the Fatiha and then delivered a special prayer for the martyr, proclaimed in a thunderous voice, which was heard by all those standing behind him, that what Muslims had seen ascending to heaven had been Qara Qul Mansur's spirit on its way to paradise. His body, the spirit's temporary abode, would decay with time, like any other edifice. What need did a spirit that has been freed of its fetters have for them? He announced that the favor bestowed on Qara Qul Mansur by God's angels, who bore him to the sky up the shaft of light, was a rare one that would permit him to join the ranks of immortal saints. Actually, people who had known Qara Qul Mansur personally harbored many reservations in their hearts about the matter because the man had been a deceitful and malicious alcoholic. Since God had chosen him in the manner that people had witnessed, however, His choice must have been based on some wisdom that escaped people. Those who had quarreled with him during his lifetime regretted that they had not recognized his true worth, which had been displayed by his death.

Then emotion seized hold of people till they lost control of themselves, along with all their sense of right and wrong. They attacked the grave, men and women, and began groveling in its dirt.

The blind washed out their eyes with its soil till they could see the light. Cripples crawled across it so strength would return to their legs and hands. Barren women, enveloped in their wraps, stuffed handfuls of dirt from the grave up their vaginas so they would bear children. Those afflicted with tuberculosis, syphilis, hemorrhoids, typhoid, and cancer swallowed some of the dirt to cure themselves of their maladies and pains. Young men seized this opportunity to throw themselves upon the women, squeezing against their soft buttocks or grasping their quivering breasts. This human offensive swelled ever greater as thousands of people from every direction shoved past each other toward the grave, struggling to reach it. Everyone who had heard the news pushed forward as stories and miracles were devised, detailing feats that not even the Messiah had ever performed. Country folk crowded in from nearby villages till it seemed that Judgment Day, which had been predicted by some leaflets distributed in Kirkuk a few days before, had dawned. The advancing swarms crushed underfoot those who fell, and thus some pregnant women suffered miscarriages and children were suffocated. The young athletes from the Chuqor community initially tried to take charge of the situation and fired into the air to frighten people back from the grave, but the crowds, whose consciences had been knocked out of kilter by Qara Qul Mansur's miracle, swept them away. So they yielded to the waves of people surging from everywhere. Only because Kirkuk's community leaders retreated in the nick of time did they escape death by asphyxiation. This was thanks to the courage of Chuqor's youth, who forcibly cleared a path for them to quit the cemetery, saving their lives from imminent danger.

Although the government had no wish to intervene in this affair, which was none of their business, at first three helicopters went up and hovered over the human throngs that surrounded the grave, pouring cold water on people to alleviate the impact of the intense heat, which was causing people to faint. No one knew exactly what was happening at the tomb, for the human mass surrounding it extended for a long way in every direction. Khidir Musa was afraid of the consequences of allowing public access to the grave and contacted the governor to explain the necessity of intervening to bring the situation under control while that was still possible. The governor was forced to ask for assistance from the second brigade's commander, who—with his officers—devised a plan to retake control of Qara Qul's grave, dubbing it "Operation Holy Month of Sha'ban." Accordingly, parachutists were dropped on the grave and took possession of it after fighting off the people who surrounded it. At the same time, tanks were stationed at the ends of the streets that led to the cemetery to prevent more people from reaching it, but the soldiers who forced the crowds to withdraw found the grave empty. The corpse of Qara Qul Mansur had vanished. Someone had already made off with it.

The officer in charge of the operation ordered his soldiers to fill the grave with dirt again in a desperate attempt to keep something secret that could not be. The governor was upset by the disappearance of the corpse and decided to get it back, no matter the cost. He declared, "A corpse can't vanish into thin air." Finally the director of public security contacted the governor to tell him that his men had discovered that residents of the nearby village of Tawuq were responsible for abducting the corpse in hopes of burying it in their village, which did not have the sepulcher of any saint to bring it blessings. Armored police units rushed off to the village, which lay no more than half an hour from the city and surrounded it from all sides, firing into the air. The abductors, who numbered more than twenty armed villagers, decided to resist and withdrew into nearby orchards and woods, dragging the corpse, which they had wrapped in a quilt fastened with ropes. The pursuing policemen traded shots with them. During the battle, which lasted more than an hour, two villagers were killed and three others wounded. One policeman took a direct hit to his heart and fell over on his back, dead. Another was wounded in the shoulder. As the abductors fled by a route that led through fields and orchards, the knot in the rope with which they had secured the quilt came undone, and the corpse, which was totally naked since people had plundered its shroud when it was taken from the grave, rolled down into an irrigation ditch. One of the villagers reached out, grabbed the corpse's foot, and dragged it behind him during their retreat under police fire. The men took turns dragging the corpse, as its glossy black skin was lacerated and befouled with mud and grass. They were eventually forced to abandon the body when pressure from the police intensified. Then they hightailed it away and disappeared into thick woods where the police did not dare charge them.

Thus the police rescued the body of Qara Qul Mansur, whose spirit had ascended to heaven on the back of Buraq the night before. They tossed the putrid cadaver in a Jeep and transported it back to the barracks. The government quickly printed leaflets, which they dropped by airplane over all the neighborhoods of Kirkuk, bringing people the good news that the corpse of the saint Qara Qul Mansur had been rescued from the wicked abductors and announcing that the next day would be an official holiday to allow people to pay their respects to the remains in a procession featuring both the people and the government.

This gesture of good intentions by the government caused people to forget even the battles they had waged against the police. A rumor spread that the policeman who had killed Qara Qul Mansur would be executed immediately subsequent to the funeral procession. The young men, in response to Khidir Musa's personal intercession, proceeded to release their hostages, who had been held in a room of the Chuqor community's mosque, but the rifles the insurgents had seized from the police had vanished without a trace. The chief of police was forced to keep silent about this matter and to turn a blind eye to it, until some opportunity should present itself to reclaim the rifles that had been taken by force from his men.

The following day, the funeral cortège set out from the Palace of Government building. At the front of the procession were musicians playing monotonous funeral tunes on trumpets. They were followed by people carrying black flags at half-mast. A bouquet of artificial roses had been placed on the chest of Qara Qul Mansur's corpse, which had been set in an open military vehicle that was surrounded by tanks as a precaution against a repeat of the previous attack and abduction. Behind the tanks marched a procession of government officials, prominent citizens, Kurdish feudal lords—invited by the government—and clerics representing Islam, Christianity, and Judaism. These were followed by a large military

138

contingent marching slowly to the beat of the music. At the rear came the citizens, who were subdued this time. Many, among them women and children, preferred to stand on the sidewalks and watch this awe-inspiring spectacle. At al-Musalla Cemetery, builders and construction workers were waiting for the arrival of the funeral cortège. The moment the soldiers returned the body to its grave, they began building a marble and plaster tomb, which they surmounted with an extraordinary dome that had windows of interlacing iron rods and a green door, above which was placed a bronze plaque inscribed in Kufic script: "Do not think that those who are killed serving God are dead. Rather, they are alive, receiving sustenance from their Lord." Beneath this was the phrase "Here rests the saintly martyr Qara Qul Mansur who ascended to the heavens." The governor announced in a brief statement, delivered in front of the sepulcher, that His Majesty King Faisal II had decided to appoint a director general to oversee the sepulcher's affairs and to allocate enough funds to rebuild the tombs in al-Musalla Cemetery of all the dead Muslims whose families could not afford to do so, as a way of honoring the martyr Qara Qul Mansur, whom he hoped God would honor too. He also said that a police detachment would guard the tomb night and day to prevent anyone from profaning the sanctity of the graves of saints.

This was, in fact, more than people had been expecting, for the governor had displayed extravagant, almost incredible generosity. Even so, their hearts were still unsettled because they wanted revenge on the killer of their martyred saint. This was a matter that left the officials in a quandary. They knew that the people would be satisfied with no punishment short of hanging, but the police chief and the director of public security opposed that: "How can we expect our men to work if they know that acting in their own self-defense may get them hanged?" Finally the police chief proposed that the government limit its actions to whipping the man in a public square, thus leaving to the people the fate of the man, whom everyone expected they would kill. The next day the killer was taken to al-Musalla Square and stripped of his clothing. Then his chest was fastened to a post and the back of his head was covered by a red cloth that had been soaked in water. A huge sergeant stood behind him and struck him twenty times with a bamboo pole, which landed on the man's butt or back. At first the killer tried to steel himself. After the third blow, however, he began to howl like a dog—provoking laughter among people who had come to watch the punishment of the policeman who had killed the saint Qara Qul Mansur. The flogger, whose bamboo staff as it cut through the air created a swishing sound that could be heard far away, began to sweat profusely. The victim now was splattered with blood and had even ceased to moan. The sergeant sighed with relief after delivering the final blow and proclaimed, "This is the punishment for those who kill a saint." Then he untied the rope that bound the killer to the wooden post, and the men with him collected the ropes and the post and departed, after pushing the victim to the ground and spitting on him. Sensing the danger surrounding him, the man attempted to rise in a desperate effort to save himself, but his legs betrayed him and he fell on his face once more. At that, Qara Qul Mansur's two black sons, who were ten and twelve years old, stepped forward. Each of them had in his hand a straight razor taken from their slain father's barber shop. They flipped the exhausted man onto his side. One of the boys seized his hair and pulled his head back while the other one grasped his chin and tried to slaughter him. A mullah who emerged from the crowd of spectators cautioned them, "It's not right to slaughter him this way, my son." One of the brothers rebuffed him, saying, "Don't interfere. Go ahead and step aside. He killed my father." The agitated cleric responded, "I know that, my son. Point his head toward Mecca first and recite: 'In the name of God, the Compassionate the Merciful,' before you cut his throat, with God's blessing." Then he helped them point toward Mecca the head of the man who was kicking and pounding the dirt with his hands in awkward attempts to rise. The policeman, however, having heard their conversation and seeing the blade near his throat, suddenly shook himself. The two boys were startled but clung to him even tighter. Then the boys' mother, a plump black lady, came forward and sat on the man, weighing down his chest, and he ceased resisting. She told her older son, "Slay him! What are you waiting for?" So the boy cut the man's neck, severing his head from his body, and blood gushed out over the dirt like a fountain. The boy then rose, tossing the head, which had remained in his hand, to the ground. No sooner had the plump lady stood up, however, than the headless body quivered and rose to its feet. It began to run every which way, eventually colliding with a light pole. Then it fell once more to the ground, and moved no more, ever.

Seven

The mausoleum the government erected for Qara Qul had a big impact on the life of the Chuqor community and indeed on the whole city of Kirkuk because people began to flock there from every direction, eager to visit the mausoleum of the man who had ascended to heaven in a cloud of light, mounted on Buraq. At first, news about him spread to the villages surrounding Kirkuk. Then it was quickly transmitted to Alton Kopri, Chamchamal, Qara-Teppa, Sulaymaniya, Erbil, and Mosul. Next it reached Baghdad by means of traveling merchants and soldiers. From there, the news went out not merely to the other cities of Iraq but to Syria, Lebanon, Transjordan, and even to the Arabs who remained in Israel, where it was carried by livestock smugglers. Istanbul, Ankara, Adana, and Iskenderun learned about Qara Qul's ascension to heaven from Turkmen travelers, who frequented Turkish cities more often than Baghdad itself. Shi'i pilgrims from Persia and India on visits to Karbala, al-Najaf, and al-Kazimiya carried varying reports about the miracles of Qara Qul to Tehran, Qum, Khurasan, Islamabad, and Kashmir.

The fact of the matter is that these reports stirred up many disagreements among Muslim religious scholars, mujtahids, and jurisprudents, both Sunni and Shiʻi, especially in Turkey and Iran. If at first the Shiʻa refused to recognize the miracles of Qara Qul, that was because they did not believe God would bestow such a huge honor on a Sunni who was not a descendant of the Prophet's family. This egotistical approach was refuted by Sunni religious scholars who affirmed that Islam had made all people equal and that there is no superiority of an Arab over a non-Arab, since only piety counts. The way Turkish ulema looked at the matter revealed a certain taste for revenge, since they never failed to point out that Qara Qul's grandfather had worked in the service of the Ottoman governors, who had rescued him from the treachery of Arabs wanting to seize this African in order to sell him to the shaykhs in al-Ahsa' in the Arabian peninsula. This allegation was naturally denied by the Arabs, who pointed out that the man would not have been able to commit the miracles that had been witnessed had it not been for Islam, which descended on the Arabs before anyone else.

These religious disputes soon ended, however. The Shiʻa began to spread the word that the man had been Shiʻi, even if he had not made that public—for fear of Sunni reprisal, since these Sunnis believed that a Shiʻi had on his bottom a short tail, which was knotted into a kind of braid into which beads were woven. The Shiʻi change of heart occurred after Shah Reza Pahlavi of Iran presented to the mausoleum a door made of pure gold. This door was studded with gems and inscribed with verses by Saʻdi of Shiraz and by Umar Khayyam. Some people in the Chuqor community and Kirkuk whose lives revolved around the mausoleum spread a rumor that Qara Qul was both a Sunni and a Shiʻi at the same time. The goal of this strange claim was clearly to attract the greatest number of people possible to visit Qara Qul's mausoleum.

The caravansaries and the hotels filled with the visitors flocking into Kirkuk and new ones were built. Among these were the Beasts of Burden Inn, which was located by the entrance to the Chay community, the Stars Inn on the road to the railway station, and al-Alamein Hotel, which overlooked the Khasa Su River and was managed by Saqi Baqi, a tall, athletic young man from the Chuqor community. He had taken part in the battles of Gawirbaghi and the cemetery and was wounded in his right leg during both of them, so that he limped for quite a while. Restaurants selling kebab flourished and raised their prices. Students of Islamic jurisprudence from the colleges of the universities lined their pockets as they began to spend most of their time among the tombs, reciting the sura "The Cow" from the Holy Qur'an. Frequently they would do an abbreviated version in exchange for ten fils, which they received from people visiting the spirit of saintly Qara Qul. Battles flared between these students and seminary pupils who came to the cemetery bearing copies of the Qur'an and who vied with them in their pursuit of customers.

Another trade gained popularity in the Chuqor community, and the boy Burhan Abdallah monopolized it, for his skill in drafting letters became widely known. He had actually acquired this reputation even before Qara Qul's miracle because of the love letters he composed for the illiterate women of the Chuqor community. Young women who maintained emotional ties with young men living in other cities and who hoped these young men would come forward to ask for their hands would visit the boy, sit facing him on the ground, and open to him hearts torn by passion and desire. He would then transform all of that into flaming words of love and romantic confessions. Lovers in Kirkuk may not have exchanged anything like this before. He had learned about this from Mustafa Lutfi al-Manfaluti's book about the amorous poet Cyrano de Bergerac. He read the book time and again without ever tiring of it. These single girls, who were not embarrassed about spilling their emotions, were content to hand him ten or twenty fils. Married women who had secret lovers and feared a scandal would shower him with gifts to guarantee his silence. Now women came to him, not to write love letters because most of them were elderly women or married women who were neglecting themselves, but to draft letters of complaint addressed to the saint, Qara Qul. In these, they would complain of the injustice of the age and of its outrages against them, requesting him to take revenge on husbands who had left them or on their co-wives and neighbors. Then there were other women who sought the saint's mediation to obtain posts for their sons in the Iraq Petroleum Company or to secure monetary compensation for their long military service. The women would take these letters to the mausoleum of Qara Qul, weeping and lamenting before him. Then they would throw the letters through the grille of the shrine's window into the domed space containing the tomb, which was covered with a green cloth embroidered with silk thread and on top of which letters and money accumulated. They would also inspect the gold wheelchair parked beside the tomb, facing the window.

King Ibn Sa'ud had presented this vehicle to the shrine so that the Shah of Iran would not appear more supportive of Islam than he, even though the Wahhabi doctrine he advocated prohibited displays like these. The truth was that the Wahhabi Ibn Sa'ud, who had commissioned this gold wheelchair using his private wealth accruing to him from oil wells he owned in the Arabian peninsula, had not considered the end toward which this custom-made wheelchair of gold was heading. There was no rational purpose for it at the mausoleum, although no one had considered that. The fact of the matter is that the idea of commissioning this gold wheelchair had occurred to Ibn Sa'ud years before the demise of Qara Qul; on February 14, 1945, to be precise, when the king had met Roosevelt on board the cruiser USS *Quincy* in the Great Bitter Lake in Egypt, during his first trip outside his country since his visit thirty years before to Basra. The king told the American president, who was crippled and sat in a motorized wheelchair, "I feel that you are my twin brother." Roosevelt had responded, "But you are very, very lucky, because you still have the use of your two legs, which carry you wherever you want." Ibn Sa'ud, who felt embarrassed, had saved the situation by observing, "You are the lucky one, Mr. President, because my legs will grow heavier year after year, whereas you can rely on your wheelchair." Roosevelt had then answered, "I have two of these wheelchairs. They are twins as well. I wonder whether you would accept one as my gift?" All that Ibn Sa'ud could think to say was, "With pleasure. I will use it every day to remind me of the person who gave it to me: my wonderful friend."

At the conclusion of this cordial meeting, the king ordered his finance minister, Abdallah ibn Sulayman, to commission a gold wheelchair as a return present for the American president. Roosevelt died, however, before the wheelchair was completed, and then the king did not know what to do with it. So it was left out in a garden of his palace, and the children, servants, and slaves played with it for many long years, until the king heard the news of the gold door that the Shah of Iran had presented to the mausoleum of Qara Qul. Then he got the idea of presenting it to the shrine. The important thing, after all, was that the wheelchair contained more gold than the shah had put in the mausoleum door. He was hopeful that this noble deed would win him the affection of the Iraqi people and shield him against the evil of the Hashemites, who were governing Iraq. So he ordered one of his black servants to fetch the wheelchair, which was covered with mud, dust, and babies' fecal matter, and proceeded to wash it himself at the edge of the garden with a rubber hose connected to a spigot. The gold wheelchair regained so much of its former splendor and glitter that he toured the wings of his women's quarters with it, provoking the laughter of the younger children, who chased after him and sprang on his back. Then a delegation of important figures from the kingdom's political and religious establishments undertook to deliver the king's golden gift to the mausoleum of Qara Qul. It was a gift for which King Faisal II personally thanked him.

People from everywhere, men and women, headed for the mausoleum to toss their letters through the window into the domed area along with coins or currency. They would go hungry so they could save something to donate to Saint Qara Qul. Those who were unable to come to Kirkuk to visit the mausoleum of Qara Qul would post their letters, which the letter carriers, who rode bicycles, would deliver to the mausoleum and empty through the window's grill. These letters were written in many languages: Arabic, Turkish, Farsi, and Urdu, but there were also Hebrew letters mailed by Jews who had emigrated from Kirkuk. There were even letters in Russian, English, German, and French. These were written by Christians who had been guided to Islam and had embraced it.

In reality this mausoleum turned into a shrine that caused as much harm as good, for the people of the Chuqor community and Kirkuk became crazy about acquiring money, and this caused many arguments and disputes among them. Mullah Zayn al-Abidin al-Qadiri, who was finagling to be appointed as the shrine's director, quarreled with Khidir Musa, accusing him of not putting sufficient effort into lobbying the authorities to appoint him to this post, which he believed he deserved more than anyone else, but this accusation was unfair. When Khidir Musa had proposed his name to the governor, he was convinced of the success of his effort. There was a glitch, though. The governor forwarded the matter to the ministers of the interior and of religious endowments, expecting that a decision about the appointment would be forthcoming, but it was delayed for a long time because the minister of the interior, who transmitted requests in a routine fashion to the public safety administration, had discovered that there was a dossier on Mullah Zayn al-Abidin al-Qadiri, who had been accused of Communism. Khidir Musa had concealed this matter from the mullah to avoid arousing his anxiety. The mullah only learned the truth when the police summoned him to conduct an investigation of his character. They then wrote a report that cleared his name of the charge of Communism and established his loyalty to the monarchy and to King Faisal II.

Mullah al-Qadiri still felt frustrated and could scarcely sleep on account of the nightmares that oppressed his heart. His zest for life did not return until Khidir Musa sought him out two weeks later in the coffeehouse and told him, "I wanted to be the first to congratulate you, Mr. Director General, to appease your anger at me." All the distraught mullah could find to say was, "Has an appointment order been issued for me?" At that, Khidir Musa handed him the text of the appointment, observing, "You can read it yourself and then you must invite us to have tea." The mullah cast a quick glance over the document. Then he rose and kissed Khidir Musa on the forehead. He apologized for his conduct, which he said made him feel ashamed. Khidir Musa, however, gently stopped him: "That's enough, man. Even friends quarrel." The mullah directed the proprietor of the coffeehouse to bring a tray with baklava and to serve tea to all the patrons, who on learning about the matter came forward to congratulate him on his new position.

The next day, Director General Mullah Zayn al-Abidin al-Qadiri sought out the governor, who congratulated him on obtaining the post and offered him a temporary office in the Palace of Government, along with two clerks from Import/Export, until a private office could be obtained for him and the employees he needed could be appointed. The mullah, however, rejected this idea, asserting that the last thing on his mind was ostentation and pomp. If he had wanted to oversee the direction of the affairs of the mausoleum, his reason had been to stay close to it, not in order to imprison himself in a room in the Palace of Government like any other government employee. The governor responded, "The matter is left to you. Make the decision you think best."

Afterwards the mullah headed to the cemetery, where three soldiers emerged from a long room they had converted into a guardhouse near the tomb. They saluted him, since the news of his appointment as director general had reached them that very day. Two of them accompanied him on a tour, during which he inspected the mausoleum and the tombs near it before returning once more to the guardhouse, where he took a seat on a chair out in the open by the door to the long room, in which four cots had been placed. He watched the visitors who streamed in from everywhere in order to obtain the miraculous blessings of Qara Qul.

The mullah grew accustomed to sitting in this chair every day during the period while masons erected the building for the headquarters of his agency. This building, which was constructed of stone and plaster and which was located behind the police guardhouse, faced the domed mausoleum. Over its entrance flew the white, red, black, and green Iraqi flag with its twin stars representing the Tigris and Euphrates rivers. On either side of the entrance were facing rooms furnished with Persian carpets, which Iranian pilgrims had presented to the shrine, and embroidered cushions that al-Hajj Ahmad al-Sabunji had donated. The entry vestibule opened onto a courtyard containing in the center a marble basin with a fountain, from which water flowed constantly. It ended with a spacious open porch, which was also paved with marble. Placed in it was a coffin that the mullah had brought from his mosque in the

Chuqor community. He used it as his desk, from which he directed the affairs of his agency. He received his visitors and contacts while sitting inside it. Indeed, he would occasionally sleep in it too while enjoying the noon siesta he found indispensable, especially when the courtyard was sprinkled with cold water. This strange custom aroused the disapproval of many people, who accused Mullah Zayn al-Abidin al-Qadiri at times of feeblemindedness and at others of exhibitionism and self-promotion. Although the governor considered this conduct inconsistent with the status of a high-ranking state official, the mullah insisted on his position, affirming that a person ought never to forget for a moment death, which—no matter how high time may lift him—lies in wait for him at the end.

The mullah said in a sermon, which he delivered one Friday in his mosque and which became famous as "The Coffin Sermon," that what destroys a man's heart is not the temptation of life but a forgetfulness of death. Every living being has a right to enjoy his time, but this enjoyment wins goals that seem imaginary when he realizes that death lies in wait for him. Once people remember this reality, no ruler will tyrannize his subjects, no notable will take pride in his glory, and no rich man will be stingy with his wealth. Mullah al-Qadiri also said, "True wisdom is revealed twice in this lifetime: first when a person is born and next when he dies. Each of us is condemned to be born; each of us is condemned to die. Anything over and beyond that is foam left by the wave on the shore." Mullah Zayn al-Abidin al-Qadiri was so touched by these realities, which were revealed to him all at once without his ever having thought about them, that tears poured from his eyes as he said, "Now that I have become a director general, I must not forget this truth. There has never been a prophet or a saint who did not carry his coffin on his shoulders. Why should I not also have a coffin, for my part?"

This influential sermon, which dumfounded the rumormongers and silenced them, in point of fact raised the standing of Mullah Zayn al-Abidin al-Qadiri, who had displayed extraordinary brilliance in the acquisition of metaphysical wisdom. Even the governor himself, some days after this sermon, the text of which was published in the newspaper *Kirkuk,* was forced to pay a courtesy call to his office, where the mullah received him in his customary way: reclining in the coffin, which he had outfitted with a pad and feather pillows. The governor sat in the open porch, which the mullah had furnished with carpets and cushions, in the style of Arab divans. He drank two cups of bitter coffee, which a man served to him from a pot with a curved spout. The fellow, obviously a servant working for the agency, held the pot in his hand. The governor started the conversation with a jest: "I didn't know you had such a restful office. At least you won't suffer the way I do from back pain." The mullah, who had reared back a bit, raising his head to look up, responded: "I tried it for two days without a pad, and my back was almost destroyed from the pain. It was truly unbearable. May God be merciful to the dead, who are placed in it naked, with only a shroud to cover their body."

The conduct of Mullah Zayn al-Abidin was an innovation that no one before him had practiced. It demonstrated to the residents of the Chuqor community, however, that the wellspring of light they had heard about for generations had not run dry, despite the corruption that the flood of Iranian, Indian, and Turkish pilgrims introduced to the city. Men neglected their employments, and teenagers fled from their schools in order to hover around the shrine and pursue the foreign women visitors who had come to seek the intercession of Qara Qul. Some of them devised novel ways of attracting women's attention and tempting them—wearing a cloak and a turban, for example, along with a fake beard. Some of them also claimed to possess a gift for magic and the ability to slay the jinn that trouble women's bodies and prevent them from bearing children. On dark nights they would entice these women to the deserted area of al-Musalla, at the far edge of the cemetery and stage what they termed "A Night of the Jinn."

Whether these desperate women visitors followed these young men in the belief that their destiny awaited them there or from a desire to contact the world of spirits, they all were convinced that a world existed where the boundaries between possible and impossible disappeared and where everything could turn into its opposite, so that the world was in effect turned upside down. They wished to reach this world, which would perhaps provide deliverance to them.

Women wrapped in cloaks would slip through the dark night, between the tombs, while reciting the opening prayer of the Qur'an on their way to the ruins of a nineteenth-century gristmill, guiding themselves by the feeble light of a candle placed on the ruin's wall facing the city. Inside the mill, candles were burning on the giant, circular grinding stone in the center of the room. Atop it sat a man who was completely naked except for the red veil covering his eyes. He was reciting in Arabic in a monotonous fashion—between singing and howling—distorted verses from the faux-qur'an of the Liar Musaylima and from an Arabic verse translation by Ahmad al-Safi al-Najafi of the quatrains of Umar Khayyam. From time to time this man would strike a cheap container made of aluminum. Nude young men, weeping and pounding their chests with their palms, circumambulated the millstone. Women arriving at the mill were commanded to remove their cloaks and to circle the millstone until they were overcome by fatigue. Then the man sitting on the millstone descended with a dagger in his hand, seized one of the women by her hand, and forced her to climb onto the millstone, where he extinguished the candles. Then each of the other young men embraced one of the women in a gloomy corner of the mill and together they raised the monotonous, communal, bestial cry "Out, out," while the woman standing on the stone swayed right and left until she entered a trance state close to inebriation. Then the young man climbed up, still carrying the dagger, and removed her clothing, one piece at a time. So the other women imitated her. Next the woman on the millstone stretched out and the young man threw a cloak over her, covering her body. He climbed inside it, repeating cryptic phrases, which were closer to Satan's language than to that of human beings:

Ta'am, Labam, Bacho Halam
Ser ya Majal, Taj Mahal
Jan Qadar, Sunbul Bahar
Bulbul Dalam, Qalbul Jalam.

Meanwhile, the other women were also stretching out on the ground in the corners of the mill. The young men covered them with cloaks, beneath which they then crept to begin slaying jinn. On average, each youth found that more than one jinni was possessing the woman he was treating. Yet he was able to slay all of them. One young man even slew—with a single thrust—five rebel jinn lurking in one woman's womb. After that, the young men wrapped around each woman's wrist an amulet of green scraps of cloth to protect them from the evils of the jinn forever. Next the women reached their hands into their pockets and paid liberally, kissing the youths' hands for saving them from Satan's evils. Then they slipped away, enveloped by their black cloaks, and disappeared into the night.

It is true that people continued to praise Qara Qul, who had benefited them more dead than alive, but the sight of the riches raining down on his mausoleum caused them to forget even his miracle of riding Buraq and ascending to heaven. Many of them felt more entitled to this wealth than a stone tomb was because it did not eat, whereas their children were hungry. What would Qara Qul—who must currently be in a circle of angels seated in a garden of riches in paradise, singing the praises of God—do with gold, silver, Iraqi dinars, Iranian tomans, Turkish liras, and Indian rupees?

These demonic thoughts tempted them until they no longer paid any attention to the principles of Islam. In fact, they forgot Islam's five pillars and substituted for them other principles, which they said they were compelled to follow. The first to be seduced by this wealth were the letter carriers, who started opening letters addressed to Qara Qul, looking for the banknotes that women normally placed inside the folded sheets of their letters. Their example was followed by the policemen guarding the mausoleum. They imposed on each male or female visitor to the shrine a fee for the visit. This was decreed by the deputy lieutenant in charge of the guardhouse. Although this tax was a trivial sum, Director General Mullah Zayn al-Abidin al-Qadiri abrogated it, threatening to inflict the stiffest penalties on anyone whose soul seduced him into placing a barrier between Muslims and the tomb of Qara Qul. The souls of these policemen did not find any rest until the director general decided to appoint Abbas Bahlawan and Mahmud al-Arabi as supervisors for the mausoleum in recognition of their heroism in the battle they led against the police in defense of the grandfathers' cemetery—or that was what he said. As a matter of fact, he was motivated by his fear of them. This was an attempt to ensure their loyalty to him.

Actually, Abbas Bahlawan and Mahmud al-Arabi did not even have recourse to a go-between. They met the mullah one day in the Chuqor community and told him half in jest, "We heard that you had appointed us supervisors for the mausoleum. You shouldn't have done that, Mullah, without at least consulting us. All's well that ends well, however; we accept." Disconcerted, the mullah apologized, "I knew you would accept; I would not think of accepting the post of director general without you beside me."

A deep friendship between Abbas Bahlawan, Mahmud al-Arabi, and the policemen in the guardhouse began the very first day they worked in "The General Directorate for the Shrine of Qara Qul." This was the official name, which Hashim al-Khattat—the most famous artist in Baghdad—had undertaken to paint in Neskhi script on a silver plaque that Mullah Zayn al-Abidin al-Qadiri affixed to the curved façade of his directorate's entry, which he painted green. When the policemen vented the complaint that was troubling their heart—the abrogation by the director general of the visitation tax—Abbas Bahlawan laughed and commented, "If your worries involve money, you can forget them from now on. Each of you will have a share of the money Qara Qul receives. Why should you think that a locked door, the key of which the mullah places in his pocket, will hinder us from accessing the wealth that fills the tomb? I wonder what Mahmud al-Arabi has learned during his lifetime if not the care of locked doors." Mahmud al-Arabi, who was enjoying a tumbler of tea in the police guardhouse, replied, "There's always at least one way to solve any problem."

This assurance, which restored hope to the hearts of the guardhouse's men after the unhappiness they had suffered, led the deputy lieutenant to rise and embrace both Abbas Bahlawan and Mahmud al-Arabi. He observed, "I've expected only the best from you two from the very beginning. I knew that you would think of us." His men followed his example, and a policeman from Talafar, his emotions getting the better of him, went so far as to kiss Mahmud al-Arabi's hand, saying, "Son, God bless your hand, which will keep

153

us from having to beg from everyone who comes along and which will preserve our dignity." Abbas Bahlawan and Mahmud al-Arabi were touched by the sentiments of these men, for they realized that their meager salaries would not even feed their children. It was true that government service offered a status that others in society envied, even if it was only that of policeman, but how could a man provide sustenance to his children when all he had to show for a month's work was seven dinars, which would evaporate during a single week?

The two men circled round the mausoleum after that, examining everything about the place, as though checking out the strengths of an adversary. As he glanced at the twin locks on the mausoleum's door, Mahmud al-Arabi confided to Abbas Bahlawan, "It would not be difficult to break these locks, but that's not what we want, since the mullah would discover the matter the next day. There is a much easier way than breaking the two locks. We'll obtain what we want without even opening the door."

Abbas Bahlawan responded jestingly, "I know you're a thief, but if you're also a magician, that's news to me."

Mahmud al-Arabi cast a speculative glance at Abbas Bahlawan and contracted his bushy eyebrows. Then he said, "The matter requires intellect, not magic, and this is precisely what you lack."

Abbas Bahlawan cursed him affectionately, "And this is precisely what you must prove exists in your empty head."

Mahmud al-Arabi replied, "Fine! You'll see that this evening when people cease visiting the shrine."

The method that Mahmud al-Arabi contrived to reach the cash inside the mausoleum was truly simple. He brought a long stick, stuck a piece of gum on one end, and poked it through the grille on the shrine's window. He used this to pluck banknotes and coins, one after the other, deliberately leaving some behind so that Mullah Zayn al-Abidin al-Qadiri would not catch on to the scheme when he opened the door, normally each Friday morning, to collect the donations, which were recorded by the Islamic law student from his mosque—Aziz Shirwan, whom he had named as his personal secretary—in a large ledger that the mullah had purchased for him for this purpose. He considered these funds to be contributions to a religious endowment for the shrine. Naturally there was no safe where the mullah could place this income. He simply had burlap sacks that he carried to his house, where he placed these in large jars he buried beneath a non-fruiting date palm. He asserted that the funds constituted a trust for which he was the guardian, and that a man had as great a duty to protect trust funds as his own money.

As a matter of fact, the gifts presented to the shrine and received by Mullah Zayn al-Abidin al-Qadiri were so varied that it would be difficult to list them: gold liras, gem-studded necklaces, silver bracelets, rare watches from China, and objets d'art from Syria. Mullah Zayn al-Abidin al-Qadiri placed all of these in additional jugs, which he buried beneath the sole palm tree in his home's courtyard, keeping them secret even from his wife, whom he deliberately encouraged to visit her sister's house or the neighbors, so he would be alone, after bolting the door. There were, however, also other gifts he could not bury. Villagers brought many eggs, chickens, goats, and sheep. Merchants presented sacks of sugar, rice, and wheat and boxes of tea. Of course not all the gifts found their way to Mullah Zayn al-Abidin al-Qadiri because the policemen, joined by Abbas Bahlawan and Mahmud al-Arabi, greeted people bearing gifts at a distance and urged them to place these in the police guardhouse, on the grounds that this was Qara Qul's very own guardhouse. Many people refused, however, insisting on delivering the goods directly to the shine's window and then having them officially recorded by the receipts clerk. At this stage as well, a portion of the gifts was divvied up by the clerk and the other employees, including the director general's secretary Aziz Shirwan, who handed over most of the eggs, chickens, lambs, sugar, tea, rice, and wheat to the city's Communist leadership. These boons caused the head of the organization to affirm, "Had it not been for this saint Qara Qul, the Party would have starved to death." He therefore suggested they recommend to the central committee the award of the Red Star Medal to the dead man once the Party came to power.

Mullah Zayn al-Abidin al-Qadiri was perplexed about what to do with the gifts that did not fit well inside his jars. Truth be told, he had at first begun to distribute these to the poor in the Chuqor community and other neighborhoods. Then he turned away from this. Believing that excessive generosity would corrupt the poor, he began to sell these goods to shop owners, adding the new money to the buried funds. Eventually, in the small souk, he opened up a shop, which his unemployed son-in-law managed, to put on sale the shrine's gifts that defied burial. He named it "The Depository for the Islamic Shrine."

Despite the zeal Mullah Zayn al-Abidin al-Qadiri displayed with respect to the Muslims' riches, which he described as his sacred trust, he was not immune to gossip and innuendo. This is customary in a city like Kirkuk, where the residents are renowned for their envy, and Mullah Zayn al-Abidin al-Qadiri, who had never risen above the mentality of a mosque imam even after he became a director general, committed more than one error in handling his high post. It would, for example, have been appropriate for him to forward some of the shrine's benefits to the governor, the police chief, and other high-ranking officials in the city, but he had not done this. Indeed he had even forgotten the ministers of the interior and of religious endowments, as if they were "a couple of scarecrows," in the words of Khidir Musa, who alluded to the matter in one of his coffeehouse sessions with Mullah Zayn al-Abidin al-Qadiri. The mullah, however, rebuffed him in such a way that he never returned to the topic again: "So you want me to pay a bribe taken from assets that do not belong to me and to abuse the trust that Muslims have placed in me?"

The other matter that inflamed people's sentiments and stirred their resentment was his use, when he went out every afternoon, of Ibn Sa'ud's gold wheelchair to convey him to the coffeehouse, on the pretext that his legs hurt dreadfully from rheumatism and that it would be hard for him to walk. Even though he took two armed policemen with him to guard the gold wheelchair, children followed him, screaming and singing all the way to the door of the coffeehouse. Men who encountered him en route would stop, overwhelmed by what they saw, and women would dart to the doors of their homes to catch a glimpse of the mullah steering his gold wheelchair.

Mullah Zayn al-Abidin al-Qadiri did not shortchange the plump widow of Qara Qul or their four children, even though rumors reached his ears that strangers visited her home, that she adorned herself inappropriately, and that this was not right for the widow of a saint. He would merely respond, "Some suspicions are sinful." Each week he sent her all the sugar, tea, rice, and chickens she needed, in addition to a monthly salary of fifteen dinars, which he had allotted her and her children and which she would come and pick up herself. Nonetheless, Satan whispered his temptation to her and she proceeded to demand—incited perhaps by her lovers and neighbors, or even influenced by the flood of African-heritage visitors who came to her home from Egypt, the Sudan, Ethiopia, Senegal, and the Ivory Coast—a real share of the donations presented to her husband's tomb, pointing out that her young, orphaned children had more right to ride in King Ibn Saʿud's gold wheelchair than Mullah Zayn al-Abidin al-Qadiri, who was afflicted by senility and love of ostentation.

Relying on an attorney known for winning all the cases he represented by bribing judges, she presented a claim in the second court of first instance of Kirkuk. In this she asked Kirkuk's shariʿa judge to award her four-fifths of the gifts presented to her husband's tomb, relying in this claim on Islamic jurisprudence, which sets the share of the public treasury in any profit or business as a fifth. That enraged Mullah Zayn al-Abidin al-Qadiri so much that he publicly accused her of turning her home into a brothel where men and women met and of practicing black magic, which was something out of keeping with the standing of Qara Qul. The plump, dark-complexioned widow asserted, without anyone believing her, that Mullah Zayn al-Abidin al-Qadiri had attempted to seduce her more than once, although she had kept quiet about it for fear of a scandal and out of respect for her husband's lofty status. Mullah Zayn al-Abidin al-Qadiri almost went crazy when he heard this accusation relayed to him and began to scream at the top of his lungs, "I'd rather sleep with a cow than touch this black bag's pussy." After gaining control of himself, he commented, "I don't know why God afflicts his righteous worshipers with fallen women like this widow. Behind it, there must be some wise purpose that our limited intellects do not comprehend. God assisted Qara Qul, who had to live with this whore, but—Glory to Him and may He be exalted—He compensated him for his worldly life with the hereafter, where he now lives in paradise, surrounded by beautiful companions. How disparate are the beauty and manners of these heavenly companions from the ugliness of this widow and her morals."

The city of Kirkuk split into two rival factions, each supporting one side in this dispute, which many considered to be linked to their own destiny. One faction thought that all the wealth was the personal property of Qara Qul himself, and this meant legally that it all accrued to his wife and children, since he was unable to receive it personally, once he was transported to an abode in paradise. Many religious scholars declared in a statement they released—at the prompting of her attorney, who was hopeful of winning the case—that the commerce of a Muslim devolves on his children after his death and that the government has no right or standing to seize and confiscate this commerce. They affirmed their rejection of Communism, which—unchecked by morality or conscience—would plunder the riches of the Muslims or nationalize them. In their declaration, these scholars demanded that the government reinstate the rights of the family and that Mullah Zayn al-Abidin al-Qadiri be removed from his position, in view of his offenses against the principles of religion.

Mullah Zayn al-Abidin al-Qadiri sensed the peril threatening him and understood that he was in danger of losing everything. He was forced, once again, to fall back on Khidir Musa, broaching the matter with him. Khidir Musa, who had been annoyed with the mullah ever since the day he had refused to offer a cut of the shrine's proceeds to government officials, accusing him of attempting to corrupt him, remained aloof, however, as if the matter was no concern of his. The only comment with which he favored Mullah Zayn al-Abidin al-Qadiri was: "I knocked myself out getting you this post. Beyond that, you're on your own." These few words sufficed to cause the mullah, whose nerves were already shot, to explode into an angry tantrum that surprised even Khidir Musa: "I know you envy me the blessing I've achieved. Don't forget that you were once a shepherd and that that's how I'll always think of you." Khidir Musa replied disdainfully, "I'll never forget that." Then Khidir Musa rose and left the coffeehouse, returning home.

The mullah was afflicted by a bout of severe coughing that left him weeping. He realized that he had gone too far and that he had risked everything by being insolent to the man to whom he owed everything he had achieved. Although the mullah felt defeated, he resolved to combat the greed of Qara Qul's widow and her attorney. A difficult battle was confronting him now that he had rebuffed the friendship and protection of Khidir Musa. He thought of going to apologize to him for what he had blurted out, but his embarrassment at what he had done prevented him: "Perhaps I can do that tomorrow. I'll do it eventually, unless I lose my mind and go off the deep end." He paid for the tea he had drunk and went out to the street, overcome by the feeling that he was nothing more than a corpse walking on two feet. The mullah had scarcely reached the nearby barbershop when he saw Hameed Nylon emerge from the salon. Traces of powder were still visible on the back of his neck and he smelled of cologne. Hameed Nylon asked, "Do you like my haircut, mullah? This young barber Yawuz has fingers that know how to cut hair. His problem always is the lice people bring him in their hair."

The mullah's features relaxed: "You know what, Hameed? You know how to coexist with this damn world."

Hameed replied in jest, "You can learn how if you want." His round eyes, which resembled the ones children draw in their notebooks, gleamed affectionately.

"No, I'll never learn that. The devil lives beneath my tongue. The moment I open my mouth out spills the scent of the dunghill."

Hameed Nylon thought to himself, "The old man's gone senile. It's really sad. He's still living in dreams. Why does a person keep hopeful to the end? What does this mullah want from the world? Perhaps he thought he would live forever. He's a Muslim, at any rate: 'Live your life as if you would live forever.' Me, I live as if would die tomorrow. I shouldn't tell him that. A man dies the moment he loses hope. This old guy still has the ability to hope."

The mullah stepped forward and placed his dry palm affectionately on Hameed Nylon's shoulder. Then he suddenly noticed something: "Just a minute." With his thumb he felt the other man's sideburn. "Your barber should have cut your sideburn shorter than he did. Young men are growing their sideburns long today, just like the Jews. Oh, that doesn't matter. Why don't you come to prayers at the mosque, Hameed? All you lack is guidance toward God."

"Do you really believe that the mosque is God's house? I believe that He applauds residence in hearts, rather than in your mosque, where men fart with every prostration."

The mullah replied beguilingly, "What a free thinker you are! But without that, you're not worth a single fils."

Hameed stopped in front of a store that resembled a hole in the wall and purchased a tin of Black Cat cigarettes. He offered one to the mullah, who said disdainfully, "You smoke Tomcat cigarettes and comb blue pomade into your hair. Young men are always this way. Old fellows like me are content if God shelters them with his expansive mercy."

Hameed Nylon lit his cigarette. Evening was beginning to fall gradually over the city. Mullah Zayn al-Abidin al-Qadiri said, "If you don't have anything else to do, we could sit in the coffeehouse. I would like to invite you to have a tumbler of tea at my expense."

"I thought you wanted to invite me to a banquet of roast lamb. What's on your mind? I know you're upset about Qara Qul's whore. Come now; tell me. She's a slanderous viper. You shouldn't have gotten involved with her."

"Yes, the matter concerns this whore, but I made a mistake with Khidir Musa. I was rude to him. He refused to listen to me and I lost my head."

"This is a major error, mullah. You know we're all indebted to him, and you in particular. But let's skip that for now. What's with the whore?"

"I'll lose everything. I've damaged my reputation. A whore like Qara Qul's widow has shown that she is more judicious than I am. Even the Muslim scholars have fallen into her snares. They've issued a fatwa against me, wishing to steal the shrine of Qara Qul from me."

"It's true; she is more judicious than you. You've changed a lot, mullah. The money's changed you. You no longer know any god beside coins. Don't get angry. I just need to tell you this. You know— no one will defend you as long as you consider the riches of the shrine as your personal wealth. The government won't accept that and neither will the religious scholars or the citizens of Kirkuk. If you want the truth, Qara Qul's widow has more right than you to these riches because at least she was his wife."

The mullah, who was summoning the waiter to order tea, blushed: "While I remain director general of the mausoleum, they will have to accept my rules. These riches are certainly not mine. They are the Muslims' riches and a trust that I bear. I am not ready to renounce it. This government is not an Islamic one to which I can entrust the wealth. As for Qara Qul's whore, she's irrelevant to the matter. The mausoleum is not a shop that her husband owned and that her children can inherit."

Hameed asked calmly, as though he wished to confide something he did not want others to hear, "Fine; when do you want to return the trust to its people? Distribute the wealth yourself to the people, and then they won't have any argument against you."

Mullah Zayn al-Abidin al-Qadiri laughed sarcastically to disguise the anger that was beginning to shake his entire body. "So you want me to be a Communist, Hameed? You want me to distribute God's wealth to the people, just like that, in exchange for nothing, so that they can spend it drinking wine and sleeping with prostitutes?"

"Fine; if you want the riches of Qara Qul for yourself, why should we stand up for you?"

Hameed Nylon rose, intending to leave the coffeehouse. There was no longer any benefit to be gained from sitting with the mullah, who was as stubborn as a donkey that suddenly stops running. Night had fallen over the small souk, where stray dogs began to snap at each other outside of closed butcher shops, fighting for bones that had been tossed out on the sidewalk. Other dogs that were ravenous with hunger had stepped aside and begun to eat leftover watermelon slices that shop owners had thrown in the street. In the coffeehouse that towered over the sidewalk, on a bench a person reached by climbing up two steps, the faint light cast shadows over the faces of the few customers, some of whom were playing dominoes. As he stood up, Hameed Nylon noticed the pallor of the mullah's face. It was difficult to say whether it was it from rancor or fear. The mullah, who appeared to want to be friendly, called to him, "I don't want to quarrel with you as well, Hameed. I've begun to lose the people closest to me. You mustn't get angry at me. I'm older than you are."

Hameed replied jokingly, "You've shattered my nerves, mullah. I need to drink some glasses of arak to regain my composure. If I weren't afraid of angering you, I'd invite you to taste the forbidden along with me."

The mullah felt delight flow through him, for he saw that Hameed Nylon was teasing him, after he had feared for a moment that he might have offended him, too. The mullah regained his composure and began to repeat affectionately, "God's curse on you, Hameed Nylon. You want to drag me into depravity and iniquity as well. Our conversation's not over. I want you to pass by me tomorrow so we can go and mend fences with Khidir Musa. I'll think over what you've said. Perhaps you're right. Do you believe, as my adversaries say, that I'm a senile old fool?"

Hameed replied mischievously, "Everyone knows that. There's no doubt that you're senile. But why are you worried about this? We'll take care of the matter tomorrow. Relax."

The mullah laughed as he chastised him fondly, "No one has your way with words, you son of a bitch. You're Satan himself."

Hameed had scarcely left the coffeehouse when Mullah Zayn al-Abidin al-Qadiri once again felt lonely. He wanted someone to converse with, anyone with whom he could share his woes.

"I've become annoying; that's clear. They all seek to avoid me. Hameed Nylon has left me too and gone off to drink arak. Doubtless I am senile. I've begun to neglect everything. I should have shined my shoes. They've been dirty for days. That's not the way I should be. The plump whore has shattered my nerves. I should have slept with her to buy her silence. Will Hameed Nylon be able to sort out a matter like this? Do you suppose he will agree? God's curse on Satan. Fine, it seems a bribe is unavoidable. But why should I bribe the small fish? Truly, why the low-ranking men? If a bribe is necessary, then I'll bribe the king himself. But, no; that might anger Khidir Musa, who is close to the king and who would consider that a personal insult. Perhaps it would be best if I became a Communist, as Hameed

Nylon suggested. I'll distribute Qara Qul's money to the people. But why should I do that? These people will accept my gifts today and then curse me tomorrow. I know these people very well. They are ungrateful infidels. 'Give, sir. Give!' Poor Qara Qul escaped by the skin of his teeth from this prostitute, who looks like a rotting sack. But why did he ascend to heaven on Buraq? Why did God choose him—him in particular—for a miracle like this? The truth is that the man was a liar and a cheat and that his broad nose, henna-tinted palm, and the earring on his right earlobe—as though he were Antara ibn Shaddad—were downright annoying. But God must know what He's doing. He chose him especially. I can't offer a prayerful complaint because the man's death was a blessing that descended upon the city, except for the she-ghoul he left behind."

As Mullah Zayn al-Abidin al-Qadiri left the coffeehouse—having decided to return home after he heard his tummy growl and only then realized he was hungry, since he had forgotten to eat anything all day long—he thought, "I'd better forget the whole thing now. Hameed Nylon is right. I too must learn how to coexist with this damn world. I'm going to have to learn everything afresh."

It was not past nine in the evening when the mullah found himself once again in the street, which was almost empty of people. He might have gone back home but was on an emotional rollercoaster, like a child who did not know what to do. "I could return to my house, where nothing but sleep awaits me."

Night, however, had fallen over the city. Nothing remained but dogs chasing from one street to another and cats meowing as they leapt from one ruin to the next. "No. I won't go home. What would I do there? I wouldn't even be able to sleep. Hameed Nylon's gone to quaff arak. So where will you go, mullah?" He mocked himself, saying out loud, "Your ship is about to sink, Mullah Zayn al-Abidin al-Qadiri, all because of a whore whose old man ascended to heaven." The mullah considered heading for the home of Qara Qul's widow to seek to placate her. "I must buy her silence. I won't be mean to her. She might agree to withdraw her claim if I offer her more of the money. She could wreck everything. She could harm even herself. Who knows? The government could use this whole affair as a pretext to assume control of the shrine. Then we would all have slain the goose that lays the golden egg."

The mullah found himself heading toward the widow's house, in spite of himself, as if driven there by an alien force that was dictating his actions. In the darkness, which feeble streetlights hung from widely spaced poles dissipated a little, the mullah's legs, which were afflicted by rheumatism, struck the ground haphazardly, pulling behind them a cloak, the tails of which dragged on the ground. One could almost feel the silence that reigned over the neighborhood. After some minutes, the mullah stopped in front of Qara Qul's widow's house. His heart was pounding violently as he approached the door to knock on it. He stretched out his hand, but something made him hesitate, for strange voices reached his ears through cracks in the wooden door. The mullah thought, "They must be her lovers." He leaned over so that one eye could see into the house through a crack in the door but then drew back in alarm. Summoning all his strength, he cast inside another thoughtful look that caused him to lose even the force to repeat "In the name of God" or to ask God's protection against the devil. What he saw was so upsetting and weird that he rubbed his eyes time and again and then looked back through the crack. Qara Qul Mansur was seated beside Dervish Bahlul in the home's courtyard on two aluminum chairs, drinking tea with three dead men, who were sitting on a carpet spread on the ground. Their white skeletons gleamed in the light of a lamp, which was suspended on the wall over their heads. He struggled to hear what they were saying, but in vain, because a radio resting near them was broadcasting a song by Sadiqa al-Mullaya. A shudder convulsed the mullah's whole body, while his head filled with questions: "If Qara Qul is in heaven, what would make him return to his widow? What is Dervish Bahlul doing here with these dead people?"

The mullah slipped back, retreating awkwardly. Then he began to run in the dark as though a wild beast were chasing him, as though the three dead men had noticed him and begun to pursue him. He fell to the ground more than once but kept on running, even though he was coughing and gasping and dogs were barking at him.

Eight

During the night when Mullah Zayn al-Abidin al-Qadiri saw—at the home of the widow of Qara Qul—the terrifying sight that caused him to take to his sickbed and left him unable to speak, Hameed Nylon kept moving from one place to another. To begin with he passed by the coffeehouse frequented by auto mechanics at the garage located on Railroad Station Street. The patrons there took him along with them after dark to a tavern, bringing with them bottles of arak purchased from liquor stores run by Christians. Hameed Nylon had not even thought about having something to drink. What was important to him was being with people. "There's always a desire to show ourselves to others' eyes. It makes us feel self-confident. This is what they call conviviality."

Hameed Nylon sat with two young men who were discussing lottery tickets. One of them had won ten dinars, receiving only nine because the vendor had kept a dinar as his tip or perhaps as a tax. One of them placed a glass before Hameed Nylon, saying, "Drink, Hameed. The nine dinars are still in my pocket."

Hameed Nylon raised the glass and took a large swig from it and then said, "Here's to the first prize, which I hope you win next time."

Yashar, who was wearing dark glasses even though it was night, because he believed they would attract Turkmen girls, shrieked, "Oh my God! A thousand five hundred dinars in one fell swoop!"

Hameed Nylon cast him a conspiratorial look, and remarked, "You would definitely marry. You would be able to ask for the prettiest girl in Kirkuk. Who would be able to refuse a young man who had that many dinars in his pocket?"

"Yashar has a girl who's waiting for him," said Jamal, the other young man seated opposite Yashar.

Hameed asked, "Really?"

Yashar said tipsily, "She's from your community, Hameed."

"Who is she?"

Yashar sighed, exhaling deeply, "Layla, a student in the girls' middle school."

Hameed asked, "Layla, the daughter of al-Hajj Ahmad al-Sabunji?"

"Yes, that's exactly who she is."

Jamal interjected, "He waits for her every day when she leaves school."

Hameed Nylon asked, "Have you spoken with her?"

"I tried, but she rebuffed me, saying that she doesn't make a habit of speaking to young men in the street. I know she loves me, Hameed. Her eyes reveal that. Every time I walk behind her, she turns and looks at me stealthily."

Hameed Nylon said, "She's truly a beautiful girl, and well bred."

Yashar invited Hameed to accompany him when he returned home, in order to cast a glance at his sweetheart Layla's home before going to sleep, but Hameed politely declined, saying apologetically that he would be spending the night elsewhere. He was thinking about seeing Ahlam, the prostitute he visited once or twice a week. Hameed Nylon consumed another glass of arak before he slipped out to the street. Patrons from the movie theaters, which had concluded their last show, were dispersing through the dark streets, returning to their homes while a dark silence prevailed over the city. Hameed Nylon focused his attention on this silence, which darkness always inspires, since this matter puzzled him. People were walking along quietly, and only their footsteps on the sidewalk or the street's asphalt were audible. Night watchmen shouldering rifles stood beneath light poles. Most of them were Arabs from al-Hawija.

"It's hard for a man to do anything in this city. All the doors and gates are closed. This city is certainly not Baghdad. There a man can spend the night in the thousand and one bars that stretch all along Abu Nuwas Street. Here there are only Arab night watchmen. Everyone feels out of sorts. But they love their vexation because that's all they know. This is why they get such childish ideas, exactly like Mullah Zayn al-Abidin al-Qadiri. Khidir Musa didn't do him any favor by nominating him to be director general because the man doesn't deserve to be anything more than the imam of a mosque. Director general of a tomb? Imagine that. No, no. What's that all about? Qara Qul's tomb is a gold mine that has fallen on Kirkuk from the heavens. It's our second leading source of income, second only to oil. For this reason the mullah has fallen prey to childish fantasies and madness. All these riches that flow between his fingers! Why doesn't the government act to seize this wealth, which the mullah considers his own riches—his meaningless protests about a sacred trust notwithstanding? I need to discuss this matter with Khidir Musa. We've got to do something before Qara Qul's widow gains control of these riches. Khidir Musa will refuse to intervene in the affair. After his visit to the king, he won't meddle in small issues. He won't wish to dirty his hands in a lawsuit that might harm his reputation. With riches like those the mullah is hiding I could outfit an army for a guerrilla war, an army to liberate Iraq the way Mao Tsetung's army liberated China."

Thoughts and dreams collided with each other in Hameed Nylon's head on his way home so that he was oblivious to the passage of time. Even at home, when he was in bed, the beautiful dream did not quit him. He could not get to sleep but tossed and turned in bed, waiting for morning to arrive so that he could take his first step on the road to revolution.

In fact, the first thing he did in the morning was to hunt out Faruq Shamil, who worked in the municipal print shop. After stepping aside with him among the rolls of paper and the containers of ink, Hameed proposed that Faruq and the other members of the union quit their jobs and leave for the countryside with him to start a guerrilla war against the government. The idea shocked Faruq Shamil, who appeared flabbergasted, sank into silence, and began to gaze in bewilderment at the face of Hameed Nylon, who asked, "What's the matter, Faruq? You don't seem to have been expecting anything like this."

Faruq Shamil answered anxiously, "You certainly have taken me by surprise, Hameed. Let me think about the matter. I'll pass by you this afternoon. It's a great idea but needs some mulling over. You know that revolutionary adventures can lead to back-breaking disasters."

As Hameed Nylon left, he said, "It's a sure thing. Since the people are against the government, they will certainly follow us. You know that."

Faruq Shamil did not know that or at least was not certain of it. Indeed the thought of Hameed Nylon leading a revolution made him want to laugh, but he said in a serious tone, "You're the only one to have thought of a revolution. Where did you get this idea?"

Hameed Nylon answered in a way that embarrassed Faruq Shamil: "Thoughts don't come to a man. He goes to them."

Hameed Nylon departed, leaving Faruq Shamil contemplating with relish this phrase, which Hameed Nylon had heard once from Dervish Bahlul. It had stuck in his mind.

That evening Faruq Shamil led Hameed Nylon through dark alleys that he had definitely never visited before, past young Kurdish men whose faces were barely discernible. They were wearing the baggy shorts that Turkmen derisively called balloons. The men leaned against the wall, staring into the void, waiting for nothing, day after day. Faruq Shamil whispered to Hameed Nylon, "These are the Wall Men. Perhaps you've heard about them. They're all unemployed and have nothing to do. They stand leaning against the wall all day long and part of the night, saying nothing. They return home only to sleep. There, brothers, sisters, father, mother, grandfather, and grandmother are crammed into a single room. They are trying to escape from life itself."

Hameed Nylon and Faruq Shamil traversed other narrow alleys filled with muck and stinking water. All that a person heard there was the barking of dogs that chased around aimlessly and the meowing of cats that leapt from wall to wall.

Faruq Shamil had notified the Communist leadership in the city of Hameed Nylon's suggestion, asking their opinion and advice. This action had prompted the Communists, who considered themselves experts on making revolutions, despite the fact that they had never organized a single revolution during their entire history, to request a meeting with Hameed Nylon that same day in order to discuss armed revolution with him. Hameed Nylon was not a Communist but had demonstrated his leadership abilities in the Battle of Gawirbaghi and had agreed to represent the Communists, although he had never told anyone, in the delegation that headed to Baghdad and met with the king. He had also attended the memorial service the Communists had held in one of the mosques of Qara-Teppa when Joseph Stalin died. He had recited the opening prayer of the Qur'an for this pure spirit while tears welled up in his eyes. He had noticed that others were shedding tears too. Despite his friendship with the Communists, he had remained outside the Party because he believed that the Communists were all talk and no action and that they hid more than they disclosed. The Communists, who were awed by his magical influence on the people, considered him an exemplary and spontaneous rabble-rouser. This was a type that was hard to squeeze into their mold, which relied first and foremost on the principles and theoretical laws that the great Marxist scholars had devised. Hameed Nylon, to whom the idea of the revolution had suddenly come, needed them now. If they truly were revolutionaries, they should join him or at least grant workers in the union the right to choose. The Communists were eager to learn the truth about this affair, which was new to them. They had spent so many of the previous years in cellars that some had forgotten there was another world beyond the basements where they lived.

Truth be told, however, Hameed Nylon—like many other people—had only a murky idea about the cellars that the leaders customarily inhabited. Faruq Shamil had told Hameed Nylon, "It seems that the idea of a revolution has created quite a stir among the leaders. That's why they want to meet you today, if there's nothing to prevent that." Hameed Nylon had replied, "That suits me fine, for there's not much time for us to waste on trivialities."

In the darkness that a pale moon overhead was beginning to affect, down one of the alleys, Hameed Nylon and Faruq Shamil approached a ruined house that not even the devil would have suspected. Faruq Shamil whispered, "We've finally arrived." Hameed Nylon stared at the ancient wooden door covered by cobwebs, beneath which a dove was sitting on her eggs. Over the screen door stretched a gray viper of terrifying size.

Hameed Nylon was unnerved and felt afraid: "This house is abandoned, Faruq. There can't be anyone here."

Faruq Shamil smiled, "Don't be deceived by appearances, Hameed. Wait a minute."

He walked up to the door and said in a rather loud voice, "Open, sesame." The viper raised its long, heavy head and gazed for some moments at Faruq Shamil's eyes. Then it lowered its head and slipped into a large crevice above the door. Faruq Shamil looked at Hameed Nylon and explained, "The viper has gone inside to inform the comrades of our arrival. A perfect camouflage. One of our comrades is a snake charmer with amazing ideas about clandestine work."

The door creaked open and Faruq Shamil and Hameed Nylon entered quietly, for fear of disturbing the dove, which was sleeping on her nest on the doorstep. A young woman whose features Hameed Nylon could not make out greeted them in the dark and then led them inside a deserted house that smelled of neglect. She cautioned them that the area was infested with scorpions and mice, "But you needn't fear them. They're all very well trained." Then looking at Hameed, she said, "I hope the viper at the door didn't upset you. She's very gentle but occasionally likes to tease. As a matter of fact, she's the angel who guards all of us." The girl pushed on a door, which opened onto an illuminated stairway descending into a deep cellar. Hameed Nylon had a chance to get a glance at the woman who was leading the way. A pretty girl, she wore a short black skirt, a red blouse, and black high-heeled shoes. Hameed Nylon wondered, "Where do Communists get pretty girls like this?"

Inside the cellar, everything was the opposite from the exterior. It really was not a cellar, although it was below ground. It was an elegant new construction, which reminded him of the offices of the English oil company. There was a long hallway with beautiful crystal chandeliers hanging from its ceiling. On each side was a row of rooms with handsome doors. Above each of these was a small bronze plaque. These clearly were offices. The girl pushed on one of the doors. It opened to reveal a man seated behind a table. The man, who was staring at the girl through his glasses, said, "The comrade must have arrived. I must record this in the arrivals' register." Then, opening the large ledger in front of him, he turned to Hameed Nylon, who was standing in front of the door, "Your Party name, please."

Hameed Nylon was surprised by this question, which he did not understand. He thought he was being asked his nickname. He tried to mask his discomfort with a laugh: "The whole world knows me as Hameed Nylon. If you wish to give me another, better name, I'll have no special objection." Then he turned to the girl who was standing beside him, "I don't know how you can receive a person whose name you don't know."

The girl shook her head flirtatiously enough for Hameed Nylon to forget his objection: "Hameed, there has to be a bit of bureaucracy. That's life." Then she turned to the man who was sitting perplexed behind his ledger: "Write down any name. You know your work better than we do." Then she grasped the hand of Hameed Nylon, who thought she was flirting with him and squeezed back.

She led him to the end of the hallway, on the walls of which were hung white cloth banners with gleaming red lettering: "A Free Nation and a Happy People," "Long Live the Iraqi Working Class," "Long Live the People's Struggle under the Leadership of the Great Soviet Union," and "Taiwan Is an Inseparable Part of the Chinese Homeland." At the end of the hallway, the girl pushed on a door that opened onto a spacious chamber with a huge, circular table at the center and many elegant chairs. In the corners were piled many bundles of pamphlets and booklets—obviously prepared for transport elsewhere. The walls were decorated with pictures of strange faces, which Hameed Nylon had never seen before, except for the portrait

171

of Stalin, whose stern peasant's face and bushy mustache anyone would recognize. He almost asked the girl about the other bald man and the two awe-inspiring old men—who resembled Dervish Bahlul—with beards that came down to their chests, but felt embarrassed, fearful of displaying his ignorance to the young woman, whose attention he was wondering how to attract.

Another side door opened and two men entered. One was plainly Kurdish and the other Arab. They shook hands with him first and then embraced him, kissed him, and invited him to have a seat. The girl, who had also taken a seat, placing before her a pen and a stack of onion-skin paper, which they used for recording reports to make it easier to conceal them, introduced them to Hameed Nylon, who kept looking back and forth from the bald young Kurd to the elderly Arab, who was so fat he could scarcely move his legs. The young Kurd thanked the girl, whom he referred to as "Comrade Intisar," asking her to take comprehensive minutes for the meeting. Then he turned to Hameed Nylon, saying, "I've heard a lot about you and have thought more than once about inviting you to visit me in this cellar of mine. But I was afraid you might be someone who is uncomfortable in cellars."

Hameed Nylon smiled, focusing his eyes on him: "Your cellar's not as bad as you think. It's better even than the governor's office itself: this beautiful construction, these enchanting chandeliers, and this elegant office."

The elderly man interjected, "This demonstrates the force of Communist ideas. Everything you see here is a gift from the people. The design of the cellar was undertaken by the great patriotic, democratic engineer Rif'at Chadirchi, whose design won the first prize in the Berlin competition for young architects. The crystal chandeliers that you see were given to us by the great Czechoslovak people. As you know, crystal in Prague is as cheap as dirt, and for that reason the central committee has proposed in the five-year plan a program to pave all the roads with it. The wood products were donated to the headquarters, as you know, by a famous furniture-making establishment in the city."

The young Kurd volunteered, "It's a gift from the shop of Shukr the woodworker."

Hameed Nylon said, "I know him. He built a bedroom for me when I got married."

The elderly man interjected again, "We must affirm to the bourgeoisie that Communists have a right to a decent life too. Do you know about the vicious torture to which our comrade Salim was subjected in the Ba'quba prison? He has a right to enjoy life now that he's escaped."

Hameed Nylon said, "I've heard that. People refer to him as the hero of the torture chamber."

These emotional words deeply affected the young man, who removed the shirt he had been wearing without any undershirt to show Hameed Nylon his chest and back, where the scars of beatings with sticks, whips, and electric cords, as well as cigarette burns were clearly visible. Hameed Nylon took out his pack of cigarettes and offered each of them one, but they declined.

The young Kurd observed, "Anyone who's imprisoned is forced to give up smoking. This is actually one of the benefits of imprisonment."

Intisar raised her head to look at Hameed, "But you could offer me a cigarette. I haven't been to prison yet."

Hameed Nylon apologized as he offered her one, which she lit herself. Then she started blowing smoke rings in the air. Hameed Nylon's heart was pounding vigorously and he almost forgot why he had come. The old man interrupted his tender dream: "Comrades have informed us that you are thinking of organizing an armed revolution in the countryside. What makes you think that such a dangerous operation will succeed?"

Hameed Nylon noticed for the first time that Faruq Shamil had not entered the room with him, but did not ask where he was. It was obvious that the two men wanted to discuss the matter with him, in person. Hameed Nylon replied with the calmness he had learned from Khidir Musa, "Success hinges on the people themselves. The question concerns rights. Do we have the right to revolt or not?"

The young Kurd raised his hand as he said, "Look. I know the Kurds very well. The time has not come to start a Kurdish revolution. You know that General Mulla Mustafa al-Barzani headed for the Soviet Union many years ago to train in guerrilla war tactics. It seems that he has not yet completed his training. The Kurds are waiting for him and will not accept a revolution he does not lead."

Hameed Nylon, who found this logic absurd, was exasperated: "It never occurred to me to undertake a Kurdish revolution. As you know I am half Arab and half Turkmen. I certainly would not object if my daughter wished to marry a Kurd. I'm an Iraqi, first and foremost. The revolution will be Iraqi."

The young Kurd shook his head disapprovingly: "These are fantasies. The revolution can only be Kurdish. Nationalist sentiments trump class sentiments. This means recruiting the shaykhs of the Kurdish tribes and the Democratic Party of Kurdistan for our side. But who can accept that?"

Hameed Nylon observed, "It seems that our goals differ. I don't believe that the Arabs or Turkmen are any less patriotic than the Kurds. All that Iraq needs now is for someone to fire the first shot of the revolution."

Pushing for a compromise, the elderly man interjected, "Our comrade's intention was consideration of the practical side of the revolution. No revolution that is detached from a nationalist movement can succeed. Comrade Fahd said, 'Strengthen the organization of your party. Strengthen the organization of the nationalist movement. For this reason I ask you to join the Patriotic Democratic Party or the Democratic Party of Kurdistan, if you don't have enough class consciousness to join the Communist Party.'"

Angry, Hameed Nylon lit another cigarette: "What are these strange parties that you ask people to join? I'm not here to join any party. I have come to ask you a single question: Can I count on your support if I begin the armed revolution in the countryside?"

Attempting to sweeten the bitter tone of the discussion, the elderly man replied, "The matter's not as easy as you believe. We've investigated the matter more than once in the central committee after seeing that the idea of revolution was spreading even to Arab countries. Indeed, we even sent one of our comrades to our brothers in China and the Soviet Union to obtain their consent for a revolution, in tandem with other nationalist forces. Do you know what they told him? You won't believe this. They said the world situation does not permit the occurrence of any revolution inside the Baghdad Pact because the Pact might use this revolution as a pretext for a nuclear attack on the mighty Soviet Union. And they're right."

Hameed Nylon shook his head scornfully, "Such convoluted matters don't concern me. I don't believe, however, that Mao Tse-tung would ask us to refrain from revolution, especially if he knew that the revolution would burst forth from the countryside—just like the Chinese Revolution that he himself led."

The young Kurd intervened: "A revolution requires rifles and money. Where are you going to get those?"

Hameed Nylon, who was assailed by doubts about the two men's intentions, replied, "God is generous. Iraq is filled with good things. We'll eat dirt if we must."

"These vague phrases mean nothing," said the Kurdish youth.

Hameed Nylon was disconcerted by the way the two men spoke: "If you're not thinking about the revolution, then why do you lead people along to the point that they lose their jobs and go to prison? These sacrifices are meaningless then."

The young Kurd replied, "We are faced with historical necessity. Only the petite bourgeoisie hesitates to make sacrifices."

Hameed Nylon felt obliged to tell the two men, "You use words without knowing the people. The important question is: Are you with the revolution or against it?"

The old man looked at empty space for a time before saying, "Comrade Stalin said, 'Dialectics require a person to be for a thing and against it at the same time.' This is our position regarding any revolution that might flare up in Iraq."

Hameed Nylon was not able to comprehend what the man had said but got the gist of it. "Does this mean that I should love Nuri al-Sa'id and hate him at the same time?"

The old man laughed. "You're trying to embarrass me. Dialectics do not apply to traitors. How can a man think of revolution without memorizing the greatest number of Marxist texts possible, especially those important text digests published by Novosti Agency? How can a person consider revolution without first learning by heart the poems of the great Turkish poet Nazim Hikmat, who divorced his

Turkish wife and married a Russian woman because he loved the Russian revolution so much? Have you read anything by our new nationally known poet Comrade Abd al-Rahman al-Qalqali? Do you know that his poems have been translated into Korean and American as part of a campaign of solidarity with the poor people of the world? This is the real revolution, Comrade Hameed. As you can see, we don't waste our time in the cellars for nothing, contrary to the rumor that our classist adversaries spread."

It was difficult for Hameed Nylon to follow this way of speaking. For this reason, he felt obliged to object, "I believe that there's not a poet in the whole world who can compare with Dada Hijri. It's not a good thing for a man to praise himself, and you Communists do that night and day. As a matter of fact, I like love poetry better than anything else. By the way, what do you think of the poetry of Burhan Abdallah? In my opinion, he's more important than any of the poets you've mentioned."

The old man asked, "Burhan Abdallah? I've never even heard his name."

Hameed Nylon replied with the calmness of a victor, "Of course you don't know him. He's my relative and publishes his poems under pseudonyms to avoid angering his mother, who considers poets beggars who lack self-respect. As a matter of fact he disguises his identity by using many different pennames, like Nizar Qabbani, Badr Shaker al-Sayyab, Muhammad Mahdi al-Jawahiri, and Husayn Mardan. He's even published many poems in English, naturally under assumed names. He shares all his secrets with me; I'm family, after all."

The old man burst out laughing so hard the young Kurd was afraid his laughter would be audible outside the cellar. "What are you saying, man? All the names you've mentioned are real poets whom I know personally. Comrade Fahd has more than once commended the poet al-Jawahiri to our attention, and two years ago I shook hands with him with this very hand. But he's a mercurial man. You can't depend on him. Al-Sayyab's a skinny young man from Basra, weak-willed; he was a member of our party but we threw him out after we discovered his link to the police. And everyone knows who Nizar al-Qabbani and Husayn Mardan are. They are licentious, existentialist poets who represent the decadent values of the bourgeoisie. What relation does all that have with your nephew, whose name I don't know?"

Hameed Nylon lit a cigarette and gazed at the young woman, who was recording the minutes of the meeting. Placing a pack of cigarettes in front of her, he said, "I don't want to call you a liar, but perhaps you've been the victim of swindlers, who attribute the glories of other people's efforts to themselves."

The young Kurd said, "Thank God that Abdallah Goran spent four years with me in the same cell in the Ba'quba prison; otherwise I'd believe he was a con artist too."

Hameed Nylon raised his hands in the air and said, "It's not about any particular individual; it's a general problem. Once the lie becomes a universal system, nothing's left but ghosts. I apologize for borrowing this aphorism from my relative Burhan Abdallah, who also writes occasionally under the name of Kafka, which sounds like a Kurdish name to me."

The young Kurd corrected him, "I don't think so. Perhaps your nephew was writing under the name of Kaka and you got mixed up."

The old man, who was irritated, intervened, "We mustn't waste precious time discussing tangential affairs. What concerns us is learning the truth of the next step you are planning, Comrade Hameed."

Rising to leave, Hameed Nylon said, "The revolution has remained on hold for a long time. It won't hurt it to wait a bit longer. I'll think the matter over for a time and perhaps we'll meet again."

The old man said flatteringly, "That's a must. We'll definitely learn a lot from each other."

Hameed was agitated when he left the secret bunker. On his way out he startled the dove perched outside the door when he almost crushed it with his foot in the dark. It fluttered its wings a little before settling back on its nest. The startled viper had raised her head, but when she found that everything was copasetic, she stretched out again over the screen door, sound asleep.

On the way back, Hameed Nylon did not exchange many words with Faruq Shamil, who asked him when they reached the street, "Curiosity's almost killing me. Tell me: how was the meeting?"

"It seems the Communists believe it's impossible to do anything without them, but as soon as you try to cooperate with them they place impossible obstacles in your way."

Faruq Shamil answered regretfully, "I knew they would refuse. You know that what counts for struggle in their view is withstanding prison. Up till now they've not even been training for a revolution."

Hameed Nylon said sorrowfully, "Right. I once heard some Communist workers happily singing, 'Oh prison darkness, reign. / We love the dark.' I don't see how it's possible for a man to court prison and love the dark. Faruq, this is the ultimate form of despair of life."

Silence enveloped them again. Faruq Shamil was certain that Hameed Nylon was not the sort of man who would easily renounce what he had decided to do, no matter how unwise or difficult it appeared. He also knew that Hameed did not have the power to persuade the Communists to wade into these hazardous adventures. Moreover, Hameed Nylon did not even have a gang with which to impose himself on the others. If the men in the bunker had listened to him, that had been merely from curiosity or a desire to know what was happening in the outside world. They longed to understand its workings from inside their secret cellars. He did not want to tell his friend that, because he was confident that Hameed Nylon would end up like many others—disillusioned even before he took the first step on the journey of a thousand miles. Faruq Shamil was wrong this time, however, because Hameed Nylon believed that there was always a way out—even when a man was trapped in a circle—and that true skill lay in finding this escape route, which might be invisible. It was also not difficult for Hameed Nylon to devise his exit strategy now.

After another sleepless night, while he ran back over his plan time after time, stretched out in bed beside his wife, he rose before dawn and slipped outside without waking her, so that he would not be forced to resort to lying when confronted by her many questions. He climbed into his vehicle, which he normally parked near his home, and started the engine. Then, filled with a new spirit stirred by the chill morning breezes coming to him through the open window, he headed off to the place where he thought the revolution was waiting for his arrival. He began to sing out loud, like someone who had suddenly found happiness. He was driving along a dirt road lined by meadows.

Although his wife Fatima was somewhat rattled by his sudden disappearance, she did not pay much attention to the matter because Hameed Nylon frequently disappeared for days and occasionally for weeks, only to reappear without ever providing much by way of explanation. She had become accustomed to this, as had his two daughters, Nadya and Su'ad. They would ask their mother once and then not ask again because they always received the same answer: "Papa's gone on a trip and will return." No one in the Chuqor community paid any attention to the absence of Hameed Nylon except for Khidir Musa, who asked after him. Fatima told him, "You know Hameed. He disappears and appears like the devil. Three days ago, when I awoke I found he had left the house. No doubt he's traveled to Baghdad or some other city."

The community was preoccupied with following the struggle raging between Qara Qul's widow and Mullah Zayn al-Abidin al-Qadiri over ownership of the gifts presented to the mausoleum. The situation became considerably tenser when Qara Qul's widow, whose black cloak was open and trailing behind her and who was followed by her four children, who were brandishing sticks, headed for the home of Mullah Zayn al-Abidin al-Qadiri. She stood before its door, surrounded by women of the community along with its children and men, and cursed the mullah, who—she said—was living on the wages of sin, since he had taken what rightfully belonged to her orphaned children. When Mullah Zayn al-Abidin al-Qadiri did not appear, her children began throwing stones at the closed door, screaming, "Come out here, Mullah Dinar!" People's attempts to calm the widow failed, and her screams were heard throughout the community.

Matters became even worse when the wife of Mullah Zayn al-Abidin al-Qadiri peered down from the roof. This sixty-year-old woman began exchanging insults with Qara Qul's widow: "Whore, go to your black lovers and stop attacking us!" She threatened, "If you don't go away, I'll come down and put your filthy face in the sewer."

Qara Qul's widow replied, "Come down here, whore, and bring that pimp of a mullah with you!"

179

People protested, "Shame! This is no way to talk. What will people say about you?"

The widow's children then began pelting the mullah's wife with stones, but the men grabbed hold of them and stopped that. The mullah's wife disappeared for some moments and then returned with a jerry can filled with dirty water, which she poured over the head of Qara Qul's widow, who was standing in front of the door, cursing. Qara Qul's widow was startled by this, and began attacking the door, kicking it with her feet. "I'll kill this mullah!" When the door would not open, she called to one of her sons, "Go call your uncles. Blood must flow today!"

Women from the community dragged her aside. "This isn't right. You're a saint's widow. Leave the matter to God."

The woman, who was foaming at the mouth, cast herself on the ground, however, striking her fists against her head and thus revealing her short, curly hair. "If Qara Qul had any sanctity he would slay this sinner. Where are you, Qara Qul? Defend your faithful wife! Where are you, Qara, you saint of all saints?"

Three semi-naked black men suddenly appeared, wearing only white shorts. Their dark black skins glistened in the last rays of the setting sun. They brandished axes with sharp blades and shouldered bows and arrows. They were preceded by Qara Qul's son who had slain his father's killer with a razor several months before in the community of al-Musalla. No one in the Chuqor community had seen these men before. They clearly were foreigners and from Africa or some such place. The community's children, who had seen them before at the cinema, appeared to recognize them and began shouting and howling, "Savages! Savages!"

Qara Qul's widow, who was sitting on the ground, pointed out the home of Mullah Zayn al-Abidin al-Qadiri and said something that none of those in the circle around her understood, because the words were strange to them. They believed that the woman was perhaps raving, but one of the three black men said something back to her and she replied with strange words. At that point, the men of the community—and the women too—were convinced that these people were speaking another language, which was clearly a black language. At this moment, the mullah's wife appeared again on the roof and began meting out insults to Qara Qul's widow, who raised her hand toward the roof and said—in the black language— "Dushan." The children, who had seen many American films about savages, said that this word meant "enemy."

In the blink of an eye, one of the black men took out his bow and shot an arrow at the mullah's wife, but she had noticed the danger threatening her and had retreated, howling. The arrow passed over her head, hissing through the empty space. This was more than the residents of the Chuqor community could stand. They felt that these black men had infringed on their own honor and had meddled in affairs that did not concern them. Since Qara Qul's widow was one of them, she had a right to fuss, but these foreigners—savages at that—had no right to shoot arrows at the mullah's wife.

First off, the community's women reacted explosively to these strangers, screaming insults at them. Then the children joined in, throwing stones and Namlet bottles at the black men. Instead of withdrawing, however, the black men began to dance in a circle, swinging their axes over their heads while emitting savage cries. The children said it was a war dance. Abbas Bahlawan and Mahmud al-Arabi arrived then, having heard the news of the fight on their way home from the shrine. One of the black men leapt high, threatening the crowd and waving his axe in a way that terrified the women and children, who were caught off guard by this gesture and retreated, falling over one another.

Qara Qul's widow, who was still seated on the ground, leaning against a wall, called out at the top of her lungs, "Lying Mullah, if you're a man, come out of your house, where you're hiding." Then she muttered some words in the language of the blacks, and the three men attacked—as she had done—the door of Mullah Zayn al-Abidin al-Qadiri's house. They began to strike it with their axes, attempting to smash it. This caused Abbas Bahlawan and Mahmud al-Arabi to dart out of the crowd. Each of them held a meat cleaver taken from the community's butchers, who were watching the spectacle.

Abbas Bahlawan called out to the three black men as loudly as possible, "Savages, you're going to be slaughtered like ewes today."

These words had no impact on the black men, whose eyes glinted with malice. One of them attacked Abbas Bahlawan with an axe, even before he completed his sentence. Abbas Bahlawan, however, ducked to one side at just the right moment, and the other man lost his balance. At that time Abbas Bahlawan directed a kick to the nape of his neck, causing him to fall on his face on the ground and his nose to bleed. Loud applause resounded from the crowd. Mixed with it were laughter and calls: "Come on! Finish off the savage!"

Abbas Bahlawan and Mahmud al-Arabi were joined by the oil worker Abdallah Ali, who held a spear that had once belonged to his ancestor Hanzal, who had fought countless battles in Arab raids against merchants' caravans in the nineteenth century and who had lost his left hand in a battle with the Turks on the banks of the Tigris. One of the women shouted, "Now, the fight will be fair: three against three."

Abbas Bahlawan threw himself on the black man who had fallen to the ground and pulled his arms back and beat him between the shoulders until he almost passed out. Then he dragged him to the young men with whom he deposited the prisoner to have his hands and feet tied with rope. He returned again to the square, where Mahmud al-Arabi and Abdallah Ali were locked in a fierce battle with the two remaining men.

Mahmud al-Arabi was now engaged in hand-to-hand combat with one of them, after surprising him with a blow that had knocked the axe from his hand. Then he himself had thrown the meat cleaver to the ground, thus demonstrating even in this rough situation his lofty morals. The two rolled around on the ground and then rose once more. Then the black man leapt in the air, attempting to land a kick on Mahmud al-Arabi's chest. He missed his target, however, struck a wall, and fell to the ground, unconscious. Meanwhile, with his grandfather's spear, Abdallah Ali had cornered the third man and forced him to throw his axe to the ground, thereby announcing his surrender.

The Chuqor community went wild with applause and cries of, "O God, praise to our master Muhammad." The young men led the three captives to the nearby ruin, where the athletes normally trained. They tied them to three stakes they set in the ground. Then they brought a huge cauldron, which the community normally used for boiling grain, which was eaten during the winter, filled it with water, and lit a fire beneath it. Then some other young men smeared their faces with red oil and started dancing around the three black men, leaving them with the impression that they wanted to eat them. The children who had crowded in roared and the women watching this scene from the far side of the ruin's low wall laughed. This did not last for long, however, because an armored Jeep arrived and three policemen got out. They laughed along with the crowd but then released the captives from their bonds and handcuffed them. They took them off to a nearby police station located in the Jewish neighborhood.

Nobody had noticed the disappearance of Qara Qul's widow, who had slipped away with her four children to avoid being taken prisoner on discovering that she had underestimated her foe's strength. She was, however, mistaken in this belief, because no one in the Chuqor community could have harmed her and her four black children, despite the impudence of her tongue, because in their eyes she was still the widow of Qara Qul, the greatest saint the city of Kirkuk had witnessed in its entire history, and it would not be easy for them to forget this fact.

People did not realize that Mullah Zayn al-Abidin al-Qadiri was absent until the end of that rowdy day experienced by the Chuqor community. It would certainly not have been appropriate for the mullah to exchange insults with Qara Qul's widow, but his absence—even after the battle ended and Qara Qul's widow withdrew—excited people's curiosity and questions. He ought to come out and thank the three men who had risked their lives to defend the honor of his home. Indeed, some people said that the mullah ought to increase the salaries of Abbas Bahlawan and Mahmud al-Arabi, who were employees of his agency, or should at least award them a compensatory bonus in view of the heroism with which they had confronted the three black savages, who would have broken into the mullah's home and torn him limb from limb—had it not been for these two men.

Abbas Bahlawan and Mahmud al-Arabi informed the men—who had spread a carpet in the street in front of the mosque to sit there and enjoy a recital of the battle's details—that the mullah had not been seen at the agency for three days. The mullah had also ceased going to his mosque to perform the evening prayer, a rare occurrence. Suddenly the men realized that something must have happened to the mullah to cause him to sequester himself. A visit to Mullah Zayn al-Abidin al-Qadiri in his home now appeared a must.

When the men knocked on the door of the house, his wife opened it, her eyes swollen from weeping. She said, "I don't know what's happened to the mullah. For three days he's not uttered a single word. I believe he's lost the ability to speak." The men sat down in the long room where the mullah squatted in a corner, gazing at the void. He did not seem to be sick, but his eyes roamed around, as though he had departed from the world. In fact, he did not even respond to his visitors' greeting. He seemed not to recognize them. Khidir Musa said, "A doctor's got to examine him. We can't simply rely on destiny."

Half an hour later, a doctor came to examine the mullah. He did not find any cause for alarm, except for the muteness, which he could not explain. He opened the mullah's mouth and felt his tongue and larynx with a wooden tongue depressor, and found everything there in good shape. Then he turned to Bakr, the mullah's oldest son, and told him, "I believe your father has had a shock, and this has nothing to do with medicine and prescriptions."

The mullah opened his mouth as though he had been waiting for the sentence the doctor uttered. "I saw him. He was there."

The doctor said cockily, "This problem has been resolved too. You see: the mullah is talking." Then with a gentle smile he asked, "Who did you see?"

The mullah gazed at his face for a time before replying, "I saw everything."

Then he stood up, put on his jacket, which had been hanging over his head, donned his shoes, and slipped outside, repeating time and again like a tape recorder, "I saw everything."

The men with him at his house followed him all the way to Qara Qul's mausoleum, where the policemen at the guardhouse greeted him warmly. The guard opened the locked door of the directorate and he entered. The crowd that had been walking behind followed, and he headed for his desk, casting a thoughtful glance at the coffin that sat in the center of the space. His eyes were bathed in tears as he embraced each of the men on taking leave of them: "I want to spend the night here, close to Qara Qul."

Then he stretched out in the coffin, asking the men to turn off the light on their way out because he wanted to sleep. The men withdrew silently. He listened to the sound of their footsteps retreating into the darkness, and then closed his eyes and fell asleep.

Nine

Mullah Zayn al-Abidin al-Qadiri was carried to his house in the very same coffin in which he had died so that his widow could weep for him and the Chuqor community could bid him farewell. When one of them was snatched away, their emotions remained disturbed and unsettled until they witnessed the death. Women of the Chuqor community normally mourned the deceased for three days, while consuming many pastries made with dates. The family of the deceased would distribute these even to strangers who chanced to pass by the door of the home, believing that the sweets would leave a final pleasant memory of the deceased in people's hearts.

The very first day that the mullah's death was announced, a professional mourner arrived from the Shatirlu community. She was renowned throughout the entire city for her skill in composing elegies that made even the hardest of hearts grieve and women's eyes fill with tears for the dead, to whom she would attribute every virtue, whether accurately or not. Her brilliance, however, lay in portraying scenes that her imagination devised. Although this funeral performer had never seen the mullah, she learned everything about him from the community's women and from his widow, who gave her ten

dinars, saying, "I want you to make the whole city weep for him." So
the mourner drew from the bag in which she carried her equipment
a loudspeaker, which she herself set up outside the door. Then she
began to wail and to strike her face while she enumerated the mullah's merits to a monotonous beat. The women who filled the home's
courtyard began their lamentations: striking their faces, tearing their
garments, exposing their chests, and rubbing dirt on their heads.

The men of the Chuqor community lined up in the street in front
of the mullah's house and proceeded to listen to the qualities that the
lamenting praise-singer allotted to the departed mullah until many of
them felt a twinge of conscience for not having sufficiently appreci-
ated the mullah during his lifetime. Custom decreed that the deceased
should be washed in the mosque, where prayers were said for him.

This was followed by his funeral and burial, all in the same day.
Mullah Zayn al-Abidin al-Qadiri, however, was not merely someone
like those who died every day. His son Bakr told the men wishing to
limit his funeral to a single day, "Don't forget that he's a director general. The government will inevitably come once the news reaches
them. Who knows: the king himself may come. Don't forget he
knew him personally. And Kirkuk's citizens who loved him have a
right to a final viewing of his pure body."

Abbas Bahlawan and Mahmud al-Arabi, who were sensible of the
favor that Mullah Zayn al-Abidin al-Qadiri had done them, suggested that the mullah and his coffin should be placed inside a glass
box for a period of three days and displayed to the inhabitants of
Kirkuk and to the visitors who came from all over the world to the
shrine of Qara Qul, so that everyone could be blessed by seeing him
lie in state. The two men, who enjoyed great respect in the Chuqor
community in deference to their role in defending the community
against aggressors, said, "It's true that the mullah was a man like us,
but he was chosen to be custodian of the tomb of Qara Qul and his
caliph on this earth. And who will forget that the mullah himself had
his own miracles? Remember the miracle of the deluge that Kirkuk
experienced after a long drought back when the mullah led a procession from the Chuqor community to the plain of al-Musalla,
beseeching God to send rain to the city? Then the skies filled with

clouds even before he finished his prayer. Kirkuk had not experienced rain like that since Noah's flood."

The points raised by the two men started people thinking once more about the life of the man they had lost. They began racking their memories for everything the mullah had said or advocated during his life. They remembered his rain sermon, his sermon about resisting the English, and his coffin sermon. They remembered his wisdom in deciding to use a coffin as his desk, unlike other administrators who supervised the activities of their subjects while seated on swivel chairs. They remembered his wisdom in utilizing the gold wheelchair when he went to the coffeehouse. His son Bakr said, "I believe he died because he saw the Unknown open up before him." The Chuqor men remembered that the mullah, before his death, had kept repeating, "I saw everything." They confirmed that the curtain screening the Unknown had lifted before his eyes, causing him to lose the ability to speak and his eyes to roam in terror. Even without falling ill, the man had died in response to a call that originated in the Eternal.

The coffin containing the mullah's body was placed in a sealed glass box, which was filled with ice blocks brought from the ice plant that his family owned, to keep the corpse from decaying or decomposing while exposed on a high bench that was built on the street in front of his mosque. The box was surrounded by tens of colored lamps that blinked on and off once some workmen drew electrical power from a pole at the corner of the street.

This affair, which was an entirely new observance for the city of Kirkuk, attracted thousands of people coming to see the mullah, who almost looked like he was sleeping. He was covered with the Iraqi flag and his turban had been placed on his chest. Actually, all that showed of the mullah were his pale, elongated face and his sunken eyes, above which bushy eyebrows met in the middle. His long, white beard had been combed and trimmed with scissors to look neater, since the mullah had paid especial attention to this while alive. People passed by the box, casting at it what they termed their "final look," although many circled around to take another peek. The children took particular delight in this. They would pass by, imitating their parents, whose tears flowed as they stood before the box.

As always happens, Muslim religious scholars disagreed this time too about placing the mullah inside a glass box and displaying him to people. Some thought that Islam forbids turning a Muslim believer's remains into a spectacle for people—as if he were a monkey in a zoo. Something like this would inevitably lead to error. These men said that their hunch was confirmed when some people began to claim that the mullah had winked or smiled while in his coffin. Indeed, the women who persisted in paying their respects throughout the three nights, striking their faces and weeping, reported that at dawn after the second night they had seen the mullah lift his head, adjust his position a little, and then fall asleep. Of course none of the men believed these women, whose mental and spiritual horizons were limited.

The anger of the ulema intensified when they heard that the Chuqor community was thinking about embalming the mullah's corpse and leaving it inside a glass box so that future generations could look at it too. They emphasized that this would turn the mullah into an idol worshipped by the people and that this was not something that would please God or His Messenger. What made things worse was that the Communists began to noise it about that the mullah was a nationalist symbol in the struggle against English imperialism and that embalming him would consecrate this symbolic status and establish a place for him in the people's hearts. They asserted that embalming leaders was a mark of civilization and would necessarily spread throughout the world and that the Russians were the first to set this precedent, which they copied from the pharaohs, when workers and peasants embalmed both of the great leaders, Lenin and Stalin. This custom would certainly be followed by all other leaders. The attorney for Qara Qul's widow issued a statement that opposed embalming. In it he slandered Mullah Zayn al-Abidin al-Qadiri and referred to the suit filed against him for misappropriation of wealth not belonging to him. A number of members of the Afterlife Society, even without investigating the matter, sought refuge in a mosque where they said they would starve themselves to death unless the government intervened to stop the embalming operation.

This groundless and fabricated commotion, which rested on certain rumors that were possibly fomented by Qara Qul's widow, forced the mullah's family to issue a statement celebrating Mullah Zayn al-Abidin al-Qadiri and announcing that an oratorical and poetic festival would be held prior to the mullah's funeral and burial in the courtyard of Qara Qul's agency. The governor allocated a prize of a hundred dinars to be awarded to the finest poem recited during the festival. Poets came from throughout Iraq and from Syria, Egypt, and the Sudan—countries renowned for poets who composed panegyric verse. Tucked in their pockets, they brought protracted odes. Even though Mullah Zayn al-Abidin al-Qadiri was buried on the third day that he was displayed in the glass box—after the ice had melted and his body had begun to decompose and smell—the celebration lasted for seven more days so the poets could deliver their elegies, from which the newspapers published excerpts together with photographs of the guests of honor seated in the front row flanking the governor, who was always at the center.

There was something approaching a fracas when the awards committee, consisting of the governor, the head of the municipality, the director of public safety, and the minister of religious endowments, relying in their judgment on the amount of applause that each poem received and also bearing in mind the geographical distribution of the countries from which the poets hailed, declared a tie among four poets. These were Abd al-Ta'ib Abd al-Gha'ib, Salman al-Safin (who was known as the people's poet because he worked at the People's cigarette factory in al-Atifiya, Baghdad), Ayman Sultan al-Ayman from Syria, and an Egyptian psychiatrist named Girgis Rami. Even the winning poets rejected this unfair division, and each of them sent a telegram to the governor requesting his just intervention to award the whole prize to that one poet himself.

Verbal battles broke out between the winning poets and the losers, one of whom alleged that Abd al-Ta'ib Abd al-Gha'ib was a Satanist and therefore ineligible to eulogize a Believer of Mullah Zayn al-Abidin al-Qadiri's stature. Others accused al-Safin of being a spiteful Communist and also demented as a result of his lengthy stays in prison. Some of the losing poets said that the winning Syrian poet was an Isma'ili esotericist accustomed to writing panegyric poems in honor of just about anyone, moving from ruddy- to olive- to dark-complexioned patrons in search of a living. The Egyptian poet Ahmad Rami, who did not participate in the festival, denied that there was any relationship between him and the winning poet Girgis Rami, declaring in his Egyptian accent, "He's a clown of a doctor, with Umm Kulthum as my witness." Only then did the prize committee realize their error, which they saw no way to rectify. They had named Girgis Rami as one of the winners thinking that he was the poet Ahmad Rami, with whom the governor himself spent the first Friday night of every month, placing before himself a bottle of arak and submerging himself in the voice of Umm Kulthum as she sang one of Rami's masterpieces. The poets' row did not quiet down until Khidir Musa donated three hundred more dinars, and each of the four poets received the hundred dinars that had brought him to Kirkuk.

This affair upset the young Burhan Abdallah, who had believed that poets were a sophisticated group. Now he saw them as they really were: beggars who would praise even the devil himself in exchange for a handful of dinars. They were jesters who moved their hands and feet on any dais, declaiming the most inane words. Khidir Musa jestingly asked his nephew Burhan Abdallah, "Do you still want to be a poet after everything you've seen of these poets, Burhan?" Burhan Abdallah replied a bit smugly, "There's always a distinction, Uncle, between a poet and a beggar, and all of these were beggars, not poets." What the boy said, however, was empty puffery because the shock caused him to stop writing poetry for many years, until he was inspired by reading a copy of the Holy Bible he had chanced upon. Burhan Abdallah then found that the life of the mullah had contained many spiritual lessons that deserved to be related as part of the evolving history of mankind. For that reason, he closed his eyes and began to imagine the mullah as another messiah planting his upright stalk of wheat. Words got mixed together in his head until he no longer distinguished between past and present: "As it is inscribed in the prophets, here I descend before your eye my imam who prepares the way for you. 'The voice crying in the wilderness: grow a healthy stalk of wheat.' The mullah traveled from one district to another. All the people of the Islamic region and of the Chuqor community went out to him. With him, they washed their sins away in the Khasa Su River. The mullah was wearing 'camel's hair, and a leather girdle around his waist; and his food was locusts and wild honey.' At that time he saw the mountains split apart and 'the Spirit descending upon him like a dove.' So he shuddered and his heart split asunder. The spirit immediately drove him out into the wilderness. And he was in the wilderness for forty days, tempted by Satan; and he was with the wild beasts; and the angels fed him manna and quail. He threw a net into the water and told the fishermen who gathered around him, 'Follow me, and I will make you fishers of men.'"

This gospel-style introduction to the life of the mullah made Burhan nervous instead of confident about his abilities to discover the message that Mullah Zayn al-Abidin al-Qadiri had brought to the Chuqor community. He asked himself what the mullah had really seen. It was hard for him to know what was true, for the secret had gone with the mullah to his grave. He was sure, however, that the mullah would not have died had he not seen what he ought not to have seen. Is this man's destiny then? His sorrow reached an extreme because he too wished to see what he did not and to uncover the secret of all secrets. Yet he did not feel prepared to die. Death resembled sleep, except that one never awoke again.

Burhan Abdallah's heart was troubled by doubt. "Does the mullah deserve to have me record his story? Can I make him into an exemplary model for people to discuss? I can't turn him into an angel because he revered money." He smiled to himself: "I've begun to rant too—just like the mullah. The mullah saw everything, but what did he really see? Perhaps he saw angels descending from the heavens or multi-colored devils with tails and beards dancing in front of hell. Perhaps he did not see anything, and the void swallowed him."

He closed his eyes and saw his own angels, the three angels, the old men who carried on their shoulders sacks loaded with spring. "Perhaps I ought to write about my own angels, these men coming from Eternity and making their long way to the Chuqor community—Chuqor, which they may never reach." His heart was filled with doubt once more. "Perhaps they aren't angels. Perhaps they're weary old men who come from some other city." He asked himself, "If God has a message, does Satan have one too?" Then he replied, "Of course not, no. Satan can't have a message. The only possible message for mankind is God's." Actually, he was not sure about this, though, for the boundaries between reality and fantasy were always collapsing.

Burhan Abdallah was standing in the desert, gazing at his three angels, who disappeared beyond the horizon, when he saw a mirror-covered white structure that rose by itself from the sand, like a legendary castle. He had often dreamed of it during his solitary nights. He stood there for some time longer, not knowing whether to advance or retreat. He thought he heard a voice that came to him from the depths of existence, calling to him, "Advance, Burhan. Don't be afraid." Something kept drawing him forward until he reached a door to which was attached a bronze plaque inscribed with a title he did not totally grasp: "Central Bureau for Existential Administration." Fearful and perplexed, he stopped before the door, which was made of gold and studded with gems, but the voice directed him once more, "Rap on the door and don't be afraid." So he knocked three times on the door and it opened. Then three angels welcomed him. He was astonished by their short, white wings, which they fluttered as they moved from place to place. One of the angels asked him, "What brings you here, Burhan?"

He stammered a bit before answering, "I've come to search for God so He can tell me the meaning of everything. Why does man exist if he's condemned to death? Why does time spoil everything? Why does God create a being that defies Him? This seems to me more like a meaningless game than anything else."

The angel smiled, "You shouldn't be overly concerned, since you're nothing more than a hero in an invented novel written by a disgruntled author." Then he placed a hand on Burhan Abdallah's shoulder and told him affectionately, "Perhaps we'll suggest to your author that he should tell you the meaning of your story, although it may not even have one."

Burhan Abdallah repressed his fury. "I've come to ask God about meaning. If you refer me to an author, he may be no more certain than we are."

The angel replied, "If you lack confidence in your story's author, perhaps you'll trust us. We'll descend to the Chuqor community to teach you what you don't know. But be on guard against a clash with reality that may be revealed to you one day." The elderly angel led him to a door and opened it. Then they were all in the Chuqor community.

Burhan Abdallah forgot the whole story, as if it had been a dream a person forgets the next day. He awoke that morning to find three strangers emerging from a house where no one had ever lived before. They carried pickaxes on their shoulders and were heading for the Khasa Su River, seeking its channels far outside the city. These three strangers with their weird clothes aroused the curious disapproval of the residents of the Chuqor community. They seemed three beings from another world with no relationship to this one.

Children followed them, afraid to draw too close. They continued to watch from afar while the men dug small ditches among the colored pebbles of the Khasa Su River. When the children grew tired of waiting, one stepped forward and asked somewhat timorously, "Why are you digging in the river?" One of the strangers—an elderly man of perhaps seventy—raised his head and said with a smile, "We're looking for gold." The children stood there a little while longer before returning home to tell their fathers and mothers what the old man had told them. The entire Chuqor community burst out laughing, mocking the feeblemindedness of these strangers. A man might find almost anything in the Khasa Su except gold. All the same, the affair aroused the suspicion of many, even if they did not dare express it openly. If these strangers had gone to dig for gold in the Khasa Su, they must be confident it could be found there, otherwise they would not be wasting their time chasing after a figment of the imagination. Suspicion turned to certainty when a rumor spread through the Chuqor community that these strangers were devil worshippers. Satan must then have been the one who showed them the existence of gold in the Khasa Su River. The next day, some fathers sent their sons to the Khasa Su River to search for gold too. This occurred two or three times without them finding anything. Then they grew bored and returned to their homes.

The presence of strangers who worshipped the devil in the Chuqor community actually excited such anxiety and fear in people's hearts that they continued to wonder whether this was possible. How could a creature worship the devil while God existed? Some rash youth considered attacking these strangers or even setting fire to their dwelling. The community's elders, however, forbade them from doing that because the issue concerned communal rights, which the Chuqor community considered sacred. In fact, according to Kirkuk's citizens who had witnessed Satanists, the matter was not entirely clear. People also differed about these strange men. It was said that they had migrated from Mount Sinjar. Some thought they were Muslims who followed their own special sect. Others said they were pagans to whom the message of Islam had not yet arrived. Scholars, however, said they were Zoroastrians who had come from Iran a thousand years before. They had embraced Islam but had shaped it to make it more like their previous creed. Apparently the spirit that people called the devil had coveted these simple folks from the moment they left the city of Yazdam in Fars, leading them along valleys, beside rivers, and across rugged mountains and escorting them past wild Kurdish tribesmen who lived in caves, to Mount Sinjar. Then they had placed young warriors at its access points and had planted their red flags on its peaks. This devil who had loved them and served as their guide was Ta'us Malak (the Peacock Angel). After many years, it became clear that he himself was the angel chief who had protested God's command when He ordered the angels to bow before Adam. This was the origin of the problem. Whereas Muslims say that the chief angel's rebellion angered God, who transformed him into a devil who deserves to be stoned, these people say that God discovered a lofty wisdom in this angel's rebellion and so raised his status. Ta'us Malak refused to bow down before Adam for some important reasons. First, God created him from fire and Adam from dirt. Second, it is wrong to bow before any creature except God, as God Himself has decreed.

This idea actually sparked the imagination of the Chuqor community's residents, who launched into heated debates with these strangers who had come to settle in the city of Kirkuk because there

195

was so much truth in their view that it was difficult to refute. As usual, the city of Kirkuk split into two factions. One endorsed God's position and the other that of the chief angel. Those who supported God's position said that there is always wisdom in everything God says or does, even if this wisdom seems obscure or even imperceptible to many. Perhaps God had wanted to bestow with this strange request a special sanctity on Adam and to grant him precedence over all other creatures. Those who opposed this position and endorsed that of the chief angel acknowledged with a courage that led them to infidelity that God had contradicted Himself by asking His angels to bow down before Adam. Any angels doing that had been motivated by limited intellect, a wish to flatter God, fear of His anger, or a desire for enhanced prestige. These opponents said that the chief angel had rejected an idea that contradicted God Himself in order to defend the truth and that this position deserved greater respect than that of the other, opportunistic angels.

From the very beginning, these strangers refused to call themselves worshippers of the devil, whom they referred to as Satan (instead of al-Shaytan), because they did not dare pronounce the letter shin (sh), which would remind the devil of them. Indeed, they went on to say that the devil was a creature God did not create. Instead, he emerged from nonexistence to combat and to mislead God's children, because it made no sense that God, who is filled with love for His children, would have created an evil being like the devil, whose only mission in life is to lead human beings to the abyss. At one time the old man told Burhan Abdallah, "I know you will see the devil one day. If only for that reason, you'll learn the bitter truth, my son. As for us—we're just poor angels like all the other angels on this earth, which is heading toward annihilation."

Burhan Abdallah, who from the beginning had sided with the chief angel's position, had determined to befriend these strangers who said things other people did not. They trusted him enough to take him with them every day to dig for gold in the Khasa Su River. Then they informed him about the Black Scripture that Shaykh Yazid had composed under the inspiration of the Malak Ta'us. Burhan's imagination was excited by texts that related the appearance of creation and the

196

emergence of the four sacred elements: fire, earth, air, and water. Finally, they allowed him into their home, after he changed his blue shirt for a white one and stopped eating heads of lettuce, since the devil lives between lettuce leaves. One evening after returning from the Khasa Su River, the old man who was known as Shaykh Yazid said something to his sons Zayfar and Bayjih in a language that the young Burhan Abdallah did not know, and then turned toward him affectionately, saying, "No one in the Chuqor community has so far entered our house. You will be the first." Zayfar approached the door and knocked on it. After a few moments, the door was opened by an elderly woman who wore red clothes embroidered with silver thread. In the courtyard, Burhan Abdallah saw a large pit in which flames were blazing. The area around the pit was spread with Persian carpets. He sat down near the fire, which warded off the dark and threw shadows on the walls. Shaykh Yazid removed from a wooden chest, which rested in a corner of the house's courtyard, a gold statue that resembled a rooster and placed this before the blazing fire. Then they all began to chant a prayer in a monotonous voice while shaking their heads to the right and left. Burhan Abdallah had never heard anything like this before.

> *Yazid is himself the sultan.*
> *He is known by a thousand and one names,*
> *But the mightiest of these is "God."*

> *Sultan Yazid perceives*
> *The water contained by the sea*
> *And the whole world before him.*
> *Taking a single step,*
> *He traverses it instantly.*

Zayfar brought out a small tambourine and began to beat it gently to the rhythm of the prayer they chanted. Little by little, Burhan Abdallah also sank into a distant dream to which he was unable to cling, for it escaped from time and disappeared into the flaming tongues of fire. Suddenly he noticed small angels the size of his hand. Silver-colored, soft fuzz covered the bodies of these winged angels, which emerged from one of the cages and danced in a circle around the gold cock. Burhan Abdallah suddenly felt terrified and thought of fleeing and leaving the house, but the old man noticed the boy's fear and took his hand, as if wishing to reassure him that everything was fine.

The prayer, which was chanted to the beat of the tambourine, had scarcely ceased when the little angels stood humbly before the statue of Ta'us Malak, who resembled the rooster. Then they called out his name in a reverberating voice: "Long live the glory of the greatest sultan in the heavens and on earth!" They turned round and greeted the people sitting there, one after the other, by name. Burhan felt almost blissful when the small angels greeted him and spoke his name, "Welcome, Burhan Abdallah, to the house of truth." Burhan Abdallah struggled to open his mouth: "They even know my name." He turned toward Shaykh Yazid, who smiled as he sipped the tea placed before him. Seeking clarification, he asked, "Did you tell them my name?"

Shaykh Yazid shook his head no. He said, "I didn't tell them anything. They know everything. Ask them anything you want. You can count on it; they see even the Unseen."

Burhan Abdallah did not know what he could ask them, and was silent for a moment. Then something came to him: "Who is the best soccer player in Kirkuk?"

The small angels said in a harmonious voice that sounded like a choir, "There's not a single finest player. There are two: the brothers Widad and Sidad."

Young Burhan Abdallah, who was excited by the answer, cried out, "My God, they're right. Widad and Sidad are truly the two finest players in the city." Then he hazarded another question: "Tomorrow Kirkuk's team plays Erbil at Sharika Field. Could I know the outcome of this important match?"

The small beings answered once more in a calm, monotonous voice, as if reading from a book set before them—an open book that contained everything that had happened in the past and that might occur in the future, "Of course you can, Burhan. Kirkuk's team will have twelve goals to a single one for Erbil."

Burhan Abdallah trembled as if he had touched a live wire: "My God, that will be an unforgettable event."

In fact, this match, which Burhan Abdallah attended the next day, having already learned the final score, became a game unlike any the city had witnessed when Sidad scored six goals and his brother Widad five. The twelfth goal for Kirkuk was scored by Erbil against itself. That made the crowd laugh a lot because the Erbil team had previously claimed that it would wipe the ground with the Kirkuk team, whose entire strength consisted of the brothers Widad and Sidad, whom the English had trained. This claim certainly contained some element of intimidation, since it called into question the patriotism of the two best players the city of Kirkuk had ever reared. The crowd could have accepted this taunt as merely sour grapes if the Erbil team had demonstrated enough skill to justify its challenge, boast, and false assertion. When it was defeated in this deplorable way, the spectators—who included even their governor, who had watched the match from a private box he had shared with Kirkuk's governor, who had forgotten himself more than once and begun to shout for his city's team—swept onto the field and attacked them, cursing. They would almost have killed the members of Erbil's team had not Sidad and Widad intervened, telling the attackers, "That's enough. Their defeat is the best punishment for them."

The police arrived, put them on a bus, and drove them to the guesthouse, where Erbil's governor was waiting for them by the door. They had scarcely entered when he ordered the door locked. He glared at each of them in turn, without uttering a word. When he finally opened his mouth, he told them, as if affirming something he had just discovered, "I wasn't expecting this from you. You have defiled my honor and your city's." The coach, who was a physical education instructor, replied, "We've worked really hard. It boils down to luck." These words, which the coach had hoped would excuse his team's defeat to Erbil's governor, whose heart was filled with shame, enraged the governor even more than the preceding events. So he raised his hand and slapped the coach, who stepped back, asking involuntarily, "What have I done, Your Excellency the Governor?" The governor called him back, gesturing with his hand, "Come!" Trembling with terror, the coach obeyed the order and took two or three steps forward. Then the governor slapped him again, prompting the coach to step back. The governor followed him, intending to kick him from behind, but his foot plunged into one of the garden's irrigation ditches, and he slipped and fell on his back in the mud. At that, the governor ordered his guards, who rushed to help him rise, to teach some manners to these men, who had defiled his city's honor.

The policemen, who had also watched the match, had been waiting impatiently for this type of order. They attacked the squad members with the batons they carried till the players were bloodied. They chased them around the garden until its roses were trampled under foot. Blood gushed from the coach's head after a Kurdish sergeant who had trained as a boxer assumed responsibility for beating him. Finally they handcuffed the players and led them to a truck that transported them back to Erbil, where they were booked in the prison on charges of harming the city's reputation.

This incident, which was the first of its kind, was repeated frequently in later years, especially during the republic that followed the monarchy. These heads of state, most of whom were afire with patriotism, considered their soccer team's defeat a deliberate offense and an attempt to cast aspersions on their own domestic policies. If the team returned with the trophy, then a new automobile would be waiting for each player at the door of the airport terminal, a gift from the government, which was not stingy in honoring its heroes. Once players had collected a sufficient number of automobiles—so that some even opened transport offices and taxi services—the government decided to give each of them a mansion for every victorious match, especially if they defeated a rival or hostile Arab state.

A loss also had a price. Men from the secret police—most of whom were boxers, wrestlers, and reformed criminals—climbed aboard the plane as soon as it touched down at Baghdad International Airport and tossed the team members out of the emergency exit onto the asphalt below. There they pummeled and kicked them, accompanied by screams from the soccer fans who wanted to break their bones. The faces of many were blood-covered by the time they were incarcerated. Behind bars, they were beaten again by fellow inmates, who were no less patriotic than the prison guards. They stayed in prison for a week or two, or even a month, and could not be released until the president himself ordered that, and he was generally preoccupied by more important matters. He would forget about the team members, and no one would dare remind him to pardon these men, whom the strong hand of justice had touched. Eventually the minister of youth and an official of the Olympic Committee would have recourse to the seamstress who made clothes for the wife and daughters of the president, to the private cook who excelled at preparing stuffed vegetables and cabbage leaves, or even to the companion who was closest to the president's heart, the man who bore the title of "Chief Taster." The president would not eat from a dish unless this man had tasted it first. One of these individuals would intervene at an appropriate moment to remind the First Lady, who normally was on the plump side, or the president himself, with a passing word or a sentence that sounded off-the-cuff, about the members of Iraq's national team. Such a hint would suffice to prompt the president to order their release and to invite them to have lunch or supper with him at his residence in the presence of his wife and daughters because he was as eager to display his affection for them as to administer severe discipline to them from time to time. He acted in precisely the same way with his children and his subjects. Occasionally he would forget that he had set them free and again order them freed, causing the head of the police some discomfort because he was forced to arrest them for an hour or two before releasing them and transporting them to the palace, where they would dine with the president.

The beautiful match that Kirkuk's soccer team experienced so fascinated the young Burhan Abdallah that it was etched in his memory for a long time. What interested him more than anything else was the masterful knowledge of the small angels that were owned by the family of Shaykh Yazid. These angels were polite and much more certain about things than the three angels whom he saw from time to time—those tired old men who carried on their shoulders sacks that they said were filled with spring. These small creatures, perhaps even without being aware of it, played a decisive role in creating the forthcoming history not only of the Chuqor community and Kirkuk, but of all of Iraq.

After Mullah Zayn al-Abidin al-Qadiri was buried, the government established a committee to search for the fortune of Qara Qul's shrine, but found nothing, even though there was no place they did not look for the treasure that Mullah Zayn al-Abidin al-Qadiri had hidden from the hands and eyes of thieves. Everyone dreamt of discovering this treasure, the location of which the mullah had not even disclosed to his wife and children. If the government wished to recover what it considered its due, the widow of Qara Qul, who resorted to black magic, thought that if she found the treasure she would be spared going to court to demand what she considered her personal right and that of no one else. The mullah's wife, who denied any knowledge of the treasure's hiding place, certainly experienced a great deal of verbal abuse from her children, who kept searching in vain for the hidden wealth. The story preoccupied all of the Chuqor community. Many even sought to entice the madman Dalli Ihsan to search for the treasure with them, relying on his well-known ties to the jinn, but he never agreed.

This fever affecting the inhabitants of the Chuqor community petered out after two or three weeks, when it became obvious to them that Mullah Zayn al-Abidin al-Qadiri had taken the treasure's secret with him to the grave, together with that other secret that had cost him his life. They stopped pursuing this interest once despair entered their hearts. Government officials contented themselves with laying hands on all the shrine's possessions that were in plain sight, and Qara Qul's widow began to hope the court would award her title to all the new gifts that were presented to her spouse's shrine.

No sooner had this fever that had gripped the Chuqor community died away than Hameed Nylon reappeared as if emerging from a void. He assured those who looked askance at his disappearance that he had been in Kuwait, where he had worked as a driver for its prince, who, he said, owned a gold toilet. As usual, no one believed him, since he showed no trace of the blessings of oil that had enriched Kuwait. As a matter of fact only a few knew that Hameed Nylon was returning from the revolution after lighting its fuse in the countryside around Kirkuk. He had granted himself a military rank and, following the custom of the leaders of world revolutions, had taken a nom de guerre—Lieutenant Colonel Anwar Mustafa—which increased his self-confidence. He had indeed even thought of growing his beard longer but had decided to postpone that till later, when the revolution would have spread to at least a few villages. He had plotted this out carefully ever since his selection as leader by the villagers who had made off with the corpse of Qara Qul and had then fled into the thickets and hills near the village of Tawuq.

In point of fact, the inhabitants of Tawuq had never once thought of opposing the government, about which they knew nothing. All they had wanted was to bury Qara Qul in their village so that their fields would be blessed and their flocks fertile. The attack that the police had launched against them, killing two of them, however, had turned them into rebels, if only to save their skins. These men, who were armed with rifles, were anxious about their future. They did not know what to do except to wait once Agha Mamand, whose influence covered tens of villages located between Kirkuk and Erbil, including Tawuq, refused to intervene to negotiate a settlement with the government, on the grounds that Tawuq was a dependency of Kirkuk and therefore fell within a region of special control by the Iraqi government, the affairs of which he felt it inappropriate to second-guess, even though he was a deputy in the parliament in Baghdad for this whole region, including the village of Tawuq.

For this reason, the arrival of Hameed Nylon in the village of Tawuq at the wheel of his car caused the children to race behind it, cheering and screaming in the dust that it stirred up. Women emerged from their houses, which were made of mud and stone and surrounded by walls at the tops of which had been planted broken bits of colored bottles to prevent thieves from other distant villages from scaling them. The men returned from the fields when they heard the continuous barking of the dogs that raced on both sides of the vehicle from the moment it entered the village.

Hameed Nylon stopped his car in front of an open hut. On either side of its wide entrance was a horseshoe-shaped, mud-brick bench, which was covered with dirty but colorful rugs of the type that Kurdish village women weave. It was obvious that this was the village's coffeehouse. The man who had been preparing tea in a corner of the hut came out and yelled at the dogs, which backed off a bit. When they saw the car door open and Hameed Nylon climb out and enter the coffeehouse, however, they lowered their heads and moved off to their former locations. Hameed Nylon greeted the three men who were sitting in the coffeehouse and ordered a tumbler of tea. He knew that curiosity would be consuming the hearts of these villagers, who would want to know the secret that brought this stranger to their village in his automobile, although they would not dare ask him. When they realized that he spoke Kurdish like them, they felt somewhat more at ease and drew him into a conversation about where he came from. One of the men said, "You must be from Kirkuk. The only people with pretty cars like this live in Kirkuk."

Hameed Nylon smiled. "Oh, it's a car like any other." Then he added, "I've come to help the village of Tawuq. I can't say any more than that. I hope you'll trust me."

Anxiety was apparent on the faces of the villagers, who normally doubted everything. They kept silent. The man who was preparing the tea, however, said, "Fine, how can we assist you?"

Without beating around the bush, Hameed Nylon asked, "How can I contact the rebels who made off with Qara Qul's body?"

One of the men asked, "Are you from the government? What do you want with them?"

Hameed Nylon smiled once more. "I can only tell them that; I'm asking you to trust me."

Hameed Nylon was forced to wait till evening, after he had placed his car in a shelter at the other end of the village, before he could make his way through fields, thickets, and valleys to the men, who had taken refuge in an orchard, which was packed with walnut, fig, pomegranate, and plum trees and grape vines and which lay between two valleys through which a small river ran. Hameed Nylon was accompanied by two armed young men who led him silently in the dark down rough paths, through thick groves, and along waterways. The only sound was their footsteps on the grass and leaves, which were wet with dew. They finally reached the hideout where the villagers who had fled from the police had taken refuge. Through the trees they saw the light of two lanterns placed in front of a large boulder before what seemed to be the entrance of a cave and specters collapsed on the ground. One of the two youths called out in a loud voice, "Peace upon you."

The ghosts, which appeared to have been taken by surprise, jerked and rose, staring. The reply came: "Who are you?"

The youth said, "It's Mahmud. Everything's fine."

Four or five of the rebels approached and greeted them, kissing the shoulders of some. They took the two bags the young men accompanying Hameed Nylon had been carrying. "We've brought you some bread, sugar, and tea," said one of the young men.

Hameed Nylon shook hands with the men, who were prevented by good manners from even asking his name. The other young man, however, said, "The gentleman has come from Kirkuk and wishes to speak to you."

The men waited for Hameed Nylon to say something, expecting that he was a government representative who had come to inform them of a pardon that would allow them to return once more to their fields and orchards because the word "gentleman," which the youth Jalal had used when introducing Hameed Nylon, had made a good impression on these villagers, who believed that anyone who wore trousers was from the government. Those were Hameed Nylon's hardest moments. In fact, this was the most difficult time in the history of the armed revolution that spread from the countryside around Tawuq. On the basis of his experience, which rarely let him down, Hameed Nylon realized that everything depended on this moment. If these villagers were not satisfied with what he said now, they never would be.

Hameed Nylon took out a pack of cigarettes from a pocket, extracted one for himself, and threw the pack to the men. He said, as though affirming an established truth, "Excellent; I've come to you to be with you. It doesn't matter that I've used **different names** in the past; the name by which the world will know me and which was granted to me by the revolutionary command is Lieutenant Colonel Anwar Mustafa. The revolution will burst out from here to engulf Kirkuk and all the rest of Iraq. From here, we will liberate the nation, one village at a time, and teach the police who have been pursuing you lessons in courage and pluck."

This was the last thing that the men, who had sought refuge by the mountain in flight from the government forces they could not confront, expected to hear. One of the men ventured to say, "We were expecting the issuance of a pardon, and then you come to invite us to a rebellion."

Hameed Nylon responded, "There's nothing easier than obtaining a pardon for you. I met King Faisal II several months ago and I can do that again. But what have you done that requires a pardon? Yes, you wanted to have a saint buried there in your village. And that's your right. But Qara Qul was buried in Kirkuk, where the tombs are filled with imams. In fact, the police continue to pursue you now for no reason at all. I've come here to tell you that Qara Qul belongs to you and that Tawuq will have him one day."

The rebellious villagers had at first viewed Hameed Nylon with some suspicion and so had concealed their feelings, but he knew how to gain their affection and trust. First and foremost they were dazzled that Hameed Nylon was a lieutenant colonel. Then, too, he promised that each of them would receive a monthly salary from a revolutionary command that they had never heard of before. He affirmed to them that King Faisal II supported this movement, which opposed Nuri al-Sa'id, Abdul'ilah, and the English, who were all enemies of Islam. The following day Hameed Nylon slipped into the village and took from the trunk of his car three rifles that the Chuqor community had liberated during the battle of the cemetery. He took these back to the base camp and distributed them to men who had no personal rifle. Into his belt he tucked a revolver he had purchased from the thief Mahmud al-Arabi.

On the first night and the subsequent ones that Hameed Nylon passed at this hideout in the valley, he was able to sleep only fitfully. He felt something between delight and anxiety because here, for the first time in his life, he was successfully taking the first step on the long road to revolution. He was not, however, totally certain about the resolve of these villagers, whose thoughts revolved around the women, flocks, and fields they had left behind. Because he had spent his whole life among people who resembled these men in every respect, he knew that nothing could ignite belief in their hearts more effectively than power and wealth. If they felt that the revolution offered this, they would not hesitate to risk their lives for its sake.

On the seventh day after his arrival, Hamid Nylon stood on a protruding boulder facing his men and made a short speech in which he announced the actual beginning of the revolution. Then he drew out his revolver and fired one shot in the air. That was the revolution's first shot. He was a bit sad that he had not been able to obtain a red cloth from which to make the flag that would flutter over Iraq. Pleased by this gesture, the villagers applauded and raised their rifles too and fired into the air, announcing their allegiance to the revolution, which Hameed Nylon termed a peasants' revolution.

From that day forward the revolution's "squadrons"—the term chosen by Hameed Nylon for his forces—went on the offensive. The men began to visit Tawuq and neighboring villages, even during the daytime, resolved to fight off any attack the police might launch against them. Indeed, they openly began to call on people to join the revolution. Hameed Nylon had succeeded in attracting a number of other farmers and school students, on whom he relied to keep tabs on the enemy.

When Hameed Nylon returned to Kirkuk, he was certain that the revolution had actually begun. He realized, however, that a lot had to be done before the revolution became an indomitable force. His heart was inundated by waves of contradictory emotions: sorrow and happiness all at the same time. What a strange life a man is destined to live! The revolution—this limitless act extending into the future—let him make it a present reality. He saw his hand reaching for the revolver that would make him famous and felt all choked up. It was spring, and the cursed particles of pollen left him so congested he had difficulty breathing. "Why is it my destiny to suffer from this allergy?" He had not killed anyone yet. "But I definitely will kill. It's not possible for a revolution to be a revolution without blood." He thought that there was always a price to be paid. On the road he saw the land of Iraq stretch before his eyes. He stopped his car and held a handful of dirt in his palm: moist earth. "This is sacred earth," he murmured to himself. Then he scattered the dirt in the air. Blood on the ground. . . . There would always be blood on this purple carpet, on this large coffin called the fatherland.

Many matters occupied Hameed Nylon's mind, which was consumed by the revolution. He knew only a little about revolutionary teachings and contacted Faruq Shamil and Najat Salim to ask them for books with information about peasant revolutions. These no longer existed, having been thrown into ovens and burned, for fear that the security men who raided homes from time to time would discover them. Faruq Shamil, however, who possessed a powerful memory, wrote down the instructions he had memorized on a piece of paper that he presented to Hameed Nylon, who stuck it in his pocket, thinking he would study it when he returned to the base camp.

News of the revolution had reached many in the city, but they made fun of the rumors that circulated concerning it: "That would be the last straw if the naïve villagers who kidnapped Qara Qul liberated us." Indeed, the Communists, whose hearts were shredded by envy, claimed that Qara Qul himself was directing the rebellion, since as usual they mocked anyone who did not agree with them. After it was too late, they regretted making this claim when they realized that many people believed it. In fact, all of Kirkuk was discussing Qara Qul's return to fight for the poor.

Hameed Nylon seized this opportunity and contacted his young relative Burhan Abdallah, who was a gifted stylist, telling him, "Great, Burhan, I believe that the time has come for you to become one of the heroes of the revolution." So Burhan Abdallah drafted the first manifesto that Hameed Nylon released. It astounded the political parties with its elevated literary language and powerful logic. Someone who worked at the Turkish consulate in Kirkuk set the type and ran off copies on a Roneo press. The police had trouble identifying the source because there was no registration for private printing equipment in foreign consulates. One night Hameed Nylon himself distributed this flyer throughout the city. He stuck it to walls in front of mosques, cinemas, coffeehouses, and government agencies and poked it through holes in the doors of homes and in the souks. Although the next day the police arrested a number of suspects who had been sitting in coffeehouses chattering away against the government, they did not have a clue as to the source of these manifestoes that called on the people to join forces with the revolution. Thus Hameed Nylon realized in one blow and in the course of a few days what many others had failed to achieve during twenty years. The Communists contacted Hameed Nylon after it reached their ears that he had recruited many of the Imam Qasim community's unemployed youth, who spent their time leaning against walls, but he informed them that he did not have enough time to conduct unproductive negotiations. He proposed to them that they should join his movement without any preconditions, if they were serious about their revolutionary claims.

In reality, Hameed Nylon's mind was not focused on anything that related to the Communists or to the many new followers who had joined his movement and been sent by him to the mountain, traveling by foot and even without any weapons, which he lacked. He was, instead, preoccupied by the treasure that Mullah Zayn al-Abidin al-Qadiri had left behind him and which no one had been able to find. As a matter of fact, everything hinged on finding this treasure. Unless he could get his hands on enough cash, everyone would leave him. He was sure of that. No matter how ebullient they were, emotions did not suffice. He would have to feed and arm his men and to provide a generous supply of food to the families they had left behind.

Everyone had totally despaired of looking for the treasure when Hameed Nylon began his own laborious search. When it did not produce any results, he too almost surrendered to despair. Although he searched in all the probable and improbable sites, attempting to assume the mullah's personality so that he could think like him and thus be guided to the hiding place he had chosen for the treasure, he failed to uncover the secret. This matter caused him to drink to excess once again, after a long abstention. He did not recover his strength until Burhan Abdallah asked him one day, when the point that Hameed Nylon had reached alarmed him, "Is this the way you want to lead the revolution, Hameed? You can't tell the difference between your head and your toes now. Why are you doing this?" Hameed Nylon blushed because the boy had made him feel ashamed, and his criticism was justified. So he replied graciously, "There won't be any revolution, Burhan, unless I find the wealth that the damned mullah hid. A revolution without capital doesn't amount to a hill of beans. Everything will collapse after a month or two unless we acquire an adequate number of rifles and pay salaries to the combatants."

Hameed Nylon was on the verge of tears. He was lamenting his revolution, which would die stillborn. He had promised his men salaries that he had not yet paid and knew he would not dare return to them unless he discovered the treasure, in which he had placed all his hope. Everyone would mock him: "This wannabe who called himself Lieutenant Colonel Anwar Mustafa." He was thinking to himself: "Fine, Lieutenant Colonel, your days are numbered," when he was taken by surprise by the smile plastered across the boy's face. "Why didn't you tell me right away? The matter may not be as difficult as you think."

"Not difficult? What are you saying?"

Burhan smiled again. "I'll help you find the treasure. That's what I'm saying."

Hameed Nylon became very alert. He asked hesitantly, "Do you know where the treasure is located?"

Burhan Abdallah shook his head, "No, but I'll know this evening."

The wind went out of Hameed Nylon's sails again. He did not even want to ask what made the boy so certain that by evening he could unravel this mystery that had baffled everyone. Realizing that the man did not believe him, Burhan Abdallah left to avoid any more questions that he would not know whether to answer or not. He waited until evening before heading to the house in which the small angels lived and rapped on the door. Silence enveloped the house in the dark of the alley, where the only light was from a lamp hung in the distance. A long enough time passed that he thought no one was home. All the same he knocked a second time without hoping that anyone would answer. He waited a moment and then started to walk away, thinking that he would return later. He noticed, however, that the door was opening and that a voice filled with affection was calling him, "It's you, Burhan. Come in. We were waiting for you."

Music coming from some place in the darkness reached his ears. It resembled the sound of men's footsteps descending a mountain. He was afflicted by a sudden terror, for no apparent reason. He even thought about running away and forgetting everything. The old man, whose face was divided by the darkness and the light, stood in front of the door, which was halfway open. Sensing the hesitation of the boy who stood there staring at him, he stretched out a thin, veined hand, gently grasped Burhan's wrist, and pulled him inside the house, which was illuminated by tongues of flame from the fire pit at the center of the courtyard. Then he closed the door behind him calmly and silently.

Ten

Hameed Nylon reached the mountain riding a mule on which he had thrown embroidered saddlebags filled with the mounds of dinars he had brought. He was wearing a military uniform that he had decorated with two red badges attached to the shoulders. He was brimming with the life that spread before him. This fresh arrival by Hameed Nylon, like a king returning to his subjects after an absence, caused the revolution to spread to neighboring villages even faster than Hameed Nylon could have imagined. He knew that nothing is as persuasive as cash. The moment he returned to his base camp, he paid back salaries to his fighters, who could not believe that their pockets were filled with all those dinars—more than they had seen in their entire lives. He said, "A revolution that fails to feed its children does not deserve to exist."

There was new life in Tawuq and the neighboring villages, which had heard that the revolution was paying salaries to combatants. Shaykhs of advanced years convened meetings in villages after receiving news of the revolution that had sprung from nowhere. Some suggested that they should contact their aghas and ask permission to enlist in the revolution. The villagers, however, categorically refused this proposal: "What connection do our aghas have to this matter that concerns our livelihood?" The meetings broke up, leaving the decision to individuals to do as they saw fit. That was exactly what many had been expecting because fighters had initially come individually, sneaking away to the base camp under the cover of darkness and then in groups, after people became convinced that the salaries paid by the revolution were more profitable than growing onions and tomatoes and better than working for the government itself. This truth tempted many policemen, municipal workers, soldiers, and students from seminaries and caused them to come and ask to enlist. Even county managers and lieutenants fled from their service and came to Hameed Nylon, who received them graciously and then sent them back to their posts to work as undercover agents. He promised that they would receive an extra salary from the revolution while they sat at their bases.

Confronted by this crush of humanity, Hameed Nylon was finally forced to call a temporary halt to new enlistments, rejecting even recommendations from his fighters and endorsements that potential recruits brought from village headmen whose names Hameed Nylon had already added to the roster of salaries to be paid at the end of each month. In reality, this was a step that had to be taken to keep matters from getting out of hand because the number of combatants had grown so large that some sought out their women at night or went missing for days at a time without anyone noticing. The villagers also continued their traditional practice of stealing from nearby villages, which they would attack at night. This caused Hameed Nylon to imprison them in a mud hut he had constructed at the end of the valley. In fact he was forced to flog those who returned to theft after being released. He knew this might scare them but not do much to change their value system, which had been passed down through many generations.

Then Hameed Nylon withdrew to study the page of revolutionary teachings, which he did not know how to implement. These abstract ideas rarely had much bearing on what he needed most. This was how to organize the revolution and to move onto the offensive. There was some useful advice along the lines of: "Depend

on the people and consolidate your relationship with the peasants"
and "Respect your elders" or "Strike the enemy and then flee."
Everyone knew these things, however. Hameed Nylon had consoli-
dated his relationship with the peasants even more than Mao
Tse-tung had. "I pay them salaries that they never in their whole lives
dreamed of." He plunged into deep reflection as he thought about
the meaning of "Strike the enemy and then flee." Then he told himself, "Perhaps it's necessary for us to do that now, but we won't do
that forever. The day will come when we march forward and liberate Iraq: village by village and city by city." Thus Hameed Nylon
decided that—like all the other revolutionary leaders whose names
people repeat—he himself would write the instructions for his
revolution.

He shut himself up in the room the villagers had built for him
from stones and plaster. As the red flag fluttered overhead, he filled
some notebooks with his thoughts on revolution in just a few days.
Then he sent these with one of his secret couriers to Burhan
Abdallah in Kirkuk to be rewritten in a refined literary style. This was
a new undertaking for Burhan Abdallah, who had always been preoccupied by learning life's secret and brooding about the stories of
prophets and leaders, but had never gained access to what he considered the essence, which must be a treasure house for all the
answers. He repeated to himself, "The answers are always deceptive
and corrupted and shade into each other until it becomes hard for a
person to rediscover an answer after the initial moment." He
thought, "There's no essence that contains the answers. There's
merely an eternity that precedes the questions. Inquiry is mankind's
destiny in this world." Burhan Abdallah withdrew to a corner of the
Umm al-Rabi'ayn Garden, stretched out on the damp grass, and
began to look over Hameed Nylon's teachings about revolution.
These were new ideas not contained by the old books. They
attempted to get to the reality inside people's hearts, rather than to
something external, and called them to become the masters of the
world. He thought, "Fine. I've always wanted to write a book about
life. This will be my first attempt to compose the book I want.
Although it's not my book, it will become part of me."

His creativity was molded by the clamorous thoughts that Hameed Nylon had jotted down and by the imagery used by oil workers at Baba Gurgur, bakers in the Chuqor community, goldsmiths in the new souk, soldiers in the barracks, and bicycle rental agents on the street opposite the citadel. Burhan Abdallah spent days thinking about drafting this book, which he wanted to be a guide to revolution, about which he actually knew nothing, although he could imagine it. He drew inspiration from the language of the gospels, which contained eternal admonitions for mankind. Thus he climbed to his house's upper room, where he secluded himself for a week.

When he descended, he had drafted the book, which he called *The Guide*. Hameed Nylon found this title unsatisfactory and changed it to *The Pocket Guide to Revolution*. Then he sent it to Turkey with a Turkmen student—from Sari Kahiya—who was studying veterinary science in Istanbul.

Ten thousand copies were printed at the Yildizlar Press. The type in them was tiny—too small to be read by the naked eye. The miniature book, which was not much bigger than a matchbook, reached Hameed Nylon less than two months later, along with ten thousand magnifying glasses manufactured by the German firm Carl Zeiss. These were sent in a separate shipment for fear the censors would detect the link between the book and the magnifying glass. Hameed Nylon really demonstrated his judiciousness in outwitting the security men because the employees of the censorship office assumed when they saw the book's cover, which was decorated with Islamic designs, that it was one of those prayer books that are normally placed inside a scrap of cloth and then attached near the elbow to protect the person wearing it from harm. These were widespread in Iraq.

Thus the book slipped past the censors and created a big stir among career leftists, who almost exploded from envy and jealousy—not because Hameed Nylon had contrived a way they had not devised to trick the security agents, but because he had composed a book in lofty literary language quite unlike the lackluster style of the political tracts that the political parties released from time to time. Although they made a show of mocking and ridiculing it, they spent their nights obsessively reading the book that Hameed Nylon's agents sold with the German magnifying glass for a hundred fils. Others, who were enchanted by the book's message, translated it to Kurdish and Turkish. Imams in the mosques subsequently took quotations from it to include in the sermons they delivered at the conclusion of the Friday prayer—naturally without any mention of the source.

This book, which listed as its author Lieutenant Colonel Anwar Mustafa, made Hameed Nylon swagger with pride and conceit because he had realized in only a few months what had escaped Iraq's political parties as a whole since the defeat of the Ottomans in World War I and the English army's entry into Iraq under the command of General Maude, who had said he came as a liberator, not a conqueror. Hameed succeeded in gaining the Kurdish tribes first. Then, capitalizing on his influence among the Arabs of al-Hawija, he gained the Ubayd and Jibur tribes, which abandoned their internecine wars and announced their loyalty to the revolution, believing that King Faisal II himself supported it.

Even after the first shot of the revolution was fired, several months passed without the revolution's squadrons engaging in any actual battles with the government forces, which had not paid any attention to this revolution, except for a few small skirmishes that occurred from time to time between night watchmen or guardhouse policemen who refused to hand over their weapons to the rebels. The situation angered Hameed Nylon to some extent. He had expected that the government would respond to him in a fashion worthy of the revolution he had announced. The government maintained its silence even when he sent a group of his men to fire—from a distance—on a school for mounted policemen at the edge of the city. A mule was killed then and a policeman was wounded in the thigh.

When Hameed Nylon observed the government's determination to ignore him—not even issuing a communiqué—he felt ever more rebellious and decided to go on the offensive. He had his men set up roving ambushes for vehicles that carried paying customers between cities. The concept his men adopted was actually borrowed from a scene that had stuck in his mind from an American film Hameed Nylon had seen. The idea was guaranteed success every time. One of his men would stretch out beside the road and hold his breath, pretending to be dead. Then passing vehicles would stop. Drivers and passengers would get out and hurry to lend a helping hand. At that, five or six men brandishing weapons would emerge from behind boulders, trees, and hills to capture the passengers, whom they forced to raise their arms. Then they would search their pockets and impound a fifth of any sum over five dinars as an alms tax for the revolution. If a person's pocket was empty or only contained a few dirhems, they would give him a dinar as assistance from the revolution for the poor, after reading him a page or two from *The Pocket Guide to Revolution*. Then they would shake hands with them, bid them farewell, and wish them a safe trip. After two or three months, however, Hameed Nylon was compelled to stop these operations, which cost the revolution thousands of dinars because the scent of dinars attracted villagers, who began to travel every day between the mountainous towns in wooden buses, exhausting themselves to fall into the revolution's ambushes. Indeed some proprietors of vehicles allowed them to ride for free in exchange for half the amount they gained from each ambush staged by the revolutionaries.

When Hameed Nylon saw that the government was deliberately overlooking his revolution, he decided to strike where the pain would be excruciating. One night he himself led nine of his men armed with rifles and slipped into the city of Kirkuk, where they knew every alley. They reached the other side of the city by crossing the Khasa Su River, which was nearly dry. Its colored pebbles glittered in the light from the stars that filled the sky. They were heading for the Arafa region, where the English enclave was surrounded by barbed wire. Hameed Nylon knew every house in this neighborhood, where engineers, administrators, and English intelligence officers lived with their families. For this reason, he had no difficulty reaching the region, which was filled with trees and expanses of green grass. He was able to surprise the neighborhood, without anyone noticing. He did not, however, wish to shed even a drop of blood. The police guardhouse was located at the beginning of the street leading to the neighborhood and beyond the railroad line over which passed the trains linking Kirkuk and Erbil. Most of these policemen were nomadic desert

Arabs who had dedicated themselves to serving the English, who were not stingy with presents. If alerted, they would start firing, and this could lead to an unnecessary massacre. Hameed Nylon, however, had no difficulty worth mentioning in taking control of the guardhouse, where the three policemen were snoring in their sleep without having posted a guard at the door. He put the manacles hanging on the wall on their wrists and feet and tied them to their camp beds almost before they woke up. Then he left three of his men there and went with the others, slipping between the trees, into the English neighborhood, which always remained illuminated.

After half an hour, Hameed Nylon and his men returned, clustered around four men and a woman who were plainly English. Their hands were tied with ropes and their mouths were gagged with scraps of cloth to keep them from speaking. They walked with staggering steps and offered no resistance. They seemed indifferent to what was happening around them because they had drunk so much whiskey, the reek of which made the villagers, who were unfamiliar with this dizzying odor, sniffle. Hameed Nylon, who—like his men—had wrapped green cloth around his head, so that only his piercing eyes were visible, and who—unlike his men, who had buried their bodies inside dark, baggy Kurdish pants— was wearing a military uniform, issued his orders to the three villagers who had their rifles trained on the policemen, who were shackled to their beds. "Excellent! Raise our flag over the guardhouse and collect all their rifles and revolvers, because the time has come to withdraw." The street was totally empty and a pervasive silence, which was occasionally broken by the barking of a distant dog, ruled over the city. Hameed Nylon cast a thoughtful glance at the street, and then they all slipped in a single procession toward the Khasa Su River, crossing the dirt embankment over which the train passed. Inside the guardhouse they left behind a few copies of *The Pocket Guide to Revolution*, to which Hameed Nylon had appended delicate dedications for the governor of Kirkuk, the chief of police, and the director of public security. He had signed these with his nom de guerre: Lieutenant Colonel Anwar Mustafa.

The men, together with the five prisoners, traversed the Khasa Su over small pebbles partially buried in sand and waded through shallow water from time to time, without exchanging a single word. The Englishwoman stumbled more than once because of her high-heeled shoes, which skidded on the pebbles and sank into the sand. She pulled them out with a nervous wriggle of her feet. Then she bent over and picked up both shoes. Hameed Nylon smiled in the starlight and told her affectionately in English, "That's better. Now you can enjoy this outing." The night breezes that stung their faces and carried with it the scent of the countryside had dissipated all the influence of whiskey in the heads of the prisoners, who noticed, apparently for the first time, that they had been kidnapped. They stopped walking and shook their heads, making sounds that were muffled because of the rags bound around their mouths. The villagers shoved them with the butts of their rifles, but Hameed Nylon told them comfortingly, "Don't worry. No one will harm you. We'll treat you like guests. You'll see that we are more humane than you think."

Then he stepped forward and untied the knot in the cloth placed over the Englishwoman's mouth, asking her, "How are you, Mrs. McNeely?"

The woman shook her head in disgust but said coquettishly, "Oh, thank you Mr. Hameed." Then she asked him gently, "What do you want to do with us?"

Hameed answered reassuringly in his own special way, "Oh, nothing. Nothing at all." He added conceitedly but with a light sarcasm that was hard to detect, "In my capacity as commander of the revolutionary army, I have the honor to inform you that you are now my guests."

Addressing her words to her husband, who was walking behind her with his mouth lightly gagged, Helen McNeely said, "George, did you hear? Our friend Mr. Hameed has become the leader of a revolution."

Silence reigned again in the darkness that revealed less and less of the city, which was sinking into the night's abyss like a legendary specter whose pulsations, which blended with boundless nature, were wafted along by the wind. They crossed the Khasa Su at the far side of the city, moving from it to fields that were fragrant with the scent of grass and earth. This daring operation led by Hameed Nylon caused the city's authorities to lose their nerve and to swear to take revenge, after the prime minister contacted and cursed them in language that was anything but polite, threatening to cut off their heads if the kidnapped Englishmen did not return unharmed. At noon ten armored Jeeps crammed full of policemen shouldering rifles set forth, heading toward the village of Tawuq, which the government held responsible for this attack.

The police chief, who led this operation, knew that there was no hope of discovering the kidnapped Englishmen because these villagers would not open their mouths no matter what the consequences. He would be forced, all the same, to demonstrate the government's brutality and strength first, before negotiating with these simpletons, who—he was sure—knew exactly what had happened. The force surrounded the village and then entered it, encountering no resistance. Many people even stayed huddled in their homes as though the affair was none of their business. This unjustifiable nonchalance caused the policemen to fly off the handle. Thus they burst into the houses that did not even have the doors latched and forced all the men and women out onto the dirt road that ran through the village, amid the barking of the dogs that gathered in a circle around all the people. The policemen waved their rifles in the faces of the villagers, who calmly continued smoking. When they grew tired of standing, some of them squatted down on the ground. Finally the police chief drew his revolver and fired into the air, causing the dogs to retreat in alarm. "We have come to inform you that the government has decided to kill all of you after you kidnapped the five Englishmen. But I will overlook everything if you return them to us. You've already created enough problems for us."

Silence reigned for a time until an old man, who was clearly the village's headman, stepped forward. "May God preserve the King for us. I believe that the King would not order us killed. We are poor villagers and have nothing to do with the English, may God curse them. We are Muslims and follow the way of God and His Messenger."

The police chief, who was trying very hard to restrain his rage, replied, "I'm talking about the Englishmen you kidnapped last night. All I want is the truth. Show me where they are and I'll pardon you."

The headman shook his head apologetically, "This is a matter I'm hearing about for the first time. What need do we have of Englishmen that would lead us to kidnap them? Our village needs an imam to watch over it, not damned English infidels." The man stopped for a moment and looked the police chief in the eye. "Perhaps the revolutionaries did that. But the village has no tie to the matter. You must know the places where they are hiding." Then he waved his hand beyond the village. "They are there in the mountains. That's all we know."

No sooner had the headman stopped talking than the village's children began singing their beloved anthem, which they had learned at school:

> *Our King, our king,*
> *Our lives for yours.*
> *Live safe and long,*
> *Your vision strong.*

The police chief was forced to order his men to lower their rifles. Then he said, addressing the villagers, who continued to stare at him, "You can go now. It would be better for us to negotiate with the village's headman and elders than to listen to anthems."

He went with the headman and three other villagers to a hut that served as the village's coffeehouse. The policemen surrounded them, and the rest of the villagers followed, squatting on the ground to listen to the discussion. The police chief, however, ordered his men to shoo them away because he did not want anyone to know what might transpire in this meeting. Participating in it were the police lieutenant and two deputy lieutenants who commanded this force of more than fifty policemen.

The police chief knew that the only way to free the English prisoners was through a deal with the village men. He was certain that they would be able to assist him, but did not want to show all his cards at once. "I don't want your village to be harmed. What the rebels did last night was outrageous."

The headman asked, "I don't know why the young men do such stupid things. What's to be gained from acts like these?"

The police chief was forced to say, "Good, I'll assign you the task of getting the prisoners back before sunset. You're the village's headman and the person responsible in the state's eyes for everything that happens in your village."

The headman suddenly burst out laughing. "What are you saying, man? Is someone who opposes the government going to listen to what a poor headman like me says? Imagine that, Mr. Police Chief. Imagine that." The lieutenant intervened, "Headman, we know everything. We're not blind, contrary to what you think."

Then the police chief said, "What you say may be true, but you can assist us by contacting the rebels so an understanding can be reached with them to release the prisoners."

The headman gazed at him for a time before replying, "That might perhaps be possible. I'll do everything I can. What do you want to say to the rebels?"

Without beating around the bush, the police chief answered, "To send someone with whom we can negotiate so we can learn their terms."

The police chief could not abide the flies that kept stinging and droning in the hot air, so he stood up, saying, "I'll wait inside my car. The heat here is killing me." He left, heading for the Jeeps that were parked at the center of the village. His men surrounded him, brandishing their rifles once more, for no apparent reason.

The police chief had expected to meet some revolutionary before evening but waited for three days before achieving that. News of the police attack on the village of Tawuq reached Hameed Nylon that same day, but he saw no reason to hasten to respond to the police chief's request because he knew the police would be unable to do anything to harm the village. The police chief's only option would be to wait.

As a matter of fact, Hameed Nylon, who had never savored the taste of true love in his life, suddenly found himself a prisoner of the emotions unleashed in his body by Mrs. Helen McNeely, when she gave herself to him even before he asked. "What a fool I was, Hameed, to toss you out!" she said, adding, "I know you risked your life to get me. Tell me that you organized this revolution of yours for my sake." Hameed Nylon burst out laughing because this was the last thing that anyone could say about his revolution. He pounded her on the back jokingly and said, "When I'm with you I feel the revolution conquering my body. Where do you get all this fire?"

Helen McNeely stayed in the command post, which was Hameed Nylon's room, refusing to be reunited with her husband and the three other prisoners, who were detained in a cave at the foot of the mountain. From the moment she arrived at the base camp, which was located in a forest between two mountains, she had told Hameed Nylon in front of the others, "I want to be with you. I think you won't refuse the request of a lady like me." It seemed to her that she was in a deadly dream and she did not want to wake up. Hameed Nylon, however, realized that this enjoyment of his would be short-lived and that he would eventually need to release his prisoners.

The conditions that Hameed Nylon laid down were straightforward and allowed no room for confusion. He presented them in a list to the police chief, who in turn passed them on to the governor, who for his part dictated them over the telephone to the minister of the interior's special aide-de-camp. These conditions caused the cabinet officers, when they learned about them, to choke with laughter. The prime minister commented on Hameed Nylon's characterization of the government as one of occupiers and thieves by saying, "The man seems to know all about us." Hameed Nylon had requested the government's resignation, the formation of another government of patriots, and recognition of the People's Republic of China. During the negotiations that lasted three days, however, he settled for the conditions proposed by the government. These were to grant him the rank of a real lieutenant colonel in the army and to appoint his rebel villagers as guards for the villages surrounding the city of Kirkuk. Indeed, the government had gone so far as to offer to recognize the village of Tawuq's right to priority when visiting the mausoleum of Qara Qul.

The government's concessions caused the villagers to swagger proudly and fire into the air. Hameed Nylon considered this a first step on the journey of a thousand miles toward the state of his dreams. People from every nook and cranny marched toward the village of Tawuq, which celebrated this victory while waiting for the arrival of the captives and the army commanded by Lieutenant Colonel Anwar Mustafa. Hameed Nylon entered the village like an emperor of some other era, seated on a litter borne by the prisoners, who had insisted on that themselves in order to expiate the sins they had committed against the rights of the Iraqis, their false boasting, and their racist arrogance. Helen McNeely, for her part, danced before the litter, inspiring delirium in the men's hearts and arousing the curiosity of the women and children. Joy overwhelmed everyone, and the police chief himself got out of his vehicle and embraced Hameed Nylon with such fraternal affection that it brought tears to his eyes. Then these two men participated in a dabke line dance performed by men of the village of Tawuq in honor of the English captives, who were deeply touched as they departed in the special vehicles the English consulate in Kirkuk had sent to the village to transport them back to their homes. Helen McNeely clung to Hameed Nylon's neck, planting a hot kiss on his lips and whispering, "I'll return to you again." Hameed Nylon felt sad as he watched the motorcade slowly move off into the distance over the horizon, which fell away at the end of the plain that spread out like a colored carpet. All the same, he was joyful because this was the first victory he had scored since the revolution began.

Three weeks later, on a midsummer day, Hameed Nylon entered the city of Kirkuk in command of a force comprised of more than twenty of his village fighters, who were armed with rifles carried on their shoulders and daggers thrust into their belts. They were received as legendary heroes, and masses of humanity swarmed out of the narrow alleys and ancient neighborhoods, and even from goat-hair tents that nomadic Bedouins had erected at the edges of the city, to see the man whom the Kurds reckoned a Kurd, the Arabs an Arab, and the Turkmen a Turkmen, relying in this on indisputable historical data. The governor, the police chief, and the director of public security went out to welcome Hameed Nylon, who had allowed his beard to grow long and who was wearing a khaki field uniform and a red beret tilted to the left. Together they toured the city's streets, which were filled with people, amid flags and banners held by veiled young men. Then they took him to the Government Officials' Club, where a long banquet table had been set up in his honor in the open air. Hameed Nylon more than once went out to the street to greet the human throngs that had gathered in front of the club and that had begun to shout his name. When the crowd kept insisting on standing in front of the club for no apparent reason, he climbed atop the club's wall and made a brief speech in which he demonstrated his capacity for modesty and his flexibility in leading the revolution, which was still in its initial phase. Thus he announced that he was but an obedient servant of His Majesty King Faisal II, may God preserve him, and that he wanted nothing more than to elevate the name of Iraq among the civilized nations. The governor and the other important city figures standing near him at the gate of the club applauded these sagacious words that Hameed Nylon delivered to quiet the ardor of the people, who lingered on there for some time before bowing out and departing.

Hameed Nylon returned to the table, where he sat near the governor. The armed villagers who had accompanied him sat in a circle on the grass beneath some trees, surrounding plates filled with all the most delicious and appetizing dishes. The villagers, who consumed everything placed before them and then stretched out to rest in the grass, all suddenly felt acute indigestion and rushed, one after the other, toward the washrooms located on the far side of the garden. They were grasping their quaking bellies and paid no attention to the policemen who were lying in ambush for them behind the trees and who captured them silently, handcuffing them and shoving them inside trucks hidden behind curtains of oilcloth.

Hameed Nylon had himself received a letter from the prime minister inviting him to enter into negotiations with the government instead of resorting to combat. Even though Hameed Nylon placed absolutely no trust in the government or its promises, he did not believe that the offer constituted a deliberate conspiracy. A blanket pardon had been issued for the rebels, but other secret documents had reached the city's responsible officials, requesting them to arrest Hameed Nylon and his men, without making any fuss about it. The director of public safety himself had devised the plan, and the governor and police chief had approved it. They nearly choked because they laughed so hard when they heard about it. It would be necessary to relieve the rebels of their weapons before they were seized, for fear they would try to resist. The director of public safety could think

225

of no simpler way to achieve this objective than to mix into the food served to the armed villagers a large quantity of a powerful laxative that would make them writhe in pain.

Hameed Nylon did not notice that his men had disappeared until three plainclothes detectives approached from behind and put their revolvers to his head and back. Then one of them said rather politely, "The party's over. Come with us."

The governor pretended to be amazed: "Young men, what are you doing? That's not right. He's our guest."

One of the three replied calmly, "Orders from above, Your Excellency."

The police chief rubbed his hands together, saying, "Since you have orders from above, there's nothing any of us can do."

They withdrew Hameed Nylon's revolver from his belt and dragged him by his shirt collar to a gray Ford parked in front of a flowerbed. It shot off the moment Hameed Nylon was inside. The surprise had deprived him of the power to speak, but his mind was still alert. Crammed inside the car between two men who had their revolvers trained on him, he thought, "The dove should not have trusted the fox's promises." He was sad but not afraid because he knew that everything would end in some fashion and that it was his duty to be what he had always wanted to be.

That same evening, the government issued a statement saying that Hameed Nylon, who called himself Lieutenant Colonel Anwar Mustafa, had violated the rules of Arab hospitality by ordering the rebels with him to open fire on the government dignitaries entertaining him, so that three guards had been seriously wounded and taken to the hospital. The government claimed that divine intervention had shielded the dignitaries none of whom had been harmed, pointing out that the vigilant security men protecting the citizens' lives had been able to strip the rebels of their weapons and to capture these men, who would receive the punishment reserved for all who are ungrateful.

The lies the government published about Hameed Nylon did not deceive anyone in the city. People had discovered the truth even before the government issued its statement, which it broadcast time and again. Along the length of the Khasa Su River, which split the city in two, battles broke out between young men from the old quarter and Bedouin policemen, who had occupied the streets. The young athletes from Chuqor launched abortive attacks on the location of the barracks where Hameed Nylon and his followers were being held, leaving behind them three wounded men, who also disappeared into the locked building. Overnight, the village of Tawuq, together with other nearby villages, marched against the city from the east. The army was compelled to bar the advance of the attackers, who found tanks blockading the roads that led into the city. Once dawn came, airplanes made raids against the rebels and forced them to pull back. They also bombed the village of Tawuq and the woods where the revolutionaries were hiding, terrorizing the villagers, who fled to the ravines of the nearby mountains.

After three days of running battles, the government forces broke the back of the resistance, which continued to fight on without any objective. There were just a few isolated snipers who shot at policemen and security officers from the cover of the tall minarets scattered throughout the city. This forced the government forces to bombard them with cannons, which frequently missed their targets. Then neighboring houses were struck, reducing them to rubble and ashes. Some people rushed to the shrine of Qara Qul to seek his protection, while others wandered through the open countryside, fleeing from the soldiers and policemen, who broke into random houses and arrested everyone they encountered—after beating him with the butts of their rifles. Anyone who resisted them was slammed against the nearest wall and shot. Fear caused women to stand in front of their homes, holding up pictures of the king and cheering the government forces.

Everything was lost, but Burhan Abdallah had not lost hope because falsehood could not triumph over the truth, no matter how many weapons it possessed. He had spent three days and nights with the insurgents, whose cohesion was shattered. He did not want to return defeated and vanquished like the others, who would continue with their lives as if nothing had happened. He had suddenly grown up and felt that the resistance must continue. He closed his eyes to search for his three angels, the old men who were proceeding from eternity to eternity, but they had disappeared. He found only the expansive desert, deep footprints in the sand, and the cries of jackals—nothing else. He told himself, "They've vanished too. What sage advice could these old men provide me in a city flowing with blood?"

Evening had fallen over the city and he began to move from one alley to another, avoiding the black watchmen who were bristling with weapons—killers looking for victims. "Hope lies in freeing Hameed Nylon. That's the only thing that could free the city from fear." Everyone had been defeated, but Ta'us Malak and his little angels that knew everything could never be routed. Burhan Abdallah did not know whether his friends the angels would be able to intercede in a matter like this. All he wanted from them was to rescue Hameed Nylon, nothing more than that. In some sense they had been part of the revolution. Without them, he would not have discovered Zayn al-Abidin al-Qadiri's treasure, with which Hameed Nylon had financed his blood-stained revolution. He repeated to himself, "They're as responsible as I am. We're all complicit."

He gradually drew nearer to the house that was filled with secrets, passing through the Piryadi community to the alley that led to the Chuqor community. Then he turned left into the alley where, opposite the ruin, the house was located. He wiped his eyes with his hand, staring again into the gloom. "This can't all be true." He walked closer and stood looking for a long time. There was no trace to indicate that any house had been there. There was nothing but a void submerged in the gloom of the night, which was illuminated by pale starlight. Burhan Abdallah leaned against the wall and started weeping. "All this fantasy! All this truth!"

Eleven

More than two years passed after the disappearance of Hameed Nylon, who was banished to the Naqrat al-Salman Prison, which is a large fortress erected in the middle of the western desert, where it stands like a dreadful sign, planted in the sand and surrounded by camel's thorn and Indian figs. At night all a person hears is the yipping of jackals circling the walls, attracted there by the scent of human beings. Everything had ended. The insurgents whom the revolution had attracted fled farther into the mountains or took refuge with their tribes, which were beyond government control. The city's young men who had been captured during the battles had been released after a month or two of instructive beatings while confined in leg vises and after being made to cheer three times a day for the king's long life. Joy returned once more to the city, which obeyed the governor's call as men, women, and children came into the street to applaud the victory processions that bore aloft the Iraqi flag and pictures of the king in celebration of the city officials' deliverance from the conspiracy hatched by the insurgents and their defeat. The procession was led by flag bearers, who were followed by the desert police on camels, the mounted police on horseback, and the mountain police, who pulled mules behind them. Next came a procession of secret agents, who had covered their faces with masks. The people applauded at length for the statesmen, led by the governor, who was seated in the gold wheelchair that Mullah Zayn al-Abidin al-Qadiri had used to visit the coffeehouse. Right behind the statesmen's procession came the dervishes, each of whom carried in his right hand a broken bottle, which he was happily munching and crunching. Then came the delegations of athletes who performed entertaining Swedish calisthenics, metalsmiths who banged on their copper vessels, and gravediggers who carried on their shoulders a red bier labeled with white letters in decorative Thuluth script: "The Revolution."

The anarchy prevailing in the city had ended and there was even a diminution of the feverish visitation of Qara Qul Mansur's mausoleum, which the government had returned to his wife, who mismanaged its affairs. After some months it turned into just another saint's tomb like all the other forgotten ones in the wilderness of al-Musalla. In the city center, where the Second Army Division's fortress was located, summer cafés that stayed open until midnight appeared as well as winter coffeehouses that filled with billiard players waiting for their turn at the green tables. Shops selling lottery tickets proliferated under the auspices of the Red Crescent Society. There were two drawings—the weekly and the monthly. A sheet with the winning numbers was fastened to boards placed on the sidewalk, where passersby could read it. Tailors and seamstresses imported styles from Paris, London, Beirut, and Istanbul, and trousers with tapered legs became popular. Assyrian girls who came out for an afternoon stroll along Texas Street wore short skirts that rose above the knee. A man from al-A'zamiya in Baghdad opened a restaurant consisting of a single small room on al-Alamein Street. It resembled a dry-goods shop with its long, glass display case, which he used as a buffet. He began selling sandwiches, which were consumed by patrons, standing, with Pepsi-Cola or Coca-Cola. Kirkuk had never experienced anything like this before. Many kebab restaurants were forced to close their doors, after the young people hankering for modern life deserted them.

Khidir Musa had vanished from sight even before Hameed Nylon had left for the mountain from which he had directed his abortive revolution. People no longer saw him except by chance, when he was walking along the street alone, looking grave and lost in thought, or when he was out in the countryside for an evening stroll with his two friends Dada Hijri and Dervish Bahlul, who looked like ghosts divorced from any place or time. They always walked single file and gazed at the flocks of sand grouse arriving from. the west, or gathered bouquets of colorful wild roses and then sat on boulders and discussed the sunset. At night, they returned to the tower Khidir Musa had built atop the Sufi house to which he had once retreated, years before, and where he had heard the voices of his two captive brothers calling to him from Russia. This time too Khidir Musa had to contend with the outbursts of his wife Nazira and her mother the sorceress, who from time to time attacked the monastery over which the tower rose. They would start by cursing Dada Hijri and Dervish Bahlul, who—they would say—had enticed Khidir Musa to withdraw to this high tower, where they were unable to climb the stairs, because they were so obese. They stayed there below, cursing the three men in a loud voice, deliberately involving other people who usually counseled them to stop this ruckus. None of the three men would respond. They kept silent as though the matter did not concern them.

People believed that the former shepherd had come down with another bout of Sufi fever and withdrawn from life. This was a frequent occurrence with ageing men in Kirkuk. They were, however, mistaken this time because the tower that Khidir Musa had built over the monastery was actually the secret headquarters for a conspiracy that the army was organizing. No one could have detected that this was the case. Dervish Bahlul had proposed its construction after Khidir Musa confided to him what had been suggested by the Commander of the Second Brigade, Lieutenant Colonel Adnan al-Dabbagh, for whom he had felt a special affection since meeting him at the Officers' Club. When Khidir Musa had visited him subsequently at his office and then at his residence, all the inhibitions separating these two men had fallen away and the lieutenant colonel had begun to ask his advice on military matters. On the day Hameed

Nylon was arrested, an enraged Khidir Musa sought out the lieutenant colonel to ask his intervention to stop the killing of peaceful civilians. The lieutenant colonel, however, took his hand, sat him down beside him, and said, "Not now. The time hasn't come yet. We must wait a bit longer." Then, after hesitating, he added, "We need you. I hope you won't disappoint me."

Life returned suddenly to the face of Khidir Musa, who rose and embraced the lieutenant colonel. "I'll gladly sacrifice my trivial life for my country. Tell me what must be done. I can accomplish a lot."

Lieutenant Colonel Adnan Dabbagh smiled: "I am confident of that, Khidir."

There was not much for the three men to do in their tower, from which they flew a green Islamic flag, except to safeguard the secret documents containing the names of the officers participating in the conspiracy and the two plans: one operational plan and another for emergencies. There was also a short list of names of people who would need to be arrested the first day. Khidir Musa handed all these documents to Dervish Bahlul, who placed them on the shelf with the Preserved Book he consulted each day before leaving for his work, which was endless. The small printing press that Hameed Nylon had obtained from Baghdad during his visit to the king was placed in a corner of the tower. It had sat neglected at the entrance of the house until Dada Hijri saw it and asked for it so that he could print his many poetry collections, for which he could not find a publisher in Kirkuk. Thus the first manifestos that rocked the government and made it tremble were released from the tower and signed by the Free Officers. Dada Hijri himself carried these to a house in the citadel, where he left them. Lieutenant Colonel Adnan entrusted civilian leadership on the day of the revolution to Khidir Musa, who felt confident that the entire city would follow him when the zero hour arrived.

The night before the revolution, which took almost everyone by surprise, Dervish Bahlul descended from the tower, carrying in his right hand the bag that contained all his belongings. On the stairs, he met Khidir Musa, who was returning from his evening excursion, and told him joyfully, "Praise God you've returned in the nick of time."

In the half-light that enveloped the stairwell, Khidir Musa asked, "Why are you carrying a bag? I wouldn't think you would desert me on a day like this."

Dervish Bahlul placed his hand on Khidir Musa's shoulder affectionately and said, "No, I must leave you on a day like this. There is much work awaiting me in Baghdad tomorrow." Then, with a smile, he added, "You know I'll return in the end."

Khidir Musa realized that a lot of blood would flow the next day. All night long he thought about what might happen on the morrow.

That night, the soldiers descended on the city of Baghdad, where King Faisal II and the government officials lived. They slipped like thieves from their distant base and then occupied every corner of the city, even before anyone noticed that something had happened. At dawn, a detachment of soldiers stormed the king's palace, where he was snoring in his sleep. They stood in the reception chamber, waiting for the king to emerge, overwhelmed by anxiety. A few minutes later a door opened, and Dervish Bahlul peered out. He cast a silent glance at the soldiers, who aimed their rifles at his face, their fingers on the trigger. Then, as he disappeared down a hallway with red carpets, he told the officer in charge, "I'll go and wake the king."

Dervish Bahlul opened the door to the bedroom of the king, who was sleeping in his pajamas. Stepping forward, he placed a hand on the king's head, whispering, "The time has come. Here I visit you a second time, Your Majesty."

The king opened his eyes and shook with surprise. "What are you doing in my room?"

Dervish Bahlul answered regretfully, "Rise, Your Majesty. I've come to take you with me."

The king said thoughtfully, "Welcome, Dervish Bahlul. How did you reach me?"

Dervish Bahlul replied politely, "I'm Death, Your Majesty. I've come to lead you to your slayers, who await you in the reception hall."

The king said sadly, "So, the hour has arrived, Dervish Bahlul. Isn't that so?"

Dervish Bahlul replied somewhat emotionally "Yes, Your Majesty. It is the inescapable hour."

The king pulled a dressing gown over his pajamas and then went out, leaning on Dervish Bahlul's shoulder, hoping that this was all a dream from which he would eventually awaken.

That morning, which people remembered for many years, the soldiers opened fire on the king, who was twenty-one. He fell to his knees, mumbling. He gazed at Dervish Bahlul, who supported him on his shoulder to the stable, which was attached to the palace. In front of it, as always, stood the royal carriage, which was ornamented with gold. He placed the king, whose many wounds were bleeding, inside the carriage, where the seat's fabric became stained with blood. The king opened his eyes for a last time and said in a feeble voice, "Farewell, brief, beautiful life."

Dervish Bahlul smiled as he looked at a watch he took from his pocket, saying, "You still have another minute, Your Majesty."

The king extended his blood-stained hand to take Dervish Bahlul's, saying, "Be compassionate to me, Mr. Death," and squeezed his hand.

Dervish Bahlul waited briefly until the alarm on his watch rang. Then he took a ledger from his pocket and crossed off the king's name. Next he brought two stallions from the stable, hitched them to the carriage, in which he shot off through the open gate to the city, which was still slumbering, sunk in a stillness interrupted from time to time by rattles of gunfire.

Dervish Bahlul passed three days without savoring sleep for a single moment because the city had been seized by madness on hearing the statements that a lieutenant colonel, of whom no one had ever heard before, delivered by radio broadcast like bolts from the sky. These were interspersed by military marches that rattled inside the heads of people suddenly facing death. The people's dejection ended and they poured into the streets as if to a giant party that encompassed the whole world. They emerged from ash-gray alleys in al-Fadl, al-Shawaka, and al-A'zamiya, from Christian strongholds, from New Baghdad, al-Taji, and Madinat al-Sara'if—beating large drums and clay hand-drums, while government employees, who had left their agencies and descended to the streets, danced. Villagers, who had brought black flags from their many commemorations of the martyrdom of al-Husayn, danced the dabke in the middle of the streets and public squares and sang for the revolution, about which they actually knew nothing at all.

The city filled with monkeys, bears, lions, cheetahs, and tigers that their trainers brought from an Indian circus that was performing every evening at a venue outside the city. Nightclub dancers gave free recitals of Oriental dance for the exhausted soldiers. The excitement became so great that the dancers stripped off their costumes and engaged in sexual acts on the scorching grass amid the screams of the people who rushed to see these thrilling scenes. Some women spectators, however, turned their eyes away in embarrassment. Others observed, "Finally we've been liberated." Zeal got the better of people, who became so agitated that they attacked anyone they considered an enemy. They stormed the magnificent palaces and killed the inhabitants with blows from sticks and feet, plundering everything they could carry. A human wave poured forth and flooded the Rihab and al-Zuhur palaces, which filled with corpses that they bound with ropes and began to drag—naked—through the streets. They hanged them on light poles at the Eastern Gate, crying out, "There'll be no conspiracy as long as there are ropes." Three days later only the bones were left. A butcher climbed up and severed Crown Prince Abdul'ilah's penis, which was dangling between his thighs, and shoved it up his asshole as the crowd applauded and roared with laughter. Other men carrying axes climbed up and began to hack off the corpses' hands and feet, throwing these down to the villagers, who fought for a piece of them.

On the third day, Dervish Bahlul returned to the city of Kirkuk, where everything had changed. It almost seemed that the world was engaged in a perpetual feast or festival that carried on night and day. Khidir Musa had donned a military uniform, placing a red badge over his wrist, after being appointed commander of the popular defense forces of the republic. He moved between the many coffeehouses that the volunteers, who were armed with sticks, knives, and ropes, had made their headquarters, asking them to keep their eyes wide open because the English might attack again from the Habaniya or Shu'ayba camps, where their forces were stationed—as had happened seventeen years before. The city of Kirkuk did not actually witness the kind of bloodbaths that Baghdad did, even though people went out into the streets once they heard the news that the republic had been proclaimed. They only attacked the American Cultural Center, which cultured people and greengrocers looted of most of its books. The intellectuals had known the value of these books for some time, and the grocers found them to be an inexhaustible source of paper, which they needed to make packets for the tea and spices they sold.

The Communists emerged from their many cellars, lifting high their banners, which dazzled people with slogans that many did not comprehend. The sight of the red flags with the hammer and sickle left people with the lasting impression that the Communists had directed the revolution. Thus many people began to boast to each other that they had always been Communists. This claim upset many others, who believed that they had been responsible for the revolution. So the city split into the Communists, who generally sat in coffeehouses playing chess or reading the newspaper *al-Nur*—which Khalid Bakdash published in Damascus and which was sold as if it were a rare commodity at the al-Jabha coffeehouse in Kirkuk—and the Turanian Turkmen, whose watchword was Iraqi-Turkish unification, versus the Baathists and the Arab nationalists, who went into the street to demand an immediate Arab union.

This upset the Kurdish nationalists and prompted them to advocate the creation of a state of Greater Kurdistan. The Armenians from the Tashnag Party held up a placard demanding punishment for the killer Turks and the incorporation of Armenia into Turkey. The Assyrian Christians, to whom the English had promised their own state in northern Iraq, began to sing gleefully in the streets, "Telkeef won its independence; Muhammad's religion is nonsense." This state of affairs scared the Afterlife Society's members, who placed all the blame on the Communists, attacked their coffeehouses, and set fire to their placards, on which they had written, "No more dowry after this month; throw the qadi in the river." The Afterlife Society distributed to young Turkmen golden medals to place on their chests. These displayed black cats with their fangs bared to eat the white doves of peace on the medals that the Communists usually affixed to their chests or hung from their necks.

In the first months following the revolution, when emotions escaped reason's grasp, the Communists ruled most of Kirkuk's working-class neighborhoods, which they declared to be autonomous democratic people's republics, and many security agents and policemen joined their ranks. These men would frequently parade through the city streets in orderly processions, chanting loudly, "Ask the police: What do you want? A free nation and a happy people." Zeal motivated security agents from time to time to arrest bystanders who did not applaud, charging them with conspiring against the republic. They would beat these people until they finally confessed to conspiracies they had been hatching in secret against the foremost lieutenant colonel, who was opposed by another lieutenant colonel who himself wanted to be the foremost lieutenant colonel. Then he was arrested and beaten until he tearfully agreed to accept an appointment as ambassador to Bonn. That made singers mock him, gloating in a popular song that was broadcast three times a day, "He's going to be ambassador to Bonn. He's weeping for the offense."

The man, however, would not leave the Bonn-Cologne Airport where his plane landed. He would reboard the same plane that had transported him and be arrested again because his wife, who had a saucy tongue and who was feared by the women of his community, had stormed into the Ministry of Defense, where she had begun to curse the foremost lieutenant colonel and his mother, who used to borrow money from her and then not repay it.

The foremost lieutenant colonel delivered the other lieutenant colonel to a loud-voiced military judge who spoke exclusively in verse. He confronted the defendant standing in the cage: "What do you say, you dusty cur? / Have you come to weep or to purr?"

The public prosecutor, however, intervened to save the session from an ode that might have lasted for hours or even days because each verse would normally be followed by a poem by one of the popular poets, who came in droves to the court, and would be accompanied by the public's applause, the women's trilling, and the reverberating chants of the peasants. The prosecutor announced that the foremost traitor, who was standing before the seat of justice, was too insignificant to defend his many crimes against the people's rights and that his tears were merely those of a crocodile living in brackish waters. He proposed executing him in Tahrir Square so he could serve as a lesson to future traitors.

The people were enchanted by these festivities, which became their sole entertainment. Each community established its own special people's court, which was convened at any hour of the night or day. This madness spread to the Chuqor community too, and so Hadi Ahmad, the young man who had been blinded in his left eye during the Battle of Gawirbaghi some years before, was named head of the people's court that had yet to find anyone to try, although many conspiracies had been discovered in other locations. People were astonished to see Hadi Ahmad, who never let the machine gun leave his shoulder, lead his aged father and two neighbors to the open space in al-Musalla and force them to dig their graves with mattocks prior to their execution on charges of mocking the revolution. The three men were rescued only when the women of the Chuqor neighborhood caught Hadi Ahmad off-guard and attacked him, biting his hands and shoulders until he dropped the machine gun and fled, cursing and threatening to get them back.

The revolution had really enchanted people. They changed and did things no one would have expected. Many began to sleep by day and stay up nights. The young men grew long beards, and senior citizens tinted their hair with henna. Virgin mothers gave birth to many babies who spoke and astonished people with their wise sayings at the moment of their arrival in this world. Children of some ethnic groups grew extra teeth. This phenomenon excited the interest of physicians, who drafted comprehensive studies about the event, which was not unprecedented.

With the new freedom, which took people by surprise, the wardens of the prisons were forced to open their locked gates. Former prisoners quit the jails and returned to their cities, which welcomed them like legendary heroes whose exile had ended. Hameed Nylon and his men, who entered Kirkuk carrying red flags, stood in a central city square where people had gathered and presented vivid displays of the torture they had endured in the prisons and concentration camps where they had resided. Hameed Nylon removed his blue and white striped shirt, revealing his hairy chest and scarred back, where whips and burning cigarettes had left their marks on his flesh. The other men who had been with him in prison staged realistic, dramatic demonstrations of the forms of torture common in Iraq. Some interrogators came out of the truck where they were being detained and stood before their trembling victims, who were forced to endure the experience one final time. Some young women in the crowd of spectators volunteered to join the victims, many of whom had their hands bound with ropes. The interrogators beat them with switches made from a skein of wire, paying no attention to the spurting blood that stained their hands. Although they felt embarrassed, the victims found themselves screaming and pleading with the interrogators to stop beating them, but to no avail because the interrogators had regained their former spirit, which had never really deserted them.

This spectacle, which was presented in the open air, was thrilling and entertaining and the crowd demanded to see everything. Thus the interrogators were forced to bring out their leg vises and to beat their victims on the soles of their feet. Then there were the bottles that they rammed up their victims' anuses, and the nail-pulling pincers. They even brought out ceiling fans, which they hooked up to the light poles. They tied their victims' hands behind their backs and, lifting them off the ground, fastened them to the fans, which they ran at full speed until the victims' shoulders were dislocated. The interrogators beat them with batons while they turned, striking them at random and chortling with laughter. The clothes of the women volunteers were torn to shreds and they were raped in front of all those present, and yet they did not utter a single word about their secret cells. Then the interrogators forced those who had collapsed because they were incapable of enduring the torture to stand in a line and howl: once like stray dogs on a moonlit night and again like hungry wolves or jackals that grew excited on nearing the edges of villages.

This demonstration of human frailty caused the crowd, which was smitten with the heroism that had propelled the revolution, to lose their nerve and attack the devastated traitors, whom they beat until the victims' howls mingled with their own curses, which arose from every direction: "We'll cut off the hands of any traitor who betrays his people." Only Hameed Nylon's eloquent intervention, amplified by a megaphone, saved the situation. He thanked the people for their zeal and pointed out that their anger ought to be directed against the interrogators, not the victims, who had sacrificed everything they had of value for the sake of the nation's freedom.

The moment the interrogators heard these provocative words, they took to their heels. People with sparks flying from their eyes caught up with them and killed them with blows from sticks and feet, then they stripped them of their clothes, fastened ropes to their feet, and dragged them from one street to the next. Children pursued them, singing and cheering, in imitation of the grown-ups. Some men who were fastened to vehicles that dragged them regained consciousness and began kicking, trying to escape from the ropes. Three or four of them succeeded in freeing their legs, rose, and ran off naked through the streets, exciting the laughter of the crowd, which stopped pursuing them. Others were hanged from trees or fastened to electric and telephone poles.

The city of Kirkuk, for its part, had become addicted to death like other cities, in keeping with the desires of the lieutenant colonel, whose thoughts changed from time to time. He was influenced by a spring of light that flowed from his spirit like inspiration falling on him from the heavens and that took the form of stern directives provided to the security agencies, which ran death squads of every type and variety. When it seemed that the lieutenant colonel was turning Communist, the squads began to patrol the cities, delivering anyone whose chest was not decorated with a hammer and sickle to butchers who hanged them by their feet with meat hooks beside the carcasses of their lambs. When the lieutenant colonel turned against the Communists, as frequently happened, the other factions attacked them and took them prisoner, forcing their own mothers and fathers to slay them with knives and bayonets. Many, however, were burned alive at civic parties, where women handed around chocolates, candy, and bonbons to the crowd, which always cheered the prevailing tendency.

After some months, the lieutenant colonel, who had filled the city with his portraits and statues, changed course again and issued a number of papers, each of which attacked one of the factions, saying that the lieutenant colonel himself stood above all of them. Laws were issued that forbade anything that was not linked to the name of the lieutenant colonel, who had dedicated his entire life to the people's benefit. These laws forced popular singers to insert his name into songs of love and romance. They would flirt with their beloved, who refused to sleep with a man who did not love the foremost lieutenant colonel. Women would experience painless childbirth if the midwife recited to them the lieutenant colonel's teachings and sage maxims, published in countless tomes and distributed to school children, government employees, and labor unions, and popularized in the poetry collections of the poet Abd al-Ta'ib Abd al-Gha'ib, who in his odes pioneered the notion that the lieutenant colonel was seated on the cusp of eternity with his legs spreading over history.

To tell the truth, all the factions were stricken by something close to languor in their charred spirits. When members of the Afterlife Society attacked the Communists, they shouted first of all, "Long live the lieutenant colonel, the foremost Muslim, the victor over Communism and internationalism!" The Communists replied to them with the slogan "Long live the foremost lieutenant colonel, the victor over reactionaryism!" When the Baathists differed with the Nationalists, they yelled loudly, "Long live the foremost lieutenant colonel, the founder of the Arab Socialist Baath Party!" to drown out the cries of "Long live the foremost lieutenant colonel, leader of Arab Unification and liberator of Palestine!" The Kurds usually intimidated the Turkmen with the slogan "Long live our brother the foremost lieutenant colonel, unifier of Kurdistan!" They responded with the slogan "Long live the foremost brother lieutenant colonel, liberator of the Turks from the rabble!" The conflict was not limited to this war of slogans, which hid behind the lieutenant colonel's name. People began to kill each other in plain daylight with bullets, daggers, and axes and to set fire to their foes' homes during the night. Fire would devour them and frequently spread to neighboring houses too, reducing them to ashes.

Khidir Musa, whose heart was distressed by the devastation that had settled over his city, seemed to be a lost soul. Everything had escaped from his control, and he could no longer find anyone who would listen to him. The world fell apart before his eyes in one fell blow when security agents on one occasion led his two aged brothers to the station and beat them, accusing them of promoting atheism in the Chuqor community. He was obliged to seek out Lieutenant Colonel Adnan al-Dabbagh, who intervened to get them released. He advised Khidir to send them back to Tashkent, where they had once lived. They preferred, however, to seek out the holy city of Mecca, where they appropriated for themselves a corner of the courtyard of the Ka'ba, which shelters all those who seek its protection. Once Khidir Musa had been deserted by the last hope in his heart, he withdrew again to his tower above the monastery, after first changing out of his military uniform, which he returned to Lieutenant Colonel Adnan al-Dabbagh. He cut his ties with the secular world and dedicated the remainder of his life to the remembrance of God, in the company of his two friends Dada Hijri and Dervish Bahlul, who joined him, seeking to distance themselves from the evil rampant in all parts of the city.

The three men no longer ever left their tower. Everything seemed repetitive and monotonous. Death followed death, and insanity succeeded insanity. The city lost its innocence and became filled with scoundrels and killers. The three men refused to receive anyone other than Hameed Nylon and Burhan Abdallah, who brought them food and cigarettes every day. Eventually it seemed people had totally forgotten these men, whom no one thought of anymore. Dervish Bahlul scaled back his work. He was content to keep his watch with the alarm beside him so he would remember to cross off this name or that from the Preserved Tablet, which he placed beneath his pillow. Dervish Bahlul was not being deliberately neglectful, but people no longer paid attention to death. They began to die so nonchalantly that it seemed they had lost any sense of life's significance. They handed themselves over to death without ever growing weary of it, and even composed songs they chanted in the streets, like, "The people die, the lieutenant colonel lives," and, "Execution, execution, the people so will it, execution, execution." The lieutenant colonel, who had some peculiar characteristics, replaced the nightingale that warbled before the radio programs commenced with the Metro-Goldwyn-Mayer lion, which roars at the beginning of each of the studio's films, to frighten his enemies. Along with death, superstitions the lieutenant colonel's astrologers popularized spread like fire through chaff. Thus many villagers who lived in reed-mat huts purchased a spyglass that they directed at the moon every night so they could see the lieutenant colonel, who was said to look down from there, granting light and affection to the world.

People had changed so much that it was difficult to get to know them. Each of them had stumbled upon some new cause that shaped his life until he no longer remembered the past from which he had developed. Everything seemed new. It was like a virgin land that dazzled newcomers enter, trailing guides who know everything—past, present, and future. It became a popular custom to worship idols, which the new priests often colored with henna and placed on benches in the corners of streets and alleyways and in front of coffeehouses and bars, as if they were signs warning of the advent of a time when earth and sky would unite.

Hameed Nylon broke with his village fighters, whom he left to their new destiny. Others pursued them and made them join peasant collectives that raided and plundered cities from time to time, with or without a pretext. Prison had left many scars on Hameed Nylon's spirit. He had gone out like an ember under the influence of time or his defeat, but no one else noticed. Many believed that he had increased in wisdom and maturity. For his part, though, the world seemed like a play performed by comic actors of every type. He would tell himself, "Now that they've all become revolutionaries, what role is left for you, Hameed Nylon?" He began to sit every evening in the Oil Workers' Union Club drinking arak, sunk in his memories. They had proposed to appoint him head of the Oil Workers' Union, which was no longer a covert organization, but he declined that. He was chosen its honorary president, even without anyone asking him. His visits to the tower where Khidir Musa, Dervish Bahlul, and Dada Hijri lived multiplied. He was gripped by the discussions that these men conducted. Each time he left the tower he would burst into tears, filled with emotions of uncertain origin—like a man awakened by distant cries.

The revolution had changed Hameed Nylon, as it had changed many others, so that friends became enemies and even traitors. A man would pass another and raise his hand in greeting, "Good day," and then draw his revolver and shoot him. The police did not ask for witnesses. They would always arrest the person closest to the dead man, accusing him of the murder, while the perpetrators stood watching. Things came to a devastating end when a man shot Dalli Ihsan, whom everyone knew to be some other type of being—not human. The moment the three bullets pierced the body of Dalli Ihsan, it was transformed into an awe-inspiring fountain of fire that ascended toward the heavens, emitting thunder and lightning. The earth shook and quaked so that people fell down on top of each other. The fire spread to markets and homes, which were reduced to ashes. From the fire descended Dalli Ihsan's kinsfolk: angels of death mounted on horses and motorcycles, raining destruction on the cities, one after the other. This attack, which no one had expected, lasted three days. Then another conspiratorial armed force spread its control over the capital, which planes from the Air Force had attacked after taking off from the base at al-Habaniya. The foremost lieutenant colonel was arrested and executed by firing squad. His corpse was thrown in the Tigris River.

Although the tribe that had descended from the fire withdrew, satisfied with the destruction they had brought to Kirkuk and the other cities, the new lieutenant colonel delivered a speech—broadcast by radio and television in both Arabic and Kurdish—in which he cursed those who, from ignorance, had supported the foremost lieutenant colonel, who ranked twenty-seventh in the secret faction of Satan. He announced that he himself was the foremost commander and derived his legal authority from his spirit, which soared over the mountains, rivers, and deserts. It had traversed the generations, extracting the essence of the revolution. He added modestly, however, "Even so, I'm a human being like you, even if my ancestors were angels." He called on the people to go out into the streets to delight in the return of the man whom mankind had so long awaited.

The terrified people, who had witnessed the devastation visited upon them by the angels of fire, sought refuge in their houses and barred the doors behind them. The soldiers, however, donned their helmets and began to break down the doors with their boots and their rifles, storming into houses. They led out the young men, lined them up against the walls of their homes, and shot them. Gallows were erected at the entries of alleys and streets, and hanged men dangled from them. In the prisons and concentration camps, bands of national guardsmen arrived from every place and every era and hosted memorial services that surpassed anything anyone had previously imagined. Each day they led out three or four prisoners whom they slaughtered and then fed to the others. Even so, they frequently organized musical soirées at which they raped the youngest prisoners in front of their comrades, who were obliged to applaud and sing.

People were forced to flee to the mountains' gullies and ravines, hiding from death, which stalked them from place to place. Hameed Nylon returned to his combatants once again to lead the revolution in which he no longer believed. The few Communists left alive sought refuge in new, even more secret cellars, after lengthy confessions had jeopardized the old ones. The soldiers surrounded the tower where the three old men were living, blocked its door and windows with cement, and turned it into a tomb.

Just as many others had disappeared, so did Burhan Abdallah. Many believed that he might have been slain and his corpse buried hastily somewhere inside some mass burial site. He disappeared so unobtrusively that he might never have existed. Many years passed without his giving any sign of life. Rumors spread that soldiers had killed him when he lobbed a Molotov cocktail at them in the Piryadi community. Others claimed that he had been killed during attacks he launched, with others, against the Ministry of Defense in Baghdad. Someone else announced that an airplane had opened fire on him, striking him, as he attempted to cross the border to Turkey. Although his mother heard all these tales, she categorically refused to believe them. She kept saying, "I'm more confident of what my heart says than of what people say. I know that my son is alive. He has simply disappeared. He will return one day." Even so, Burhan Abdallah remained absent for so long that the memory of him faded from the Chuqor community, which withdrew into itself in response to the succession of invaders that stormed it from time to time, leaving festering wounds in its smothered heart.

Twelve

Suddenly everything calmed down. An unusual yellow suffused the heavens. Was it the end or the beginning? Burhan Abdallah returned once more to his native city, which—after he had buried himself in diverse cities and continents, experiencing lethal depression and exuberant vitality—seemed no more than memories cast into time. He had become an old man who supported himself with a cane, and—after forty-six years spent traveling from one place to another, from airport to airport, from a city lost in fog to a city where the sun sparkled over its temples—he wore a gray hat to cover his baldness. Had it really been forty-six years? He felt he had left his city only the day before. He had not matured, because the only time he possessed was that of his memories. Even so, he had endured millions, even billions of centuries. He had endured all of eternity, which had left its traces on his scrawny body but had not touched his spirit, which continued to be subject to whatever lay behind the essence of things. His teeth had taken turns falling out and his head retained only a little of its hair, which hung off the sides. His hands were wrinkled, and their veins showed clearly. Through the prescription eyeglasses he wore, he saw nonexistence and what preceded it: the first dark atom that exploded and filled existence with galaxies and suns. "My God, I was there too."

He found it odd that he—a descendant of light and darkness—should be shackled with hands, feet, a trunk, a head, two eyes, two ears, and a nose. He thought, "What kind of game is this: that I should be everything and also nothing?" The matter seemed to him totally risible but also serious enough to be a curse. Lifting a hand he took off his glasses, which he wiped with a cloth the optician on Schönhauser Allee had given him. "This hand, which moved by itself even without an engine to regulate its powers and which looked almost like a fish, was—in some sense—a fish." It occurred to him that he had perhaps read that somewhere . . . in a poster on a wall, in a detective novel. It did not matter where all that had happened. What happens, happens as a matter of habit. Human beings are always like that. Ideas always exist. To have ideas, all a person needs to do is to look. And he was looking.

In his long years of exile he had learned the humor of vision, or what he called "the self-contradictory nature of meaning," seeing all of life as a drop of condensation on his spread fingers, which had knobs like the fingers of a robot in an exhibition. It is, however, a life heading toward death. Over the course of generations, people have been born and then died. In a hundred years at the most, no one we now know will be left alive. "There will be others whom we will never know at all: workers, prostitutes, writers, painters, commanders, rulers, and soldiers, but what interest are they to me, when I no longer exist? None at all, although I might linger on as a memory or a secret gesture in this comical celebration called life."

Burhan Abdallah's heart had been numbed, although he had survived because he never ceased for a moment to hope for a return to his city, which he had fled. For forty-six years he had sat, day after day, in a room in a remote city, listening to news bulletins, thinking he might hear something about his city. There were many things to make him anxious, for over the expanse of these years many upheavals had occurred in succession. One dictator had followed another. Finally, human beings had disappeared from the cities and streets after the dead emerged from their hiding places to occupy everything.

For forty-six years, wars had flared between them or against the others. The ancient dead hated the more recently deceased. The nineteenth-century dead hated the eighteenth-century dead. A new order developed and pushed many of them to resort to violence. The dead who considered themselves civilized refused to associate with the dead of the first human epochs, even those from the stone and bronze ages, on the grounds that their skeletons more closely resembled apes' than humans'. Indeed, there were some who did consider them apes and unrelated to human beings. On account of this struggle, which led to many crimes, the dead from the two factions attacked each other with jerry cans of kerosene or gasoline, which they lit. This was the only way to kill the dead.

The dead originated sects that advocated the absolute equality of all the dead because the deceased possessed no distinctive characteristic save that of being deceased. This in and of itself should suffice to guarantee the solidarity of the dead and their brotherhood. Actually, these dead people displayed some wisdom too by allowing the continued existence of many of the living, so that they would not cut off the stream that provided them with renewed powers every day. Unfortunately for the dead, they could not procreate. For that reason, they were forced to depend upon the living, who bred, gave birth, matured, and then died, thus joining mankind's greatest army: the eternal dead.

All the same, Burhan Abdallah never abandoned his hope that he would one day return to his city to meet the last of the living, who had never lost their appetite for life. He was not afraid of death but of becoming one of the dead. For this reason, he directed that his body should be cremated and the ashes scattered in the Tigris River. He also realized, however, that a man does not die until he loses hope in life. He had not lost this hope and was incapable of losing it. He would awake each morning in exile, where he had spent forty-six years, and gaze out the window of his room at the white snow piled in the streets and on buildings' roofs. Everything was pure and white, affording a glittering light. Black crows would soar here and there, rising high into the air, and then descending to peck at the snow in search of a non-existent morsel of bread or grain of wheat. He paid attention to each morning and evening throughout the forty-six years, as he moved from city to city, from street to street, and from coffeehouse to coffeehouse. He saw all the cities of the world.

In South Africa he fought for Zulu rights. In Zanzibar he lived for years on spices. In Yemen he joined a Sufi dhikr circle in the Great Mosque in San'a. He became a guide for explorers crossing the Empty Quarter by camel. He worked as a chef on a German steamship. He transported tea from Ceylon. He led the student revolution in Paris, even without anyone calling attention to him by name. In London he worked as an escort for rich people from the Gulf Region, accompanying them from the hospitals to the dancehalls of Soho. Then he was a secretary for an astrological scholar, who read horoscopes, conducted spiritual séances over the telephone, and investigated the supernatural. In Mecca he organized an international gang of pickpockets to prey on pilgrims. Then he fled with a forged Saudi passport to New York, where he resided for a year or part of a year in one of the tunnels of the Statue of Liberty. At his wits' end, he returned once more to Europe, where he chose to work as a translator paid by the word for an establishment that owned a building almost next to the Berlin Wall.

Each time he moved, he lost his books and furniture. He would leave them and never return. All the same he never relinquished his transistor radio, which he carried with him. It was a black, German-made, Siemens radio with eight shortwave bands. Day after day he would sit searching for broadcasts with news that would restore life to his snuffed-out heart. In his homeland, each war was followed by another. Wars overlapped occasionally so that it was difficult for a person to distinguish between one war and another. There were wars between the dead and wars between the living, wars in the mountains and wars in the cities, wars in the marshes and wars in the deserts.

During these conflicts, each new commander seized the one before him and slew him, feeding his flesh to his courtiers, who ate even the crotch, oblivious to the difficulty they had digesting this. From time to time, festivals were held to immortalize the accomplishments of the new ruler. Each had his own idiom, which differed from the others'. Thus it became customary to compose books about the genius that this ruler or that displayed in his use of language. Each had his special habits. One would eat boiled lettuce and another would sprinkle sugar on his food. One's taste was so depraved that he smoked a cigar while sleeping, and this became the people's compulsion too. They were all demigods. This was more or less understood until someone came along who disdained these pagan practices and proclaimed that there was no god but God. Naturally he was God.

Burhan Abdallah went almost every day to the coffeehouse, where he had a cup of coffee and smoked, waiting for someone who might chance to come and bring him some news from his distant city. He occasionally met another exile like himself and listened to his words, which he knew by heart. Even words lost their meaning with time. When he spoke, he addressed only himself, as he always had done. He existed in his past. His memories weighed him down, but he did not want to become a narrator of his memories, like some old man who is the laughingstock of his community. At times he would ask, "Is there any new information about our homeland?" The other person would reply a bit anxiously, "You must have heard the news. They've resorted once again to striking each other with atomic bombs. This is the second bomb to explode in a week." He would say, "Yes, I heard that. Basra was hit, isn't that so?" He was not very interested in learning the answer because he knew that death was everywhere in his distant country. Years ago, they used to strike each other with chemical weapons, but now they had changed over to atomic bombs. He would ask himself, "Is there any difference between a man dying of a bullet, cannon fire, a chemical rocket, or an atomic bomb?" He would repeat to himself a fragment of poetry: "The causes have multiplied, but death remains one."

Emotion frequently overpowered him and brought him to the verge of tears, but he would turn his face and flirt with the German waitress Cornelia, "Connie, would you bring your lover another cup of coffee?" She would reprimand him, "You know I only like young men, you fugitive from the cemetery." Was he dead too without knowing it? Not at all. Never. He would tell her, "If you allow me to visit you once,

I will compress a whole lifetime into a single night." She answered pensively, "I might do that some day. You really tempt me."

But all that was finished now, like a curse whose magic was exhausted. He awoke one morning to hear the stunning news that he received so coolly it might as well not have been true. For a long time he had lost the ability to feel delight because he had waited so long, like a man no longer interested even in losses. For the first time, however, he felt that he had liberated himself from a nightmare that had consumed his entire life. He listened once again to the broadcasts that carried news and lengthy reports about the dead, who had finally surrendered to the living, who had built crematories for the dead— who were no longer able to die—in every community and city. They stood in long lines in front of the crematories and leapt into the blazing fire. Life had finally triumphed over death. During a single week, every trace of the deceased was eliminated from his country.

In his coffeehouse, located in the Alexanderplatz square in Berlin, for the first time in forty-six years, he saw his angels, the three old men coming from eternity, carrying spring inside hemp sacks on their shoulders. This time they were traveling across the rolling steppes that stretched to the outlying communities of Kirkuk. They smiled at him affectionately and scolded him, "You shouldn't have deserted us for all this time."

Burhan opened his mouth with difficulty, "I didn't think there was a spring in store for Kirkuk. It seemed to me that all you were just a fantasy I had created for myself."

The three men responded, "You shouldn't have done that, Burhan. Don't you see that we've finally drawn near to the Chuqor community? We want you to be our guide when we arrive."

He heard Cornelia say as she placed another cup of coffee in front of him, "It seems you didn't sleep very well last night."

He opened his eyes once more, "It's true; that's always the way it is."

Through the glass façade of the coffeehouse, he cast a look at the street, where people were descending to the subway tunnels, which traversed the city, and climbing out of them. "I wonder where they're going." It did not matter to him whether he discovered the answer to his question. He said, "They're coming from everywhere and going everywhere. As for me, should I follow my three angels, who have never reached Kirkuk?"

Now he was on his way to Kirkuk in the front seat of a taxi. When they were within walking distance of the city, he stopped the vehicle and got out. He was afraid of the surprise and felt self-conscious. He thought he was returning to his roots again, but saw the city stretching into the distance before him in the sunset, spread out like a legendary bird. He climbed a nearby hill and sat down on its red dirt, from which grass sprouted. He filled his chest with this ancient scent that he had smelled throughout his childhood. He was choked up with sorrow over his long absence: "Burhan, why was it necessary for you to leave for all these years? No one banished you, but you were afraid of death and fled, abandoning your pearls to the dogs. But that's all over now. The life that you squandered in the world's hermetic cities has ended. Everything has ended. Here you return, carrying your old age in your heart to a city that knew you only as a child." He was not even able to weep.

In the gloom that descended over the distant city, Burhan Abdallah left the hill, heading toward the minarets as their crescents glowed in the red sky. His steps were heavy, but his eyes remained fixed on the distant, blazing fire. He waded through a grassy creek and crossed through two orchards he had not seen before. Step by step, he listened to the wind as it rustled through the leaves of the trees. It was a city that had piled up on itself, an unknown conglomeration that breathed with life, sounding almost like a storm heard from the bottom of a well. So this was his ancient city. Invaders had passed through it, leaving their mark on the stones of its houses. Do you suppose it had died and ended, like everything else? His steps took him through darkness unlike any he had ever seen before. This darkness united with the sky, which was almost blue but smudged with red clouds. It descended upon the earth as if it were a transparent crystal.

For forty-six years he had never written a letter to anyone in his city or received one. He had wanted to be as absent as anything else, hidden, leaving no trace behind him. He was almost certain that everyone who knew him had died. Who could defy death for forty-six years? Who could freeze time? He cut his way through the night with his cane, the way Moses cleft the sea with his staff. For the first time he noticed the barking of dogs coming from the heart of the black conglomeration. He listened to the saddening silence, one he recognized from sleeping outdoors on the roof of his family's house in the Chuqor community. "There's no one left in my city. So what will I do in the streets and houses?" He thought he would retrace his steps. "I shouldn't have returned and dredged up all this pain." Then he composed himself: "All there is to the matter is that I listened to my destiny forty-six years ago and here I am listening to it again." He realized that there was nothing more that he could lose, after losing his entire life. His body began to shake and tremble as he kicked at the gloom with his two heavy feet. "No one's waiting for you there. Only your memories. No one will even know your name." He felt dizzy, sat down on the ground, and burst into tears, filled with a happiness that flowed from giving vent to sorrow.

He sat there, staring at the arc of fog and smoke, wrapped up in himself, until he felt fatigue close his eyelids. So he fell asleep, resting his head on his small carry-on bag, into which he had stuffed a shirt or two, pajamas, a toothbrush, shaving supplies, and a diary. He awoke to find the dawn's cold stinging him. That was more like a dream he had seen somewhere else, but could not remember. He felt he was experiencing this for the second time. In a certain sense, he knew what was awaiting him. Was he truly here? Had he also returned before now to this city that lay in the distance? Had he walked along this very road? Had he entered it like a thief in the night? That did not make sense, but he knew he had been here. He felt a lump in his throat. He tasted a bitterness on his tongue each time. So it was spring then. Early-rising sparrows were soaring from one place to another, chirping with the first rays of sunshine. "My God, it's the spring I've dreamt of for so long and which I've never found anywhere else in the world."

He pulled a cigarette out of the pack he had placed in his pocket. He lit it and inhaled the smoke until he felt it touch the pit of his lungs before he exhaled again. He sensed a slight buzz in his body. The doctor had advised him, "At least don't smoke until you've eaten breakfast." But of what importance was that now? A man would die some day, whether he smoked or not. It was all the same to him whether he lived a hundred years more or died in only a hundred days. Here spring, which the three old men had brought after they had called to him for so long and spoken to him, was bursting forth again over his city. They certainly must have arrived now. They must have opened their sacks and let spring spill forth. He felt he had gained control of his city once more. The ending merged with the beginning in a way that made separating them difficult, just as day fades into night.

He stood in front of a garden encircled by a fence coated with green paint, which was still wet. He smelled its scent and sat on a stone bench plopped among the trees to gather his strength. Then he saw two men walking in the street, each in a different direction. Their footsteps were almost in cadence. It truly was spring. Scents that mingled with each other roused him: the fragrances of familiar dew and of the still, cold air. There was nothing real about what he saw. Everything seemed a fantasy or perhaps mimicked his memories. Everything resembled images spilling from his imagination, almost as if he were in a dream.

Two eyes saw trees. Two arms stretched toward an island over which awoke a dawn he recognized. Countless birds shot up, soared a little, and then settled back on the bank. A pole rose there. A woman was climbing a mountain that almost touched the sky. Fluttering over its right corner was a Turkish flag, and, before a cannon that had been left on a hill, soldiers sat eating canned food. On the far side, the desert began. Shepherds were playing reed double-flutes and children coming from the alleys followed them all the way to the water. Here was the city once more.

A curtain went up and a naked woman on a gray horse looked down. She was traveling between Friedrichstrasse and al-Musalla community, from Unter Den Linden to the Chuqor community. Khidir Musa was standing in front of an assembly of men and women in the Lustgarten opposite the Palace of the Republic in Berlin, talking about his two brothers who had gone to Mecca and not returned. His mother, Qadriya, was strolling in her black wrap through Saint Germain in Paris or sitting in the Milano café in

Cyprus, gazing at the waiters, who always brought a glass of water with the coffee. The scent of intoxicating spring awakened him. "All this affection when you remember the Assyrian girls, coming out of one building heading for another, like an opening in a cloud." Here is the student of Islamic jurisprudence on his donkey, with its frayed saddlebags, pouring drops of jasmine perfume on the meadows from a bottle in his hand as he travels from village to village. "Oh! Another day, another awakening! Everything is here. They are all here: dead friends and living ones, those I know and those I don't. The trees, always the trees. The plastered houses always and the light that picks out their tops . . . and as usual, always, me."

He awoke from his slumber and wiped his face with his hands the way he habitually did. He wanted to rise, go to the kitchen, and put some water on to boil before he headed to the bathroom but stopped. "There's no kitchen here." He opened his drowsy eyes. Kirkuk stretched before him. He felt both terror and anxiety. He was seized by a feeling that had afflicted him during the past forty-six years as he moved between continents and cities with forged passports or real ones. Time had vanished—like a bubble that pops when you reach a finger toward it. It seemed as though he had never left his city.

He went over to a water tap in the garden and put his head under the water the way he had done in the garden in al-Musalla whenever he passed by it. Raising his head, he found his three angels standing in front of him, smiling. He was so perturbed he did not know what to say. One of them, who was holding a towel of Aleppo velvet, offered it to him, saying, "Dry your face with this, Burhan."

Burhan stammered and then said, "I didn't believe that all this was real. I didn't believe that all this was possible."

The three old men answered calmly, "What are you saying, Burhan?"

Burhan corrected himself, "Nothing. I must have said something silly. Old men are always like that."

One of the three men put a hand in his bag and drew out a handful of seeds, which he scattered into the air. Then the earth was carpeted with flowers and the garden was filled with colorful birds. One of them lit on Burhan Abdallah's shoulder and head. Hedgehogs, rabbits, and squirrels emerged from their lairs and began to frolic among plants that sprouted instantaneously. He started with alarm when he saw life creep into the stone lions that stood at the entrance to the garden. He stayed put because the blood had frozen in his veins as he looked at the three angels, but the two mild-mannered lions approached and lay down at his feet. One of the angels told him, "There's finally peace, Burhan."

A type of enchantment had settled over the city. "This is more than I expected," Burhan told himself. Then he placed his hat on his head, and a small sparrow lit on it and began to peck at what it thought was a hole. The three old men, who looked so much alike that it was hard to tell them apart, laughed. One of them said, "Seeing you like this will make everyone in the Chuqor community roar with laughter." Another added, "Fine, we'll wait for you there, Burhan." The third placed his hand on Burhan's shoulder, saying, "You must enter the Chuqor community alone, just as you left it alone." Then they headed for the far side of the garden and disappeared among the olive trees that hid white stone-and-plaster houses that gleamed in the light.

"Definitely not; I can't stand all this tenderness. It surpasses what's required. It's more than I deserve. Not even the mind of God would conceive of such a happy ending." Images from distant memories mixed together in his mind with dreams so arresting he felt like weeping. Through a crack in a door, he was watching a woman comb her hair and rub her breasts with a lemon. A man sat in a coffeehouse and surreptitiously counted his money. A security officer dismounted from his motorcycle and asked a young man as beautiful as a girl his name. Satan was seated at a table in a restaurant filled with smoke. Pupils were fleeing from their schools to pinch girls' bottoms in demonstrations.

"I normally become intoxicated after the first glass. I dance till I fall asleep on a woman's shoulder. When I awake in the morning I find that an executioner is leading me to some square to chop off my head, but he normally leaves me alone while he goes to a farm to eat greens. My God, how beautiful our days were when we hunted for angels among the trees and pursued demons among the boulders. Once I saw a machine-gun at the rear of an airplane fire on shepherds. Naked women, men, and children at the shore of Grünau in Berlin conduct a memorial service for me. A man with a glass eye reads from a newspaper that almost touches his face. Hamlet's mother stands at the door, wearing a black evening gown that reveals her shoulders while she distributes smiles to soldiers carrying heads on bronze trays. Is this the head of John the Baptist? The man who incited us to rebel against time? Oh, I once saw myself in a sanatorium with blood on my palm."

He was cast into the spring that had taken the city by surprise after being delayed. He was caught up in his emotions and memories as if in some nameless passion. Here finally was Kirkuk. The dead had quit it, as if it had never experienced death. They had vanished, just as everything else vanishes. They had entered the crematories, leaving no trace behind. Burhan Abdallah's eyes were bathed in tears as he crossed Kirkuk's stone bridge: "My God, it's still standing, even now. Nothing has changed at all." He leaned on the railing, studying the roaring waters of the Khasa Su, which swept along with them tree trunks, the bodies of wild animals that the floods had over-whelmed, and empty containers. He smelled the scent of the mud and experienced the light dizziness that had always afflicted him as a child whenever he crossed the bridge. He noticed coachmen whip-ping their horses that pulled carts behind which boys in ragged dishdashas leapt at each other.

At the far end of the bridge was the citadel, to which a person climbed by steps on either side. He thought of heading to the Chuqor community by ascending to the citadel, but wished to pass through the great souk. He turned right and walked in front of the shop of the Armenian prosthetic dentist. The man was still sitting on a chair that he had placed in front of the entrance on the sidewalk. Burhan Abdallah greeted him by politely raising his hat. The man returned his greeting, rising from his chair, astonished to see an old man wearing a European hat in a city like Kirkuk. Through the glass, he saw the Turkmen barber Tahsin lather with a barber's brush the chin of a man reclining in a chair. He passed a lame locksmith, who had covered the wall of his shop with pictures of Egyptian actresses like Fatin Hamama, Samia Gamal, and Shadya. He saw the Kurdish goldsmith

Abd al-Samad seated on the ground, stretching his legs in front of his bellows. In the area leading to the great souk, he saw porters transporting sacks of wheat to the great warehouse, which lay opposite a plant that produced large blocks of ice, which children carried on their shoulders. The metalsmiths were still beating their copper and bronze vessels. He passed people selling tea on the sidewalk, kebab restaurants, and shops offering just about anything. The old smell of Kirkuk intoxicated him. Almost everything was mixed into it, and it comprised a blend that went to the head before reaching the lungs.

Nothing had changed except that the colors had become brilliant. He was struck, however, by the dogs that were playing with cats after forgetting their instinctive hostility, the crows that entered stores, and the storks that had descended from the minarets to stand on the sidewalks. The garden's two stone lions were following him like two old retainers, but what interested him was not the lions but the Chuqor community, from which he was separated now only by al-Qaysariya, which had a rotten smell and the passageways of which he still knew by heart. He had scarcely passed through al-Qaysariya and caught sight of the alley that was the beginning of the Chuqor community when he was surprised by something he had never even imagined.

They were all standing there, waiting for him, holding roses. It was all the old faces, as though impervious to time, and they embraced him, one after the other. There was his mother, who looked younger than he did, and his father, who was wearing his Arab clothing. There was Hameed Nylon, who as usual delivered a humorous speech. Abbas Bahlawan brandished his revolver and fired in the air. The thief Mahmud al-Arabi presented him with a skeleton key that would open any lock. Drummers were drumming while the women placed bonbons, chocolates, and candy on the heads of people in the crowd. "My God, how did they learn of my return? I didn't tell anyone." Burhan Abdallah wondered about this. "My angels, the three old men, must have been the ones who arranged this. They were the only ones who knew I was returning." He was certain that this was the case when he saw the three men walking through the surging crowd. Burhan Abdallah looked for his maternal uncle Khidir Musa, who had been sealed up in the tower along with Dervish Bahlul and Dada Hijri so that they were buried alive. The drumming continued, women in black wraps trilled, and dervishes poked skewers into their bodies. Here the pilgrim was returning from his long journey to Mecca, after forgetting the hardships of the trip. The deadly days that had subdued Chuqor had ended, and the faces had regained their original innocence. The curse that had settled on the city, blocking spring for forty-six years, had ended. The evil sorcerer had been manacled. They had bound him to a large rock and thrown him in the river.

"You shouldn't have lost hope, Burhan. Your angels have instructed you since you were an adolescent that they were carrying the spring of eternity in hemp sacks to Chuqor, where not even memories are limited. Sorrow? There is no sorrow worse than that of a waiting heart. What sorrow is ruder than that of the newborn's longing for his mother's womb? All forms of waiting have ended: the waits of a forlorn life, of pointless excursions, of trains in snow, of friends in coffeehouses. That is all over now, for the soldier has returned from the war. All of them are returning: living friends and deceased friends, as spring spills over the earth."

The next day Burhan Abdallah headed for the tower in which Khidir Musa, Dervish Bahlul, and Dada Hijri had been interred. All night long while he was in his family's house he had continued to think about the three men, whom everyone had forgotten. They must at least be given a proper burial. With the pickax he had brought he began to strike at the door, which had been covered with concrete. The delicate wall, which humidity had damaged and weakened, collapsed. The lock broke, and he pushed on the door with his foot, oblivious to the pains convulsing his body. He knew that he would discover the skeletons of the three men who had been buried alive. This scene had never left him during all the years he had spent far from the city. They must have died one after the other. He thought of the last words that they had perhaps exchanged. There is nothing worse than for a man to be buried alive. That was an unalloyed evil.

The door opened partway. At the center of the room a candle was burning, throwing shadows on the walls. Burhan Abdallah pushed on the door with his hand and it opened wider. He continued to stand there, not daring to enter. The three men sat there calmly, leaning against white pillows and smoking. One of them asked, "Why are you standing there, Burhan? Come on in."

Burhan Abdallah entered, filled to overflowing with grief and terror, stunned by the unexpected spectacle. He heard a voice tell him, "Why don't you come greet your uncle Khidir, who's been waiting for you all these years?" Burhan closed his eyes and then opened them again. They were sitting there just as he had left them. Khidir Musa was playing chess with Dervish Bahlul while Dada Hijri sat leaning over a large notebook, which he had propped on a pillow, transmitting to paper what appeared to be the last of his poems. Burhan Abdallah stood there, baffled but filled with bliss. He found nothing to say. The words had died on his lips. Then he found himself laughing boisterously, like a child playing happily.

This enormous happiness that filled his heart did not, however, last long. He awoke one morning to find that spring had died away like a fire that turns to ashes. "My God, was all that a fantasy, too?" The air had become stagnant, and the sky had turned yellow, emitting sickly yellowish rays. He no longer heard the chirping of sparrows or the rustling of the wind. Everything was still, as though death had settled over the city. He had difficulty breathing. He pulled on his clothes and went out to the street after being gripped by an anxiety that had afflicted him throughout his long years of exile. He would open his eyes to discover his corpse, over which other people were weeping. He would be unable to scream to them, "Why are you weeping? I'm still alive!" He was alive and dead at the same time, without being able to dispel this confusion. As a matter of fact, he was unable to bear happiness because he knew that happiness always conceals the threat of its annihilation, just as a glass might fall to the floor and shatter, by accident.

In the days following his return to Chuqor, he was filled with a dream-like happiness because the world had suddenly changed. Spring, which had been withheld from the city for long years, had come to earth. So here it was, glowing green. The trunks of trees that the blinding sun had scorched had regained their vigor and put forth leaves and flowered, stretching boughs out in every direction. Their

261

twigs interlaced, forming corridors without beginning or end. Light penetrated through these, and colors washed with mist were reflected, almost forming a portrait of nature in the first days of its creation. The wolves left their dens and went into the meadows, where they began to graze on grass with the sheep. Meanwhile the shepherds sat on boulders found in the countryside and played the nay. Layla returned to her grandmother in the forest and the wolf opened the door. He fixed her some soup and then curled up on the floor beside the grandmother's bed, listening with a smile while she told Layla the story of the evil wolf that ate grandmothers, wrapped a kerchief around its head, climbed in bed, and then waited for little girls who were picking flowers in the woods. Lions, cheetahs, elephants, foxes, hyenas, jackals, monkeys, stags, gazelles, skinks, anteaters, hawks, penguins, tapirs, and rhinoceroses left their hiding places and returned to the cities from which they had been chased. They presented free, humorous shows to amuse children, who often rode on the lions' backs or clung to the talons of eagles, which lifted them high into the air. They would sit on the clouds before returning to the earth once more. What delighted them most, however, was the performance of the vipers with bells. They would hold themselves erect and make music to the beat of which even men and women danced.

During the days that Burhan Abdallah spent in Chuqor, he was haunted by the feeling that all this could not be true, but it felt so true that he wept from happiness. The earth had suddenly exploded with springs that began to flow with milk and honey. People came and ladled as much from these as they wished. Chuqor was filled with shops and stores that were open day and night but that lacked salesmen. They were filled with merchandise from all over the world. People would enter them, take what they needed, and then leave. No one thought about money, which people began to toss in trash bins, making fun of the days when a man could go hungry if he lacked some colored slips of paper stuffed into his wallet. The women and girls of the Chuqor community removed their wraps and wore jeans, deliberately cutting holes in them in areas that would excite men's interest. Then they replaced these with short garments that revealed shapely legs. In fact, they swam naked in the many lakes that had appeared in the empty countryside of al-Musalla, lying on their bellies on the grass and reading detective stories or a book of poems. The aged Burhan Abdallah would pass by them when out for a stroll and would raise his hat in greeting, even to those he did not know. "My God, how times have changed! Is this the Chuqor community?" The cocky young women would lift their heads and whisper to each other, "He's the old guy who's returned from exile." He would smile, oblivious to everything—even his old age, which lent him a dignified air that he had never possessed before.

Although everyone—perhaps from force of habit—purchased Mercedes and Volvos, or even a Rolls-Royce or a Jaguar, they parked them in lots located near their homes, after fastening a horseshoe to the front bumper to ward off envy. They preferred to ride bicycles or to take a subway train when heading to the forests located near the city in order to enjoy their plentiful free time, which they possessed now that no one was forced to work. Unknown workers—perhaps robots made in Japan—directed everything themselves and organized it. For this reason, many people began to compose poetry, to write imaginative novels, to draw, and to dance, as though there were nothing else to live for except art.

Young men and young women immersed themselves in love, overflowing with emotions that caused their eyes to grow languid and to dissolve in delicate affection. Beyond this, no one died anymore. Death had been erased from people's history, and nobody even thought about it. That fact, which was suddenly observed by Burhan Abdallah, made him think nervously and agitatedly, "This could only happen in heaven." He was certain, however, that he was in the Chuqor community and that everything was real. "Time has changed. That's all there is to the matter. I shouldn't be so skeptical."

He did not grasp the secret of this transformation until Khidir Musa, Dervish Bahlul, and Dada Hijri visited him one day in the room he occupied in his family's home. They said they had come to have tea with him. His mother prepared tea with cardamom and mixed in some dried rose petals. As they drank the tea, they chewed on sugar cubes after each sip—the way old people do. Dervish

Bahlul withdrew from his breast pocket a large ledger with a black binding and handed it to Burhan Abdallah. "Take this. It's my gift to you. I no longer need it. I've lost my employment, as you can see."

Khidir Musa commented sarcastically, "There's nothing better than retirement. We've grown old, Burhan."

Dada Hijri nodded his head and added, "It's hard for a person to endure what Dervish Bahlul has survived to this point. A person needs a heart of stone to accept what has been delegated to him."

Burhan Abdallah was astonished by this conversation, which seemed cryptic to him. He commented, "I've scarcely understood anything you've said."

Dada Hijri interjected, "That's because you haven't opened Dervish Bahlul's ledger and glanced at its contents."

Burhan Abdallah examined the ledger for the first time and flipped through its pages at random, scrutinizing lines that seemed to tremble before his eyes. Then he said, "My God, this resembles the register people have called for ages the 'Book of Destiny.'"

Dervish Bahlul replied, "That's actually what it is."

Everything seemed weird to Burhan Abdallah. Life got mixed up with dream in his head. The dervish's presence alarmed him greatly. Then he opened his mouth rather hesitantly, "It doesn't seem to me that you're God."

Dervish Bahlul let out a resounding laugh and then said as if whispering an important secret, "'Thank God I am not God!'"

Burhan Abdallah felt so perplexed after the three men had left that he wanted to see them again, for no particular reason. But they were inscrutable men who appeared when no one was expecting them and disappeared when everyone was requesting them. As a matter of fact, Burhan Abdallah had entertained doubts about the reality of these old men since he demolished the door to the tower and found them sitting there. These men could not really be Khidir Musa, Dervish Bahlul, and Dada Hijri. Those men had died forty-six years earlier, when they were buried alive in the tower. "I wonder why Dervish Bahlul gave me this ledger, which he says is the veritable Book of Destiny? Death has ended. What meaning is there then to destiny? What shall I do with it?"

He turned the pages of the thick ledger, which he placed on the table before him. There he saw all of human history: men, women, and children—being born and then dying. Tribes and nations appeared like water moss sprouting and then disappeared into the heart of time. There were wars without end, treasonous conspiracies like murder mysteries, epidemics that swept over cities snatching the people away, tyrants and commanders who erected gallows in cities' old markets, executioners who chopped off heads, and cooks who threw their victims into kettles of boiling tar. Innocent young children burned to death within the walls of besieged cities, and soldiers with lances ripped open the bellies of pregnant women. There were kings who lost their heads to guillotines and prophets who were slain or burned, leaving behind ashes that were cast into the wind.

Dervish Bahlul had described everything so precisely that Burhan Abdallah could see time's realities parade before him like an endless video loop. Happy moments turned into catastrophes, and loyal relationships led to betrayals. Heroism was forgotten after the end of the celebration, and beauty withered in its bloom. Burhan Abdallah pondered the events that were described in the book before him and then was overwhelmed by a kind of tremor in his body: "The only history is the history of victims."

He felt a deep and overwhelming affection for Dervish Bahlul, whose feet had traveled the earth since the first man appeared on earth. He would seek out his trembling victims and place a firm hand on their brows, before crossing out their names. "My God, how this man has suffered! How do you suppose he has endured all that?" He kept reading till he reached the time when spring settled over Chuqor and death ended. There were no longer any victims. Evil suddenly disappeared from the world and the demons whispering in people's hearts vanished as innocence triumphed—just as saints, prophets, and the proponents of the great ideologies had predicted. Burhan Abdallah thought, "Perhaps it's been a return to the sacred beginning. Perhaps this has been a return to paradise, from which Adam and Eve were expelled. What of it? Mankind has paid an exorbitant price already in order to make their way to their lost paradise."

265

He quickly turned through the pages of the book to discover whether the spring that had settled over Chuqor would last eternally. What mattered to him now was to learn the ending of the story he was reading. He felt that way at times when reading detective stories. When he could not bear to wait to discover the criminal's identity, he would jump to the final chapter in which the story's complication is resolved. He would normally lose his desire to read the chapters he had skipped, however, because once he had learned the secret, the other details were superfluous.

Unlike other books, this book did not have a last chapter. Instead, there was a blank chapter that lasted to the end. It began with one word: "suddenly." Then there was nothing but white paper. Burhan Abdallah felt rather exasperated. "What a cunning dervish! He's left everything open-ended. He must have kept another ledger, one that contains the story's final section." He felt anxious as he looked time and again at the word "suddenly," which stirred terror in his heart. Everything could end suddenly. A man might die suddenly. Suddenly the earth might slip from its orbit and plunge into the depths of existence. He did not attribute much significance to chance occurrences but knew that chance was a realistic possibility, one with which even the computer had to reckon. This time it was not a question of chance, but of a destiny recorded since eternity. It was a destiny that he was sorry to see blank, as if it were an incomplete act.

Suddenly he watched the final chapter fill with the events it had been missing. He stood there appalled. He could scarcely believe his eyes. Chuqor had turned into ruins where owls hooted, into remnants of a past glory that time had so effectively erased that it might never have existed. Lions, wolves, hyenas, and jackals prowled around the caves where the last survivors had retreated and tore apart the corpses that had been thrown into alleyways once people even lost the desire to bury their dead.

He heard a resounding voice blow through a horn to announce the end of the false spring. Burhan Abdallah himself was in danger, but the pain affecting his heart made him forget even the peril threatening him. From behind the boulders where he sought shelter, he saw little green creatures coming from everywhere. They were attacking the dead city and torching even its stones. These creatures wore military uniforms with stars adorning the shoulders. He thought, "Perhaps spring has not totally abandoned all the city." They were, however, bombarding the city with atomic and chemical weapons. With tears in his eyes, he asked himself, "Why are they doing that? Everything's over. What can they want?"

He noticed that a man, who was almost naked and resembled a wild creature with his unkempt hair, was creeping toward him between the rubble on hands and knees. Burhan was startled, but the man reassured him, "They pass here every day, burning everything they find."

Burhan Abdallah felt he had to ask the man, "But who are they?"

In a voice like a howl, the man replied, "What did you say? It's clear you're a stranger to this city."

Burhan Abdallah said, "I've spent forty-six years in exile. That's all there is to it."

As he crept away, the man said, "They are Gog and Magog. Perhaps you've heard of them. You should never have returned to this accursed city."

Burhan Abdallah continued to lurk behind the boulders, not daring even to lift his head. A pack of wolves had crossed the Chuqor community behind him, and beneath a leaning light post he watched the two stone lions from the garden rip apart a donkey that seemed to have lost its owner. "That was a false spring—the one I saw," he realized. "Perhaps I didn't see anything at all. Perhaps that was all a fantasy I created during my long nights in exile." Like a feverish invalid, he began repeating, "I should never have returned. I should never have listened to my three angels. I was deceived the moment I clung to a hope derived from fantasy. I've spent my whole life waiting for a false spring. Yes, there was a spring, but it was dead on arrival, perhaps because the three angels were late, perhaps the time that spring spent sealed inside their hemp sacks ruined it. Oh, these men for whom I've spent my whole life waiting." The earth shook under his feet with a terrifying and resounding concussion, which was followed by a storm of red dust that drilled into his face. In the distance, he saw an appalling mass of fire that rose toward the clouds. They must have dropped a new atomic bomb somewhere.

He raised his head toward the heavens and almost went crazy. He began to repeat without interruption, "That can't be. It seems impossible." He saw the sun rise from the west, but this appeared to be a different sun, a sick one that reminded a person that everything is ephemeral.

To stay clear of the hyenas and wolves that were ravaging corpses with their fangs, he dragged his exhausted body to shelter amid the ruins, which were crawling with vipers, fire ants, and reptiles. What frightened him most, however, was the possibility of being discovered by Gog and Magog's soldiers, who were slaying all the human beings they found or stringing them up and leaving them bound beside the road. Burhan Abdallah did not know where to go. There was no longer anyone in Chuqor. Many people must have hidden in holes, caves, and cellars. He would have to return home. "I'll hide there and wait." He laughed at the idea of sitting there and waiting. What could he wait for this time? In the past, the distant past, he had always waited for the arrival of his three angels. It was certainly true that they had been delayed for a long time, but he had definitely not lost hope that they would arrive. What could he wait for now? In a voice that was almost a scream, Burhan exclaimed, "No one! No one at all!"

While the raging wind—sweeping with it empty containers that had been tossed in the deserted streets—howled, raved, and ripped apart palm stalks and thorny plants that had been torn up by their roots, Burhan cast a final look—into space, which was stained a dark yellow—at the sickly sun rising from the west. That was more than he could bear. "I didn't believe I would see this day too." Conditions resembled those of Judgment Day, which everyone assumed would eventually come, but he did not wish to acknowledge this. He was not so much afraid of death as terrified by the thought that he would witness the death of a world he loved so much it made him ill.

"Everything can't end like this in a single blast. In that case, everything will have lost its meaning."

He dragged himself to the tower where Khidir Musa and his two companions had lived. Perhaps they could calm his spirit. They might disclose to him the secret behind this horrific ending, which had taken him by surprise. Perhaps God has been toying with mankind. He remembered that Einstein once said, "God does not play dice." What does He play then? Someone must play dice: all these galaxies, the innumerable suns, stars, moons, cosmic expanses, these existential explosions, these endless endings and these beginnings without a beginning, these braggart human beings, who are born and then die, these leaders who believe in glory, heroes who fasten medals to their breasts, children who are stillborn or who die as infants, the male lovers and passionate women, the troubled generations and the happy ones, these cities and villages, the Arabs and the Jews, the primates that leap from tree to tree, these clouds, thunder and lightning—perhaps they all possess some meaning. Perhaps they have none. Perhaps the meaning they possess is to have no meaning. Burhan Abdallah was breathing with difficulty and stood at the brink of what appeared to be death, that unique stupor. So—like a fish a hand had pulled from the water—he opened his mouth and whispered to himself, "Definitely not. I never play dice."

Time had shaken the tower and left it a deserted, historic ruin. The walls were breaking apart, the stairs were demolished, and many of the stones had slipped loose and lay piled in corners. Dog shit and empty Coca-Cola cans, the remains of old newspapers and magazines that no one remembered, books of prayers and magic in manuscripts that would turn to dust the moment a person touched them, rats gnawing stone and iron, spider webs, black or small yellow scorpions standing in front of their holes. . . . The effects of time, moisture, and termites, which had tunneled through it vertically and horizontally, had eroded the door of the room in the tower. For this reason, he had barely shoved the door with his foot when it fell into the room, creating a cloud of dust that filled the space and a clamor that caused swarms of owls and bats to panic and soar through the gap of the door that had opened before them, as some of the bats bumped into him.

He opened his eyes to find himself confronted by three skeletons, tossed in a corner of the room. He stood there frozen. He could scarcely focus on anything. He felt like saying something but his mouth remained closed. Then he found himself stuttering for the first time in his life: "No, no, no, no, tha, tha, that's not possible. Th, th, this isn't true." He felt a violent desire to laugh, remembering a friend who always stuttered whenever he talked about a girl he loved. Burhan's thoughts stuttered too: "Bbbbbuttttt he didn't, didn't, didn't see corpsesssss, llllike me." Burhan Abdallah felt feverish. He left the tower, descending to the street, having forgotten his stuttering.

He continued to slip between the deserted alleys, which seemed covered in ashes, and glimpsed women, men, and children who were hiding behind boulders or inside the ruins of their former homes—like ghosts that were frightened even of themselves. Artillery fire could be heard resounding in the distance as the wind howled like a procession of women garbed in black, and the sun went dark, even though it was still midday. Then creation was lit up by a brilliant light. He raised his head and saw three prodigious stars. These fiery agglomerations thundered in the sky, approaching each other, as though a supernatural force were attracting them, and then collided with a massive reverberation. The earth shook beneath him, and he was hurled into emptiness before falling again to the ground, where he lay, stretched out on his back, unable to rise. The sky started to rain down drops of flaming fire, as people began to flee from one place to another, bowing their heads as they screamed in unison, almost weeping:

"Oh, when?

"Will the Absent One appear?

"Oh, when?"

He thought, "O my God, they're still waiting for their Absent Mahdi who will restore order to the universe." He stared at the heavens again. He saw moons rise only to be flung roaring into existential gloom. Stars exploded, suns were extinguished, formidable galaxies collided, and days and nights passed in succession. He smiled like a child when he witnessed these fiery, existential games. Then he muttered, "Someone is playing somewhere."

He knew that there would be some time of Reckoning in the final act of this drama, followed by a definitive and terrifying ending in which gloom settled over the steppes of hoarfrost and ice. He knew that the terrestrial sphere would begin its long death agony some day in the distant, mysterious future, but what concerned him was not its timing but its meaning. It did not matter whether the end came now or in a billion years. "If this planet is doomed to die and go out at the end of the journey, then what meaning remains for glory, love, suffering, and passion? For warriors making their way through the deserts and across the ice? For interrogators whipping their victims and leaders delivering orations? What meaning is left for the work of geniuses, adventurous explorers, and the fatigue of inventors?" He would sit and weep at times. "We can't lose everything in a throw of the dice." He would always console himself, however: "Millions of years separate me from the end. There's a lot of time for life. If there's no other meaning in this world, then life itself is the meaning, even if it is doomed to die and even if life is hopeless." But here Judgment Day had arrived prematurely, perhaps because someone had miscalculated a move or perhaps because people like him had been waiting for springtime to descend upon the earth, even if it was a false spring, a spring that ended like any other one.

He moved between the ruins or hid behind the charred trunks of trees, fearful that the soldiers of Gog and Magog would seize him and cut out his tongue or take him away with them. He had contracted a fever, and dreams and images passed through his head, roaring as if they were a river sweeping everything away with it: Khidir Musa herding a flock of sheep behind him along the Kudamm in Berlin and crossing with them to Knightsbridge in London; Mullah Zayn al-Abidin al-Qadiri haggling with a prostitute who leaned her wrist on a windowsill overlooking the street in Pigalle, in Paris; Hameed Nylon placing a rifle on his shoulder and traversing the dark forests of Bolivia; combatant Ansar landing on Mount Uhud from a zeppelin and rescuing the besieged Prophet; Mirage, Sukhoi, MiG, Skyhawk, and Tupolev fighter jets soaring overhead and bombing the Sasanian Persians' elephants at the Battle of al-Qadisiya while pursued by processions of nomadic Arabs coming from the Empty Quarter of the Arabian peninsula; wolves tearing to bits mothers left in the wasteland in Abadan; traitors placing their parents in flaming tar skiffs and throwing them into the Tigris.

Burhan Abdallah leaned against a tree. "No, I'll never give in." Then he took a nap, as he had so often done during his lengthy exile. He was resting on a sofa, gazing at the screen of the decrepit television that allowed him to forget what was being presented before him because he was so involved in seeing personal images he saw on the screen of his imagination. Occasionally the dividing lines between the two screens dissolved and the images merged. Then the following day he would tell his friends about events that had not actually occurred.

He awoke to the ruckus of drums being played to a military beat. Trumpets were being blown, and there was a heavy tramp of footsteps. He raised his head cautiously to find a soccer field, which was crowded with crosses, placed one next to the other. The little green soldiers were dancing with delight as if celebrants at an ancient Bacchanalia. Along the length of the playing field, little green women stood applauding the soldiers and handing out bonbons to the troops. Removing his hat, which he grasped with his hand, Burhan Abdallah proceeded to crawl closer to the pagan playing field. He adjusted his spectacles and stared for a time at the bodies nailed to the crosses. His body was wracked by fevers and terror. He felt nauseous. They were all there on their crosses: Khidir Musa, whose skeleton he had seen in the tower; Hameed Nylon, who had returned from the woods; Dalli Ihsan, who had been killed and who had changed into a ball of fire; Mullah Zayn al-Abidin al-Qadiri, whom they had brought in his gold wheelchair; his own father, Abdallah, who had continued wearing an oil worker's uniform to the end; Abbas Bahlawan, who still had his revolver at his waist; the thief Mahmud al-Arabi, who had not relinquished his keys; Dada Hijri, who had perhaps been drafting a poem that no one would know. They were gazing at him and smiling, as if they wished to tell him, "Farewell."

His body shook once more when he saw something that made him burst into tears. They were there as well. He bowed his head: "That can't be true." He removed his glasses and wiped them with the bottom of his shirt. Then he replaced them. "How is that possible?" His three old angels were dancing in front of the green troops of Gog and Magog. They had turned into devils with erect horns and with tails that dragged behind them. This was a shock he had never expected. He was furious with himself and repeated, "What an ass I've been! I've spent my whole life following angels that are nothing but persuasive devils." He was grief-stricken. The moment the truth was revealed, however, he felt a new force that he had never possessed at any time in his life: freedom.

He dragged himself once more to the ruins where the other human beings had taken refuge. Even his fear had left him, but he was choked with emotions he had never known before. Amid the debris of his room, which had been hit by bolts of lightning, Burhan Abdallah discovered the book that Dervish Bahlul had given him. He dusted it off. Everything in it had been erased. Nothing was left but blank pages devoid of words. He said, "It's just a white notebook like any other." He thought he would take it with him to use as a diary but declared, "There are lots of notebooks. What would I do with it?" En route, he tossed it in a blazing oven, "What was once a ledger for death will go up in flames." He thought about another ledger for life but corrected himself, observing, "What need does life have for ledgers? It is itself the greatest ledger." He ended up in an alley filled with people. They were frightened, but one of them recognized him, perhaps on account of his gray hat and prescription glasses, and cried out, "The Absent One has returned!" They crowded around, asking him, "Were you really absent and have you returned?" Burhan said, "Yes, I've returned after forty-six years in exile." He had scarcely uttered these words when he saw that other people were gathering around and touching him. Then, in a fury of temporary insanity, they exploded with a chant in unison:

The Absent One has appeared.
And it seems
That he endures
Forever.

That was the last thing that Burhan Abdallah was expecting. O these poor wretches! They had encircled him, revolving around him. They were singing as tears poured from their eyes. The women began to trill, as if they were at a wedding. Burhan Abdallah turned to them and said, "You're mistaken. I'm not the Absent Mahdi you're await-ing. I feared for my life and fled into exile. I'm worse off than you are. I'm more afraid than you are."

These words caused the crowd to grow more zealous and turbulent. An elderly man approached him and said lovingly, "A sign of the Absent One is that he denies his identity. And now you've done that."

Burhan Abdallah, who was becoming exasperated with the fool-ishness of these people, began to scream, "I swear I'm not the man for whom you wait. I'm a forlorn man, who doesn't even know him-self." But his voice was lost in the hubbub and he remained standing there, not knowing what to do. He saw thousands of women, men, and children emerge from the rubble and from holes in the ground to swell the ranks of the human swarm that kept expanding. They were banging on tambourines and drums. A man rose to say, "The Absent One will conquer the army of Gog and Magog and restore order to the universe." Burhan Abdallah thought, "My God, what a dilemma! They're clinging to a straw! I should never have returned to this city."

The tumult had attracted Gog and Magog's troops, who sur-rounded the area, demanding that the last human beings return to their hiding places behind the boulders and amid the rubble. Panic crept into the hearts of the men, who threw down their tambourines. The women swallowed their trills, and even the children stopped crying. They all withdrew, crawling away on their bellies to hide in holes and pits and among the boulders, until they seemed almost not to exist at all. Burhan Abdallah stood his ground, waiting for the approaching soldiers, who brandished the bayonets of their rifles. He assumed that they would spear him repeatedly. "So this is the end, then." The sol-diers drew closer to him with each step. "It wasn't possible for me to obey their orders and bury myself in holes, like the others." That was more than he could bear. He was alone and the soldiers were advanc-ing on him, waving their bayonets. He said sadly, "I can't die. I can't imagine myself dead, even if the whole world has ended."

He felt a tyrannical love for life and it brought him close to tears. The little green soldiers were only steps away from him. He could see their round eyes, which were washed in blood, burning and staring into his eyes. He raised his hands up high, like a man preparing to die. Just when he had lost all hope of salvation, he noticed that his hands were changing into prodigious wings. He beat the air with them. He lifted himself higher . . . higher . . . higher . . . until he soared into the sky, and disappeared.

Author's Note

This novel was written between April 12, 1987, and September 2, 1990, in Berlin and Nicosia, although small sections of it were written in Damascus, Tripoli, and Sana'a.

Translator's Acknowledgments

As the character Burhan Abdallah observes in slightly different phrasing in this novel, each of my translations—even though the original works are not my books—becomes part of me. It is always a privilege to work with an Arab author, and each of my books is special to me. Having said that, I need to express my deepest thanks to Fadhil al-Azzawi for his encouragement, close reading, and corrections of my drafts of each of the twelve chapters of this novel, which is full of the kind of local color that can trip up even a translator with the best intentions. The glossary has been compiled from footnotes written by the author or the translator. I would like to thank Dr. Gaber Asfour, who invited me to the Cairo conference where I met Fadhil al-Azzawi in 2005. I also need to thank the National Endowment for the Arts for the literary translation grant for 2005–2006, during which period I completed the bulk of this translation. I thank Appalachian State University for allowing me to translate full-time during Spring Semester 2006. As always, I appreciate my family's tolerance of my enthusiasm for translation; so thank you, Sarah, Franya, and Kip Hutchins.

Glossary

Ababil birds: Reference to the way an Abyssinian attack on Mecca was repulsed miraculously circa A.D. 570.

Abdallah Goran: Important twentieth-century Kurdish poet.

Abu Naji: A common Iraqi nickname for an Englishman during the period of the Iraqi monarchy. The original Abu Naji is said to have been an Iraqi friend of the influential British official and author Gertrude Bell. What Abu Naji used to say about British policy reflected British intentions in Iraq. See "Returning to Abu Naji," Khalid al-Qishtini, *al-Sharq al-Awsat,* London, no. 9010, 30 July 2003.

afreet: Jinni or genie.

Bahlul: Clown or buffoon.

"Beyond the mountains . . .": Ibrahim al-Daquqi, *Irak Türkmenleri* (Ankara: Güven Matbaasi, 1970).

Buraq: Heavenly steed believed to have carried the Prophet Muhammad on his miraculous ascent through the heavens.

"Camel's hair, and a leather girdle . . .": Matthew 3:4 (Revised Standard Version).

Glossary

Captain Chesney: Francis Rawdon Chesney (1789–1872) was a British explorer, soldier, and entrepreneur. The narrator's account differs from that of General Chesney, whose iron steamship, the *Tigris*, sank in the Euphrates River "at the rocky pass of Is Geria" due to freak weather, not because of an attack, although some of its survivors later, when on board the sister ship the *Euphrates*, were attacked in the Lamlum marshes by Arabs, who allegedly attempted to kidnap one Mrs. Helfer. See Stanley Lane-Poole, ed. *The Life of General F. R. Chesney . . . by His Wife and Daughter* (London: W. H. Allen & Co., 1885), 326, 335–36.

". . . concern and a striving after the wind": Paraphrase of Ecclesiastes 2:11 (RSV).

dabke: Levantine line dance.

dervish: Sufi, Muslim mystic.

"Do not think that those killed serving God are dead . . .": Qur'an 3:369.

"Don't weep . . .": Ibrahim al-Daquqi, *Irak Türkmenleri* (Ankara: Güven Matbaasi, 1970).

"The faux-qur'an of the Liar Musaylima . . .": The Prophet Muhammad challenged others to attempt to reveal another sacred book like the Holy Qur'an. Musaylima, his contemporary, was one of those who attempted the feat.

"Follow me, and I will make you fishers of men": Matthew 4:19; Mark 1:17 (RSV).

"God does not play dice.": Albert Einstein, "Letter 81," in *The Born-Einstein Letters,* translated by Irene Born (London: Macmillan, 1971), 149.

Gog and Magog: Hostile forces contained in the distant past but predicted to threaten human civilization once more as a sign of the end of the world.

al-Hajj/al-Hajja: A man or woman who has performed the pilgrimage to Mecca.

Ibn Sa'ud: Abdul Aziz ibn Sa'ud (1880–1953) was founder of the Saudi Arabian monarchy; See: Wilhelm Kopf, *Saudiarabien: Insel der Araber* (Stuttgart: Seewald Verlag, 1982), 78–79.

jamdaniyat headcloths: Turkmen-style headcloth.

jinni: Afreet or genie.

kaka: Kurdish for "elder brother."

Kakaiyeen: Members of a Muslim religious sect in northern Iraq.

Khidir: The name of a pre-Islamic prophet associated with fertile, green, life forces.

Kudamm: Kurfürstendamm Street in Berlin.

al-Maydan: Baghdad area that was famous for brothels until 1960.

mujtahid: Islamic jurisprudent authorized to think independently about Islamic law.

Namlet: An Iraqi soft drink from the 1950s, similar to Coca-Cola.

al-Nas: The final chapter of the Holy Qur'an, sura 114: "Mankind." It is a command to seek refuge with God from the devil's whispered suggestions.

nay: A reed flute.

"Oh, when? / Will the Absent One appear? / Oh, when?": Shi'i chant repeated in religious processions in southern Iraq.

Peacock Angel: The chief angel who refused to bow before Adam, according to the Yazidis.

qadi: Islamic judge.

"The rose's bed . . .": Abd al-Latif Bandar Ughlu, *al-Turkman fi 'Iraq al-thawra.*

Ruq'a, Farsi, and Kufic: Styles of Arabic calligraphy.

Samanchi Qizzi: Popular, twentieth-century Iraqi dancer who eventually married a diplomat.

Sayyid Qizzi: Famed female miracle worker.

"The Spirit descending upon him like a dove": Mark 1:10 (RSV).

"The spirit immediately drove him out into the wilderness . . .": Mark 1:12–13 (RSV).

"Ta'am, Labam, Bacho Halam . . .": A magical formula, used by some magicians in Iraq. It has no meaning and its aim is to make things seem secret and vague.

"Thank God I am not God!": Allen Ginsberg, "Lysergic Acid," *Kaddish and Other Poems 1958–1960* (San Francisco: City Lights Books, 1961, 1982), 87.

Throne Verse: Qur'an, 2:255. A commonly recited celebration of God's omnipotence.

"The voice crying in the wilderness . . .": Isaiah 40:3 (RSV).

"Yazid is himself the sultan": Verses from a religious poem of the Yazidis in Mount Sinjar in northern Iraq. Shaykh Ali, "Hawl al-Yazidiya," *Majalla al-thaqafa al-jadida,* no. 205, January 1989.

Yazidis: Northern Kurdish religious minority also known as Dasini, misdescribed as devil-worshippers, who hold a syncretistic set of beliefs based in part on Sufi and ancient Iranian influences.

Yunus Bahri: Iraqi journalist who worked for Berlin's Arabic Service during the Nazi era. He died in Baghdad at the beginning of the 1980s.

Zurkhaneh: A traditional Iranian system of physical training that involves a "pit" or ring for exercises.

About the Author

FADHIL AL-AZZAWI was born in Kirkuk, Iraq, in 1940. He holds a Ph.D. in cultural journalism from the University of Leipzig and is the author of more than twenty books of fiction, poetry, and translations, including *Miracle Maker: The Selected Poems of Fadhil al-Azzawi* and *Cell Block Five,* a novel to be published in English in April 2008. In Iraq, he was a member of the Kirkuk Group of poets in the 1960s. He has lived in Germany since 1977.

WILLIAM M. HUTCHINS is the principal translator of Naguib Mahfouz's *Cairo Trilogy* and has most recently translated Mohammed Khudayyir's *Basrayatha,* Naguib Mahfouz's *Cairo Modern,* Ibrahim al-Koni's *The Seven Veils of Seth,* Duna Ghali's *When the Scent Awakens,* and the forthcoming *Cell Block Five* by Fadhil al-Azzawi.

The Last of the
Angels

A Modern Iraqi Novel

Fadhil al-Azzawi

Reading Group Guide

A Conversation with Fadhil al-Azzawi

ABOUT THIS GUIDE

The following reading group guide and author interview are intended to help you find interesting and rewarding approaches to your reading of *The Last of the Angels*. We hope this enhances your enjoyment and appreciation of the book. For a complete listing of reading group guides from Simon & Schuster, visit BookClubReader.com.

READING GROUP GUIDE FOR
THE LAST OF THE ANGELS

Discussion Questions

1. How does the rumor of Hameed Nylon begin? What are the consequences of this rumor? What does this reveal about the prejudices and stereotypes?

2. Khidir Musa leaves the village after he had "received from the spirit world a message to set forth to search for his two brothers, who had been missing since World War I." (p. 67) What do you make of his sign? What is the significance to Burhan?

3. How do the villagers feel about the road being constructed by the British? What will this mean for their village?

4. The number three comes up a great deal in *The Last of the Angels*. There are three angels, the three brothers returning to the village, and the three men in the tower, just to name a few examples. What do you think is the significance, if any?

5. Khidir Musa meets an aging dervish in a cave, which we later learn is Death, who tells him: "Don't forget that the matter concerns the dead first and foremost, not the living. The dead too have a right to voice their opinion." (p. 101) Why is it fitting that Death is making this pronouncement? What is its importance to Khidir? How does this relate to the rest of the novel?

6. Khidir Musa leads an expedition to King Faisal in order to stop the building of the road through the cemetery, and Dada Hijiri composes a poem about their meeting:

The rose's bed:
Come let us seek the rose's bed.
I sought the rose's bed
But found thorns bedded there instead. (p. 115)

What does the poem mean? How does this relate to their situation?

7. How does Khidir Musa change over the course of the novel? How does Hameed?

8. Why does so much violence break out after the death of Qara Qul? How does the sectarian violence in the city mirror what's going on today?

9. Mullah Zayn al-Abidin al-Qadiri comments to Hameed, "You know how to coexist with this damn world." (p. 159) What is he trying to say to Hameed? What is the significance of the mullah's vision at Qara Qul's widow's house?

10. Why do you think Hameed Nylon is so insistent on starting a revolution? He claims not to be a Communist because he feels they are "all talk and no action," but what attributes does Hameed share with the Communists? Why is he so frustrated after he meets with their leaders in the cellar?

11. When Burhan questions one of the angels as to the meaning of life, he replies: "You shouldn't be overly concerned, since you're nothing more than a hero in an invented novel written by a disgruntled author." (p. 193) What does the angel mean by this? What does the author?

12. In an effort to get the government's attention, Hameed and some of his followers kidnap a few Englishmen. Do you think this was a personal vendetta for having been fired by his English boss, or did he capture them because of what they represent? How is Hameed a sort of patsy of the government?

13. Upon returning after forty-six years in exile, Burhan Abdallah says, "I've spent my whole life following angels that are nothing

but persuasive devils." (p. 273) Following the moment when the truth was revealed, he felt, for the first time in his life, freedom. How is Burhan finally free? Do you find the ending hopeful?

14. Why do you think this novel was banned in Iraq when it was originally published? Have you ever read any Arabic literature before? After reading *The Last of the Angels* are you interested in reading more?

A CONVERSATION WITH
FADHIL AL-AZZAWI

Which character in your novel *The Last of the Angels* do you relate to the most?

It is without a doubt Burhan Abdallah, the young boy, who finds himself in a world full of wonders and tries to grasp the meaning of everything around him. He resembles me in many aspects of his life: His father is a worker in the same oil company that employed my father, he lives in the place I did, and he goes to the same school I attended. Also, his life in exile reflects somewhat my own experiences in exile: He lives in Berlin and sits, as I often do, in a café in Alexanderplatz and talks with his Iraqi friends about the war in his homeland. He dreams of returning someday to his lost paradise. He sits and waits, day after day, year after year, for a miracle: the end of the hell raging in his country.

You left Iraq for Germany in 1977, after being jailed for three years for your political activities. What do you miss most about your homeland?

To be sure, I miss a lot of things, but they are things that no longer exist. The land now is not the same land that I left behind in 1977. Everything there is changed. The long nightmare of the dictatorship and the subsequent successive and bloody wars have blinded the people to reality. The greatest dream of everyone in Iraq now is only survival. Iraqis from different parts of the country tell me that each time they dare to go to work or to step outside their doors, they do not know if they will be able to come back home at all. I miss of course my mother; my friends; the cafés, bars, and nightlife of Abu Nuwas in Baghdad, but I know that my mother has already died without ever seeing her prodigal son again; many of my friends have been killed in the battlefields, jailed, or obliged to flee the country; and the cafés and bars in Abu Nuwas are closed.

The last section of my novel *The Ancestors* (2002) is entitled "Returning to No Return to It." The main character returns from exile to Baghdad to find that "his" Baghdad exists only in the dreams he had during the long nights of his exile. I have received many invitations in recent years to visit Iraq, but I have found myself unable to accept them. For thirty long years I waited day after day for paradise, so what can I look for now in hell?

Were you surprised when the book was banned after its initial publication in 1992?

Not at all, because all of my works were already banned in Iraq under Saddam's regime. In 1979, this regime began a campaign of terror targeting specifically intellectuals and writers who supported democracy and were not ready to accept the regime's nationalist and ideological guidelines on culture and literature.

In 1980, I founded, with some other Iraqi writers, a group called The Union of Iraqi Writers for Democracy in Exile. In response, the regime withdrew my passport and later confiscated my family's house in Baghdad. These measures failed to prevent the Iraqi people from reading my books. Most of the books, which I had published abroad, were smuggled into the country, copied, and sold in secret. I have met people who have been arrested simply for possession of my books. This shows not only how vulnerable and ridiculous the dictatorship was, but also the real nature of the conflict.

The whole struggle in Iraq, but also in the rest of the Arabic and Islamic world, was and is a struggle between two choices: to live in the past or in the present. To carry the heavy burden of ancient history on our shoulders, or to liberate ourselves from our own demons and promote creativity and craft in this modern age. All the nationalist and religious movements preach about a certain "Golden Peak," on a "Sacred Mountain," that gleams and shimmers somewhere in the remote past and should be attained at any price, in their opinion. For me, my ascents lie only in my own lifetime.

What would you want first-time readers of Arabic literature to understand about Iraq and its people?

Iraq is more than the journalists' reports of daily explosions, acts of terrorism, and sectarian violence against innocent people. It's a land with more than five thousand years of civilization and one of the leading cultural centers of the Arab world. It is rich not only in its natural resources, but also in its thousands and thousands of well-educated people. The bloody daily picture doesn't reflect Iraq's real human and modern spirit. Saddam's regime destroyed all the democratic and progressive parties and forced a great part of the intelligentsia to flee the country. The current struggle in Iraq is not taking place among ordinary people—who are eager to live like everyone else in the world. It's a struggle between certain religious groups with their maniac and terrorist ideologies, who are trying to control the country in the political vacuum following the fall of the dictatorship. The American administration has committed a big mistake in allowing these religious groups to rule the country in a very primitive way. It is very important now for Iraq and America to put an end to this war together and give the Iraqi people the chance to live in peace and dignity.

This edition of *The Last of the Angels* was translated by William M. Hutchins. How closely do you work with the translator?

William M. Hutchins is one of the most important translators of modern Arabic literature. To work with him is a real pleasure for me.

When he finishes translating a chapter, he emails it to me and asks me to read it to check the language. And each time I do this I discover how accurate, wonderful, and astonishing his translation is. He divines the deepest spirit of the text and creates it anew in the English language.

The novel ends with Burhan's hands changing into wings as he lifts himself "higher . . . higher . . . higher . . . until he soared into the sky, and disappeared." (p. 275) What do you intend for the reader to take away from this statement?

I usually do not like to give the reader my own interpretation of specific situations in my novels. I leave them open, preferring to give the reader the chance to derive his or her own conclusions and enjoy these discoveries. Anyhow, as Burhan decides at the last moment not to run away from the soldiers of destruction, to face them and accept even his own death if necessary, he liberates himself from his chains and discovers his own craft. The soldiers fail to kill or arrest him. With his wings soaring into the sky, he gives us new hope and lets us know that the story is not yet finished and it will, in fact, go on without end.

What writers would you say influenced you?

I have read countless Eastern and Western writers and have learned from them. The first, most important book in my life was *A Thousand and One Nights*. I read it as a child many times, and each time I found more pleasure in its stories. I was taken, not only by its magical world, but also by the eroticism of its language. I read also as a schoolboy, besides the Arabic literary canon, *The Odyssey* by Homer, *The Divine Comedy* by Dante, most of Shakespeare's plays, and the work of many other writers and poets.

The writers who have influenced me most are Kafka, Nietzsche, Dostoevsky, Proust, Joyce, Faulkner, Hemingway, Sartre, Camus, T. S. Eliot, and Rilke.

Because I speak four languages (Arabic, Turkish, English, and German), I carry within me something from the literary and cultural values of all these languages and their great writers. I consider my writings as a kind of unifying bridge between different cultures.

You've written several volumes of poetry, six novels, and three books of criticism. Have any of your other works been translated into English?

Yes. In 1997, the *Quarterly Review of Literature* (Vol. 36) published my poetry collection *In Every Well a Joseph Is Weeping,* translated by Khaled Mattawa, and in 2003, BOA Editions published my second poetry book, *Miracle Maker: The Selected Poems of Fadhil Al-Azzawi,* also translated by Khaled Mattawa. My second novel, *Cell Block Five,* translated by William M. Hutchins, published by American University of Cairo Press, is to be released in April 2008.

What is the most important thing you'd like readers to take away from this novel?

I'd like my readers first of all to read this novel as a literary work. *The Last of the Angels* is a journey inside Arabic and Islamic culture, mythology, and religion not only as it exists in Iraq, but also in the entire Middle East. It describes the different forms of struggle between traditional beliefs and the reality of the modern world, with all its ideological illusions and dreams. All his life Burhan Abdallah follows the advice of three old angels who carry the spring to his city. But at the end he discovers that they are not more than disguised devils. The truth alone liberates him from the temptation of his false angels (symbolizing the ideological prophets of our modern times) and enables him to find his own human strength.

What's next for you?

I am writing now a novel about Iraq under the occupation, which follows the tragic destinies of several different Iraqi and American characters who find themselves standing on different fronts in a war not of their own waging. I hope to finish it within months.

My novel *Cell Block Five* will be available in English in April 2008 from the American University in Cairo Press. I hope also to see my novels *The Ancestors* and *City of Ashes* translated into English. The first one tells the story of four dictators in Iraq and the rise of each from the dead, while the second is about the complicated relationship between the executioner and his victim: a novel about love, friendship, betrayal, and loyalty.

Enhance Your Book Club

1. To learn more about Arabic literature and its history, check out http://en.wikipedia.org/wiki/Arabic_literature.
2. You can learn more about the author and his other works from this article: http://www.thewitness.org/printArticle .php?id=27.
3. Try making authentic Iraqi cuisine to enrich the discussion of this novel. Many great recipes can be found at http://www.recipezaar.com/recipes/iraqi.